MYSTERY

RAN AWAY

The Benjamin January Series from Barbara Hambly

A FREE MAN OF COLOR
FEVER SEASON
GRAVEYARD DUST
SOLD DOWN THE RIVER
DIE UPON A KISS
WET GRAVE
DAYS OF THE DEAD
DEAD WATER
DEAD AND BURIED *
THE SHIRT ON HIS BACK *
RAN AWAY *

* available from Severn House

RAN AWAY

A Benjamin January Novel

Barbara Hambly

This first world edition published 2011
in Great Britain and in the USA by
SEVERN HOUSE PUBLISHERS LTD of
9–15 High Street, Sutton, Surrey, England, SM1 1DF.
Trade paperback edition first published
in Great Britain and the USA 2012 by
SEVERN HOUSE PUBLISHERS LTD

British Library Cataloguing in Publication Data

Hambly, Barbara.
 Ran away.
 1. January, Benjamin (Fictitious character)–Fiction.
 2. Free African Americans–Fiction. 3. Private
 investigators–Fiction. 4. New Orleans (La.)–Social life
 and customs–19th century–Fiction. 5. Murder–
 Investigation–Fiction. 6. Detective and mystery stories.
 I. Title
 813.6-dc22

ISBN-13: 978-0-7278-8082-6 (cased)
ISBN-13: 978-1-84751-382-3 (trade paper)

All Severn House titles are printed on acid-free paper.

Severn House Publishers support The Forest Stewardship Council [FSC],
the leading international forest certification organisation. All our titles that
are printed on Greenpeace-approved FSC-certified paper carry the FSC logo.

MIX
Paper from
responsible sources
FSC
www.fsc.org   FSC® C018575

Typeset by Palimpsest Book Production Ltd.,
Falkirk, Stirlingshire, Scotland.
Printed and bound in Great Britain by
MPG Books Ltd., Bodmin, Cornwall.

PROLOGUE

December 1837

Word flashed through the town like pebbles flying from an explosion. Americans, French Creoles, slaves and the *gens de couleur libré* all seemed to know it at once. 'He strangled them with bowstrings,' the Widow Levesque announced, over morning coffee and beignets at the house of her son, 'and pitched them out the attic window.'

'Who did?' Benjamin January paused in the pantry doorway, a pitcher of cream for his wife and his mother in his hands.

'The Turk, of course.' There could not have been richer satisfaction in Livia Levesque's tone if she'd been divulging her own acquisition of railway shares.

In a city reeling from the impact of the business depression sweeping the country, the Turk provided – to white New Orleans society and to the blacks, slave and free, who coexisted with it – a welcome combination of diversion and largesse. The house he'd purchased on Rue Bourbon had been the site of a dozen stylish entertainments since his arrival in November. All the best of New Orleans society, both Americans and French Creoles, were invited, and all came: the Turk's first action upon his arrival had been to acquire one of the best cooks in the city. The penny-pinching evident even in the houses of such notables as the Marignys and the Destrehans these days was nowhere to be seen under the Infidel's roof. A representative – it was rumored – of the Sultan of Constantinople, the Turk was educated, convivial, spoke flawless French and displayed manners that most of the American planters (said the French Creoles) would do well to copy.

Moreover, in addition to being excellent company when present, in his absence he provided an unending source of whispered speculation, for his household included – as well as the French cook – a number of slaves brought from his homeland, a wife, and two concubines, young women never glimpsed but reputed to be of breathtaking beauty.

The fact that most of the bankers, planters, and brokers in New Orleans had concubines themselves – slave women whose duties included sleeping with the master – was not deemed the same thing, somehow: one bought them for their housekeeping skills, and anyway, they were black. Even the ladies of the free colored demi-monde – the mistresses to those same bankers, planters, and brokers – were fascinated.

Society matrons, though utterly charmed by the Infidel's polished manner, opined among themselves that no good would come of it.

'Both his concubines.' Livia Levesque took the cream pitcher from January's hand. 'Murdered and thrown from the window.'

'Who says this?' Rose demanded, and offered her mother-in-law a plate of pralines.

'That's ridiculous,' added January.

The Widow Levesque scratched with a critical nail at a chip in the edge of the creamy queensware plate and took one praline, which she laid on the edge of her saucer. 'Did you make these yourself, dear? I don't see what's ridiculous about it.' She regarded her son with velvet-brown eyes. A former demi-mondaine herself – though nowadays she would never admit such a thing – Livia Levesque kept into her early sixties the striking beauty that had saved her from slavery over three decades before. She was, January knew, inordinately proud of her white father's blood and generally tried to pretend that her son by a fellow slave in her youth – as African-black as his father – was no relation of hers. Only Rose's production of a grandchild in October had brought that portion of her family into her good graces again, although she had been heard to hope that Baby John would not inherit his mother's nearsighted-ness: *So tedious and silly-looking, having to wear those awful spectacles . . .*

'I could have warned them,' she declared. 'Turks have no regard for women. They simply use them and cast them aside – and are madly jealous as well, though Heaven knows the man kept the poor things prisoners in that attic, so closely that they never had the opportunity to make him jealous . . . Not that *that* makes any difference to a Turk.' She shrugged her slender

shoulders in their wide sleeves of straw-colored silk. 'I dare say
he tired of them . . .'

'If he was tired of them he'd have sold them, surely.' Rose's
voice was dry. 'He'd certainly have found a buyer.'

'Not a Turk, dear,' corrected Livia darkly. 'They would sooner
kill a woman than believe that she's been taken by another man.'

'No,' said January.

His mother regarded him, eyes widened with surprise, as if she
weren't quite certain what the word meant in regard to herself.

'I will not believe it,' he went on quietly. 'I know the man—'

'Nonsense, Benjamin, of course you don't.'

'—and he would not do such a thing. He saved the life of my
wife.'

'Don't be silly. Rose has never even met—'

'Not Rose,' said January. 'Ayasha.'

ONE

'**M**âlik?'

January opened one eye, squinted against the light in the room.

He'd woken briefly just before dawn, when Ayasha had risen to pray – a habit she'd retained from her childhood, though she had become a Christian and went to Mass as dutifully as any of the other inhabitants of the building. He'd heard the bells of St Séverin strike seven before he'd slipped back into dreams. It was broad daylight now.

Not satisfied with this tepid response, his wife yanked wider the bed curtains, pulled up her skirts and flounced on to the bed in a great whoof of petticoats, straddling his body on the faded coverlet. Offended, Hadji the cat sprang from the pillow, retreated to the window sill that overlooked – far, far down – the Rue de l'Aube, and commenced washing, with the air of Pontius Pilate: *I haven't the slightest idea who those creatures are.*

'*Zahar?*' January drew his hand from under the blanket – the October morning was bitterly cold – and groped for her brown knee.

Her fingers closed on his wrist, strong and warm as a child's. Her black hair, braided and tucked in a great curly pile on her head, had come down in wisps around her face: she looked like a desert witch, inexplicably masquerading as a housewife in a dress of green-and-white muslin. 'There is one who needs your help,' she said.

'You want me to break into the harem of Hüseyin Pasha and see one of his concubines?'

'The girl is ill.'

'I'll be even more ill if I'm caught. I've seen his guards.'

'You won't be caught, my husband. The Lady Jamilla – his wife – will let us in—'

'Oh, he'll understand *that*.' Shuddering with cold, January washed with all possible speed in the basin before the hearth which served the big room for both heating and cooking and, on spring nights when all the *gratin* had left Paris for their country estates and there wasn't quite enough money for candles, sometimes lighting as well. The nobles who had returned to Paris in the wake of the Bourbon kings a dozen years previously valued January's talents as a musician, and Ayasha's as a dressmaker, sufficiently to afford them a living decent enough, and at this season they were flocking back to the city demanding entertainment and new clothes. So there was coffee, soft cheese, butter and jam on the domestic end of the long work-table. In a huge willow basket beside the door, January saw shining lengths of silk, blonde lace, gauze like a breath of lilac mist, covered with a towel against the depredations of Hadji and Habibi. Ayasha had been visiting a customer.

Ayasha poured coffee, plucked chunks of sugar from the tin box on the table and added a dusting of cinnamon. 'Hüseyin Pasha has forbidden any in his household to see *farangi* doctors,' she said. 'He says they will bring evil ideas with them and corrupt the household. I told the Lady Jamilla that you were not like the others; that you were taught by wise women as well as by idiots at the Hôtel Dieu, and that you don't bleed and puke and stick clysters up peoples'—'

'In other words, that I'm not a doctor at all,' said January. 'Just a surgeon – a bone-setter.'

'Yallah! She'd never let you near the girl if I said that. The girl is with child,' pleaded Ayasha, her great dark eyes filled with distress. 'She is far from her home, *Mâlik*. *Sitt* Jamilla fears that one of the other wives has poisoned her because the Pasha is away in London. Please come.'

January pulled his shirt and trousers on, and a warm, if shabby, waistcoat that dated from his first days in Paris, when he'd still been under the impression that *liberté, egalité,* and *fraternité* applied to men of African descent in the medical profession.

He'd arrived in France from his native Louisiana in 1817, aged twenty-two. The long wars between England and France had just ended: the likelihood that a sea voyage undertaken by a man of his color would end in some planter's cane field in Barbados had shrunk to an acceptable minimum. Armed with an introduction from the *libré* who'd taught him surgery in New Orleans, he had been admitted for training at the Hôtel Dieu, and later had been hired there as a surgeon.

But by that time he'd learned that he could make far more money playing the piano at the entertainments given by such families as the Polignacs and the Noailleses – recently returned to France after living abroad since 1789. This had mattered little to him then. He'd shared a garret in the Rue St-Christopher with two of the other junior surgeons and had been perfectly content. But one morning an eighteen-year-old Berber dressmaker had brought into the clinic one of the girls from her shop, bleeding from a botched abortion.

When he'd emerged from the hospital not long afterwards, he had found the young dress-shop keeper weeping in an alley for her dying friend and had walked her back to her rooms.

To take a wife, a man needed more money than could be got as a surgeon in a clinic.

As a musician, he didn't make a great deal – not enough to purchase a new waistcoat for everyday wear. But the room in the Rue de l'Aube was only a few doors from Ayasha's shop, and times – January hoped – would improve.

Provided he didn't get himself beheaded by the Pasha's guards for breaking into a harem in the Rue St-Honoré.

'What's the girl's name?' he asked as they descended four flights of narrow stairs – seventy-two steps in all – to the street. On the landing of the *deuxième étage* – back home the Americans would have called it the *third floor* – the door of the upholsterer Paillole's chamber stood open and Madame Paillole could be heard berating her eldest son for Heaven only knew what transgression. With Jacques-Ange it could be anything. On the *premier étage* the wives of both Renan the baker and Barronde the lawyer, who despised one another, stood listening intently, and they leaped apart at the appearance of January and Ayasha. Madame Barronde vanished into her husband's apartment – which occupied the whole of the *premier étage* and was the most elegant in the building – and Madame Renan ('Such a woman would not have been called *Madame* in *my* day,' Madame Barronde was rather too fond of saying) went downstairs to her husband's shop.

'Her name is Shamira,' Ayasha replied. They crossed the tiny yard behind the bakery, where moss grew on grimy cobbles amid smells of bakeshop and privies, circumvented the pump, ducked under the laundry of the students who occupied the attic, and followed the damp little passway out to the street. 'She is the youngest in the harîm, only seventeen. Hüseyin Pasha bought her only a few months before he left Constantinople for Paris, just after the New Year. He has brought the whole of his harîm, and both his wives . . .'

'And a platoon of scimitar-wielding guards?'

'Only ten, Lady Jamilla says.' Ayasha's blithe tone indicated that she considered her husband more than a match for ten scimitar-wielding Turks any day of the week. '*Alors, copain*,' she added, in slangy street-French, and waved to old Grouzier who ran the Café l'Empereur on the other side of the narrow street. 'And anyway, he has taken four of them to London with him,' she went on, as if this improved matters. 'And two of those who remain are eunuchs. There are four other eunuchs in the household: two to serve in the harem, and one each for the Lady Jamilla and the Lady Utba, who is also with child.'

She ticked off these facts on her strong brown fingers: short, like a child's, though her small square palms were as wrinkled as an old lady's. 'Hüseyin Pasha is a great friend of the Sultan – so great that His Highness merely sent him to Paris when he spoke out against the Sultan bringing in men of the West to train the Army and teach young men science and medicine. He is a great hater of all things of the West and says they foul the hearts of the true followers of God's Law . . . Is it true that the Sultan's mother was French?'

'Not *French* French.' January smiled, with a trace of pride. 'Creole French, from the sugar islands. She was kidnapped by pirates in the Mediterranean on her way to a convent and sold to the Sultan's father back before the Revolution. I've heard she was a cousin of the Empress Josephine, but that's always sounded to me like the kind of story someone would make up.'

'I'll bet her father sold her himself for two centimes.' Ayasha adjusted the ribbons of her bonnet. In the raven cloud of curls her earrings glinted, gold cut in the primitive spiral patterns of the desert where she'd been born, like the flicker of a pagan smile.

'He won't let them leave the grounds – Hüseyin Pasha won't let his wives leave, I mean – and has forbidden them to wear Western clothing: *For whom does a woman wear these garments*, he has asked, *save for her husband, who hates the sight of these immodest shapes?* It's why I was called upon today, while he's away—'

'To make the Lady Jamilla a Turkish *entari* of Lyon's silk?'

'*Sahîf*.' She poked him with her elbow. 'That's what the Lady Utba thinks – and what *she's* having me do. But the Lady Jamilla looks ahead to the time when the Sultan will summon them back and *make* Hüseyin Pasha dress his wives in the style of the West. She plans to have the fashions of Paris all ready, to shine down every woman of the court. Which she cannot do,' she added encouragingly, 'if she lets harm befall *you*.'

'That sound you hear,' responded January politely, 'is my sob of relief at the assurance that all will be well.'

The hôtel rented by Hüseyin Pasha stood amid handsome gardens on the Rue St Honoré, near the city's northern customs barrier. It was an area that still boasted market gardens and drying grounds among the small cottages of artisans; garden beds lay fallow in the chill flash of cloud and sunlight, and there was a strong smell of backyard poultry and cows. A lane flanked by a yellow sandstone wall ended in a stable gate. 'We're here to see Bellarmé about the milk,' Ayasha casually informed the single groom they met as they crossed the stable court toward the kitchen.

January raised his eyebrows. 'You told Madame already that we'd be coming?'

'I knew you would not turn your back on a girl who is in trouble and afraid, far from home.'

'When I get sewn in a sack and thrown in the river I'll take comfort in the thought of my virtue.'

'*Mâlik* . . .' She looked up at him – compact and voluptuous, she stood almost a foot shorter than his towering six-foot-three – with the expression of an adult being patient with a child's fears of the platt-eye devil beneath the bed at night. 'The guards are as lazy as other men. With the Pasha gone, they scarce even trouble to patrol—'

And immediately gave the lie to her words by yanking him through the doorway of the stone-flagged dairy beside the kitchen to let a servant pass: a black man whose slim build and sharp features marked him, to January's eye, as of the Fulani tribe. Hüseyin Pasha's ordinance about proper dress seemed to extend to his servants: the man wore billowy Turkish pantaloons – *salvars* – and a long tunic of bright orange wool, his shaved head covered by a scarlet cap. January wondered if this man had consented to come to this chilly Infidel country, or if, like the girl Shamira, his master had simply ordered him to pack.

Ayasha slipped from the dairy, glanced through the door of the kitchen, then motioned January to follow her. The kitchen – considerably larger than their room on the Rue de l'Aube – was redolent of saffron and cinnamon, and of the straw-packing of broken-open boxes in which, presumably, the master's favorite spices had been shipped. They passed swiftly through and went up two steps into a pantry scented with coffee. So far, only the aroma of spices hinted that the house was occupied by other than some French noble and his family. The dishes on the white-painted shelves were Limoges, the glassware Bavarian crystal. When Ayasha pushed open the door at the far end of the long, narrow room, January caught a perfectly French glimpse of pale-green boiseries and an oil portrait of a disconsolate-looking gentleman in a powdered wig.

But from the table beneath the portrait a woman sprang to her feet, dark eyes above the edge of her veil flooded with relief. 'You have come!' Her French was heavily accented.

'Did I not promise?' The woman followed Ayasha back into the pantry, and January bowed. '*Sitt* Jamilla, this is my husband, Benjamin, *al-hakîm*.'

Her eyes touched his, then fleeted aside. 'This way, please come.' Her voice was a beautiful alto. 'It go bad for her. Fear . . .' She gestured, as if trying to summon from air words that she was too shaken to recall; long slim fingers, polished nails stained with henna. Then she gathered her veils about her and led the way to the backstairs. As he followed her up the narrow treads the drift of her perfume whispered back to him, French and expensive.

In French he asked, 'Is she poisoned?'

'I think.' She touched her finger to her lips as they passed the door on the *premier étage* – what they would call the *second floor* back in Louisiana, the main level of salons and reception rooms – and ascended to the private apartments above. Frankincense pervaded these upper reaches, penetrating even the confines of the enclosed stair. January had already guessed the Pasha kept his concubines on one of the upper floors of the house, but the ascent filled him with the sensation of being cut off from escape. One could leap from the windows of a salon on the *premier étage* and risk no more than a sprained ankle. A drop from one of the dormers on the roof would be a serious matter.

'Vomit—' In the thin light that came from the stair's few small windows, the Lady Jamilla's slim hands conjured the meaning, in case she had the word wrong. 'Bleed in womb, little . . .' Her fingers measured half a thimble-full. 'Fall down. Hear noise.' Then she pressed her hand to her chest, drew two or three gasping breaths.

January nodded his understanding. 'She has not lost the child yet?'

The Lady shook her head, reiterated the gesture: *only half a thimble-full.* 'Yet so afraid. All afraid.'

All except the equally-pregnant Lady Utba, I'll bet . . .

At the top of the backstairs the Lady paused to listen at the door. The smell of incense was stronger here, even through the shut door, but could not cover the stink of sickness. She opened it, led him through into what had probably once been a servants' hall, now converted to the usages of the harîm. A low divan and a scattering of floor pillows touched January's consciousness even as he crossed toward the single door that stood open, his boots sinking into four or five layers of carpet, in the Eastern fashion. A huge brass brazier radiated gentle heat from the center of the room; a second, much smaller than the first, stood in the smaller chamber to which Jamilla led him.

A skinny maidservant in black knelt beside the divan that had been built around three sides of the little chamber. The pillows that heaped such low benches during daylight hours were still piled at both sides, and a young girl lay among the sheets and quilts of the longer central section. Jamilla said something to the maidservant, who sat back on her heels and shook her head. Between the *hijab* that concealed her hair and the *niqaab* that veiled her face – both businesslike black cotton – dark eyes stitched with wrinkles wore a look of grief and defiance; she responded in

something that might have been peasant Turkish, but the disobedi-
ence was as clear as if she had spoken French.

Jamilla waved toward the door and repeated her order, and the
maid shook her head violently. The girl on the divan, January saw,
had been dressed in a long gown that covered her from throat to
ankles, a servant's *camisa*, he guessed: black, substantial, and all-
encompassing. She was veiled, even her hair. The room stank of
vomit and sickness, the sheets were stained and wet, but the
garments and veils were dry and clean.

*Do they really think I'll be overwhelmed with lust at the sight
of a poor girl spewing her guts out as she aborts her baby?* Anger
swept through him, at the insanities of traditions that branded
every woman as nine times more passionate than the poor men
whose lusts they commanded; that cautioned that all Africans were
animalistically lascivious – as the educated and philosophical third
President of the United States had so tastefully put it.

Or were Jamilla and the maid simply doing what they could to
maintain their innocence, should word of all this reach Hüseyin
Pasha? *The girl was never unveiled before the Unbeliever, and
never left alone with him . . .*

He wondered if that would save them, or the girl.

And God only knows, he reflected, *what the girl herself thinks,
or feels . . . or what language she speaks, even.* If the Pasha bought
her only a year ago, how much Turkish would she have learned
to speak to the servants? Or with her master . . . if he considered
conversation with his bed-mates a part of their duties.

January knew most American masters didn't. 'Does she speak
French?' he whispered, and again the Lady made the little half-
a-thimble-full gesture with her fingers.

'Only little. Egypt – Cairo. Family is Jew.'

He knelt beside the divan. 'Mademoiselle, can you hear me?
You're going to be all right.'

The fatigue-blackened eyelids stirred. In broken French she
whispered, 'I'm sorry—'

'It's all right.'

'My Lady . . .' Jamilla knelt beside January, took Shamira's
hand. Her reply was gentle, as if she spoke to a younger sister.

Shamira whispered something else – an apology? Perhaps,
because Jamilla gripped her hand encouragingly, stroked the girl's

hair, dislodging the veil, and said something else, in which January heard the words *farangi* – a Frank, a European – and *hakîm*.

The girl whispered, in a voice hoarse from vomiting, 'My baby?'

January guessed from the symptoms that the girl had been poisoned with quinine and guessed too that quantities enough to do this to her would trigger an abortion within hours. 'Do not worry about this now, Mademoiselle. First it is your life which must be saved.' He turned to Jamilla. 'When was she sick? When did this start?'

'Night. End of night. Before first prayers.'

He felt the girl's hands – the servant looked horrified – and found them icy, and her pulse, thready and weak. 'Is no one else sick?'

Jamilla repeated the question to the servant, then translated the reply. 'Ra'eesa say, all well. Others—' She turned to Ayasha to translate, but it was scarcely easier. The Osmanli tongue spoken by the upper classes in Constantinople was an elaborate combination of Arabic, Persian, and Turkish, only half-comprehensible to a young woman who'd grown up speaking the mix of Arabic and Tamazight common to the Mahgrib.

'She says she sent the other women away to the cottage at the far end of the garden,' explained Ayasha at last. 'There are three other concubines and their maids. Ra'eesa – the maidservant – says that the Lady Utba is there too now.'

January turned to Ra'eesa and said – a little hesitantly – ''*afak zheeblee lma* . . .' When the maid went out into the other room and returned bearing the copper water-pitcher that January remembered seeing on the low table there, he said to Jamilla, 'Not the water in the other room. Fresh water, clean, from the kitchen.'

It was clear to him that the elder wife knew at once what he meant, for her eyes widened with shocked enlightenment. She took the ewer from Ra'eesa and gave her a quick instruction, and realization flared in the older woman's face as well. When the servant left, Jamilla handed January the pitcher and gave Ayasha a rapid and urgent explanation.

'She says they have given Shamira water twice from this pitcher today,' Ayasha translated. 'It is many steps down to the kitchen, you understand . . .'

'Oh, I understand.' January sniffed the water and tasted it. Beneath the sugar and the attar of roses, a familiar bitterness.

'That's exactly what someone was counting on. Chinchona,' he explained to Jamilla. 'Peruvian bark. An abortifacient, but it can easily kill. We must induce vomiting once again, with charcoal this time –' he took a packet of it from his satchel – 'and then I will give Mademoiselle Shamira something to strengthen her heart.'

Ayasha explained hesitantly, half in French, partly in Arabic, partly in signs, while the servant woman returned, panting, with a jar of water from the kitchen. She also carried – January was delighted to see she had that much sense – a clean, empty jar. He performed the gastric lavage on the semi-conscious girl – touching her as little as he could and ordering the servant to do most of the lifting – then mixed a tiny pinch of a foxglove compound, barely enough to strengthen the heart, and administered it as well.

'*Sitt* Jamilla says you are wise in the ways that women are wise, *Mâlik*.'

'You may tell *Sitt* Jamilla that my sister is a wise woman, and that she and I both learned from an old Auntie in our village when we were tiny, about herbs and how to use them.' The faint, dry scent of the foxglove brought before him the face of old Auntie Jeanne, fat and toothless and covered with wrinkles and 'country marks' – tribal scarring . . . He and his sister Olympe had been furiously jealous of one another over the old woman's herb lore, each wanting to know more than the other, and Olympe, even at six years old, spitefully triumphant because she was a girl and as such had a greater share of the woman's teaching.

And that old slave mambo, probably dead for a dozen years, had handed him the key that would save the life of a young girl in a land Auntie Jeanne had never set foot in; a girl who for all her silk cushions and beaded veils was just as much a slave as the cane hands in the quarters on Bellefleur.

And Olympe . . .

It had been years since January had even thought of his sister.

He returned his attention to the girl Shamira. Her veil was now soaked with water and dabbled with vomit, but the maid kept readjusting it, to keep it in place. She had replaced the veil over the girl's hair, too: thick black hair, curling.

Weakly, Shamira disengaged her hand from his and pressed it to her belly. She had not wept since those few tears she'd shed when she'd whispered in French, 'I'm sorry . . .'

Now her face transformed with relief and joy, and her body shook with sobs. 'Lord of Hosts,' she whispered, 'oh, God of Abraham and my fathers, thank you . . . Thank you. I felt him move,' she added, looking up into January's face. 'He lives. My son lives.'

January fought back his first impulse to lay his own hand against her side, knowing that it made no difference. With that much quinine in her system, abortion almost certainly would commence before nightfall.

'The Lady Utba is with child as well.' Ayasha translated another spate of Osmanli from Jamilla. 'The fortune teller said that her child would be a girl, and that Shamira would bear a son.'

'Oh, that must have set the cat amongst the pigeons.'

'My lord *only* son.' Jamilla spoke up, picking her words carefully. 'Shamira have all she want: sweet, necklace, this room her own.' She gestured around them at the comfortable little chamber, the cushioned divans and embroidered hangings of pink and green. 'Lady Utba also still delight the heart of my lord.' She pressed her hands to her heart, miming a man in a swoon of love, then put her hands over her eyes.

January said, 'I see.' He turned to have Ayasha explain – because he wanted there to be no mistake – but she had gone into the larger outer room, to investigate the platter of sweets on the low table there. He called out after her, 'Don't touch those!'

She called back, 'Do I look like an idiot, *Mâlik*?'

To Jamilla, he said, 'Can you keep Shamira from the others, until your lord comes home? Separate food, separate drink?'

'Not easy.' The chief wife frowned. 'Girls eat from one dish. Yet, I say her disease still catching.'

'Good.' January had to restrain himself from taking this woman's hand in thanks, or patting her on the shoulder as a gesture of comfort, such as he would do to the wife or girlfriend of one of his friends. 'Tell them this is the command of the doctor.' He glanced toward Shamira, who had drifted off to sleep, and lowered his voice. 'I am afraid there is a good chance she will lose her child,' he said softly. 'I'll leave you medicines, to strengthen her in case . . .'

'It is not first time,' said Jamilla, and sadness filled her eyes, 'that woman in this house lose child. This, I can help. I can do.'

'Thank you. If there are any complications, or any more of this sickness, send for me—'

'*Ibn al-harîm!*' Ayasha swore – practically the only Arabic January knew – sprang down from the window seat in the outer room and dashed to the door of Shamira's chamber. 'People on their way across the stable yard. Two women – and six guards.'

TWO

January reached the window just in time to see the foreshortened figures of women and guards disappear past the corner of the house. They'd be climbing the servants' stair in literally seconds. 'Can you get us—?'

Jamilla caught his hand. 'No time. Come!'

She drew him to the backstairs in a striding billow of pink and topaz silk and threw open its door, and though he knew there was no way he could avoid meeting the oncoming guards halfway down he followed. She was right, there was no time for a second's hesitation: he must trust this woman, or fight his way out against long odds with the certainty that Jamilla, Shamira, the maidservant Ra'eesa and quite probably Ayasha as well would die in the aftermath of Hüseyin Pasha's vengeance.

Which, he reflected sourly, was the Lady Utba's goal.

At the floor below, Jamilla pushed open the servants' door and thrust January out into the hall. Even as she closed the discreet portal behind her, he heard in the echoing stair a door open below and booted footfalls pounding. At the same moment voices rang in the grand staircase that lay at the other end of the hôtel's long central hall. Without hesitation, Jamilla opened the nearest chamber door and pulled him inside.

'Ayasha—'

'Safe.' The woman touched his lips with her hennaed fingers. The room, he saw with alarm, was obviously her own chamber, stripped of whatever Western furnishings it had once contained and refurbished with hangings and divans. 'No harm woman.'

Which was more than could be said of what the Pasha's guards would do to him if they caught him on this floor, much less in the bedchamber of Number One Wife . . . or even her dressing room, through which she next hustled him. Given the diplomatic understandings between France's King and the Sultan, it wasn't likely that the death of an intruder into the Assistant Plenipotentiary's *maison* would even be reported, much less investigated. He could easily imagine the bored shrugs of the police inspectors, should an enraged young Berber woman storm into the local prefecture with the demand that a prominent Turkish diplomat be arrested for having his guards kill a man who broke into his house . . .

For that matter, he reflected, with a glance at the woman beside him, if the guards caught him up here, Jamilla's only protection would be screams and an accusation of rape.

Sweat chilled his face. But Jamilla led him straight through into the next room – a library furnished in the Turkish style, with low tables and the ubiquitous divan covered in enormous cushions, and a great hanging of crimson and indigo: stylized mountains and stars. She pushed him down on to the divan and began covering him with cushions. January comprehended – Jamilla had clearly forgotten whatever French she knew – and stretched and squashed himself as flat as he could to assist matters. Before she put the last big pouffes over his face she gestured with both hands – *stay* – and he nodded.

'*Eeyeh,*' he said, hoping that was *yes* in Osmanli as well as in the Mahgribi that Ayasha spoke. '*Fhemt.*'

Jamilla looked absolutely baffled.

'I understand.'

She put the last pillow in place, and he felt, rather than heard, her dart back across the library to the dressing room, curly-toed golden slippers soundless on the piled carpets.

Soft boots thudded in the hall. The door opened, long enough for the guards to glance around the room. Then it closed.

He heard the bedroom door beyond opened likewise, and for no longer a span of time.

Not enough guards – or, anyway, not enough eunuch guards – to thoroughly search the house at the first sweep. They'd be back.

Women's voices in the hall, a shrill chatter, like birds. He could almost hear the words. Protesting, denying, demanding how they could think such a thing.

Allah pity the guard who tries to question Ayasha about the large black gentleman who accompanied her . . .

Slippers whispered on the rugs. *Sitt* Jamilla yanked the cushions off him, took his hand. 'Man in yard.' She led him back through the dressing room, through her chamber, and to the backstairs again, a faint perfume rustling from the folds of her veils. 'Watches. Look in kitchen, look in room of – of *keten*. You stay.'

Above the edge of her veil, her eyes held his. *Seeking what? Courage and resolution? The nerve to stay in hiding, possibly for hours, until the guard walks away?* Maybe only seeking a sign of trust. If he did not trust – if he panicked, tried to flee or to fight – they would all be doomed.

'I stay.'

The dark eyes shut for a moment in relief, and her hands tightened on his, the way he would have slapped a friend on the arm and said: *Good man.*

She tugged him down the backstairs, through the pantry, into the kitchen. Beyond the wide kitchen window he glimpsed the man in the yard, squat and formidable in a rough combination of French jacket and Turkish trousers, his head shaved. In addition to a curved Turkish sword and a dagger the man bore a very businesslike rifle.

Not a man to argue with about what you were doing in the house.

A small door led from the kitchen into the linen room, long and brick-floored and lined with cupboards, and smelling of cedar and scorched sheets. From her belt Jamilla took a key, opened the big armoire at the far end of the room. It was a close fit, but January unhesitatingly curled his six-foot three-inch height on to the lowest shelf – four feet long and some two feet deep – and Jamilla closed the doors on him at once. He heard the lock click. So still were these rooms at the back of the house that he heard the pat of her slippers retreat across the brick floor to the kitchen.

It had all been as neatly accomplished as a military campaign: *well, a military campaign by a general who knew what he was doing – Caesar or Alexander or Frederick the Great.* The one military campaign which January actually witnessed – at the age of nineteen, crouched behind redoubts made of cotton bales at the top of an embankment, while a British army three times the size of the defenders attempted like idiots to charge uphill at them into a wall of rifle fire – would have had any proper general tearing his hair.

For a moment he smelled the fog again, heard the steady beat of the British drums, invisible in the cinder-colored darkness, and the sneeze of a man somewhere down the line to his left. After the battle, working in the infirmary tent among the captured wounded, he had felt such pity for them as they were carried in, soaked in blood and mud and begging for water – men he'd shot himself, or bayoneted: 'You can't think about it,' one of the surgeons had advised him, a Scot from one of the British regiments who'd permitted himself to be captured, so that he could look after the prisoners. 'When you start to think about the battle, just imagine yourself closing a door on it, so you'll be able to work.'

The Lady Jamilla, January felt sure, would never have ordered a stupid charge like that.

He smiled.

You'd have thought she was sneaking very large men in and out of her lord's harem all her life.

A childhood in slavery had given January plenty of experience in hiding, so he knew prolonged stillness would very quickly result in agonizing cramps. Michie Simon, the owner of Bellefleur Plantation, had been a drunkard who thought nothing of rawhiding a six-year-old. What to the white children of the parish were merely the finer arts of hide and seek had been to January and his sister almost literally life-or-death skills. He knew how to ignore the cramps, keep still and wait.

He knew how to listen, too.

Voices of the guards in the yard, little chips of sound. (*And what language is it THEY speak?*) Ayasha's voice, raised in angry imprecation as she passed through the kitchen and went on outside without pausing. For her to linger would have been as good as an announcement that she still had an accomplice in the house – the groom in the yard would remember an immense broad-shouldered black man in a brown corduroy jacket. For Ayasha to flounce through the stable gates and down the lane without a backward glance was the best corroboration that could be offered to the statement: 'Who, Benjamin? He left an hour ago, *muti . . .*'

But it left him utterly at the mercy of that dark-eyed woman in the saffron veil, who had so cared for her husband's concubine that she'd risked her own safety – perhaps her life – to bring in a Western doctor.

There was a clock in the kitchen. Through the open doorway its notes drifted faintly: noon, then one, then two. Cook and kitchen maids came in and chattered in French, wooden clogs clattering on the bricks. 'Intruders . . . heathens . . . they say that he whipped a concubine to death for looking at one of his guards . . . Hand me that cream, would you ever, dearie?' The smells of garlic sautéed with onions. 'Is it true Jojo's marrying that Chinese?' (*Chinese???*) He wondered what was happening above stairs and whether the search was still in progress.

It was well past three when someone shut the door between the two service-rooms and approached the armoire with pattering slippers. January hoped his cramped legs would still bear him.

The lock clicked. Jamilla gave him her hand to steady him as he rose – he needed it, and caught her shoulder as he staggered. She led the way to the outer door, opened it and pointed toward a tall hedge. 'Garden,' she whispered, and gestured: *straight through, then over the wall.*

'*Shukran jazeelan*,' he whispered, another of the few Arabic phrases he knew. 'Thank you. Shamira?'

'It goes better with her.'

He nodded, turned at once, and strode across the open space of the deserted yard to the gate in the hedge. When he glanced back, *Sitt* Jamilla was gone.

The hedge didn't completely conceal the garden from the yard, but at least he was no longer in the house itself. He spent the minute or so that it took him to cross the formal rose-beds, the graveled walks, inventing an indignant explanation. *What, I in the house? Never! I waited in the lane for my wife and have come back to seek her—*

And of course the guards probably haven't a word of French . . .

Old vines covered the brick of the garden wall and easily took his weight. Only when he slipped over the top and dropped down to the lane on the other side did he breathe easily again.

His fellow musicians at the Opera, he reflected with a grin, would hang themselves with envy at the story: *I invaded the Pasha's harem, eluded his guards – we won't speak of hiding for four hours in an armoire in the linen room – sprang over the garden wall . . .*

And we won't speak of any of it at all, of course. The other thing he'd learned in the small, gossipy world of that African village in Louisiana's cane country was not to *ever* say *anything* that could get someone hurt, no matter how good a story it made.

You never knew who was listening. Or how trustworthy they were when they'd had a drink or two.

The better the story was, the likelier it was to be passed along.

Like Hüseyin Pasha killing a concubine only for glancing at a handsome guard – but that was a story that might possibly be true.

This was an adventure he'd have to keep to himself.

'Perfidious woman,' he said, when he reached the Rue St-Honoré and Ayasha sprang from the table of a café on the other side of the street. 'If you wanted me out of the way could you not simply have arranged to be taken in adultery with M'sieu Barronde? I'd have given you a divorce. I'm aware of your undying passion for M'sieu Renan—'

The baker, who lived behind his shop on the ground floor of their building, was sixty-two, enormously fat, and – owing to the loss of most of his teeth – drooled.

'*Sahîf.*' She slipped her arm through his. 'If I just let you divorce me for adulterating M'sieu Barronde I wouldn't get any of your money.'

'Let me tell you, Madame,' said January severely as they crossed the street, 'I have registered it in my will that if I die at the hands of the Pasha's guards, or in fact the guards of *any* Mohammedan potentate whatsoever, you shall not get a centime.'

'Oh, curse!' Ayasha pressed a dramatic wrist to her forehead. 'Oh, spite! I am undone. I shall just have to think of something else, then.' They turned their steps, not toward the river, but toward the Étoile and Napoleon's pretentious half-constructed triumphal arch, beyond which lay the non-taxed wine shops and inexpensive cafés of the *banlieue*. The chilly afternoon was already growing dark, and the district beyond the limits of the old tax-wall had a country stillness to it at odds with the liveliness of that place in summertime. But it was still possible to get a good dinner of stewed rabbit and fresh-baked bread at the Café Marseillaise before returning to the Rue de l'Aube so that January could change for the Opera.

The performance was Mozart's *Abduction from the Seraglio*, a piece that Ayasha regarded with scorn, knowing from experience what it was to actually grow up in a harîm. Through the evening as he played, January's thoughts returned many times to the low-ceilinged chambers at the top of that walled house, and the sweat-soaked Jewish girl on the divan whose face he had not even been allowed to see.

The following day Ayasha came back late from work at the shop, with the news that she'd walked out to Rue St-Honoré to ask how Shamira did. 'She is well, the child also,' she reported, and covered the mix of fish and onion on the small brick *potager* built into the corner of the room. 'Allah be praised . . .'

Freezing rain had started last night on the way home from the Opera, and all day it had hammered the gray cobbled streets. Kneeling by the hearth, January stirred coffee beans in the roasting pan over the fire and cringed at the thought of making his way to the theater again that night.

'She didn't lose the child?'

His wife shook her head. '*Sitt* Jamilla spoke well of you. It isn't every man, she said, who would follow a woman he had never before met, without stopping like an imbecile to ask questions that would have got them killed.'

'What would have happened to Shamira,' asked January, 'if I'd been found there? Surely no one would think that in her state she'd be receiving a lover.'

'That isn't the point, *Mâlik*.'

'For that matter,' he added – though he knew she was right – 'in France, Hüseyin Pasha has no jurisdiction over those girls, not even the command a man has over his wife.' He shook the pan, judging the color of the beans as the indescribable miracle of their scent filled the long room. 'No matter what he paid for them back in Constantinople, they're free women here.'

'Free to do what, *Mâlik*?' She brought out dishes from the cupboard, rested them on the tiled counter that edged the cook hole, barely wider than January's palm. 'Free to find work in a sewing loft, without a word of French to their names? Free to find a *gawaad* – a pimp – to protect them while they earn money the only way they can?'

The autumn day was already dark, and the warmth of the hearth and the little *potager* didn't penetrate even to the other end of the room. *Mine enemy's dog,* King Lear had said, *though he had bit me, should have stood that night against my fire . . .*

'They have a place to stay,' Ayasha went on softly.

'That isn't the point, *zahar*.'

It rained the next day, and the day after. Homicide, the beggars called this season. The Opera went into rehearsal for *La Cenerentola*, and January was out most afternoons, playing piano for the ballet company. Since frequently he was hired to play at balls that started when the performance was done, he and Ayasha saw one another only in passing. It was a life they were used to. They both complained of it, loudly, but when he'd stop home, between rehearsal and return to the theater with his cornet, he'd find bread, cheese, and apples waiting for him, and the room filled with a fantasia of tulle, silk, muslin pattern-pieces. He'd leave a new comb, or hair ribbons, on the pillow for her and carry up the coal and water, seventy-two steps, to be ready for when she returned.

In Paris, as in New Orleans, this was the rhythm of winter as the town filled with the wealthy and their money ran out like water from a squeezed sponge. All the musicians' wives and mistresses understood that one dipped up the water while it flowed. Summer would be dry.

Then on the Sunday morning – St Hilarion's Day, and four days after what January thought of as the Adventure of the Seraglio – while he and Ayasha drowsed in bed, someone knocked at the door.

'Tell him we're dead.' Ayasha pulled the blankets up over their heads.

And, when January – always conscientious – rolled from beneath the quilts and caught up the second-hand velvet robe against the cold outside the bed curtains, she thrust aside the curtains and shouted at the top of her lungs, 'Go away! We're dead! Coward,' she added as January crossed to the door.

Standing in the dark of the landing, wrapped in what looked like twenty cloaks and veils, was the maidservant Ra'eesa. Relief, anxiety, pleading mingled in her dark, wrinkled eyes.

With the air of a schoolchild repeating by rote a memorized verse, she said, 'Shamira gone.'

THREE

RAN AWAY, was how an advertisement would start out in New Orleans, reflected January.

He'd seen thousands of them – they had been among the first things he'd learned to read, after he'd been given his own freedom.

A little illustration of a fleeing slave, a description, and a reward.

Only, no American would ever admit that the fugitive in question was a concubine.

At the Café La Marseillaise on the Boulevard de Passy they waited while Ra'eesa scurried like a black beetle across the Étoile and vanished between the tall stumps of Napoleon's Arch. Madame Dankerts, who knew them well, brought sweetened cream, griddle cakes, plum compote and coffee, and within half an hour, Ra'eesa reappeared through the Arch, accompanied by *Sitt* Jamilla, cloaked and veiled against the clammy fog.

'Will your coming bring you trouble?' Ayasha asked at once.

The Lady looked about her at the café with great curiosity: the plastered walls painted a vivid yellow, the tin-sheathed wooden counter that separated the little kitchen from the common room, the few working men and their wives and girlfriends drinking coffee and consuming Madame Dankerts' excellent griddle-cakes at the plain little tables. The sight of Ayasha, and of those other women in their Sunday bodices and high-crowned, beribboned hats, seemed to reassure her. This was obviously a place where it was appropriate for a woman to be.

She shook her head. '*Sitt* Utba know not. My lord come Friday from London. I will say, Shamira gone, I fear some harm to her. This – me – he will forgive.' She sat, and Ra'eesa took the chair at her side with the air of one who has never done such a thing in public before. 'Shamira he will not forgive.'

'When did she leave, *Sitt* Jamilla?'

'Night. Ra'eesa –' the Lady touched the maid's wrist gently – 'sleep beside her. Shamira walk about the house yesterday. Better.

I watch, cook watch, Ra'eesa watch, that Lady Utba give no poison—' She shook her head, her eyes filling with concern. '*Taryak* –' she gestured, trying to summon the French word – '*dawâ – ma'jûn* . . .'

'Opium,' provided Ayasha.

'Opium, yes. Opium in water. Girls all asleep. Shamira gone.'

'Was the Lady Utba drugged as well?'

'Lady Utba, her lady, her eunuch—' She lost the word, pantomimed the shape of the house with her hands, which were astonishingly expressive.

'The girls are at one end of the house, the Lady Utba at the other,' provided Ayasha. 'The Prophet has said, a man may take unto himself more than one wife only if he provide them with equal households.'

'So the poison was only administered to the harîm upstairs?'

Ayasha nodded.

'Could Shamira have done this herself?'

Jamilla was silent for so long after January asked this question that he feared she had not understood. But when he began to repeat it, she shook her head, raised her hand. *I understand* . . .

At last she said, 'I do not know.' She brought her dark-blue veil a little away from her face and lifted up under it Madame Dankerts' prosaic white pottery coffee-cup, to drink.

'Is there opium in the house?'

'Yes. Key of chest . . .' Beneath her cloak she jingled them slightly on her girdle. 'Lady Utba also. I look in chest; I think not any gone. But, Shamira walk about the house. And girls . . . Raihana –' she named one of them – 'always a little opium, here, here.' Her slim hands conjured an invisible pillow, an invisible jewel-box, little packets of the drug tucked secretly inside.

'Was any of her clothing gone?' asked January. 'Her shoes?'

'None.'

'Or the clothing of any of the other girls?'

Another emphatic head-shake. Then, with the first wry flicker of a half-smile in her eyes: 'Girls watch clothing. Always taking.' She mimed snatching something and snatching it back. 'Watch like misers. No thing gone.'

Ayasha rolled her eyes at some memory of her own upbringing, and January smiled. Even in the slave cabins of Bellefleur Plantation,

where one would think no one would possess anything, he recalled
how his six-year-old sister Olympe nearly tore the hair off Judy,
the daughter of the other family that shared the ten-by-ten cabin
with them, for 'borrowing' her hair ribbon.

No wonder the Prophet mandated that the households of wives
be kept strictly apart.

'*Sitt* Jamilla,' he said. 'Do *you* think she has run away?'

Again silence, while the Pasha's chief wife considered. The omens
had predicted a male child, and had given young Shamira precedence
over the other women who lived beneath the Turk's roof. But the
woman to whom a girl had been predicted was still a legal wife,
not a concubine, and still 'delighted' the master's heart.

Reason enough to flee.

'If she run,' Jamilla said at last, 'it will go hard, when the master
return. Our master a good man, but of the old ways. Child –' the
expressive hands groped for a concept – 'Hüseyin child in Sultan
palace, raise up to serve, together like brothers. Sultan read French
book, look to West. Hüseyin Pasha read French book, but say: *It
is pollution. Only in Blessed Qur'an is there truth.* But if Shamira
not run, if she *taken* away—'

'Who would take her away, *Sitt* Jamilla?' January spoke quietly,
for in the woman's voice – and in her dark eyes – he detected no
hint that this was melodrama or far-fetched speculation, but a real
possibility.

'Sabid al-Muzaffar.' The slim hands cradled the coffee cup,
seeking warmth from its smooth sides. 'Man of new ways. Father
siphari – own land, own peasants, very rich. Not slave like Hüseyin.
School in France, school also in Egypt, school in London. Bridges,
steam machine, printing book about stars, about sun. Napoleon
law, English gun. Our master say to Sultan: *Send Sabid away.
These Infidel things make men turn from Allah, become like Infidel,
who believe not in Prophet, not in Allah, also not in own God any
more. Without belief, Empire will die.* Sultan . . .' She made a
sweeping gesture, as if of a man scornfully knocking a tableful
of objects to the floor. 'Sabid flee. Now Sabid in Paris.'

'You know this?'

She nodded.

'And your master knows?'

'My master know.'

'Do you know where?'

'Charenton.' Her pronunciation of the little village was surprisingly accurate. The suburb was a small one. A Turk in residence would be remarked, and his house pointed out, without trouble.

'Do you think this Sabid could actually have entered your master's house and taken Shamira?'

Her brows drew together again, troubled. 'I know not. I think not. I know . . .' She shook her head helplessly and held out one expressive hand. 'Shamira flee, Hüseyin Pasha very angry. This she take, his only son.' Her eyes dark with concern, she looked at her other palm as she held it out also, as if balancing the weights of two invisible situations. 'Shamira flee, Sabid hear of it—'

'And he will,' broke in Ayasha. 'A man like that would have a servant, perhaps more than one, in his pay, in the household of his enemy.'

Melodramatic as it sounded, January knew this was almost a certainty. It was not uncommon for even the wealthy ladies of the French aristocracy whose daughters he taught piano to have the maidservants of social rivals on their payroll.

'Sabid find her,' went on Jamilla softly, 'before our master return from London, then he have only son of Hüseyin.'

Only after Ra'eesa had escorted her mistress back to the house – veiled, and dressed in coarse black outer garments, the Lady could have been any anonymous servant – would it be safe for January to go up to the house himself. 'Allah forfend,' muttered Ayasha cynically, 'that the Lady should emerge from its gates, or look upon any man but her master.'

'Shamira could have gone out the same way.' Through the cold-misted window of La Marseillaise, January watched the two black nameless bundles disappear into the confusion of carts from the country, herds of geese, donkey-loads of firewood, and vendors of everything from old shoes to country apples that milled around the city customs-tollbooth on the other side of the Étoile.

'Were such the case, the garments would be missed.' Ayasha mopped up cream and compote with the remains of her third griddle-cake. 'Frenchmen all think there is a great pile of *burqa* and *hijab* lying about somewhere in every Muslim house, all of them alike. But in truth, though the Lady borrowed the garments of a servant, I think that any servant who had her garments borrowed would know it. A lady like *Sitt* Jamilla might possess a half-dozen *burqa* and a dozen veils to choose from, but even a favored concubine would have but a few. My father's maids each had only one, and he was not a poor man. It is the same even in the wealthiest of houses. If Ra'eesa says that no garments are unaccounted for, I think Shamira did indeed have them brought in from somewhere else, or went forth without them.'

'And if someone brought her clothing,' murmured January, and finished his coffee, 'that same someone could have brought in opium as well. Are the kitchen staff French or Turkish?'

'There are two cooks, one French and one Turkish. The undercook is a Turk. The French cook's wife acts as housekeeper.' Ayasha slung her shawl around her shoulders and shook out her skirts as January counted out coin to leave on the table. 'They would have dealings with the Lady Jamilla, but not, of course, with the concubines.' Pale sunlight brightened the leafless trees. As they left La Marseillaise, the bells in the little Convent of St Theresa, on the other side of the thin woods in the village of Batignolles, began to ring sweetly.

'Do you know anything about the girl Shamira?' January quickened his step to dodge past the *diligence* coming in from Rouen, laden with passengers and mail. 'Is it usual for Jews in the East to sell their daughters?'

'There is selling and selling.' The young woman shrugged and tucked up the coarse dark tendrils of her hair beneath her bonnet. 'My father would not have said that he was selling me to be concubine in the house of a man with whom he did much business, but without Labib ibn-Yusuf's camels, Father would have had no means to pay his debts. Then again—' She sprang lightly out of the way of a high-wheeled chaise, driven around the Étoile at a great pace by a very sleek young dandy in a pearl-gray English driving-coat. '*Naghil*!' she shouted after the chaise, and made figs with both fists.

'Then again,' she went on, turning back, 'I had met no boys beyond my own family. Why should I not wish to marry this greedy man who never washed? I think my father must still be wondering about it.'

January remembered the morning he'd been called on to the

back gallery at Bellefleur Plantation, at the age of seven, and informed that his beautiful mother had been sold to the sugar broker St-Denis Janvier. When he and his sister Olympe had been told that they were going to be free and go live with their mother in New Orleans, he recalled, Olympe had spat on M'sieu Janvier's shiny shoes and run out of the room. Growing up in New Orleans, ebony African black among the variegated little quadroons and octoroons at the 'back of town', January had been well aware that many of his playmates' older sisters took 'protectors' – or were taken by them – who were business partners of their white fathers, without much regard for the preferences of the girls. Their mothers, technically free like his own, could do little about this. Why raise a flurry over a daughter's tears when your own house and income might be taken from you as a result?

Tears were a girl's lot.

Ra'eesa met them at Hüseyin's stable gate and led them across to the kitchen quarters. The scullery maids were assembled in the laundry room, as tough and snaggly-haired a gang as January had ever encountered in ten years of living in Paris. Even girls of the lowest classes would fight shy of taking up service in the house of a man who had three concubines and six veiled maidservants who were his to use as he pleased. Annette, Babette, Colette, and Quatorze-Julliet were the sweepings of the Faubourg St-Antoine, and they glared at the cook with wary hostility when they were introduced to January and told to answer his questions.

No, not a single one of them had taken any kind of note in or out, to or from any of those girls upstairs. The very idea!

'We ain't never seen 'em, an' that's a fact,' explained Annette. 'You'd think the world ended at the pantry door.'

'It's true.' Quatorze-Julliet hitched up her skirt to scratch her posterior matter-of-factly. 'Half the time His Excellency's got one of his guards stationed just outside that door, an' if one of us so much as puts a foot through it's: *Go back! Go back!*' She imitated the clumsy French of the guards. ''Fraid we'll give 'em Christian lice or somethin'.' She laughed loudly at her own wit.

A childhood spent in the quarters had told January that the guards were less concerned with lice (Christian or otherwise) than with the coffee beans, sugar, tea, and vanilla stored in the pantry – not to speak of the linen napkins and silver spoons. Any of these could be sold or traded to the rag-and-bone dealers who trolled the streets in any wealthy neighborhood, wailing: *Old grease! Old tea . . .*

Honest cooks jealously guarded the right to sell cooking grease, used tea-leaves and coffee grounds as a perquisite of their office. Less honest ones would peddle tea leaves and coffee beans in a more pristine state – or cooking grease while it was still in the meat – if they thought the mistress of the house wouldn't notice. Even a cook engaged in such commerce would not welcome the amateur depredations of scullery maids, lest such behavior provoke an investigation of the kitchen account-books.

Bribing one of these damsels to purchase opium and bring it in would be child's play.

'The ones you ought to watch is the laundresses,' provided Annette, and she jerked her blonde head toward the door of the room in which January had taken refuge earlier in the week. Two of the armoires there stood open, displaying shelves stacked deep with pressed, folded, and numbered sheets. The great square wicker hampers lined along the wall, in which soiled linen was taken away and fresh brought back clean, gaped empty, like the mouths of cotton-lined hippopotami.

'His Nibs has a heathen woman to do veils an' turbans an' panta-loons,' the girl went on. 'Thinks we'll stink 'em up with our Christian breath, I reckon. Sheets an' towels, they sends out. Yesterday a whole parade of 'em was in and out. It's always like that Saturdays. Baskets all over the room, while the girls went around lookin' for Ma Boudin – that's Cook's missus – to get paid.'

'Do the Turkish girls – the servants, not the concubines – come down to the laundry room to fetch sheets and towels?'

The girls glanced at each other, then nodded. 'Always all veiled up,' added Quatorze-Julliet, 'lest one of 'em get looked at by one of the stablemen an' find herself pregnant.'

'Do you know the laundresses by sight?'

'Some of 'em.' Annette shrugged. 'They comes an' goes. My cousin Fantine an' her Ma, they use pretty regular. Others I've only seen once or twice. My Ma's always pullin' in cousins or the daughters of her friends or whoever she can get, to do deliv-eries. Ma Boudin don't tip worth a Protestant's fart, so there's always different girls.'

*   *   *

'So anything could have been smuggled in.' Followed by Ra'eesa, January and Ayasha exited the back door and retraced the route of January's precipitate flight of four days ago through the gate into the garden, past the low beds of fallow vegetables, across the small patch of lawn and then in among the rose beds, where a very old black gardener was carefully wrapping the pruned bushes in straw. 'On any Saturday, for that matter,' added Ayasha after a moment's thought. 'If that's the day the laundresses are in and out and all over the grounds—'

'So a note could have been gotten in – or out – to make arrangements. Could the girl write French? Or read it?'

'You're very sure she fled of her own accord.'

January looked back across the stable yard, satisfying himself that his estimate of four days ago was correct: it would be almost impossible to cross the yard from the kitchen doors to the garden gate unobserved from the stables. As in any big house – in France or America or, he guessed, Constantinople as well – all the activity went on in the rear quarters. The guards probably occupied the upper floor of the stables. Their windows overlooked the yard between the kitchen door and the gate.

A lantern hung over the gate. Did it remain lit all night?

'*Entia non sunt multiplicanda praeter necessitatem*,' he said after a moment's thought. 'The simplest explanation is best.'

'The simplest explanation being that you cannot resist showing off your Latin?'

January grinned. 'That, too.'

The gravel walk among the roses was fresh, impervious to tracks. 'It's probably possible to break into the grounds, and then into the house after it's locked up for the night,' he said thoughtfully. 'But that would take concerted planning and an inside confederate – a gang, in fact. And I can't imagine how you'd get a woman, even one drugged with opium, down from those chambers under the roof. You'd have to drug the guards in the stable, and Jamilla didn't seem to think that had been done. But whether Shamira actually left on her own, or whether she was lured away . . . There.' He stopped, pointed down to the moist clay of the path.

Back here near the vine-covered wall the gravel was older and deeply trodden into the underlying soil. The rose bushes here, though they'd been pruned, had not yet been wrapped up for the winter. The clay was undisturbed since the previous day's rain, and in it, a narrow foot had left a mark.

'A laundress?'

'If you think one would come out all this way on her rounds wearing fashionable shoes.' January knelt on the grass verge. 'No one with her, so she's not out here with romantic intent. A narrow heel and a thin sole – look how dim the edges are. Would you walk all day in such a shoe? It's an expensive one, but old. See where it's been repaired on the heel?'

Ayasha drew up her skirts to consider her own stout shoes. Deliberately, she set her foot down in another patch of clay nearby and considered the track.

Clay from the path smeared the tough vines on the wall, close to where January had clambered over. 'Here—'

Ayasha plucked a thread from a broken piece of vine. 'White,' she said. 'Cotton, not silk. A petticoat, not a veil or pantaloons—'

'So one of those laundry hampers brought in yesterday contained clothes for her.' January moved a foot or so to the right, where the vines were stout enough to bear his weight. 'Shoes, too . . . I can tell you, here and now, that things can be concealed in those cupboards in the laundry room for hours while guards search the house for intruders. If Shamira were veiled as a servant, and knew which cupboard to look in, she could be in and out of that laundry room in moments. *Allez-oop.*' He set his foot into the toughest part of the vines, scrambled to the top of the wall and leaped down on the other side. Ayasha followed him, in a great whoofing umbrella of petticoats, and left Ra'eesa standing in the garden behind them.

The narrow shoe with the mended heel had trodden deeply in the soft soil at the top of the ditch that separated the wall from the road. January leaped across and knelt again. 'Here.'

Ayasha followed, skirts caught up like a schoolgirl.

'Two-wheeled chaise.' January studied the ruts and hoof prints where the edge of the roadway was soft. 'Here, she's jumped across the ditch and slipped.'

'And here is your answer,' added Ayasha. The mark of a man's boot was dim, owing to the hardness of the roadbed. It was about four feet back from the rear hoof-print: where a man would stand to help a woman into the chaise. 'Look,' she added, pointing into the weedy ditch, 'she's left her lantern behind . . .'

And indeed, half-submerged in the stagnant brown water, January found a small brass candle-lantern – untarnished – whose intricate latticework could only have come from the East. He turned it over, dripping, in his hands and pictured the scene in his mind's eye: last night's foggy darkness, the creak of harness buckles as the chaise came down the narrow road. The walls of the next house – grounds and garden, and the tops of trees – shut off the view toward the Étoile. An English phaeton passed across the end of the road where it debouched into the Rue St-Honoré, amid a great clattering of hooves and the cracking of the driver's whip, and a moment later a slower coach, with a sprinkle of Sunday excursionists even in this raw autumn weather, trundled along in the same direction.

RAN AWAY. Reward.

'And so ends the tale.' Satisfaction rang in Ayasha's voice. 'She left with a man.'

'If she was merely a discontented wife –' January straightened up – 'deceiving a jealous shopkeeper, that would be one thing. But if Hüseyin Pasha pursues her – as he will, if she is carrying his only son – it will go badly for her if she's caught. And worse,' he added, 'if this enemy of his – this Sabid – is the one who finds her. I doubt the Lady Jamilla will want to leave the matter at that.'

FOUR

True to its heritage – for decades its name had been synonymous with libertinage in Paris – the Palais Royale on a Sunday night was lit up like a fairground and twice as crowded. Light from thousands of lamps filled the elegant colonnade that surrounded its enormous central garden, where shoppers for lingerie, silver, watches and gloves swirled past the tables of a myriad of cafés. From the stairways that led up to the upper chambers – gambling rooms, naughty theaters, expensive bordellos – dark-clothed gentlemen ascended and descended, like the angels in Jacob's dream, impervious to the confusion on the lower level through which they passed. In the colonnade clerks, journalists, students, and police spies jostled shoulders with artists, models, actresses from the Comedie, and the artisans whose skills had for centuries made Paris famous. Little grisettes and hat makers hung on each other's arms and chattered like bright-hued birds; young journeymen gaped at the prostitutes who beckoned from the bare gardens. Music drifted from doorways – January could sometimes identify a particular trick of playing: he'd accompanied Jeannot Charbonnière at enough balls to recognize at once the erratic lilt of his flute, had only yesterday morning at ballet rehearsal worked his piano around the lively fiddle of Fructidor Dumay.

His hand clasped in Ayasha's, he nodded to friends and acquaintances at the cafés, stopped to exchange opinions while Ayasha greeted dressmakers, actresses, artists – 'Benjamin, if your wife does not consent to pose for me I shall cut my throat – I promise you I will! – and throw myself into the Seine!' Someone immediately proffered the painter a knife from somebody's dinner, and the artist made a huge show of stabbing himself repeatedly with theatrical stage-blows, like Romeo on hashish, to wild applause from all sides.

Ayasha stood with arms folded and her nose in the air. 'That is the best you can do, Carnot? I've seen better deaths at the pantomime!'

'He lit himself on fire for *me*,' added a flaxen-haired hat-maker, 'only last Tuesday . . .'

January left Ayasha to flirt outrageously with young M'sieu Carnot and his friends, and stepped into the gloom of the White Cat.

His eyes met those of Bourrèges behind the bar. The little hunchback made no further acknowledgement of acquaintance, but when, in time, January picked his way among the close-set tables to the back of the room, he found the cellar stairs unlocked.

The reek of pipe smoke and the murmur of voices rose to meet him as he descended the narrow twist of steps toward the dim blur of a few candles, bright against the utter blackness of the stair.

'Soon, we're not going to be able to feed our families at all,' a man's voice was saying, urgent against the background mutter. 'Does the King care? No more than his fat brother did.'

'We need more than talk, Maurice,' said someone else. 'Votes are what we need! And those fat Ducs and Marquises would sooner sell their mothers than open up the Chamber of Deputies to anyone who isn't their brother or their cousin.'

'We must have education—'

'It's useless to talk of education if it is only for men!' chimed in a thin, dark young man in a corner. 'The whole system must be reformed! Women, too, must be educated—'

'Education won't do us a damn bit of good until we have the vote!'

'The vote won't get us a fart in hell until the king makes it possible for wheat to be brought into Paris at a cost that poor men can afford to pay!'

Heads turned as January appeared in the dark of the doorway. Someone started to shove a stack of pamphlets out of sight behind a bench, then recognized him – by his height more than anything else, the only thing discernible in the tobacco fog. The speaker at the center table, a tall fair man like a denatured Viking, nodded a greeting and immediately went back to his harangue on the price of potatoes. After a short pause to let his own eyes grow accustomed, January saw the man he sought at a table near the stairs. Round-faced, smooth-haired, and genially epicene, he seemed as out of place among the working men and journalists around him as a *pêche glacée* in a soup kitchen. The rough shirt and short corduroy jacket that hugged those plump shoulders had more the air of a disguise than of garments in which actual work had ever been done.

January had helped break in that jacket when it was new, lest those who habitually gathered at the White Cat to defy the royal statutes against discussing politics should mistake its wearer for a police spy, and an incompetent one at that.

'Benjamin!' Daniel ben-Gideon held up one moist, plump hand to shake. Though suitably dirty, it was soft as a maiden aunt's.

'You're never going to convince anyone you're poor until you grow some calluses.' January clasped the ladylike fingers in greeting. 'And lose some weight.'

'My dear Benjamin, not a soul in this room – saving your excellent self – has ever spared me so much as a glance from the speaker, the newspapers –' the plump man gestured to the enormous pile of journals and pamphlets heaped on the table before him – 'and whoever it is he's arguing with. I could come in here in a court coat and knee breeches and no one would look up. Besides –' ben-Gideon moved his chair aside as January leaned closer to hear over the sudden flurry of shouting around the speaker – 'I tell anyone who asks the truth: I am the proverbial Rich Man's Son. My heart has been captured by the writings of M'sieu le duc de St-Simon, and my father has hired detectives to keep me away from the cause of the working man.'

'That's what you call the truth?'

'Well, it's true that I am a rich man's son, anyway. Shall we go upstairs? Once Maurice gets started on internal tariffs not a great deal else gets "discussed".'

They reascended, bought a bottle of wine from Bourrèges, and settled in the darkest and least noisy corner of the White Cat. It was marginally less black than the cellar – mostly owing to the lamps out in the colonnade – and the air marginally more breathable, and, January reflected, if the place got raided by the secret police there was a far better chance of getting out. Bourrèges paid a substantial bribe to the local Prefect of Police every week to make sure that the insurgents of the 'Political Reading Club' could talk sedition in his cellar in peace, but with increasing unrest throughout the city, this was no real guarantee.

'I'm looking for a girl,' said January.

'In the Palais Royale? Benjamin, I'm shocked.'

January mimed boxing his companion's ears – something that would have gotten him arrested in his home city of New Orleans, one reason that he had no intention of ever returning to New Orleans again as long as he lived, secret police or no secret police. 'If a Jewess from the East – her family comes from Cairo, I gather – were to find herself in need of help in Paris, where would she go?'

'To her family,' replied ben-Gideon promptly.

'I'm not sure she has one in Paris.'

'Benjamin, my mother spends eleven and a half hours out of twenty-four going from sister to sister, from aunt to aunt, from the houses of her sisters-in-law and second-cousins to the grand-parents of my father's old business-partners, lugging my sisters along with her, and what do you think they all talk about? Family.' Ben-Gideon ticked off subjects with his fingers. 'Who's marrying whom. Who shouldn't have married whom and why not. Who's expecting a child and who isn't bringing their children up properly. *Oh, was she the one who married Avram ben-Hurri ben-Moishe ben-Yakov and is now operating that import business in Prague? . . . No, no, that was the OTHER Cousin Rachel who married Avram ben-Hurri ben-Moishe ben-CHAIM and THEY'RE in Warsaw, where THEIR son is a rabbi . . .* Every rabbi from Portugal to Persia will tell you that women's minds are incapable of the concentration required for study of the Torah, yet I guarantee you that not a single word of this lore is forgotten. You can drop any Jew over the age of seven naked in the dark out of a balloon anywhere in Europe, and he or she will locate family in time for breakfast. Who is this girl you're looking for?'

'Her name is Shamira,' said January. Any one of his Aunties back on Bellefleur Plantation, for their part, could tell him where their brothers and sisters, nephews and nieces, former husbands and parents and parents of former husbands, had been sold to, and no traveler came up or down the river but that his valet and groom made their way out to the quarters with word from Cousin Rasmus in Ascension Parish or Aunt Felice in Mobile. 'Her family hails from Cairo, but her father had business connections with Constantinople. I think they dealt in wheat.'

Shamira had spoken little of her family, Ra'eesa had said.

Certainly, she had never given her father's name, out of shame at what had become of his daughter.

'Her father died last year, and Shamira went into the household of Hüseyin Pasha—'

Ben-Gideon's brown eyes opened wide at the mention of the Plenipotentiary's First Deputy.

'—and that is *not* for mention abroad. The girl has fled his household. If she's retaken, I don't believe the King will stop the Pasha from taking fairly serious revenge.'

'And for whom are you working?' Ben-Gideon's round face – smeared artistically with a little lampblack, to counterfeit, in the low light, the stubble that would be out of the question in his daytime incarnation in his father's banking house – lost its child-like quality behind a watchful mask.

'The girl herself.'

The black eyebrows quirked in polite disbelief. 'She hired you to find her after running away? What an original approach to escape.'

In few words, January outlined the attempt at poisoning and the circumstances of the girl's flight. 'It's hard to see how the girl could have genuinely fled with a lover,' he concluded. 'She hasn't been out of the grounds. According to the Lady Jamilla, the Pasha's first wife, the concubines are permitted outside only in the garden under a guard of eunuchs. She has neither seen nor spoken to anyone not of the household since her arrival.'

'Yet the escape sounds extremely well planned.'

'Exactly. So it must either have been set up by someone in her family, or someone whom she *thinks* is in her family. And there lives in Paris an enemy of Hüseyin Pasha's, a man named Sabid al-Muzaffar, whom Hüseyin caused to be exiled. I – and the Lady Jamilla – would like to satisfy ourselves that the girl is in fact out of harm's way before the Pasha himself returns on Friday. But I have no intention of informing anyone of the girl's whereabouts until I've spoken with the girl herself.'

Ben-Gideon considered the matter, turning the cheap pottery wine-cup in his fingers. Snatches of song from the music hall next door came through the wall. Men passed among the crowded tables, and now and then someone would emerge from the cellar and glance watchfully around before gliding out the rear door into the grimy little yard, and so away over the wall in the direction of the Halles. Raised on accounts of the *liberté, egalité*, and *fraternité* won by France, January had been vexed – but not surprised – to find on his arrival that far from being liberated, the country was once more under the control of a King and of nobles who appeared to have learned nothing from the events of 1789.

And King or no King, *fraternité* or no *fraternité*, nobody in France was any more likely than they were in the United States to hire a black man to come anywhere near them with a scalpel.

But it was something at least to be able to smoke a cigar in public, or carry a knife in his boot if he happened to be passing through an unwholesome part of town. The ferocious censorship clamped by the King on newspapers and journals was no worse than the systematic attempts of the American whites to prevent blacks from learning to read. At least here, the whites could get a taste of what it was like – those that cared, and a great many simply didn't. And there were always places like *La Chatte Blanche* where banned journals and seditious pamphlets could be read and talked about with men – and a few women – who still cherished the liberties of which neither Napoleon nor the present King had approved.

Since the old King's death two years ago, and the accession of his feckless brother to the throne, censorship had grown stricter. It was now against the law to criticize the Church, and men had started disappearing, arrested by the White Terror – the secret police – for no particular reason. Political parties – even political discussion-groups – were outlawed, and it was in fact illegal for more than twenty people to meet together for any purpose what- soever, which made parties in the painter Carnot's attic rather chancy affairs.

For which reason January found it interesting that Daniel ben- Gideon – the son of one of the wealthiest bankers in Paris – would have taken up haunting the White Cat. Were there to be trouble some night, none of the nobles surrounding the throne would put himself forward to rescue Moses ben-Gideon's son from punish- ment: a Jew, with merely money to recommend him. A jumped-up banker who'd made his fortune lending money to such appalling parvenus as the Bonapartes.

Which meant that ben-Gideon, who made it a point to belong

to every social circle in Paris and to read every one of its hundred-plus newspapers, was of the opinion that the radicals who called for the King's downfall might very well win.

'I've met Sabid,' said ben-Gideon at last. 'He's as fanatical about bringing factories and State education to the Sublime Porte as Hüseyin is about handing everything over to the *imams*. If I hadn't, I'd have said: *Good luck and leave me out of it . . .*'

'But God help anyone,' said January quietly, 'who is caught between two fanatics. Particularly a woman.'

'Amen.' Ben-Gideon stood up, plump and comfortable in his shabby clothing, a balding mama's boy of thirty-two – January's own age – who sweated when he walked and would undoubtedly call for a bath the moment he returned to his parents' very elegant town-house . . . But who had not, January guessed, wasted a moment of his evening of drinking bad wine and listening to what was being said by the angry poor.

'I'll find out what I can. My impression is that Sabid al-Muzaffar is the kind of man who would not baulk at harming the innocent to regain his position in the Sultan's good graces. But I want your word, Benjamin.' Ben-Gideon shook an admonishing finger. 'If you find this girl has located her family and gone back to them, you're not to breathe a word of it to Hüseyin without asking me first. If she's managed to get herself to safety I'll not have anything to do with sending her back. For one thing,' he added with a quick grin, 'the Rothschilds would cut Father completely if I did, and then I'd be in the street.'

January crossed the fingers of both hands, the way the children did back on the plantation for luck: 'May the witches ride me three times around the moon if I tell,' he replied solemnly, picked up his wine cup from the table and tipped the dregs on to the floor, as all his aunties said that you were supposed to do, to keep the spirits away. 'Family is family, but the Rothschilds—'

A child in the colonnade called out, 'Flics on the way!'

So much, thought January, for Bourrèges' program of bribery. Ben-Gideon said, 'Damn!' and the men at the table nearest them said things considerably stronger, and January caught his friend by the wrist and plunged at once for the back door. Men were pouring out of the cellar door, blundering into those who were trying to fight their way out and toward the Rue des Petits Champs.

January dragged ben-Gideon out the doorway, across the stinking little yard, through the gate and into the nearest doorway—

'Hey, there, mister!' protested the woman already occupying that dark niche.

A faint, youthful voice from between her and the wall added: 'Look here, now—'

'Pardon us, Mademoiselle.' January bowed, and his companion dug in a pocket for a couple of coins. 'Pardon us, M'sieu.'

In the Rue des Petits Champs voices were raised. There was the sound of blows. The police had been waiting for fugitives there.

January tested the door at the rear of the rather crowded embrasure, found it locked, and kicked it – hard. The wood jerked and cracked – 'You're paying for this, you know,' he informed ben-Gideon – and he kicked the door again. This time the lock splintered away from the frame, and January, ben-Gideon, the girl, and her customer all tumbled inside just as the owner of the establishment, an elegantly black-clothed gentleman with a countenance straight out of an antique painting and a vocabulary straight out of the sewers, strode into the tiny back-room.

'What the goddam hell—?'

'Flics.' Ben-Gideon caught the gentleman's wrist and deposited five silver francs on the palm of his white kid glove.

His face like a Flemish saint who's just bitten on a lemon, the gentleman said, 'Well, you ain't bloody goin' out through the goddam salon an' upsettin' my goddam gentlemen. This's a goddam respectable place. You stay the fuck here an' don't cause no goddam trouble. You—' He caught the girl's arm in one hand, her customer's in the other: the boy looked about sixteen, pasty-faced and terrified. 'Get back out there.'

'Oh, here.' Ben-Gideon handed the gentleman another two francs. By the sound of it, the police raid had boiled back into the alley and a riot was starting. Shouts echoed from the high walls, and the fouled cobblestones rang as roof tiles and bricks were hurled from the windows of the rooms above. 'They're with us.'

The gentleman shoved the back door more or less back into position and shot the bolts. 'Fucken Jacobins.'

January, ben-Gideon, the student – whose name was LeMoreau and who hailed from Brussels – and the whore all remained in the back room of what January guessed was the downstairs portion of the gambling hall *Au Bon Oncle* for an hour or more. Since the downstairs was mostly a wine shop, the glow of lamplight came through the curtain and with it the rise and fall of voices; upstairs, January knew, there would be new-style Argand lamps and almost total silence broken only by the rattle of the dice box and the voices of the croupiers. Here, downstairs, there were women's voices as well. Once someone asked, 'What on earth is going on out there?'

The owner's deep voice replied, 'I believe it to be police trouble, sir. Nothing to concern us here.'

'I presume he pays the police more than Bourrèges does,' murmured January.

'Nonsense,' retorted ben-Gideon, perched on a box of candles playing cards with the girl. 'Nobody pays more than Bourrèges does.'

The shouting in the alleyway reached a crescendo, then faded away. January guessed that police had come into the White Cat from the front as well as the alley, and if so, there had probably been fighting in the colonnade as well. But he guessed Ayasha had had the good sense to head straight into the dark central gardens at the first sign of trouble, and stay there.

When the disgruntled gentleman returned to the back room to give them the all-clear and unbolt the back door, nothing stirred in the wet blackness outside except a few scurrying rats, definite proof that things were back to normal. Stumbling on broken bricks and roof tiles that littered the alley, January and his companion worked their way around through the maze of medieval streets and stinking gutters that lay between the upriver side of the Palais Royal and the Butte St Roche, and so, eventually, back into the Palais gardens again. To judge by the crowds, one would think nothing out of the ordinary had happened – which in fact it had not. As he'd suspected, he found Ayasha at the café table where he'd left her, playing dominoes with Carnot.

'There!' she said in triumph. 'You owe me ten centimes!'

'Witch.' The painter dug in his pocket. 'You need to keep better control of your wife, Janvier – bloody hell, I haven't a sou. Let me paint a portrait of you—'

'You come up and carry water upstairs for me,' retorted Ayasha, 'and I'll forgive you. There was scarcely any fighting out here, *Mâlik*; Bourrèges is swearing he'll have the Police Superintendent's job for this. A hundred francs a week, he pays! Will you join us for coffee, Daniel?'

'I think –' ben-Gideon bent to kiss her hand – 'I shall decline the pleasure for the moment. Benjamin, I shall see you tomorrow night, I hope with something to tell. Heaven knows if I shall even be able to get a cab, dressed like this. I've had rather enough excitement for one evening.'

January – remembering back to the morning's abrupt wakening in the fog – replied, 'I couldn't agree more.'

FIVE

The following afternoon – after a morning spent giving piano lessons to various young ladies of the aristocracy and three hours rehearsing with the Opera chorus – January, instead of returning to dinner and, it was to be hoped, an hour of rest at Ayasha's side, made his way up the river to Charenton.

The villa rented by Sabid al-Muzaffar lay four miles from the Rue Le Peletier where the Opera stood, near the Bois de Vincennes, a detached villa in its own grounds surrounded by gardens and a pink brick wall. But January ascertained, by dint of inquiring for a fictitious brother who might have taken employment in the district, that there was no concubine nonsense about al-Muzaffar. 'As good as a Christian, he is,' proclaimed Madame Lyons, who kept the local café. 'Except for going to church on Friday instead of Sunday, and what is that, eh? But no falling on his knees five times a day and refusing to sit at my tables just because I might happen to use a little honest salt-pork in my stew. *The Lord knows what's in a man's heart whether he's on his knees or on his feet*, says he – and it's always beat me, how anything gets done in those Mohammedan countries, with everyone stopping what they're doing five times a day . . . And *I* say, the good Lord will prosper us only if we lend Him a hand and prosper ourselves, without always slacking off to pray.'

'I couldn't agree more.' January gazed consideringly through the windows at the rain-wet lane that led toward Sabid's villa, as if expecting to see this paragon of secular rationality appear at any moment. 'Yet what do his servants think of this? Surely it would be difficult for him to find men of his own faith who share his outlook.'

'He'd not have them around him, he says.' By her tone she considered this a further mark of civilization. 'He's not a man to go bringing in a lot of Infidel devils into our village—'

For the district around Charenton was much more like a village than it was like a part of Paris.

'—when there's good men hereabouts needing the work in these hard times.' She glared and nodded, as if January had announced his opposition to this view of the matter. 'Laurent – my godson, who works as a footman in his house – says the only heathen servants are the grooms, who speak no French and keep to themselves in the stables where they belong, and whether they pray or not, Modeste – that's the coachman, whose mother is my neighbor and has a tongue in her head that a Christian woman should take shame to herself to own! – Modeste has no idea. Not that Modeste could tell the difference between a priest's sermon and a donkey's bray!'

There followed an embittered diatribe against Modeste and his mother, whose father had cheated Madame Lyons' father out of farmland that would have kept her from the indignity of having to run a café in the first place, not that she had the slightest objection to honest work . . . to which January listened with patience before guiding the conversation back to Sabid and his servants.

There were five grooms, and two eunuch servants for Sabid's wife – 'Not that anyone ever sees *her*, but what can you expect? A man needs a wife, and no Christian woman could be expected to marry a Mohammedan . . . But, Laurent tells me, His Excellency keeps to one wife and doesn't go bringing in those nasty concubines. And his wife's servants are respectable old women – barrin' those nasty eunuchs, which I don't hold with, but I will say there's some in *this* land that could do with having capons in their henyards instead of roosters.'

'But this is astonishing,' exclaimed January. 'My brother gave me the impression – I don't know why – that His Excellency's circumstances were reduced. Yet so large a household—'

'Your brother,' retorted Madame Lyons, 'has no notion of how the aristocracy lives – hand to mouth and in the pockets of money-lenders, who should be outlawed from any Christian country! As for His Excellency, it's true he had to flee from Constantinople, through wicked lies that was told about him by an enemy who had the Sultan's ear. But he has friends in this country, good friends who owed him for favors he did them, and he doesn't do so badly, Laurent says. *And*, Laurent says, he's seen any number of wealthy gentlemen at His Excellency's – not those lazy nobles that hang about the King, but bankers like M'sieu Rothschild and M'sieu Bethmann, even if they are Jews, and folk like that fellow Savart who made such a fortune selling boots to the Army back under the Emperor, though what France was doing with an Italian Emperor is more than I can stomach . . . and Englishmen like that M'sieu Polders who owns all those factories and banks.'

This information gleaned, January strolled down the lane that Madame Lyons had pointed out to him and took as good a look at al-Muzaffar's house as he could without being conspicuous. This wasn't easy for a man six-feet three-inches tall and proportioned like a coal-black oak-tree, so January took care not to linger. Still, he formed an impression of a dwelling far less palatial than that of Hüseyin Pasha, with a garden to one side and a single-story stable building at the rear.

Five horses, he estimated as he turned his steps back toward the Rue de Bercy. Not nearly enough to justify the keeping of five grooms.

Bodyguards?

The house itself was two floors plus an attic. Plenty of room to keep a woman prisoner up under that tall mansard roof. If Sabid's wife had eunuchs of her own there was no reason for the French servants to even know.

A horseman was approaching him on the grassy verge of the road, but January didn't realize it was Sabid al-Muzaffar until the man was opposite him: such was the effect, he realized – looking up into the brown Arabian face, the hooked nose and aloof dark eyes – of Western clothing. The man wore neat riding-breeches and English boots, a trim coat of dark-gray superfine wool, and a white neckcloth, without a single pin or jewel or flare of color to speak of the East.

But the horse was pure Arab stock and probably had a pedigree longer than a number of the Marquises whose daughters January instructed in the piano.

And do you permit your wife to go abroad as you do, he wondered, *in the garb and character of the West?* From the opposite side of the lane he watched two very tall and beefy 'grooms' emerge from the gate to greet their master: swarthy-complected Berbers, like Ayasha, with scarred faces and gold rings in their ears. *Does she receive these Rothschilds and Bethmanns and*

Polders at your house? Will she be on your arm the next time you visit the Opera?

Or is that 'different'?

Madame al-Muzaffar certainly didn't accompany her husband to the ball that night at the town house of the Duc de Bellegarde.

January played for a performance of *La Cenerentola* which ended at ten thirty, changed his shirt and neckcloth backstage along with half the other musicians who also had balls to play at, and was ensconced with Jeannot Charbonnière, Narcisse Panchaud, Lucien Imbot and two or three others behind a bower of hothouse ferns at one end of the Bellegarde ballroom by eleven, hungry enough to eat his own sheet music.

The Duc himself had fled France before the blood of the Bastille's garrison was dry on its stones, and of his own accord he would no sooner have invited to his house anyone he had not known at Versailles in its heyday than he would have invited the relatives of his footmen. His daughter, however – married to the Comte de Villeneuf – had a daughter of her own to dispose of and was, January had heard, well aware of the financial situation of most of the ancient nobility who had returned to France in the wake of the Kings. He hid his smile as he watched the Comtesse – daughter in tow – bestow her convent-bred charm upon the assortment of bankers, financiers, and government contractors that the Old Duc so resolutely ignored. One could almost hear her saying: *Ah, M'sieu Savart, and how is your so-distinguished son . . .?*

'Even the ones without sons, she smiles upon,' whispered Jeannot to January between minuets, and he shook the moisture from his flute. 'They *know* people who have sons.'

'In New Orleans,' replied January thoughtfully, 'when I would play at the Blue Ribbon balls for the demi-mondaines to meet their white protectors, the older ladies would bring their young daughters, to introduce in just the same way. Although mind you,' he added, 'the young ladies were *far* better dressed than Mademoiselle de Villeneuf—'

'Hssh!' Old Lucien poked him in the back with his fiddle bow. 'D'you want the Duc to throw you out? Then what would we do for a piano?'

The resemblance to New Orleans balls didn't end there, January reflected as the little orchestra glided into the first exquisite bars of a Mozart contredanse. When the fed-up populace of Paris had started murdering aristocrats in the streets – or, more usually, murdering in the streets the hapless soldiers that the aristocrats had hired to protect themselves – large numbers of those aristocrats had fled to the great French sugar-island of St-Domingue, where many of them had family. Others fled to New Orleans, still a very French town though it had been ruled by the Spanish for a generation at that point. When the fed-up slaves of St-Domingue had started murdering whites – to the horror of the French originators of *liberté, egalité,* etc. – the aristocrats and every other white on the island had quickly decamped to New Orleans as well. There they had encountered a great many French who were all in favor of the Revolution, about whose opinions they could do nothing – the country being under the control of the Spanish – except write scathing diatribes against them in New Orleans' several newspapers and be as rude as possible to them at social events.

Thus, any ball in New Orleans had an air about it of a badly-made béchamel sauce, its elements separating to opposite ends of the ballroom: Republicans not speaking to Royalists, Napoléonistes snubbing Republicans, and nobody speaking to the Americans, who showed up in greater and greater numbers, with money falling out of their pockets . . .

Here in France, the old nobility resolutely snubbed the Ducs and Marquises created by Bonaparte in his years of imperial rule, the Ultras refused to speak to the Liberal Royalists, the Liberal Royalists (not to be confused with the actual Liberals, whom no one invited anywhere) turned their backs on the Doctrinaires. Nobody invited the Constitutionnels anywhere either – the rich, educated middle-class and professionals.

Unless, of course, they had marriageable sons.

'My dear Benjamin . . .'

At the conclusion of the minuet, Daniel ben-Gideon appeared on the other side of the banked foliage.

'You're in luck.' He nodded toward the elderly gentleman at the center of a group of Liberal Royalists: tasteful in dark grays in contrast to the ancient nobility, many of whom wore the brilliant uniforms of the Army. 'Jacob L'Ecolier has numerous family connections in Cairo and in Constantinople – where the family name is Talebe; Heaven only knows what it is in Egypt. They import wheat and finance slave-vessels to Brazil. And that –' he gestured with a kid-gloved hand in the direction of a stout, hook-nosed man in conversation with the Napoleonic Baron DesMarines – 'is Abraham Rothenberg, first-cousin to the primary banker of the Khedive of Egypt and related to half the Israelites in Alexandria.'

Ben-Gideon himself, perfumed and pomaded and resplendent in a beautifully-cut pale-green coat that made him look like a colossal melon, had the air of one who didn't even know where the Palais Royale *was*. 'I think Elias Haber is here as well. He's also got connections in Constantinople and family that covers the North African coast from Algeria to Sinai.'

January noticed that none of the men in question seemed to have family with them. A precaution against the resounding snub from the ancient aristocracy that awaited any woman of Jewish birth, be her husband never so wealthy? He had observed on other occasions that when the Jewish financiers and traders brought their wives, the only ones who spoke to them were the wives of their husbands' business partners, and even then – if they were Christian – not for any longer than was strictly polite. Most men understood that business is business – except for the diehard Ultras, who did not appear to understand anything whatsoever. The Marquises and Duchesses, and the female hangers-on and cousins of the great families, in their gowns of point lace and Italian silk and their elaborately wired topknots, dared not be seen to speak to those dark, quietly-dressed, often elegant ladies, lest the *haut ton* whisper: *She receives – well – JEWS* . . .

Meaning if you went to her teas or her at-homes, you might find yourself in a position of having to recognize a Jewess socially.

There are some barriers – he had overheard this more than once, while teaching little Mademoiselle La Valette or Coigny or Régnier their simplified scraps of Mozart – *that one simply must never let down* . . .

'I'll tackle Rothenberg first.' Ben-Gideon set his champagne glass on the tray of a liveried footman who passed by. 'He's a cousin of mine.'

'One other question.'

Lucien flourished into the opening bars of 'Le Pantalon'. It was time to get back to work.

'Is there anyone here connected to the French Embassy in Constantinople?' January whispered hastily, even as his fingers followed the violin's lead. 'Can you find out if anyone has recently returned from there, who might have encountered this girl—'

'While casually dropping in on Hüseyin Pasha's harem?' Ben-Gideon's eyebrows bent like neat little bows. 'I'll ask.'

For the next twenty minutes, January devoted the whole of his attention and the whole of his heart to the light-hearted glitter of chassés, jetés, rigadoons and emboittés; to the soft swish of silk petticoats and the light pat of dogskin slippers on the waxed parquet of the ballroom floor. And within seconds, all other concerns vanished. There were times when he missed the sense of helping people that he'd had, in his days as a surgeon; the joy of seeing a woman walk out of the Hôtel Dieu alive, whose life had been despaired of, or of hearing the voices of a family clustered around the bed of an injured child as that child woke once more to life . . .

The sense that he had acted, for a brief space of time, truly as a servant of God.

But God dwelled in music, too.

And there was nothing that gave him greater joy and so deep a peace of heart.

When he looked up again, as the dancers separated – the young men in their clocked silk stockings and bright cutaway coats to fetch lemonade for girls like pastel blossoms in ivory, primrose, cream – it was to see Sabid al-Muzaffar stroll into the ballroom with a young and soberly-dressed gentleman whose face seemed vaguely familiar.

He leaned over to Lucien Imbot and whispered, 'Who's the *rutin*?' with a nod in that direction.

The violinist shook his head. 'Not a clue. The one with al-Muzaffar, you mean?'

January nodded. In the course of several 'seasons' of playing for the wealthy, he knew most of them by sight, and old Lucien – who as first violinist in the household orchestra of Queen Marie Antoinette had come within twenty-four hours of losing his head in the Terror – knew them all. Which meant that this sunburnt young gentleman, whose eyes seemed so much older than his face and who bore himself with the unmistakable carriage of the old aristocracy, must be newly-returned to Paris. His plain black coat was new and exquisitely tailored – *just home, from wherever he's been, and tricked out by his welcoming family*. Thus its color was a deliberate comment on the brilliant hues of the men around him. *Church?* That would make him a younger son.

But there was something in his expression that rebuked the fashionable young Abbés and Chevaliers who crowded around the stylish Bishops in attendance at the ball.

'Arnoux de Longuechasse.' Jeannot knocked the moisture from his flute again. 'The Marquis' brother. I played for the family Wednesday night – whilst the rest of you lot were amusing the riff-raff at the Opera – a little *affaire* to welcome him home from Constantinople. Most elevated. Gluck and Salieri . . . None of your opera airs and waltzes for the Abbé.'

'Constantinople?'

'Attached to the Ambassador's suite. Almoner or something. Holier than the College of Cardinals all rolled into one. But the Marquis' valet tells me Arnoux made his name teaching French to the ladies of the Sultan's harem.'

A gigue followed, and another minuet. It was only in the houses of these ancient families that these court dances were still performed, when everyone else in Paris was doing the waltz. At intervals January glanced from his music to sweep the ballroom with his eye: the place was ablaze with a thousand francs' worth of beeswax candles, and the young Abbé de Longuechasse was easy to spot in his sober garb. Sabid remained in the ballroom, watching the dancers, though he did not himself dance. The Abbé was gone the first two times January looked for him, but on the third occasion – after the minuet – he was in conversation with Sabid again, presenting him to his brother the Marquis . . .

Which is why his face was familiar. January had played at the balls given by Louis-Antoine du Plessis-Vignerot, Marquis de Longuechasse, a score of times. The Marquis bowed stiffly, but did not offer snuff, nor accept that which al-Muzaffar extended to him in a golden box.

The du Plessis-Vignerots, January knew, were among the most Ultra of the Ultras, clinging haughtily to the old ways. January noted with amusement that the Marquis and his wife likewise snubbed both the wealthy business gentlemen invited by Madame de Bellegarde and the assorted counts and barons whose titles had been created by Napoleon. When, much later in the evening, Daniel ben-Gideon reappeared beside the orchestra, January asked him if the Abbé de Longuechasse had by any chance taught any other ladies besides those of the Sultan's household.

The banker's son flung up his hands in mock dismay. 'You don't expect he'd answer that question – or any question I addressed to him – do you? I should be lucky if he didn't fling Holy Water at me.'

'He didn't fling it at Sabid,' pointed out January.

'He probably didn't bring any with him tonight, then,' retorted ben-Gideon. 'The whole family suspects the Banque de France is part of a plot against the Pope and thinks the King should bring back the Inquisition. They'll barely speak to Protestants, let alone a money-grubbing Jew. I'm surprised His Holiness the Abbé consented to lend his countenance to the ball here tonight.'

January watched the Marquise de Longuechasse – a stout woman without a trace of the jolliness commonly attributed to stout women – herd her far-traveling young brother-in-law in the direction of the Comtesse de Villeneuf and her marriageable daughter. 'Perhaps he's under duress.'

The banker laughed. 'Perhaps he is. And I must say he's a most handsome young man, despite the sunburnt look. A shocking waste. Half the family's in Holy Orders; the only aunt that survived the Revolution is an abbess, and all three of her sisters – also nuns – were guillotined. The only reason he's not in orders himself is because he's his brother's heir. He's the last person who'd be telling tales of what went on in the Harem of the Sultan, even if he was admitted . . . I wonder if they castrated him? It would account for the gloomy expression. I shall inquire . . .'

And ben-Gideon moved off, with the same expression of perpetually fascinated interest that he'd worn listening to the would-be rebels at the *Chatte Blanche*.

SIX

On the following morning, when January woke – late – to find Ayasha gone as usual, it was also to find three buckets of water lined up in front of the fire, the largest kettle filled and simmering gently at the back of the little hearth, and a note on the shelf beside his shaving razor.

My dearest Benjamin,

Enquiry among the other members of my tribe last night unearthed no mention of a fleeing girl seeking refuge in the tents of her kinsfolk. Jacob L'Ecolier does – or did – indeed have family in Cairo who have business dealings with Hüseyin Pasha. He was aware that his second-cousin Isaac was gathered to the bosom of their fathers late last year, but because of estrangements in the family knew nothing of the fate of Isaac Talebe's wife or children. He has asked to be kept notified of any information you learn, and has offered – discreetly – to reimburse monies laid out in the search for the girl.

Scalded with the holy water that was flung in my face, and muttering curses against all Christians, I shall continue to creep about the city making enquiries after our Most Christian Abbé's adventures in the Sultan's harem.

Daniel

Thoughtfully, January shaved, bathed, and dressed in a morning costume of stylish gray; checked the contents of his music satchel; collected his cornet, since the morning's agenda included rehearsals for the Opera; and descended the seventy-two steps to the street. To judge by the outcry as he reached the *deuxième étage*, the situation in the Paillole household had not changed since yesterday (*'You cannot go on expecting your father and me to support you if you show no interest in your studies! Every morning I ask the Blessed Virgin why it was your brother God saw fit to take from us, and not yourself. . .!'*) and on the *premier*, he was delayed by a long diatribe from Madame Barronde about that worthless brat that Ayasha persisted in hiring to carry water up the stairs for her and who was just looking for what he could steal. Yes, it was Christian of her to give the boy a *sou* now and again, but only ill would come of encouraging those devil's imps of street children . . .

Poucet, nine years old, lounged on the steps of the building across the street in a spot of thin sunlight, dividing an apple and part of a loaf of bread with the little gang of younger children who ran with him. The boy saluted January cheerfully as January crossed to him. It was true that Ayasha would generally pay the child to lug water up the four flights from the yard rather than do it herself, and it was also true that Poucet or one of his gang of infant beggars probably did steal stockings if Madame Barronde's hired girl left them hanging on the clothesline. He suspected that Madame Barronde would have shot Poucet if she'd thought she could have gotten away with it, rather than have him exercise his 'evil influence' on her nine-year-old Charlotte or seven-year-old Jean-Stanislas, who regarded the juvenile rabble with awed fascination.

'*Et alors, copains.*' January returned the salute. 'Thank you for bringing up the water.'

'It's nuthin'.' Poucet shrugged elaborately, but January could tell he was pleased. 'Ma Barronde carried on like we was gonna steal it or somethin'. You shoulda heard your lady dress her down! What's a *harmoota*?'

'Just what you think it is,' said January with a grin – careful, as he always was, to address the boy by the formal 'vous' of adulthood, rather than calling him 'tu' like a child. 'You have anything going the next few days?'

'Saturday I'm speakin' before the Chamber of Deputies,' replied the boy grandly. 'An' Sunday I have to give the sermon at Notre Dame. 'Til then I'm at your service, chief.'

'Thank you,' said January. He handed him ten centimes. 'You know the Marquis de Longuechasse's house?'

'Sure thing. His coachman's a sport – lets us sleep in the hayloft sometimes, long as we're up and out of there early before Her Ladyship gets up.'

'I thought all rich ladies slept until three in the afternoon.'

'Not her!' piped in Chatoine, Poucet's sister, a tiny child almost lost in a much older boy's cast-offs. 'Has to get up early, see, 'cause the maids might steal a piece of coal while they're makin' breakfast.'

'You know the Marquis' brother?'

'The one that's been in foreign parts?'

'That's the man,' said January. 'Can you follow him? See where he goes?'

'I can tell you now where he goes,' retorted Poucet. 'He never goes no place but to the Bishop's, and to St-Louis-Le-Grand to hobnob with the Jesuits, and out to the convent in Batignolles where his aunt's a nun.'

'Batignolles?' January remembered the clear notes of the convent bells beyond the woods, the cold mists outside the windows of the Café La Marseillaise. 'St Theresa's?'

'Some saint.' The boy shrugged. 'Whoever they are, they don't like kids hangin' around the gate corruptin' the girls locked up inside.'

January thought about this for a moment. 'Does de Longuechasse have a single-horse chaise?'

'That he does, chief. Red like sealing wax, with black wheels and a black horse to draw it. What a mover! *Formidable!*'

'Find out if you can – and without anyone at his stables knowing you're asking – if the chaise went out Saturday night. Can you do all that?'

'Is he up to something?' Chatoine's bright black eyes sparkled under the short-chopped straggle of her fair hair. 'Him and the Jesuits planning to take over the country?'

'They've already taken over the country, you dumb *andouille!*' Poucet, sitting higher on the steps than she, nudged her in the back with his foot. 'But he's plotting something?'

'I think he is,' said January. 'Not a word, now.'

Hands were raised, fingers crossed for luck, and much spit expended upon the cobblestones in oaths of silence, and January handed them another few centimes before proceeding first to the church of St Séverin – where he was slightly late to morning Mass – and then to Ayasha's shop. She had rolls there – bought from Renan the baker on her way out that morning – and a small dish of butter, which she shared with the two young seamstresses and the little girl who ran errands and pulled out the basting threads ('They're no use to me if they're starving . . .'), and while he ate,

January recounted what Daniel had told him last night, and Poucet that morning.

'It would help – if you have time – to learn from Ra'eesa if Shamira was one of those who learned French from the instructor who came to the Sultan's harem.'

'And what do I say to Madame de Remiremont?' grumbled Ayasha as she stitched acres of tiny, pink silk roses on to the immense sleeves of a pink-and-black gown. 'That I have to go speak to a servant woman, and just wait here for me for two hours? Bad enough that stuck-up servant of ben-Gideon's comes knocking at the door this morning with a note before it gets light . . .'

'I said, if you have time.' At a guess, the Comtesse de Remiremont wanted her gown that evening. It always made Ayasha cross to be hurried. 'And if *I* have time, I'll walk out to Batignolles and have a look at the Convent of St Theresa . . .'

'Don't you *dare* go without me, *Mâlik!*' She flicked his elbow – the portion of his anatomy closest to hand – with a sharp little blow of one finger in its gold thimble, like one of the cats when annoyed. 'Or I'll—'

'You'll what?' He grinned across the workroom table at her.

She threw a pink silk rose at him. 'I'll sew up all the sleeves of your shirts when you have to go to the Opera.'

January pressed his palms together and bowed his head in a gesture of submission. 'Forgive me, *zahar*. Not a step shall I stir without you at my side.'

'See you don't. Now give that back.'

January tucked the delicate flower into the band of his hat and set the hat on his head. 'Even the marks of your anger I treasure as badges of pride.'

'*Nuti.* I'll give you a mark of my anger . . .'

They kissed, the three shop-girls all giggling – they had learned that for all her strictness and parsimony in matters of business, their mistress's bark was considerably worse than her bite – and January took his leave.

He kept the matter of Shamira out of his mind, and a mental door closed upon it, through the morning's rehearsals at the Opera – first with the singers for the upcoming production of *Proserpine*, and then with the dancers – and, after a hasty luncheon of soup and coffee bought from a street vendor in the Rue du Petit Luxembourg, through piano lessons with assorted offspring of the rich. Music was an exacting task, and January never quite understood those musicians – and Paris was rife with them – who could dash off waltzes and arias by rote, while chatting to someone else in the room about how they were going to pay the rent.

He put up, too, with the usual expressions of politely concealed surprise from the mother and aunts of a new pupil, that a man of color could teach and understand the finer points of the Viennese style of the pianoforte . (*What do they think I play at the Opera, the tom-tom?*) In Louisiana he'd endured the same, mostly because of his size: everyone expected a black man of his stature to be good for nothing but cutting cane.

He returned to the Rue de l'Aube at five, wondering if Ayasha would be back from the final fitting with Madame de Remiremont and if he was destined to make a dinner out of eggs, cheese, and cold couscous, and found the wife of his bosom pacing Renan's bakery-shop downstairs.

'I thought you'd never get here, *Mâlik!*' She caught him in the doorway, hooked her elbow peremptorily through his. 'We have but a few hours, to get out to the convent and see what they have to say there, before you have to go to your silly Opera—'

'So that I can pay our silly rent.' He let himself be tugged along the street toward the Rue St-Jacques. That few hours was also all he had to encompass any food he was likely to get during what was to be a very long evening, but it was at any time useless to struggle against Ayasha.

'*Yallah* for our silly rent.' She released his arm long enough to button her jacket, wind one shawl around her neck and pull another closer about her arms; the afternoon was gray, and chill wind lanced down from the river. 'Madame de Remiremont paid me, what more do we need? Ra'eesa told me that indeed Shamira was one of those who went with *Sitt* Jamilla, to learn French from the young Abbé from the Embassy—'

'De Longuechasse?'

'Even he. The ladies were all veiled, of course, and there were about fifteen eunuchs with swords stationed around the walls, in case de Longuechasse suddenly decided to improve relations between France and the Sublime Porte by ravaging the Sultan's women . . . Too, he taught his lessons at one side of the room, and the ladies sat at the other, with fifteen feet of open floor between them, and a moat of fire, belike . . .'

January let himself into Ayasha's shop as they passed it – it was too dark to work by four, and the windows were shuttered fast – and left his music satchel and cornet on the counter.

'And did Shamira ever speak to Ra'eesa,' he asked as he re-emerged, 'of the Abbé de Longuechasse?'

'She did.' Ayasha's voice was grim. 'She asked Ra'eesa to find where he dwelled, that she might use her new-found skill at the writing of French – she knew a little from her childhood, because her father was a merchant – to thank him.'

'And did Ra'eesa have any opinion of the Abbé himself?'

'She says that he is comely – which Hüseyin Pasha definitely is not – and young. And she said that upon the occasion that she spoke to him, and gave him the message of thanks from Shamira, he asked her, "Is the Lady Shamira the one who sat farthest to the right, beside your mistress?" which was indeed the case. Which means that she did something – met his eyes, leaned close to listen, a woman can always do something – that made him take notice of her. Whether she wrote to him again Ra'eesa knew not.'

'Could she have smuggled further notes out to him from Hüseyin Pasha's house in Constantinople?' They reached the river, and the Hôtel Dieu rose on their right as they crossed the bridge, Napoleon's new brickwork already dark with the soot of Paris chimneys against the raw gloom. The water that rustled beneath the hospital's pilings stank of blood and decay, and gleamed with sulfurous glints from the windows above it.

'Oh, yes.' Beyond the bridge, candles burned high in the black, gothic walls of the houses along the Rue de la Juiverie, a narrow canyon cutting the medieval mazes of the island. 'Even a rich man's harîm isn't like the Sultan's, or the harîms in the storybooks. Servants come and go. If you trust one, and you can find one who isn't afraid of being beaten by the master, you can usually get a message out.'

'But what could she have hoped for?' January asked. 'She couldn't actually have believed that a member of the Embassy staff would rescue her from the house of a high official of the Sultan's court, could she?'

He stopped at a tiny side-street, bought two pasties from a vendor – God only knew what was in them – and Ayasha promptly devoured both.

'And what did she think a member of the Embassy staff would do with her? Carry her back to France? Wed her?'

'She was just turned seventeen.' Ayasha's dark eyes were sad. 'What would seem real to her, or possible? In a *harîm*, all you do is tell each other stories. Even if you despise the other girls, and the servants around you, what is there to do but listen . . . and dream?'

The village of Batignolles lay a half-mile beyond the customs barrier at the Étoile. January and Ayasha had walked out there many times on hot afternoons in the summer, to drink cheap wine or water-lily tea. In the cold gray of a rainy evening, most of its cafés were shut, and the only activity seemed to be village boys driving cows home to be milked. The Convent of St Theresa stood at the far end of the town, and like many religious establishments in France these days it showed signs of dilapidation and looting during the Revolution. The statues on its Baroque facade had all been recently given new heads of stone five or six shades lighter than their soot-darkened bodies, and the effect was one of men and women who needed to have their robes washed.

Through the barred gate January could see the church was brightly illuminated, its doorway crowded with men and women clearly well off and dressed to advertise that fact. The elderly lay-brother who kept the gate produced a long list of reasons why he shouldn't have to go inquire of the Mother Superior as to whether she would see these decidedly un-rich visitors or not . . . And no, he knew nothing of any Jewess taking refuge in the convent. What kind of a place did they think this was?

In time, however, St Peter (as Ayasha irreverently described him) shuffled away to see if Mother Marie-Doloreuse had a few moments before the beginning of the Mass. January was reminded of the butlers in the houses of his pupils who *would see*, as they said, *if Madame were at home*, when everyone knew jolly well that Madame was at home and watching out the drawing-room window to see if she wanted to have anything to do with the caller or not.

The convent bells struck seven. January quietly gave up all hope of getting anything resembling dinner before he reported to the Opera at half-past eight. Maybe the same pastie vendor would be in the Rue St-Christophe on their way back across the island?

The judas opened in the convent gate, and St Peter announced in an aggrieved tone that the Mother Abbess would see them, and then took good care to herd them in a long circuit by the convent wall, as far as possible from the ladies in their lace pelerines and the gentlemen in their tall beaver hats in the church porch.

The Mother Abbess will see you meant, of course, that the Mother Abbess would sit on one side of a wooden window-grille curtained in purple velvet, and hear their voices, and permit them to hear hers.

'It gratifies me to learn that any soul should repudiate the Devil and flee the gates of Hell,' proclaimed the sweet, steely soprano from the other side of the curtain. 'Yet you are mistaken, if you think that my nephew Arnoux would be involved in a . . . a *deliverance from a seraglio*, like a character in some cheap romance. Though worldly considerations have forestalled him from taking Holy Orders until such time as his brother's wife brings forth a son, yet his only bride has ever been the Church, and he has been a faithful lover.'

'Perhaps,' suggested January, 'your nephew acted out of pity for the girl. If that is the case, I assure you that members of the girl's family here in Paris have expressed themselves willing to take her in.'

'What sort of Christian are you, sir?' The Abbess sounded scandalized. 'When a soul lost in darkness seeks the light, do you think that any *true* Christian would send them back into the abyss? Probably you do,' she added bitterly. 'So deep has this country gone into atheism. Even His Majesty – a priest himself and God's representative on Earth! – stands in need of a reminder of his duties.'

'Forgive me,' said January, in his most contrite voice, 'if I have expressed myself ill. When the girl's family begged me to seek her, I only asked myself if there were anyone now in Paris, whom she might have seen in Constantinople.'

'And you heard from my nephew the Marquis that his brother Arnoux taught French there, to ladies in the households of the

Sultan's officials. How that man loves to boast of vainglorious trappings! But I assure you, M'sieu Janvier: Arnoux would never compromise his family in the eyes of – I will not say the King. His Most Christian Majesty is a true Son of the Church. Arnoux would never run his family afoul of the King's ministers, hollow men, nameless souls themselves who would spit upon the Host, if by doing so they could curry the favor of those who have for five centuries enslaved and desecrated the very Tomb of Our Savior.'

January glanced sidelong at Ayasha: this was an extreme view to take of such conservative gentlemen as Villèle and Polignac and others who had approved of the Anti-Sacrilege Act, merely because they might be expected to object to giving offense to one of France's chief allies. From the wall of the parlor – recently wall-papered to cover the damage done during the Revolution – a small oil-painting of St Theresa frowned disapprovingly, as if she detected January's lie.

'Whoever sent you,' the old nun went on, 'you may inform them that neither my nephew, nor I myself, have any knowledge of this unfortunate girl. Yet you may tell them also that all Christians applaud her courage and wish that more here in France shared it. *Who is not with us is against us*, the Apostle says. If this girl should ever come knocking upon our gates, seeking the truth of salvation, we – God's *true* Church – shall welcome her among us, and let the Devil and the Sultan and all the wealthy Jews who seek to buy the King's favor with their ill-got pelf break their teeth with gnashing, that a single soul has run away to the Light.'

'So there,' said January as St Peter conducted him and Ayasha out of the cloister house and across the cold twilight of the grounds toward the gate once more.

'Did you tell her that Shamira was a Jewess?'

'St Peter might have . . . Now you've got me calling him that.' Better that, he supposed, than Papa Legba, who was the voodoo equivalent of the Heavenly Gatekeeper and whose marks had a way of turning up on the old saint's statues in New Orleans churches . . . 'But I don't think either you or I mentioned the Sultan to him.'

He stopped at the side door of the convent church, at the unac-customed sound within of applause. St Peter beckoned impatiently, but January gestured – *Let me behold this* – and the lay brother stood back, wearing the expression of a sulky bulldog, while January stepped to the rear of the crowd.

It was fortunate that he stood half a head taller than any man in France and a head taller than most, for the little church of St Theresa was packed to the doors. Those gentlemen in their swallow-tailed coats and the ladies in Brussels lace clustered up almost to the tall grating of barred iron that stretched clear across the room before the altar. Diamonds flashed around most of the feminine throats in the assembled watchers, and diamonds glittered also in the hair of the girl who stood before the altar, on the inner side of the grate: a girl of fifteen or sixteen, clothed in Italian silk of pink, rust, and gold. She had just turned toward the audience – family and friends of the family, January knew – hence the applause, and her face almost glowed with the exaltation and joy that very young girls can feel, when they are the center of attention and can make a splendid gesture with all eyes upon them and only them.

All eyes including God's.

A panel opened behind the altar. Chanting in their sweet voices, the nuns emerged in their coarse black habits, their dark veils; at their head walked a tall woman whose resemblance to the Marquis de Longuechasse was striking, even at that distance and in the dimness of candlelight.

The nuns stripped the diamonds out of the girl's hair, and from her wrists and hands, and threw the jewels to the floor at the feet of the man who stood next to the altar, the man whose crimson garments gave him a look of flame. They took the girl by the hands, led her to the open panel, where other nuns waited with a dark screen. Behind this they would, January knew, swiftly change the girl's dress from the ostentatious gown to the black habit of a novice, so that all who watched would not only *know* that their sister – daughter – cousin – friend had forsaken the world for the glory of the Church, but would also *see* it, acted out like a pageant.

Then the girl would kneel among them before the altar – or in some orders, he knew, lie on the stones with her arms spread in the shape of the Cross – as a black curtain descended on the inner side of the grate.

Your sister – daughter – cousin – friend is dead to the world. She has gone on to the wonderful mysteries of marriage to

Christ . . . Which too frequently, January knew also, consisted of endless sewing, reading the lives of saints, and trying to fit into a community of women no more educated than oneself, with very little to do.

Yet how many little girls – and he could see the boarding pupils of the convent gathered like an angel choir to one side, watching their former friend – saw only the ecstasy of doing what everyone wanted you to do, with all eyes upon you, like a bride? Like young girls dreaming of their wedding, without a thought about the life that lay beyond.

Lights, candles, sweet voices chanting. The black screen was moved aside, and the Mother Abbess led the new nun forward.

The girl's face was filled with a wild joy, which January hoped, for her sake, meant a genuine religious vocation and not simply the overwhelming thrill of the occasion.

Mother Marie-Doloreuse's face held triumph, and pride that not only glowed but burned. Not only had another soul been led into the light, but was also *shown to all* to be led into the light. And led *by her*. A lesson, to those still in darkness.

And yet with this triumph to proclaim, she took the time to tell us that her nephew had nothing to do with Shamira's disappearance, and that we should go away.

He took Ayasha's hand and backed from the church, before the black curtain fell.

SEVEN

D amp mist rose from the Seine as they crossed the Étoile. January checked his silver watch, an expensive bauble he'd bought for himself upon his arrival in Paris ten years before, just prior to receiving the news that his mother's protector – the man who was going to finance his education in France – had died. It looked like they would actually get back to their room in time for him to gulp down something resembling dinner before he had to race to the Opera . . .

Then as they passed the lane that led from the Champs Élysées toward the Beaujon Hospital two men came from the other direction, talking quietly, and turned up the lane. At the sound of their voices Ayasha looked sharply back, but January caught her arm and steered her on without change of pace. As soon as the men had gone on, however, he said, 'Can you get to Hüseyin Pasha's house? Not by that lane –' he nodded back toward the one they'd just passed – 'but going around by way of the Church of St Philippe? Quickly.'

'Those men were speaking—'

'Arabic,' said January. 'They're Sabid's grooms. The man with the broken nose is unmistakable. Go, quickly, get in through the stable gates and don't let them see you. Tell *Sitt* Jamilla I need to speak to her at La Marseillaise at once.'

Madame Dankerts of the Cafe La Marseillaise, in addition to good Flemish batter-cakes and strong coffee, cheerfully provided January with paper, pen, and ink. He had no intention of leaving his colleagues at the Opera to attempt the overture of *La Cenerentola* without a first cornet, and he fully expected to have to impart his information to Jamilla by means of a letter.

But Ayasha must have made astonishing speed to the Rue St-Honoré, for he was only up to his third batter-cake and *the only reason I can think of for Sabid to keep watch upon your house is* . . . when his wife and two black-veiled forms appeared in the café's door.

'This true what Ayasha say?' The Lady took the seat opposite in a dark swirl of gauze. 'Sabid men watch house?'

'They do. I recognized two of them – there have probably been others.'

Her brows pulled together below the edge of her dark *hijab*. 'Then is *not* he who took Shamira?'

'No. But it may mean he's looking for her; that he knows she's escaped. What would he do if he found her? If he had her in his power? Kill her?'

'Not first.' Jamilla's voice was barely a whisper. 'Sabid – Hüseyin – hate.' She tapped the faces of her two fists, like the butting heads of rams. 'Long time. Hüseyin spies in house of Sabid in Constantinople. Spies tell him Sabid take money like a street whore, from French, from English, from Austrians. Men who make gun, make steamboat, make boots. Give Sabid money. Sabid tell Sultan: to be modern, to be like West, Empire need gun, need steamboat, need boots. Sabid say, *I get them for you, for such a price*.'

'And is this true?' asked January.

'I know not. But Hüseyin tell Sultan, and Sultan very angry. Send Sabid away. But, Sultan still need *farangi* gun, *farangi* steam-engine. Hüseyin fear, Sultan call Sabid back while Hüseyin away.'

'Not an unreasonable fear. I doubt Sabid is the only modernizer in Constantinople – nor the only man around the Sultan to be taking bribes to get his favor.'

'It will go ill for Hüseyin,' said Ayasha softly, 'if this Sabid does return to favor.'

'Worse than ill,' agreed Jamilla. '*I will make you weep*, Sabid say. *I will make you curse the light of the day when you spoke against me*.'

'And he followed him all this way here, only out of hate?'

'Not hate only.' Jamilla glanced around the little room, as if she expected the hook-nosed, scar-faced grooms of her husband's enemy to be sipping coffee at the next table. 'In Constantinople, my husband hear of *farangi* – *Inglis* – send bribe unto Sabid, and later Sabid cheat the *Inglis*, I know not how. This man my husband go to England to seek. Sabid wrote the *Inglis* a letter, and this letter, my husband will send unto the Sultan, that the hand of Sabid, the lips of Sabid, the seal of Sabid all bear witness to treason.'

'And does Sabid know this?' asked January.

'I know not. My husband now careful. I careful . . .'

'And those *salopes* in the kitchen talk like monkeys,' finished Ayasha. 'Else why does Sabid send men to watch the house, save to learn whether Shamira is still there or not?'

'If he's sending men to check,' pointed out January, 'that sounds as if he isn't sure. If there were a spy regularly in the household, he would be. Is there one in the house who is of a height to counterfeit Shamira? Of a shape to be taken for her, in her clothing, at a distance?'

'Raihana,' said Jamilla promptly. 'I send her into the garden, in Shamira dress, Shamira veil. Sabid cease to hunt for her outside? Only, we must watch.' She put a hand on Ra'eesa's arm and explained something to her in quick low sentences. Ra'essa nodded, her wrinkled eyes grim.

'We must watch,' Jamilla repeated. 'For if Sabid think it is Shamira, he may take her, may kill her, only to make my husband weep. You found her not, *Hakîm*?' Her eyes, dark as a gazelle's, returned to January. 'Hüseyin return Friday.'

'There are two places where I think she might be.' January stood and bowed over Jamilla's hand. 'Those I will visit tomorrow—'

His outraged mind flung up at him the tasks already allotted for tomorrow – piano lessons in three different parts of Paris, rehearsals for *Proserpina*, that private rehearsal with the opera singer La Dulcetta that he'd worked so hard to get hired for . . . *Why am I going to all this trouble, for a girl I saw once, a girl who has barely spoken a word to me . . . ?*

Because she is alone, as Ayasha was alone when she came here. As I was alone.

Because she is a slave, as I was a slave. Because she ran away, as Ayasha did. As all those did in New Orleans, whose owners advertised for them like straying dogs.

'—those I will visit tomorrow, if I can.'

If I don't starve to death between now and then. Ayasha had just finished devouring the remaining batter-cakes.

'I must go. Ayasha, will you see *Sitt* Jamilla safely home?'

And almost before his wife had said *Yes* or *No*, January was out the door and striding as swiftly as he could back toward the Rue Le Peletier.

*   *   *

January made it to the gaudy, gilt-trimmed Opera House with moments to spare and without further dinner, ravenous yet handsomely attired in dark well-cut wool and carrying his music satchel and his cornet. After the Opera was a ball in the fashionable district along the Vielle Rue du Temple – the aristocracy was indefatigable during its season of pleasures, and from autumn to Lent January felt that he was married to an insane, many-headed monster that never slept. Because the Comte de Cruzette had been ennobled by Napoleon, most of the older aristocracy eschewed his entertainments, but the *chevaliers d'industrie*, as they were called, were out in force: bankers, manufacturers, financiers whose social-climbing wives glittered with jewels. Carriages clogged the narrow streets, the dancing lasted until five in the morning, and since, at that point, it was easier to stay up than to get up, January proceeded with Lucien Imbot and Jeannot Charbonnière to a worker's café on the Quai Beaufils for a breakfast that lasted until well after sunup.

'Who is Sabid al-Muzaffar, anyway?' he asked at one point, and Lucien gestured with a fragment of buttered roll.

'Al-Muzaffar is the best and dearest friend of such men as the Rothschilds, Lafittes, and Städels.' He named some of the most powerful banking families in Paris. 'Allegedly their agent in the Sultan's court until old Mahmud chucked him out. Quite the reformer, though coincidentally those reforms always entail large purchases of equipment through loans engineered by the Rothschilds, Lafittes, and Städels.'

'That's hardly fair, old man.' Jeannot shook back his leonine golden mane. 'You can't have an omelette without breaking a few eggs, you know. And you can't deny that the Sultan's empire could do with being brought forward into the nineteenth century.' He signed to the girl for another round of coffee.

'Can't I, though?' retorted Lucien. 'Centralize power in the hands of the Sultan so that he can more easily locate those who disagree with him? Make everything alike, as the Revolution tried to make everything alike here in France? Build factories to put artisans out of work?'

'Build factories to bring down the price of shoes so an honest musician can afford them when they wear out?' Jeannot held up his foot to display a well-cut boot. 'I only wish! I lived on bread and cheese for three months, to save up so that I could look decent enough to play in a gentleman's house. Sabid's a reformer,' he added, turning to January. 'Men with vision are always hated by the old crumblies.'

'Men with vision are always fanatics.' Lucien sipped his coffee – he'd been friends with Jeannot for years – and turned his heavy-lidded gaze along the quay, where the first of the water sellers waded down through the thinning mists to dip their buckets full from the Seine. 'Give me a kind-hearted reactionary who doesn't keep his wife locked behind iron gates.'

'Is that what al-Muzaffar does?'

'Every man follows the customs of his country.' Jeannot shrugged. 'A Mohammedan woman is used to it.'

'I know one formerly Mohammedan woman who would knock your brains out with a skillet for that remark,' said January, and both men laughed.

An old man came along the quay selling waffles, his grandson at his heels with a hurdy-gurdy, and the icy morning air transformed the yowling music into alien and ethereal beauty. Across the river, the bells of Notre Dame began to ring.

When January reached home Ayasha had already gone out – her basket of laces and silks was missing from its place beside the door. She had, however – he silently blessed her – left water simmering all around the back of the hearth in kettles, enough for a bath and a shave. January slept for an hour – something he'd learned to do in Mardi Gras season in New Orleans – then made a hasty toilette, donned clean linen and his very natty gray morning costume, and set forth for the home of the Harbonnières: a well-to-do broker of corn who owned half a score of bakeries and considerable city property.

On the way he passed within a few streets of the Rue St-Denis, where the ancestral Hôtel de Longuechasse stood. Because he had walked swiftly and was a little ahead of his time, he turned aside and stood for a while considering what he could see of that hand-some residence above its protective wall. The gate into the forecourt had at one time been a beautiful openwork of iron. Revolution and rioting had prompted the addition of iron backing-plates, but as January turned to proceed on his way, the gates opened and a stylish barouche emerged, drawn by gold-maned chestnut horses

matched like liveried footmen – with one white stocking apiece
– and check reined to within an inch of their lives. Through the
open gateway, the hôtel could be viewed for some moments in all
its baroque glory: two floors of polished and pedimented windows,
and a high mansard roof under which – like that of Hüseyin Pasha's
establishment on the Rue St Honoré – would be found rooms for
servants or lesser members of the household.

Or, January reflected thoughtfully, anyone the Marquis or his
family wanted to conceal there.

Judging by the length of the street frontage, there was room for
service courtyards on either side of the narrow court that led to
the main block of the house. He could glimpse the entrance to one
of them as the concierge closed the iron-backed street gates. But
unlike dwellings in Hüseyin Pasha's more rural suburb, the main
gate was the only way in or out.

Thus if the girl Shamira had taken refuge with Arnoux de
Longuechasse, she would be as much a prisoner in his brother's
house as she was in that of her former master.

January put the matter from his mind as he ascended the steps of
the Harbonnières' town-house and for the next hour gave his
thoughts and energy exclusively to Mesdemoiselles Eliane and
Andromaque, neither of whom had practiced since their previous
lesson and both of whom swore they had, an assertion backed up
by their mother's statement that she was usually out of the house
at the time of the girls' practice, but that neither of her daughters
would ever lie. 'Of course, Madame . . . Certainly, Madame . . .'

'It is up to you to make sure that they practice.'

'Certainly, Madame.' Actually, reflected January resignedly, it
was up to their governess, but his impression of that individual
was that she'd long ago given up trying to make her golden-haired
charges do anything.

'And I'm sure they're both much better than you're giving them
credit for, M'sieu Janvier. They're just a little nervous.'

Eliane, who had just taken a sheet of music from her sister's
folder and dropped it out the parlor window into the courtyard,
assumed an expression of soulful innocence.

'It happens to everyone, Madame. Will you stay and hear them
play?'

'I should love to, M'sieu, of course, but I'm just out to *dear* Madame Chamillart's luncheon . . . I'm positive they're just perfect, aren't you, my darlings?'

'Not as perfect as you, Maman.'

As January bowed Madame out of the drawing room, Andromaque pulled her sister's hair.

At least his next pupil – a tiny boy named Camille Fontdulac over in the old Marais district – was a joy to teach, too young to have any technical skill but with a genuine feeling for music. January had never seen the boy's merchant father, nor any member of the household but the boy's tutor, who assured him that M'sieu Fontdulac would never countenance his son following any course in life but to inherit Fontdulac et Fils.

The third of his Wednesday pupils was a fragile young lady who always gave January the impression that she would kill herself with chagrin if she played a wrong note. The parents of Desireé Boulanger moved on the outskirts of Court circles, and Madame Boulanger – who held her 'at home' on Wednesday afternoons during Desireé's lesson – was careful to let January know just how many marquises and comtesses would be among the callers whom her daughter would entertain with whatever new piece the girl was learning. The folding doors between the parlor where Madame received her callers, and the salon where the piano was located, were invariably left slightly open so the ladies might admire the lesson in progress.

Thus it was that while Desireé sought for the new Schubert lied she was learning, a fragment of conversation flickered tantalizingly from the parlor: ' . . . actually converted one of the Sultan's wives to Christianity!'

Even before January could turn his head, Desireé cried breathlessly, 'Oh, here it is! After all this I should have *died* if I couldn't have found it—'

And because under no circumstances would it be acceptable for a music master to let anyone suspect that he eavesdropped on conversations in the parlor, January was forced to turn back with a smile, and to give his fullest attention to her painstaking execution of 'The Linden Tree'.

Converted one of the Sultan's wives . . .

Or the wife – or concubine? – of some other Muslim official in Paris?

To the resounding glory of the Church – and of the man who accomplished such a coup?

The note of delighted triumph in the woman's voice was unmistakable, but he couldn't even go to the half-open parlor door to see who it was who had spoken, or who was there.

And perhaps it had nothing to do with the vanished Shamira, or the expression of radiant triumph on the face of Mother Marie-Doloreuse as she led her latest young novice into the shadows of the convent.

They might have been speaking of someone other than Arnoux de Longuechasse altogether.

And yet . . . *Is it being bruited about Paris?*

As Madame Boulanger's 'at home' would go on until five or six, there was nothing that January could do to further his knowledge at the lesson's end. He only took his money from the extremely discreet butler, bowed deeply to the ladies in the parlor in passing ('He's done simply *wonders* with her playing – would you care to favor the marquise with that polonaise you learned last month, darling?'), and made his departure.

As he descended the stair he heard someone in the parlor behind him exclaim, 'How *extraordinary* to find that sort of talent in a Negro!'

And: 'Aren't you terrified to leave Desireé alone with him?'

Some things, he had found out early, were precisely the same in France as they were in America. At least they addressed him as 'vous' – an adult and an equal – and not 'tu'.

One of the women in the parlor was indeed the Marquise de Longuechasse.

EIGHT

Ayasha was still gone when January returned to their room. She'd changed clothes, leaving her 'respectable' green-and-white delaine spread out on the bed with the two additional petticoats that she wore with it over and above the usual complement: Hadji and Habibi lay curled up together in the precise middle of this billowing ensemble. Her work basket lay beside the door, covered with its usual protective towel. After a momentary debate about whether food or sleep was the most pressing requirement, January settled for a half-hour's nap and thrust a couple of apples and a hard-cooked egg in his pockets as he went out the door. He promised himself something more substantial after the two rehearsals slated for the afternoon . . .

Actually converted one of the Sultan's wives.

Had the next words – the words he'd missed – been, *or something* . . .?

Had the Marquise – notoriously pious and notoriously proud – been boasting of her young brother-in-law?

Ayasha wasn't at the shop. She hadn't been in, the seamstresses told him, after stopping there in the morning to assign them to work. She was going to Madame Torcy that morning, then Madame Blé, and on to the Comtesse de Remiremont . . . January barely made it to the Opera before the ballet mistress arrived.

Generally ballet rehearsal – held in one of the maze of rooms behind the enormous backstage – included a number of visiting gentlemen. Young, elderly, noble, or of the wealthy bourgeoisie, they would sit on hard wooden chairs beside the door and admire the young ladies' ronds de jambes. *Lions visiting gazelles* was how the ballet mistress put it. Upon occasion one of these visitors would be Daniel ben-Gideon, who like many wealthy men in Paris kept a dancer as a mistress – a sinecure, January guessed, mostly to keep his family in ignorance of his true preferences. But he was absent today.

Since Madame Scie permitted nothing to interfere with the

rehearsal of her corps, it was not until almost four that January was able to approach the austere and beautiful ballet mistress herself – Marguerite Scie generally knew everything – and then he was forced to wait for almost half an hour after the rehearsal's end while this or that girl or gentleman or costume mistress or director of the Opera came to her with matters that absolutely *had* to be dealt with . . .

When they were at last able to speak – with barely half an hour to go before he knew he had to present himself at the studio rented by La Doucetta's protector for *her* rehearsal – Marguerite replied, 'I shouldn't be surprised if Sophie de Longuechasse is going around Paris saying that brother-in-law of hers converted the Sultan's whole harem.' She slipped on a short velvet jacket, much worn, and folded her arms. Every portion of the opera house, allegedly 'temporary' and built of wood and painted plaster, was at all times freezing, and Madame taught in the same garments worn by the 'little rats', as they were called – chemise, corset, and a short petticoat that barely came past the knees. During rehearsal black clouds had gathered, and rain now beat drearily on the long windows that overlooked the court. Gaslights had been kindled (January had a bet with Jeannot Charbonnière that the newfangled lighting would one day burn down the theater), and in the sulfurous gleam Madame rather resembled a cold-blooded Venus surrounded by attendant nymphs.

'The King depends on the Pope to make it good with the people that they have a cretin on the throne and another in line to follow him,' she went on, without bothering to lower her voice. Two of the 'lions' chatting up the gazelles were relatives of the King, but Marguerite's father, the Marquis de Vemandois, had been guillotined while the parents of the 'lions' had fled the country, so it took more than sour looks from a couple of Ducs to impress her. 'He wants, in fact, to lead the whole population of Turkey to the Light, but it doesn't do to say so to the Sultan, whose support he needs against the Austrians. Give that to me,' she added, to a middle-aged little gentleman in a bottle-green coat, who was holding out a note to her, and a couple of banknotes. 'For Musetta?'

'It must be delivered before tonight's performance.'

Madame Scie tore up the note, then the banknotes, and placed the scraps firmly back into the shocked gentleman's kid-gloved hand. To January, as if nothing had interrupted them, she continued, 'His Majesty would love nothing better than to have it seen that the scion of the old aristocracy has snatched a helpless young girl from the clutch of the Infidel.'

'And has he?' inquired January. 'The scion, I mean, not the King. Snatched a helpless young girl from the clutch of the Infidel?'

'Not that I've heard.' Marguerite shrugged. Anything that did not involve ballet held only limited interest for her. 'I know the brother – this is the Abbé we're speaking of, correct? – taught French to those ladies, but one would be very rash indeed to suppose that Arnoux de Longuechasse would get up a flirtation with even the most forthcoming concubine.'

'You know Arnoux de Longuechasse?'

'We've spoken. Like Our Lord, he'll speak to anyone. The Marquise's idiot brother brought him backstage a few days ago to introduce him to that dreadful new soprano they've saddled us with, who I believe the brother wishes to mount as a mistress. He – the idiot – was aflame over Arnoux's "conversion" of the Sultan's harem in the name of God and the King, and Arnoux corrected him. He seemed embarrassed by the praise. And perfectly impervious to the young ladies who remained after rehearsal was done, I might add, despite their interest in *him* . . . A most comely boy.'

'Cold?'

Coldness was not the impression January had received of the young man.

'No. He is filled with that singular fire you find in men of the Church, that takes hold physically as well as spiritually: I have no doubt that the boy is a virgin. And unless he is obliged to marry for the family's sake, will probably die one, after a lifetime of wearing a *cilice*. And on the subject of the fires within the flesh, how is the lovely Ayasha?'

'Well.' January grinned at her: he and the ballet mistress, half a dozen years his senior, had been lovers when he'd first come to Paris. 'Filled with ire at the newest fashions in sleeves . . .'

'I always knew her for a woman of taste.'

'And how is young M'sieu – Basile?' He hazarded the name of the most recent of Marguerite's lovers that he knew about.

'Theo,' she corrected him. 'Also well, or as well as any young man can be who has just discovered Socialism and must share his discoveries or die.' She smiled with the astringent tenderness of a woman who has been through all this before. 'At least it isn't Rosicrucianism. I'm not sure I could take another of Basile's lectures about allegories of Egyptian gods. Give my love to Ayasha,' she added as January glanced at his watch, cursed, and made his bows. 'And let me know whether this La Doucetta you're going to rehearse with can sing at all. There's a rumor that her lover's going to finance a production here of *Euryanthe* so she can star in it, and I'd like to know what we're in for.'

January was used to the musically-inclined mistresses of wealthy gentlemen, whose patrons provided them with private lessons if the Paris conservatories did not share their opinion of the young lady's talents. At least La Doucetta, a plump and statuesque brunette, though profoundly self-deceived about her own abilities, was kind-hearted and teachable, and she seemed to take a great deal of pleasure in being rehearsed for an audition of Weber's opera. Her singing master was a Viennese who made his living from such arrangements, and the location and furnishings of the rented studio on the Rue St-Dominique left January in no doubt that this young woman's lover was prepared to pay everybody handsomely to retain her good mood, so in fact the rehearsal went quite pleasantly. The tip La Doucetta bestowed at the end of the afternoon enabled January and Herr Blick to have a very decent dinner together at the nearby Serpe d'Or, before January proceeded – through the drenching black Paris rain – to the Hôtel Tambonneau for a ball.

And though the Comte de Tambonneau was a Bonapartist noble and looked with an outsider's contempt upon the old nobility which surrounded the King, between waltzes, cotillions, and quadrilles in the brilliantly candlelit Grand Salon, the talk was of nothing but Arnoux de Longuechasse and the Converted Concubine.

'A powerful Mohammedan nobleman, dearest, and absolutely savage! She took French lessons in Constantinople from l'Abbé de Longuechasse, and he managed to convert her to the True Faith, right under her master's nose!'

'Never!'

'And, when she came here to Paris, he was able to spirit her away to a convent!'

'Think of that! God's call was so strong in her, that she found a way to go to Him . . .'

'It's like a romance—!'

'Nonsense, Elvire, it's a most elevating and Christian story! Romance indeed!'

'—whole family held to the Faith in the face of the Terror—'

'—poor Clémence and Anne-Marie went to the guillotine rather than renounce God—'

'—the girl heard God calling to her in a vision, night after night—'

Fragments, snippets, glimpses of details that January knew were absurd – he knew quite well that there was no hereditary nobility in the Sultan's empire, for instance – yet it was clear that the news was everywhere. Ladies in gowns of pinks and plums, with what appeared to be entire forests of silk flowers and wired curls trembling on their heads, clasped their hands over it, with expressions that reminded January of the schoolgirls at St Theresa watching their friend become a nun in the full blaze of sanctity and attention.

It was the most romantic thing they'd ever heard.

Early in the evening January glimpsed Sabid, clothed in immaculately proper evening-dress of dark-gray coat and spotless white stockings, in conversation near the door of the salon with a man January recognized as a high official in the prefecture of police. But after that he looked for the Arab in vain.

When Daniel ben-Gideon appeared, much later in the evening, with the daughter of a prominent banker on his arm, he confirmed the rumors.

'According to my sister – who heard it this afternoon, so the story can't have started much before this morning – Arnoux "converted" this girl in the course of their French lessons, then managed to send her messages through laundresses and grocery deliveries and the woman who sells butter and eggs. He set a time and place to be there with a chaise and carried her off . . . I've always had great admiration for the organization of the Holy Church. It's astonishing what they can get people to do. Quite ordinary folk are delighted to carry notes and risk their lives poking about where they're not supposed to be, if they think God's going to take favorable notice of them as a result. One would think they all had guilty consciences or something.'

And he glanced in the direction of his young lady-friend, deep in talk with old Moses ben-Gideon and a hard-faced man whose build and nose were clearly echoed in her own. *A match in the making?*

'I thought it had to be worked through the laundresses,' January said. 'But it's ridiculous to think Arnoux would convert anyone through a French lesson under the eyes of guards, some of whom would certainly know French. My guess is that the girl contacted him after the lessons began and told him she wanted to convert. It was an appeal he would not ignore. Can Hüseyin take her out of a convent?'

'I shouldn't think so. At least, *I* shouldn't like to try to pry a prospective novice out of the fists of that frightful Mother Abbess at Batignolles. Particularly not one who's become a *cause célèbre* for the Church . . . which might be one reason for spreading the story. But if—'

Lucien poked January in the back with his fiddle bow. Ben-Gideon pére and Daniel's prospective bride started to stroll in the direction of the little orchestra, and January, with a gesture of thanks, turned back to his piano. For the rest of the evening he concentrated on olivettes and cross-passes, moulinets and brisés, and on keeping an eye on where the top couple of the set was, so as to end the dance at the proper moment – not easy when one had had only an hour and a half of sleep. Only now and then did it cross his mind to wonder whether Hüseyin Pasha, when he returned on Friday, would succeed in forcing Mother Marie-Doloreuse to relinquish her prize – and whether he would take vengeance on the women of his household, for not keeping a better watch on his property.

He wondered if he should pay another visit to the Convent of St Theresa tomorrow (*and will that be in the quarter-hour you have between rehearsal at the Opera and the first of your lessons?*); whether he should offer his assistance to the girl who, he was fairly certain, had no intention of converting.

The dancing lasted until three. The rain had ceased by then, and when he reached the Rue de l'Aube again, above the uneven medieval roofline the stars seemed to stare, untwinkling and cold. In the windows of the bakery, the first glow of the fire reflected red through the uneven glass; the smell of woodsmoke lay thick

in the misty air. As January turned down the street, the bells of
St Séverin rang for matins.

He was so tired that the thought of going to sleep on the second-
floor landing and not bothering with the rest of the stairs had a
certain appeal.

'Ben!' A tiny form darted out of the shuttered doorway of the
Café L'Empereur.

'Chatoine—'

'Ben, they got her!' The little girl caught the long tails of his
coat; she was shuddering with cold. 'The Arabs. They went to the
convent with the police and a bunch of the Arab's guards, with
guns and knives. The flics had a piece of paper, they made the
Mother Abbess let them in—'

'They took Shamira?' In his mind he saw again Sabid al-Muzaffar,
deep in conversation with the official of the Paris police . . .

The urchin shook her head violently. 'The Arab girl got away,'
she said. 'We couldn't follow – there was just the two of us, and
Poucet said to come get you. They got Ayasha.'

NINE

There was a statue of St Peter in a niche a few houses down, beside the door of the oldest house in the street; January shoved his music satchel behind it, with a prayer that it would still be there when – if – he got back. His blood like ice and all thought of sleep rinsed from his brain, he caught Chatoine's hand. 'Sabid's house? In Charenton?'

She nodded. He caught her up – she weighed no more than her namesake kitten – set her on his shoulder, and strode off toward the river in the icy dark.

At this hour even the student cafés in the Rue St-Jacques were dark, and the workers' taverns along the Quai de la Tournelle had not yet opened. Only in the Hôtel Dieu did lights burn, sullen orange dribbles on the moonless blackness. The towers of Notre Dame reared against the starry abyss, like the sterncastle of a ghost ship being swept through nightmare waters toward the uttermost ends of the earth.

'Poucet's keeping watch.' Chatoine's little fingers clung to his collar. 'This afternoon the *mec* you put us on – the Abbé – went to the convent. Poucet sent me back to tell you, but you were gone, so Ayasha came out with us, all dressed up like a servant. She went in just before it got dark, and we all stayed outside to wait for her. But she didn't come out.'

Virgin Mary, Mother of God, January prayed as he walked, *show me what to do*. The cold air cut his lungs; beneath the arches of the Pont de la Tournelle the Seine sounded thick and menacing, sable water curling against the worn stones, invisible in the darkness.

'We waited and waited, and it rained and got really cold. Poucet sent Malapatte back to look for you twice. Then just when the clock struck midnight the flics came . . .'

'You're sure it was the police?' *Virgin Mother, send me help . . . uphold Ayasha in your hand . . .*

The oil lamps that hung above the intersections of the larger streets had gone out. The Île St-Louis, with its ancient mansions and narrow streets, had the look of a necropolis across the water in the ghostly starlight: like the crowded brick tombs of the St-Louis Cemetery that January had known as a child, in that murky city where the dead could not lie in the ground.

'They were *dressed* like flics,' said Chatoine. 'I recognized old Daddy Margis from the Châtelet station, and anyway they came in the chicken wagon. That Arab was with them, Sabid, and his men, and the flics all did what he said.'

'Damn them.' How easy Sabid would have found it, to twist the story as it was trumpeted from one wealthy matron to another at Tambonneau's ball that evening. All he needed was a police official who was tired of making exceptions to the law for the benefit of the King's friends. *It is MY concubine they're all talking about, my friend, and what they aren't saying is that she robbed the house when she left it . . .*

Simple as spinning a little thread with your fingers out of wool you found caught on a bush.

The girl is a liar and a thief and has no intention of converting . . . She's making fools of those nuns and a fool of the authorities . . .

'Then there was a lot of shouting,' Chatoine went on as January's feet thudded on the Pont Marie's worn flagstones. 'Two nuns ran out from the stable gate. Only, there were lanterns by the gate, and I saw one of them was really Ayasha. One of Sabid's men came out right after them yelling to stop them. The other nun got away, and most of the men went after her, but three of them grabbed Ayasha. She was yelling curses really bad – she called the Mother Abbess a *kosefil* when she came out. A *kosefil* is—'

'I know what it is. So the Mother Abbess came out?' Starlight barely showed him the outlines of the riverbank, between the quay and the actual water – the batture, they called that marginal ground in Louisiana. The moist breath of the flood brought the stink of coal to him, and the bark of a bargeman's dog.

'She slapped Ayasha.' The little girl's voice filled with hurt and distress, that one who should have helped had believed the word of the enemy. 'She called her a *garce* and a thief, and told the men they could take her away. That's when Ayasha called her a *kosefil*. They put her in the chicken wagon with two of the Arabs and a flic. The rest of them went off with Sabid. Poucet followed them, and he told me to get you and tell you—'

'How long ago were you waiting outside my house?'

'An hour. I ran back as fast as I could.'

All the way from Batignolles, in utter blackness and freezing cold. January thought of little Mesdemoiselles Harbonnière, who couldn't even be bothered to learn their scales. *France, don't you understand what treasure you're wasting, when you leave children of this courage and this loyalty to grow up in the streets?* He slipped and scrambled down to the batture, shoes slithering in the clayey mud. The gates in the customs barrier would not open until nearly sunrise. Beyond the barrier, the remains of the ditches that had once been the city moat made an easy route to clamber back to higher ground. The old district of St-Antoine was a pitch-black labyrinth, every house barred against roving packs of thieves. Among the locked-up wine-depots behind the quay, January drew back from the movement of shapes barely seen in a narrow street; a hoarse voice whispered, 'Hey, *cossu*, where you bound, eh?' and a blade glinted in the blackness.

'Piss off,' retorted Chatoine, in purest thieves' cant, *'espèce de con*; who you callin' a *cossu*?'

'Va-t'en, sonny—'

'Va-t'en yourself! We need help against the flics – You gonna come, you gonna let us get on our way?'

The shadows melted away. Chatoine called after them, 'Hey! *Connard*! Give us a *surin*, eh? My friend don't got one.'

From the shadows, a voice asked doubtfully, 'You really goin' after the flics?'

'No,' retorted January, also in the slang of the underworld, 'we're meetin' the King for tea, and I forgot to shave.'

Metal flashed in starlight, then rang on the filthy cobbles at his feet. 'Razor one up for me, eh, *copain*?'

They were gone even as January bent to pick up the weapon. The knife was thin and balanced like a sharpened butcher's tool.

It was colder in the more open lanes of Charenton. Above the wall of Sabid's villa, the windows of the house were dark. January circled cautiously through the lanes behind the property and sensed that the place did not sleep. A smudge of yellowish light – lamp, or candle – flickered for a moment on the underside of the stable eave. Stealthy feet crunched gravel. January's heart seemed to turn over inside him at the sound.

Ayasha was useless to her captors. She'd gotten Shamira out of the convent, but Shamira was gone. If Sabid had captured Shamira, he'd kill the woman who was with her simply to avoid an encumbrance. No witness, no risk.

And if he hadn't captured Shamira, he'd come back and ask Ayasha where the girl had gone.

Dear God—

January retreated across the road. Trees grew along a crumbling boundary-wall, the shadows below them an Erebus of black. Dry leaves crunched; he whispered, 'Poucet?'

A man seized him from behind. January turned, tried to slash with the knife, and Chatoine squeaked as she was pulled off his shoulders. In the starlight he glimpsed a second man in front of him as more hands caught his wrist. His leg swept out, hooked the feet from one of his assailants; he twisted his body. *They'll have knives . . .*

'Silence!' Starlight ghosted along the bald curve of a shaved head. 'One noise and they come out and kill us all. Who are you?'

'Janvier.' January yanked his arm from the loosened grip of the men behind him. 'Who are you?'

'Abu.'

The name only meant *servant*, but the man's speech, and the smell of his clothing and that of the others behind him – frankincense and strong tobacco – caused January to ask, 'You are servants of Hüseyin Pasha?'

The man before him nodded, and one of the men in the utter black of the shadows hissed, '*Shaitan!*' and the next second, January heard the scramble of Chatoine's tiny feet darting away into the night.

'Did they bring in a woman?' he whispered urgently. 'Not Shamira. She'd have been in the black dress of a nun—'

'What know you of Shamira?' The man called Abu turned his face toward the house. Starlight showed January a jutting nose and thick lips, a mustache the size of a small raccoon and eyes overhung by a massive brow. 'The other woman they brought in between two and three.'

Four had struck some minutes before on the clock of Notre-Dame de Bercy.

'I do not know for certain,' said January softly. 'But I am fairly sure that Sabid lied to the police, to get men and a warrant to take Shamira from the convent where she had gone for refuge.'

'A convent?' Abu's ape-like brow clouded. 'She—'

'She was there.' January held up his hand. 'I know. My wife found her there and convinced her to leave, I don't know how. It is my wife that Sabid's men have taken. If they have not brought Shamira in, where she is I do not know. Has Sabid himself returned?'

Abu shook his head.

'Then we may be in time. *I* may be in time. And you, too, if you will help me . . . In the name of Allah, the All-Compassionate, will you help me? I can't get her out of there alone.'

Abu took January's arm in one meaty hand, squeezed it re-assuringly. 'Have you been in the house? Or the grounds?'

'No.'

'I have. Who is with you?'

'Only the child.'

'Leave him out of this.' Abu grunted and glanced in the direction Chatoine had fled. 'Your child?'

'A child of the streets.' As always, January used the masculine pronoun to speak of Chatoine. Bad enough Hüseyin's servants would think he would willingly endanger an urchin, without revealing that that barely-glimpsed urchin was a six-year-old girl. 'My wife was good to him and his brothers. They were helping us find Shamira.'

'Were they, indeed?' As they spoke thus, in the barest of whispers, they moved through the darkness along the wall, to where it made a corner in a thin woodland. So dense was the night beneath the trees that the wall – and the shapes of the stable roof and the taller house-roof beyond – were barely to be seen, but January smelled tobacco smoke and guessed there was a gate of some kind in the rear that led out into the woods.

And the gate was guarded.

Abu signaled them to retrace their steps to the front of the property, which was in all about a hundred meters deep. Here at the edge of the faubourgs, where the houses were thin, the frontage on the road was far wider than in the more densely built-up areas. The next cluster of buildings – unwalled – lay perhaps three hundred meters away, lightless and smelling of cows. 'And how comes this to be any affair of your good wife?'

'As a woman, my wife pitied her.' January strained his senses in the inky shadows, to guess how many men Abu had with him, or how well they might be armed. 'And feared for her, when the Lady Jamilla told us that when Shamira made her escape, this man Sabid would follow her, to make her a pawn in the fight between himself and her master.'

'And did your good wife,' returned Abu a little grimly, 'have the intention of returning Shamira to the house of her master, that Hüseyin Pasha might not be robbed of his child?'

'I know not Ayasha's intent. Perhaps neither did she. Only to keep Shamira safe from Sabid, and to speak to her. To see what it was that *she* wanted.'

Abu grunted, then stood silent for a time, listening. For his part, January heard his own voice speaking with a kind of amazement. *How can I sound so calm?* Within him his heart was screaming at God: *Don't let them harm her*—! Yet he noted, almost with detachment, that Abu and the others – there were three of them – wore the traditional Turkish garments that seemed obligatory for the servants of Hüseyin Pasha. That Abu was armed with a brace of pistols.

'I think you need to learn to school your wife, African,' said Abu at last, but there was a trace of humor in his voice.

January took a deep breath. 'If I can ever find a man who would show me how to survive such a lesson, I would think about it.'

'Hmph. A woman—'

What he would have said, January never knew, for distantly in the dark hooves clattered, and – blinding as sunlight after hours of starlight and dark – lanterns flared as they came into the lane. So bright did the light seem that for a moment January couldn't see past it: two lanterns, and the dim flash of a horse's eyes. In the same instant he heard light small feet on the dirt roadbed, and a youthful voice whispered, 'Janvier?'

'Here. It's all right,' he added, guessing that Poucet – for it was Poucet – would flee, as Chatoine had, from the shadows of the Turks.

'They didn't find her,' whispered the boy. 'Ayasha—'

'You've got to get her out!' added Chatoine's voice from the darkness.

'I didn't understand what he said –' desperate fear shook Poucet's voice – 'but you know he's going to try to make her tell!'

'Where would he have her?' January glanced back at Abu. 'Cellar or attic? Quickly, man—'

'Cellar. He has French servants—'

The riders were approaching the gate. 'How many are with you, Poucet? Do you have your slingshots? Get across the road, now, and shoot at the horses when they reach the gate.'

'You cannot expect those children—' gasped Abu, shocked.

'Run like hell the moment someone comes after you,' January went on. 'We just need the noise. Go! Now!'

Brother and sister vanished like alley cats into the night. January caught Abu's elbow, dragged him along the wall toward the rear of the grounds again. 'If there's a commotion at the gate the guards inside the house will run toward it. Can we get over the rear gate?'

'If there's no guard. The entry is arched, but the gate is flat across the top. There's space between for a man to slip through, if he has someone to boost him up.'

Weeds lashed January's calves, and he stumbled on the uneven ground along the wall. Behind them he heard the angry whinny of a horse, and then another. Men shouted curses. *Virgin Mother, watch over your children . . .*

'Would Sabid truly torture this girl, to obtain back the letter Hüseyin went to find in England?'

'The Lady told you that, did she?' Abu panted a little, striving to keep up with January's longer strides. 'He would. And anyone – even those poor children – who stood in his way.'

Their feet slithered in the ditch. So cold was the night that ice had formed there, but January barely felt it, even when it soaked his shoes.

'Sabid lost everything when he was banished,' Abu went on. 'The men who bribed him will support him in this country for a time, but he must return to power if he is to survive. And, he has his pride. He is convinced that what he does is for the good of the Empire. Such men are the most dangerous of all.'

One hand touching the stones of the wall, January turned the corner, strode swiftly until he felt the stones of a gate arch and, an instant later, heavy panels of iron-strapped wood. 'Here.' The men gathered around them: a whisper of fabric, a thick breath of tobacco and spices and sweat.

'Daud,' breathed Abu, followed by a string of instructions in

Turkish. A man grunted in reply. January had seen that one of Abu's followers was nearly as tall as he was himself, muscled like an ox. He heard the wood of the gate creak as someone – presumably the mighty Daud – leaned against it. 'Daud will be our ladder. Will you follow me over, African?'

A moment later the hinges rattled. Distantly, January could still hear commotion around the gates, and he prayed that Poucet and his siblings were able to slip away in the dark. He tried not to count the moments that he knew were all they'd have.

A hand took his arm, guided him. Like an acrobat he put a foot into a stirrup made from a man's clasped hands, and as he was boosted up – no small feat given his size – he scrambled for the top of the gate. A rope hung over it, aiding him as he went over, and he remembered to keep his head low. *All I'd need is to brain myself on the arch . . .*

A single lantern beside the stable door showed him the bulky silhouette of Abu, the dark orifices of other doors: carriage house, laundry rooms, wood cellar, wine cellar. He turned back in time to see another of Abu's men come over the gate, and a third: tough, solid soldiers in their loose salvars and short jackets, shaven heads bare. Abu drew the dangling rope to the side of the gate, so that its shape might not be as obvious in the darkness. January strained his ears to reassure himself that the tumult by the front gate continued, but heard nothing. *Because the house is in the way? Because they've already come in . . .?*

The third man over the gate carried a dark-lantern of pierced tin, which he kindled from the stable lamp.

Abu led the way at a run across the stable yard, down a brick-paved ramp to a low arch. *Wine cellar*, thought January. *Carts bring the barrels in, men roll them down below the house . . .*

Would Sabid drink wine?

The cellar was closed with a padlock and hasp, and Abu made short work of these with a small crowbar. The lantern's yellow gleam caught the flash of a blade as the henchman stepped back to keep guard on the cellar door. Then darkness, as Abu covered the light. In that darkness a thread of muddy orange shone in the cellar door's cracks, and as January's hand touched the wood of the door he heard, on the other side, Ayasha's voice scream, 'No!'

TEN

She added, in a fury of desperation, 'Son of a dog!' as January ripped one of the pistols from Abu's sash, and both he and the Turk hurled open the cellar doors.

Lantern light within the cellar showed him Ayasha, her black dress torn and her black hair a tumbled mass of night, as Sabid slashed the ropes that had held her to one of the long room's wooden support-pillars. Sabid held her by one arm – like January, he was still in the evening clothes he'd worn to the Tambonneau ball – and had just brought up the knife to her throat to keep her from raking his eyes with her nails.

Both turned as the doors slammed open, and the two grooms with Sabid started toward January and Abu.

'Not another step!' shouted January, and he leveled the pistol on Sabid.

Fifty feet separated them, a dusty, cobwebbed aisle of ancient barrels, dry bottle-racks, the broken debris of disused tables and chairs. In Captain Rory's Gallery of Self-Defense – where January practiced both boxing and target practice twice a week when he had money – he could hit a playing card at that distance every time.

With a pistol that he knew.

In good lighting.

Without the one person he loved most in the mortal world held with a knife at her throat an inch from his target.

The knife moved a glinting millimeter, and as if someone had said it in his ear, January thought: *If he cuts her and drops her, he knows I'll stay behind with her rather than pursue him . . .*

Abu stepped from behind him and called out something in Arabic, from which January only picked out the word *imrât – woman.*

Sabid answered in the same tongue, his cold, clear voice mocking. Behind him, the two scar-faced grooms kept their own weapons pointed – rifles of some kind, though it was almost impossible to see in the shadows. From his jacket, Abu drew a folded piece of paper, clotted all over with broken sealing-wax.

Silence fell in the cellar, save for the hiss of the flame within the lantern carried by Abu's henchman still behind him. January could see nothing but the thin edge of metal laid on Ayasha's brown throat.

Then Sabid spoke, quietly. Abu answered, at some length, and Sabid's mouth curled in a scornful smile.

Without knowing Arabic, January heard, in al-Muzaffar's reply, triumph and contempt.

'He says you are to carry this to him.' Abu held out the letter to January. 'Stand back from him, and hold the paper up so that he can see it, but not touch it.' In the lantern light, January saw bitterness, weariness, defeat on his ugly face. 'Then when I tell you to, give it him, but only after he has returned your wife to you. If he harms her, run with the paper back to me, and I promise you that, by it, he will suffer vengeance. It will not bring her back,' he went on softly. 'But some vengeance is always better than none. Will you do this?'

January handed him the pistol he held. The other half of the pair was already in Abu's hand. 'This is the letter, of which *Sitt* Jamilla spoke?' And that being so, he knew, too, the true name of the man before him.

Abu nodded. 'It is a letter in Sabid's hand to the directors of the British Black Sea and Anatolia Company, promising concessions of territory from the Sultan in exchange for a hundred thousand pounds to be deposited in Sabid's account in the Bank of England.'

Under the heavy brow, the Turk's face was sad. 'I traveled to London to find Mr Willard Polders of the Black Sea and Anatolia Company, and to purchase this letter of him, since the Sultan made other disposal of those concessions last year. It is not only my hatred of Sabid for an apostate that made me undertake the voyage, you understand. I love the Sultan, who is like a brother to me, and I love the land of my birth. This man –' he nodded toward al-Muzaffar, sleek and handsome in his Western evening-dress, his pomaded dark hair – 'would enslave the one and transform the other into what I saw in England. A world of uncaring machines, of smoke and steel, a world that knows not God nor the silence of God in man's heart.

'But I understand,' he went on, 'that if he takes your lady away with him, he will have Shamira's whereabouts from her sooner or later. And then I will be where I am now. Only you, who have tried to help the mother of my son for no profit that I can see, would be bereft, to no purpose.' He handed January the paper. 'So it might as well be now.'

'You are Hüseyin Pasha, then?'

The man who had called himself Abu nodded. 'Servant of Mahmud the Defender of our Faith – and of Allah the All-Merciful, the All-Compassionate One.'

Sabid snapped something, short and angry, and Hüseyin Pasha said softly, 'Go. But watch him. He is a viper, and he has in the past killed for only the pleasure of doing so.'

January took the paper, walked the length of the cellar, taking care never to step into the line of fire between Hüseyin's pistol and Sabid. Ayasha called out to him, '*Mâlik*, don't trust him! He is a son of serpents!' He saw bruises on her face and felt his whole body grow hot with rage.

'It will all be well, *zahar*.' He felt dizzy as he walked, and strange, as if he had a high fever or walked in a dream.

He stopped a dozen feet from Sabid. Unfolding the paper, he held it up in the light of the lantern held by the taller of Sabid's grooms; the man moved the light closer, to show it up. From the far end of the room, Abu called out something, probably asking: Did Sabid recognize the paper as his?

'Lay the paper down, African,' said Sabid. 'And step back one step from it.'

'Do so,' affirmed Hüseyin. 'But do not get between my pistol and that son of dogs.'

January stooped and laid the letter on the ground. As he straightened up Ayasha made a move, and she gasped as Sabid twisted her arm. Sabid snarled something through his teeth, an instruction to one of his grooms.

With shocking suddenness, the Arab shoved Ayasha at January with a violence that made her stumble. As January caught her in his arms the taller groom dashed the lantern to the stone floor; from the corner of his eye January glimpsed the other groom as the man dove to snatch up the paper. In blackness and confusion it was hard to be sure. In any case, his main concern was to drag Ayasha back away from Sabid as swiftly as he could. He heard retreating boots, the clatter of a door, and Hüseyin yelled, 'Run!'

January didn't ask questions. Just caught Ayasha's hand, and ran.

Hüseyin waited for them by the door at the far end of the cellar – January guessed that Sabid would rally his guards and kill them all if he could, letter or no letter. They fled up the ramp, across the stable yard, stumbling on the old uneven cobblestones. January boosted Ayasha to the rope and scrambled up it behind her, slithered between the top of the gate and the arch of the gateway. As they dropped to the ground shots rang in the woods behind them. He grabbed Ayasha's hand again, and they fled toward the river, where the first of the boats from the countryside were bringing in coal and wine, wood and vegetables through the wet darkness to Paris.

Daybreak found them in the Café l'Elephant on the Place de la Bastille, consuming coffee, milk and bread among a mixed crowd of bargees, furniture-makers, sleepy whores and carters. '*Was* Arnoux de Longuechasse behind Shamira's escape?' asked January, and daubed jam on the bread. His head throbbed with weariness, and now that the heat of fear was gone from his blood he felt he could have curled up under the table and slept for a week.

'He was.' Ayasha wolfed down her fourth slice and licked the butter from her fingers. He'd wrapped his coat over her torn black robe, for the morning was freezing cold, and together with January's much-scuffed evening-dress they made a grimily dissolute-looking pair. On the other side of the table, Poucet, Chatoine, and their little band of infant criminals shared their meal in silence, trying not to appear as shaken as January guessed they really were. He wondered a little if, when they returned to the Rue de l'Aube, he'd find his music satchel safe, and decided if he didn't, it was a small price to pay. It would be a nuisance to replace, but whoever found it and pawned it would probably need the money more than he did.

He was aware that God had been very good to him that night.

'I take it she had no intention of converting?'

Ayasha regarded him, puzzled, and shook her head. 'Did you see her?' she asked doubtfully.

'No. But if a girl in a Muslim household cries out in her extremity to the God of Abraham,' said January reasonably, 'I would be a little surprised to hear of her going over to the Blessed Virgin two days later. And yet, someone like the Abbess of St Theresa's would be more able than anyone else to organize an escape. And she'd need no convincing of the girl's sincerity: what Jew would not fall at Christ's feet with cries of joy, once she was shown the light?'

Ayasha sniffed. 'And every one of those laundresses and grocers and women who sell eggs would fall all over themselves to deliver messages, and never the same one twice. How not, when to do so would save their own souls and strike confusion to the Filthy Infidel?'

'It was an excellent plan.' January held out his handkerchief to her, to tie up her tumbled hair in some echo of respectability. 'And well thought out. Did she set it in motion when she was in Constantinople?'

'It would be hard *not* to think of it, with l'Abbé de Longuechasse sitting there in front of the ladies of the Sultan's *harîm* just *shining* with Christian fortitude.' Ayasha consumed another slice of bread and jam in two gulps. 'Of course such a man would have connections in the Church, whether or not he spoke of them. And even in the Ottoman lands, the Church has power. She would have known from the synagogues at her home, and the families of the Jews, what can be done when people will do what they're told without questions. She had just learned that she was with child, and she had reason to fear the Lady Utba – and also, that Hüseyin Pasha would soon take them all to France. She smuggled word to de Longuechasse that she wished to learn more of Christ, and soon after that, that she had seen the Light, and would he help her, for the glory of God and the Catholic Church? What good son of the Church would refuse?'

Ayasha held her hands over the steam from her coffee cup. On the other side of the table, Poucet and his little tribe had slipped into an exhausted doze in the unaccustomed warmth, like dirty puppies slumped in their chairs. January seriously considered doing the same.

At length Ayasha said, 'When her father died, her mother needed money that Shamira's brother might go to university . . . and so, of course, become a man capable of supporting his mother in comfort.'

January said nothing. Ayasha had told him once that when she was fourteen, she had run away from her father's house with a

French soldier, needing a protector, she had said, to get her to France. She never spoke of the man, and January sometimes wondered about those months of her life: what it had cost her to run away.

After a little time he asked, 'And how much of that did she tell Mother Marie-Doloreuse?'

'Well, if she'd told her the truth,' said Ayasha practically, 'the Mother Abbess would have given her back over to Hüseyin Pasha. He is not a bad man,' she added. 'Even if he is ugly as *Shaitan*'s pig.'

'He saved your life,' pointed out January. 'At the cost of leaving himself in danger from his mortal enemy.'

'Was that the letter *Sitt* Jamilla spoke of? That paper?'

'It was. By the sound of it, it could have gotten Sabid hanged if he'd gone back to Constantinople . . .'

'They don't hang them,' corrected Ayasha. 'If the Sultan is in a good mood, one who displeases him will be beheaded. If he isn't in so good a mood, the man will be sewn in a sack with a couple of cannonballs and dropped into the Bosphorus, or maybe strapped up in an iron cage, so that he cannot move, and hung up for the ravens to devour while he starves. Mahmud has often spoken of getting *la guillotine* – Sabid tried to convince him that it was modern and scientific. But at least malefactors are no longer boiled in molten lead.' She licked another smear of jam from her finger. 'Sometimes they'll boil a cauldron of asphalt and stick a funnel . . . Did you learn where she had gone?'

January asked gently, 'Did you?'

Ayasha looked aside. 'You would not make her go back?'

'He saved your life,' repeated January.

'That's no reason to send her back to a man she doesn't want to lie with.'

'Is he bad to her?'

Ayasha shook her head. Her voice was quiet. 'He is a good man, she says. Kind, and with great sympathy for her plight. Yet, she said, as his concubine, he has the right to use her body – however gently. But it is not what she wants. And she said that, as a woman in his household, if she said *no*, then where would she be? And he is not of her faith. Both his faith, and hers, and even yours, *Mâlik*, count a woman's soul as weaker than a man's, and more likely to be excused by God for faithlessness that she cannot help – yet Shamira dreamed still of being the wife of a man of her own people, with honor and dignity. Is this not a dream that any woman might have?'

They returned to the Rue de l'Aube and slept – January retrieved his music satchel untouched. Had any of their neighbors seen it, there behind St Peter's feet, they would have recognized it and left it alone.

January assumed that eventually Hüseyin Pasha would track them down. Either Jamilla would tell him where they could be found, or the Turk would ask at the embassy where he might reach the big African who played piano upon so many occasions at the Embassy balls. January had no doubt that Hüseyin Pasha was not a man who ever forgot a face.

Before he did – and indeed, January hoped, before he had to be at the Opera that night – he wanted to know, at least, what he was to say to the man who had saved Ayasha's life.

So before retiring to bed that morning, he had written a short note in simple French (*'Yallah, Mâlik,* you don't think anyone ever bothered to teach her to read Arabic? Or Hebrew, for that matter?'), and dispatched it – via the helpful Poucet – to an address in the district of St-Germaine. When he awoke, just after two, it was to find two notes under the door.

One was from Hüseyin Pasha, requesting that January present himself, at his earliest convenience, at his residence on the Rue St-Honoré.

The other, in a strong, elegant hand on good-quality notepaper, said:

> *M'sieu,*
>
> *Many thanks for your note. Deeply sensible of the debt that she owes to you and to your wife, my niece agrees to meet with you this afternoon at four, at this address. On her behalf, I add my entreaties, not to speak of your meeting, or my niece's whereabouts, to anyone, until you have spoken to her.*
>
> *My most sincere thanks,*
> *Jacob L'Ecolier*

ELEVEN

The town house of the banker L'Ecolier stood on a small *place* off the Rue des Tuileries, not far from the Luxembourg Palace. An elderly servant showed January and Ayasha upstairs, to a small salon at the rear of the *premier étage*. Two women looked up as the man ushered the visitors in. One was the inevitable thirty-ish female relative so frequently found in well-off households, either unmarriageable or widowed: the latter, in this case, January guessed, for she was clothed in unrelieved black and, to January's experienced eye, just beginning the fifth month of pregnancy.

The other was the girl he had last seen in the attic of the house of Hüseyin Pasha, the girl whose face he'd barely been allowed to glimpse.

She was still thin from her sickness, and very pale. Her face – unveiled now and framed in neat thick curls the color of café noir – was delicately beautiful, slightly aquiline, and illuminated by enormous brown eyes of singular beauty and intelligence. At the sight of Ayasha their watchfulness faded, and she sprang to her feet. 'God be praised!' Her French was thickly accented. 'You got away!'

The two women clasped hands, Shamira's face tight with emotion. 'I feared for you—'

'I was taken.'

The girl's eyes widened: guilt, shock, fear. And dread, at what recompense might be asked of her, for honor's sake.

'Hüseyin Pasha paid a price for my release. I do not know,' Ayasha added, as January bowed, 'if you remember my husband?'

'I do.' Color briefly stained Shamira's ivory cheeks, that he had seen her sweating and vomiting in her sickness. 'I – thank you, sir . . .'

January bowed deeply over her hand. 'Are you well, Mademoiselle L'Ecolier?'

She glanced across at her chaperone, put a hand protectively to her belly, as women with child the world over are wont to do. 'Yes. Very well.' Her eyes went to Ayasha again. 'Hüseyin Pasha send you?'

Ayasha shook her head. 'We had a note from him this morning, but we have sent him no reply. Still, he gave up the only hold he had over his enemy Sabid – the only protection he had against him – in order to save me from pain, only because I was taken in trying to help you. He does not know we are here, or that we know where you are. Yet I think you owe it to him to speak with him. Will your kinsman M'sieu L'Ecolier stand by you?'

January saw her eyes flicker again to the black-clothed chaperone, who through the whole of this dialog had merely sat tatting an antimacassar. From the lack of expression on her round, impassive face, it was for a moment impossible to tell whether she was being tactful, disapproving, sly, or whether she truly took no interest in this lovely young kinswoman's exotic affairs. Even when, for a moment, she raised her dark eyes to meet Shamira's, the look which passed between them was swift and secret. Then the whole of her soul seemed to return to her needle, flickering silver in the window's pale twilight.

Her face now flushed again with shame, and her dark eyes shining with tears, Shamira replied in a steady voice, 'M'sieu L'Ecolier know everything of Hüseyin Pasha and myself.' Her hand stole briefly to touch her belly again. 'He will stand by me. He say, by laws of France, I not sent back to Hüseyin Pasha, not by King himself.'

'But the laws of France – and of God,' said January, and he watched her face as he said it – 'will give a father some claim on the upbringing of his child, whom he begot lawfully upon a woman of his own household. He was willing to put himself into grave danger, that you and your child might be safe.'

The girl's fingers darted to her eye to catch a tear before any could see it. 'Even so.' She added then, in a small voice, 'He is good man. Please understand he is good man. He was good to me. Kind. Only I . . .' She looked to Ayasha, as if to see in her eyes the words she needed to say, and Ayasha said something in Arabic that January knew in his heart was: *I understand.*

'I want husband with honor,' said Shamira after a moment. 'Hüseyin Pasha was kind to me as a master kind to his slave. Me, I want household, children. I want . . . sit in synagogue among wives, see my son's bar mitzvah, my daughter wed with honor to good man. M'sieu L'Ecolier say he will see this so.' And turning her eyes again to Ayasha, she added, with a nod at January, 'I want this what I see you have. Husband. Life.'

And again Ayasha said: *I understand.*

Shamira led her to a small desk between the windows, which looked down on to the little town garden behind the house; took a quill from the holder, paper from the drawer.

'Please.' She held them out to Ayasha. 'Write for me.'

January and Ayasha returned to that house on Sunday, in company with Hüseyin Pasha. This time in that airy parlor, with its stylish furniture of carved mahogany and its discreet bronze and marble statuettes, Shamira sat with her kinsman, the banker Jacob L'Ecolier himself, and his bird-like little wife, as well as the black-clothed chaperone. In her high-waisted dress of gray silk Shamira looked every inch the daughter of a wealthy Jewish household, and January caught the glance that passed between the kindly-faced Madame L'Ecolier and this newest kinswoman to come under her wing: friendship, warmth, and care. When Hüseyin Pasha was shown into the parlor, the banker's wife squeezed Shamira's hand: *Don't be afraid, dearest . . .*

Shamira did not get to her feet for her former lord. Only held out her hand, as a well-bred French lady should.

This distinction wasn't lost on Hüseyin Pasha. His heavy, simian face remained impassive, but January saw the smallest of rueful twinkles in the dark eye. He said something to Shamira in a gentle voice, almost jesting; her chin came up. In careful French, she replied, 'I am French now, M'sieu.'

In the same language he replied, 'So I see.' And sighed.

'My niece bears you no ill will, M'sieu,' said L'Ecolier, when his visitors had seated themselves. 'Please understand that. My kinswoman Rachel bint-Zipporah had no business negotiating with you the contract by which Shamira came into your household. As her kinsman, and head of the family, I thank you from the bottom of my heart for treating her well and with indulgence. But I hope you understand that whatever my niece will have said to you at the time, the match was not made with her free consent.'

'I understand that there is consent, and there is free consent.' The Turk folded his coarse, square hands upon his crimson silk knee. 'Yet what woman ever gives her free consent to a match made for her by her parents? Particularly to a business partner who is forty-four years old and ugly as a horse's backside, eh? And how many girls are there who take unto themselves lives of poverty and misfortune, because they come hand-in-hand with a handsome face or a voice beautiful in song? Yet I am glad to hear, Shamira –' he turned to her and inclined his head – 'that you bear me no ill will. One thing only I ask. That you give me my son, when he is born.'

Shamira took a deep breath, glanced at the black-clothed chaperone, then nodded. In a perfectly steady voice she said, 'Yes.'

Hüseyin Pasha had clearly come prepared to have to make his case; and, just as clearly, knew enough not to make any reply at all. He only took her hand and gently kissed it.

Shamira went on, halting a little on the words, 'It is best so,' and glanced at her kinsman. January saw her fingers tighten on Madame L'Ecolier's. This was something, he guessed, that they had spoken of already. What young gentleman in the Parisian circles of Jewish bankers, merchants and financiers would wed a young widow – for he already guessed how this lovely girl would be introduced to the family social group – if she came with an infant who was obviously the child of a Turk? Easier to say: *She was wed in the East, but her baby died . . .*

Certainly, given Jacob L'Ecolier's wealth, easy enough to arrange.

It would avoid, too, whatever feeling she might carry against that child, when she bore others to that 'husband with honor' that she craved.

And yet . . .

'My niece will send you word, M'sieu,' said Madame L'Ecolier, 'when the child is born.'

'You have given me treasure beyond my deserving,' replied the Turk quietly. 'And I swear to you, Shamira, that your son will never want for education, or guidance, or whatever else lies within my power to give.'

There being nothing more to stay for, the visitors rose. Ayasha and Shamira embraced, tears again glistening in Shamira's eyes in the cold autumn light from the windows. From the little garden below, January heard the voices of children, and stepping back, he looked down, to see half a dozen boys and girls, in stair-step sizes, all clothed in black. It was unlikely that the tired-looking chaperone would ever be anything but what she was, with that brood in tow. Still, he reflected, it was a mark of L'Ecolier's kindness, that he would take them in. The girl Shamira would be in good hands.

She rose as the banker opened the parlor door himself, to see his guests away. In a small voice she said, '*Kassar Allah hairak*, M'sieu,' which January knew to mean *thank you*. 'The blessing of God go with you.'

'And with you, Shamira. You made me very happy.'

Turning, Hüseyin Pasha passed through the door and down the stair, a great gorgeous bird-of-paradise in his crimson salvars and his crimson turban and his long red-and-blue coat trimmed with fur. And all the little chaperone's black-clothed children, under the supervision of an older boy who had to be – by his round snub-nosed face – her brother, clustered at the bottom of the stairway to watch him pass, in silence and in awe.

And thus it was that Benjamin January *knew*, to the bottom of his heart, that Hüseyin Pasha would not – *could* not – be the man who had strangled his two concubines and pitched them out the attic window on the night of December tenth, 1837.

December 1837, New Orleans

Within fifteen minutes of his mother leaving the house, January was walking down Rue Esplanade in the direction of the Place des Armes. The day was gray and raw, and the air smelled like burned sugar; it was the end of the *roulaison*, the grinding season. For a hundred miles up the Mississippi, and as many downriver, every plantation worked full stretch, twenty-four hours a day, hauling cane to the cogged iron wheels of the grinding house, hauling wood to feed the hell fires under the boiling kettles. Gritty smoke always in the eyes, aching muscles, the numb exhaustion that makes for terrible accidents if you happened to have a razor-sharp cane-knife in your hand.

The plunge in cotton prices might have triggered the demise of banks and businesses across the United States, but the world could never get enough sugar.

The levee at the bottom of the Place des Armes was the most active that January had seen it in months. A dozen steamboats lay at the wharves, though compared to other years it was nearly deserted. Kaintuck farmers and flatboatmen, newly come down-river with their loads of pumpkins, corn, and hogs, prowled in disconsolate fury from buyer to buyer of the few brokers still in business, and as he crossed toward the Cabildo beside the Cathedral, January could hear voices harsh with anger: *What the hell you mean, two cents a bushel? At two cents a bushel I coulda dumped the whole load into the river an' saved myself a trip . . .*

The old man who used to sell pink roses from a basket on his head was gone.

No one had the money for roses.

The few shops still open around the square were half-deserted. Passing the head of Gallatin Street, he'd seen the bar rooms and gaming houses were all still open, but the sound of the street was different. The gaiety that tinged the sounds of drink and play had been replaced with a harder note, a threat of violence.

It was as if, along with the smell of burned sugar, the air was alive with the stink of anger, frustration, and fear.

Lieutenant Abishag Shaw was at his desk in the big stone-flagged watch room of the old Spanish headquarters of law and justice in New Orleans, patiently writing the accounts of two flatboatmen, a gambler, a sailor and three whores concerning an altercation at Alligator Sal's. Only the gambler was sober. Shaw had a cut over his left eye, and on the bench next to where January took a seat, one of the other City Guards was patching up another with sticking plaster and bandages.

'Goddam Irish bastard started it!'

'Who you callin' bastard, you dog-friggin' Whig whoreson?'

'I'm callin' you bastard, an' cheat besides!'

Through the open doors at the rear of the watch room came the crack of a whip, then a man's scream of agony, from the courtyard where disobedient or insolent slaves were sent by their owners to be whipped, at fifty cents a stroke. A man stood next to the doors waiting his turn at the whipping post, holding a girl of fourteen by the arm in an iron grip and casually smoking a cigar as he watched.

'How can I help you, Maestro?' Shaw uncoiled his tall height from behind the desk as the whole squad of the accused were herded, still shouting, from the room. He looked, as usual, like a badly put-together scarecrow, greasy blondish hair hanging to his bony shoulders, inches of knobby wrist projecting beyond frayed and dirty sleeves.

'What are the chances I might speak with Hüseyin Pasha? I knew him in Paris—'

'If *this* man is permitted entry to the cells,' cried a rich, slightly gluey voice from behind January – 'a mere Negro from the wharves, you can have no excuse for keeping the man sequestered from the licensed representatives of the Fourth Estate, sir!' January was unceremoniously elbowed aside by a very large, very fat, very unwashed and unshaven man, in a blue frock-coat only a degree less grimy than Shaw's stained green jacket and a pair of checked trousers in an alarming combination of mustard and cinnamon hues. He recognized the man as Burton Blodgett of the *True American* – until recently the *Louisiana Gazette* – the chief English-language paper of the city. 'My readers have a right to know the facts of this shocking crime, sir! And not all the gold which this verminous Infidel has showered upon the officials of this city to cover up his misdeeds can erase the rights guaranteed by the Constitution to my readers, to know the truth!'

'Maestro –' Shaw stepped past the journalist to January's side – 'walk with me a spell. Mr January,' he added as Blodgett determinedly thrust himself in front of them on the way to the watch room's rear doors, 'far from bein' a mere Negro from off'n the wharves, is Mr Hüseyin's personal physician, here to bring him news about his wife.'

'Wife?' Blodgett struck an attitude like Mark Anthony at Caesar's funeral discoursing upon the honor of Brutus and Cassius. 'And which of his *wives* is that, sir? Has he many left?'

'Just the one. Sergeant Boechter,' added Shaw, with a gesture to the officer at the desk, 'would you make sure Mr Blodgett don't wander off an' get hisself lost? If'fn you knew Hüseyin in Paris, Maestro, I would purely like to have a word with you.'

TWELVE

'Janvier.' Hüseyin Pasha raised his eyes as Shaw and January came opposite the barred wall of the cell.

Privacy was a scarce commodity in the Cabildo. What had been adequate cell-space in the days of the Spanish governors not quite forty years previously had been long outstripped by the growth of the town once the Americans had taken over the territory, and the Americans' recent insistence that white drunks, murderers, robbers and rapists not be required to share their facilities with blacks had not helped the situation. A year ago the city had been divided into three 'municipalities' – each with its own courts – and this had eased the crowding somewhat. The new jail in the process of completion a short distance away on Rue St Peter would, January knew, help in time, but it hadn't yet.

At the moment, with Burton Blodgett ensconced, loudly protesting, in the watch room, the only place available to meet Hüseyin Pasha was either in the infirmary, in the makeshift morgue below the ground-floor stairs, or in the dirty corridor outside the cell itself.

The cell which was hallowed to the incarceration of slaves and free blacks, not whites.

Anger stirred in him. Evidently a Turk did not count as a white man.

'*Sayyadi.*' January inclined his head, and the Turk's thick, ugly lips bent in a wry smile.

'So the wheel turns again, my friend. And here I did not think to see you until next Wednesday, when you were to play at my reception.'

January returned both the wryness and the smile. Hüseyin Pasha had greeted him joyfully back in November, when January had been playing for a ball at the wealthy Widow Redfern's, though few words had been exchanged. It did not do – they both understood – for one of the guests of honor to speak overlong with the musicians. Subsequent meetings had been equally brief, usually under similar circumstances. Once the Turk had asked, 'Is your beautiful lady with you?'

January had replied, 'She died in the cholera, in thirty-two. Two years ago I remarried, and my wife has just borne a son.'

Hüseyin's sympathy had been genuine and warm.

Now January asked, 'What happened, sir? For I know you did not do this thing; and I know there must be a way to find who did.'

'You are the only man in this city who believes me, then, Janvier.' Hüseyin Pasha had removed his turban – which he still affected, along with the rest of his Turkish dress – and January saw that the stubble on his scalp, like his heavy mustache, was now shot with gray. 'As for what happened, that I do not know. The two poor girls – Noura and Karida – had fled from my house on Friday night . . .'

His voice hesitated as Shamira's shadow seemed to pass between them.

'I was angry,' he admitted. 'They took with them not only the jewelry that I had given them, but also my wife's as well. Yet I did not wish to make of myself a spectacle for the newspapers in your city, and so I spoke of their flight to no one. I see now that I should have done so. And indeed I feared for them, for they spoke only slight French, and no English at all. Three men had already offered me money for them, without ever seeing them.' The heavy flesh of his face hardened, and under the ape-like brow his dark eyes glinted with anger.

'They were not dark like Negroes, yet I have seen slave women in this country even more fair of complexion, and being foolish girls, how could they judge whether a man's intentions were honest or not? I should have spoken.' He sighed, angry, January could see, at himself . . .

And who would believe him, when he only says, 'They were not in the house,' after he is accused of their murder?

Only someone who knows him well.

January understood that he himself was the only man in the city who did.

'Tell me about Sunday night. Was anyone else in the house with you?'

Under the thick mustache, Hüseyin's mouth quirked again, at

the bitter jests of Fate. 'I was to meet a man of business named
Smith that night, who had said that no one must learn of his presence in New Orleans. Given the anger over the failure of the banks,
this did not seem unreasonable to me. I gave my son's tutor leave
to take my son to the theater, and with them all the other servants
as well, saving only my wife's woman.'

'Would that be Ra'eesa still?' January smiled. 'After all these
years?'

'You could not send her away at gunpoint.'

'We been inquirin' after Mr Smith.' Shaw's voice was dry over
that most common of names. 'Mr *John* Smith. Business unknown,
address unknown – nobody in no hotel in town by that name
'ceptin' a former director of the Mobile an' Balize Commercial
Bank that don't look a thing like Mr Smith's description, even if
he *had* been wearin' dark spectacles an' false whiskers.'

'What did Smith look like?'

'A man of girth and strength, like myself,' provided Hüseyin.
'A little taller. As the officer says, with dark hair and a full dark
beard, and spectacles on his eyes.'

'French or American?'

'That I cannot say. We spoke French, but whether he spoke it
as a true Frenchman would, I am not so familiar with the language
that I could judge. The beard may indeed have been a false one
– M'sieu Shaw tells me that it is not common for men in this
country to wear beards, as it is in mine. By the light of candles,
it is not so easy to tell.'

'Had you met him before?'

'No. He sent me a letter, introducing himself, saying that he
wished to speak to me of investment. Much to my advantage,
he said, but needing the capital of my gold. Again, I have had
many men come to me in the city, offering me the opportunity to
invest my gold.'

For weeks January had amused himself at receptions, balls,
entertainments – at the Opera and the Blue Ribbon Balls of the
demi-monde – watching the businessmen of the city swarm around
the Turk: *Now, don't you be deceived, Mr Hüseyin, the Carrollton
Bank's sound as a rock – as a ROCK, sir! Just needs a little capital
to get through this rough time . . . Banks, pshaw! Nuthin' like
land to turn over a profit in this country . . . Now, a score of men*

– not a score, three dozen, easy! – have come to me offerin' to partner me in this new cotton-press, but I didn't trust a one of 'em, not a one! But I'll give YOU the opportunity . . .

Nihil tam munitum quod non expugnari pecunia possit, as January's friend Hannibal had whispered irreverently on one such occasion. *There is no fort so strong that it cannot be taken with money.*

'He arrived shortly after eight – just before the rain began,' went on Hüseyin after a moment. 'I let him in myself. As you know, my house has two entrances: the great door out on to Rue Bourbon, and the carriageway that lets on to Rue des Ursulines. We went upstairs to my study, where there was a good fire. We talked for perhaps two hours. At the end of that time we were interrupted, by the crash of something falling past the study windows. I sprang to my feet and listened – he caught my arm and said: *It must not be known that I am in town*, or something to that effect. Then there was a second crash, and men began to shout in the street.'

'Did you go to the study window?'

'It was shuttered,' said Hüseyin, 'and I did not. My first thought was that my wife, who sleeps in the room above the study, had come to some harm. Yet I knew Ra'eesa was in the room with her, and moreover I had heard no sound of footfalls overhead. Yet when the second body fell I rushed out on to the gallery above the courtyard, and so down the stairs and through the passageway to the street. By the time I reached the street door men were shouting and banging on the door. I threw it open. It was almost too dark to see, though some of the men had candles, and a lamp burned in the passageway behind me. The bodies of my poor girls lay on the bricks.'

His face twisted as he said it, and he looked aside. Shaw leaned an angular shoulder against the bars that formed one wall of the cell and spat tobacco at one of the enormous cockroaches, which even in this frigid weather moved sluggishly along the grimy wall.

'They said that I had done it,' Hüseyin went on after a moment, his voice held steady with an effort. 'That someone had seen me hurl them down from the attic window.'

'Feller name of Breche, that keeps the shop down the street. Says he saw him clear.'

'The pharmacist?' January knew the place, though he seldom went there.

'That's the one. The old man's son.'

January fished in his memory for a moment for a picture of the man, small and fair and a little tubby, grinding powders in the back while his father shouted at him: *Oliver, where's that jalap? Oliver, this cinchona has lumps in it you could choke a horse on! Can you never do anything right?*

He looked back at the Turk, who only shook his head.

'It is a lie. I told them that I was with this man Smith. Yet when I led them up to my study, Smith was gone, and with him also the letter that had introduced him to me.'

'Had the attic window been opened?'

'It had,' said Shaw. 'Was still open when I got there, which was maybe an hour after the defenestration. But naturally every livin' soul that had been in the street had gone tearin' up to the attic by that time to look for theirselves, an' the attic was trompled up like a brick pit. I had to run the lot of 'em out sayin' I'd be happy to arrest every man jack of 'em as well as Mr Hüseyin, but there was no question about what room it was nor what window.'

'Any other way to get into the attic?'

'It's what I intend to have a look at this afternoon, if'fn I can get there 'fore the light goes.'

January glanced toward the cell's single window. It was barred on the inside, with a pierced iron plate set into the stucco of the wall outside. The pallid gray spots made by this admitted just enough light for him to see his watch. It was past four. 'Will you have company, sir?'

'I'd 'preciate it.' Shaw spat at another roach, with no greater success than he'd had with the first. January had seen the Kentuckian put out a candle with a rifle ball at two hundred and fifty feet. 'Not officially, but nuthin' says you can't call on Mrs Hüseyin in about twenty minutes' time. Care to have a look at the girls' bodies? They's down in the morgue.'

Hüseyin Pasha's face worked with distress. 'What will be done with them? Noura, and Karida—'

'They'll be returned to Mrs Hüseyin.' The first gentleness January had heard crept into Shaw's voice. 'She bein' either their next of kin in this country, or their mistress, dependin' on how the courts look at your domestic arrangements. Will that suit her?'

'Very well, thank you. She was fond of them,' added Hüseyin quietly. 'You understand, there was no jealousy, no hatred. She was angry that they took her jewels, of course. But she feared for them as I did, when Ra'eesa came to tell us on Saturday morning that they were missing from their room. And I think it will grieve her, as it does me, that they must lie in foreign soil among unbelievers, with none to care for their graves.'

'That at least can be attended to.' January put a hand through the bars to touch the Pasha's shoulder. 'I will speak to *Sitt* Jamilla about what can be arranged.'

'Not that it matters.' Hüseyin Pasha sighed again. 'Not to them, may their souls rest in Allah. But thank you, my friend. I shall feel better knowing that it is so.'

'Not a man to casually murder two girls out of jealousy,' remarked January as he and Shaw descended the stair to the Cabildo's courtyard again.

Shaw glanced back at him over his shoulder. 'He's your friend, Maestro, an' he done you a good turn. But you know, an' I know, there are men walkin' around in this world who rape children an' cut their little throats, an' then weep buckets – in purest sincerity, far as I could tell – at their funerals. I don't know how they think, but I know they exist 'cause I arrested one last year in Marigny, with cuttings of their hair all done up in ribbons in a box under his bed. An' danged,' he added, without alteration of expression in his mild, rather high-timbred voice, 'if it ain't gonna come on to rain again.'

He glanced up at the gray sky as they emerged into the Cabildo court. 'I suggest you get on over to pay your respects to Mrs Hüseyin now, an' we have a look at the girls afterwards. If there was any marks left on the roof, they'll be gone inside an hour.'

January smelled the air and had to agree. 'Do *you* think he did it?' he asked as they crossed the courtyard to the watch room again.

'I don't know. But I purely want to have a talk with Mrs Hüseyin an' have a look at that attic in daylight.'

'Why is that?'

''Cause when they was throwed out that window, both them girls had been dead for the best part of a day.'

A maidservant – middle-aged, well trained, and obviously purchased from a local Creole family – answered January's knock on the courtyard door of the big house on Rue Bourbon. 'I'm afraid Madame is unwell, sir.'

January handed her his card. 'I'm a physician.' This was a lie: he was still only a surgeon, as the woman's eye told him she knew when she glanced at the pasteboard rectangle in her hand. *Mr Benjamin January.* Had he been a physician, it would have read *Dr*, but she was far too well bred to pass judgement on the veracity of any guest, even one so much darker of complexion than herself. 'I have just come from the Cabildo, from speaking to Hüseyin Pasha, with whom I was acquainted in Paris. Perhaps Madame Ra'eesa is here and would vouch for me?'

The woman's mouth pinched up at the mention of Ra'eesa's name. But she stepped aside, to let January pass before her into the covered passageway that led back into an open loggia that in its turn gave on to the central courtyard of the house. January had played at the Turk's reception only a week ago, and he'd mentally noted the layout of the place: the stables which faced the loggia across the courtyard, the ballroom built above them, the kitchen that flanked the courtyard on the left and across from it, the back premises of the shop property that made up the right-hand corner of the lot.

A small parlor where Hüseyin Pasha would deal with day-to-day business and tradesmen opened to the left from the passageway from Rue Bourbon. A stairway ascended from the loggia behind that parlor to a gallery above, on to which would open the principal rooms of the house. Another passageway, wider, led from the courtyard, behind the shop, and out on to Rue des Ursulines; as was usual in New Orleans this wide passage doubled as shelter for the Turk's very stylish purple-lacquered barouche.

Though the open loggia was cold, and from it French doors opened into the ground-floor parlor, the maid indicated that he could take a seat on one of the benches in the loggia for all she cared. Her disdain was carefully calculated so that no one could accuse her of being 'uppity' – not that a man darker of hue than herself would dare to do so. Her attitude, as she left him and climbed the stairs to the gallery above, said clearly, as if she'd shouted it: *You may call yourself a physician, MR Benjamin January, but your complexion tells me your blood is almost pure African. Your parents were slaves, if you weren't born one yourself.*

At a guess – January tried to be detached, to take away the sting of her scorn – she assumed he was a Protestant as well. Many of the American-born – and less mixed-race – blacks in town were.

There was anger, too, in the set of her back, the angle of her head, anger that she probably wouldn't own to herself. Anger that a man whose dark skin marked him as part of the slave class should be free, while she – lighter than many of the *libré* demi-monde who owned their own houses, controlled their own destinies – could be sold like a set of dishes to a Muslim Turk who wanted to impress people with the excellence of his servants.

This lessened his own annoyance. But he felt gratified when, only minutes after he seated himself on the chilly bench, another knock sounded on the passageway door, necessitating Mademoiselle I'm-Whiter-Than-You to cease whatever she was doing upstairs and come down again to answer it.

At the maid's heels came a youngish man in Turkish dress, followed by old Ra'eesa, whose dark eyes flashed with pleasure at the sight of January, though she did not speak.

The young man bowed to January as the slave maid went on to open the passageway door. 'M'sieu Janvier?' He spoke excellent French. 'My master has spoken of you on several occasions in these last few weeks. I am Harik Suleiman, tutor to young *sahib* Nasir. Lieutenant Shaw,' he added, changing to English just as pure, as Shaw's mild voice echoed in the passageway. He stepped to greet him with an outstretched hand. 'Please do come upstairs.'

The maidservant looked as scandalized as a lifetime of being superior to everyone around her would let her.

Shaw emerged into the loggia and grasped Suleiman's hand. 'Pleased,' he said.

'All has been left as you ordered it last night; the attic locked, and none admitted.'

'Thank you, sir. That's right good of you. Mr January here bein' a surgeon, I'd like his opinion as well on the look of things, if'fn it wouldn't trouble Mrs Hüseyin none?'

'Not at all. You are to have every facility, she has said.'

'Now I take that very kindly.' Shaw bowed again, like a well-mannered dustman introduced to the Queen of England. 'If'fn it wouldn't be rushin' things a tad, we'd like to have a look up there first thing, as it looks to be comin' on to rain again. Afterwards I'll want a word with Mrs Hüseyin, if she's able for it.'

Suleiman turned to Ra'eesa and spoke a handful of words, in which January caught the name *Sitt* Jamilla and the word *labbas* – *to dress*. 'I am sorry,' said January, 'to trouble Madame, if she is not well. Please let her know that all of this is vital, if her husband is to be cleared of this crime.'

'Madame will be pleased to join you when you have finished,' said Suleiman. 'And I understand that she will be happy to renew your acquaintance, Mr Janvier. She holds you in great regard.'

'You speak any Arabic?' Shaw whispered as they ascended the stairs to the gallery.

'A little. And *Sitt* Jamilla's French may have improved. My wife—'

They passed the French doors that led to the parlors on the second floor, and January found, for an instant, that he could not go on.

It was only the hanging on the parlor wall – the sumptuous pattern of crimson and indigo, mountains and stars, that he last had seen in *Sitt* Jamilla's library on the Rue St-Honoré. But it was as if he had found, unexpectedly, Ayasha's comb, still entangled with strands of her hair, or a dropped chemise that still breathed the scent of her flesh. The furnishings of the room – Western chairs, carved tables with their brass insets still polished bright – were all as they had been in Paris, and the sight of them drove like a steel dagger into his heart.

It was only a glimpse in passing. But January was still shaking inside as they ascended to the upper floor – with its low tables and divans, its lingering smells of frankincense and tobacco – and from there, to the attic above.

THIRTEEN

'We have kept the window locked, from which Noura and Karida fell.' Suleiman fitted an iron key to the door of the south-west – or upstream – of the three attic chambers, which, January guessed, corresponded to the rooms on the floor below. 'This is Ghulaam's room – my master's valet, who also serves my lady.'

Which was, January was aware, the polite way of explaining that Ghulaam was a eunuch.

'From first light this morning, men have been crossing the roof from the house next to this one—'

'Consarn it!'

'It proves at least,' pointed out January comfortingly, 'that it's an easy crossing, from that roof to this.'

'Hell, I knowed that from puttin' my head out last night.' When the door opened, the Lieutenant strode across the big chamber, to the dormers that were almost like shafts projecting out to the light.

The attic room contained a single bed, with a prayer rug rolled up and stowed neatly beneath it. The Turkish cook, the black cook – whom January had met when playing at Hüseyin's entertainment – and the kitchen boy would sleep over the kitchen; Suleiman the tutor in the *garçonnière* – the separate quarters for the young men of the household – with Hüseyin's son Nasir; and the three American-born maids in the long downstream attic whose single dormer looked out over Rue des Ursulines. The walls, and the steeply-pitched roof, were freshly whitewashed, and the room scrupulously neat, with the exception of the floor, a smeared and muddy confusion of tracks.

January mentally cursed the monkey-like curiosity of humans, that treasures its right to 'go see what happened' over the slightest consideration of preserving evidence *in situ*.

Shaw was considerably more vocal on that subject.

The window sill of the upstream dormer did indeed show scrapes in the soot beyond the edge of the sash when Shaw raised it, but there was, as far as January knew, no doubt that the girls had been thrown from here. And when Shaw leaned out, January, looking around his shoulder, could see the trail of scuffs left by dozens of boots across the slates to the brick partition-wall that divided Hüseyin's roof from his neighbor's, less than two yards away.

This partition was only a foot high, dark with chimney soot and fringed with resurrection fern, that swift-growing New Orleans pest that would take root in anything. Beyond lay the dormer of the next house, a tall, thin structure identical in height to Hüseyin's, but less than a quarter its frontage.

Still muttering curses, Shaw swung himself out the window – the dormer was quite tall – and crossed the roof, the angle of which was about forty degrees. January looked down. Rue Bourbon, nearly forty feet below, bustled with carts and carriages, children chasing along the banquettes, and *marchandes* carrying wicker baskets on their heads: pralines, apples, shrimp. The balcony that stretched along the Rue Bourbon face of the house didn't extend all the way to the property line. Anything thrown from any other attic window would have fallen on it.

Then Shaw said, 'Afternoon, gentlemen,' and January looked up to see two men emerge from the dormer of the next-door house. Their long coats and high-crowned hats marked them as 'gentlemen', but only just. Small artisans or shopkeepers, he thought: the coats out-at-elbows, the pale trousers discreetly patched. 'Mr Pavot know you's comin' up through his house, whilst he's in Baton Rouge?'

'Pavot's a friend of ours, yes, Americain.'

The other sightseer added belligerently, 'Yes, he said to Jerry when he left: *If there's any murder done in the house next door, you're to let Denys Devalier and Nic Lassurance through to have a look at the windows.* What do you think about that, Americain?'

'I think that was right neighborly of him.' Shaw spat against the side of M'sieu Pavot's dormer. 'But bein' as Mrs Hüseyin got troubles of her own right now, I'm sure you'll understand her request that visitors be kept off'n the property, no matter how friendly they might be with their neighbors – or their neighbors' house servants.' He made a gesture with his fingers, as of rubbing coins together. 'If'fn you wish, in a neighborly way, to pay your respects to Mrs Hüseyin, I think it'd be best if you was to do so at the front door like regular folks.'

Rain began to fall while the Kentuckian was speaking. When the men went back into Mr Pavot's window, he crossed back to the dormer where January stood and stepped through, wiping soot and moss stains from his hands on the thighs of his disreputable trousers. 'Well, that didn't tell me much,' he grumbled. 'It quit rainin' just after eight last night, an' I didn't get here 'til near eleven.'

'Who sent for you?'

'Breche sent his kitchen boy.'

January looked across the street and upstream, to the two-story, soot-dark apothecary shop. Under its front balcony it was impossible to see from this angle, but he knew its windows displayed the huge glass alembics which announced the pharmacist's trade; announced, too, by the color of their contents – blue – that there was no fever in the town.

'And I take it – Jerry, is it? M'sieu Pavot's servant? – has a good account of himself for Sunday night?' January drew in his head, latched the window against the increasing downpour. Only a couple of carts remained of the bustle just moments ago, the clack of the horses' hooves on the pavement bricks strangely magnified by the gray wetness of the air.

'He swears the house was locked up tighter'n a miser's purse, an' he was in the kitchen in back the whole evenin'.' Shaw slicked back his wet, light-brown hair from his eyes. 'An' it's a fact that by the time I got there, he was in the crowd around the bodies in the street.'

'And he's Pavot's only servant?'

Shaw nodded. 'There used to be a cook – this man Jerry's ma – but Pavot put her up as security on a loan over the summer, an' then couldn't pay. Pavot's the manager of a little factory over in Marigny, what makes ladies' straw hats.' Their footfalls echoed hollowly on the bare plank floors as they returned to the main attic. 'You know anythin' about Hüseyin's enemies here in town? He ain't been here but a month, but even a man what everybody likes 'cause of his gold got enemies. Or about this Smith feller?'

January shook his head. Suleiman, who had waited by the door of the south-western room, locked the door behind them. 'Hüseyin told me he'd fallen out of favor with the Sultan and was obliged to leave Constantinople. He was looking to invest in imports, for he knows merchants throughout the Mediterranean, and in land.'

'Well, he can sure pick that up cheap these days.' Shaw glanced back over his shoulder at the door of Ghulaam's chamber as they reached the stair that led down, and he halted, to close his eyes, and sniff.

January stopped, too. The attic – unlike most of those in New Orleans – was almost completely uncluttered, Hüseyin having lived in the house only a few weeks. A line of wicker boxes along one wall held a little clothing, but it was nothing, January knew, compared to what an American family's attic would be like, with trunk after trunk of dresses, for which servants would be sent up every morning when Madame and her daughters awoke. There was no old furniture, no stacks of newspapers, no piled-up household accounts. The big room that lay between Ghulaam's chamber and the maids' dormitory was for the most part bare to its walls.

He knew what Shaw was thinking. Where would you put the bodies of two girls, that the servants wouldn't find them? Wouldn't at least detect them, by the increased presence of insects or rats?

'Think about it,' he urged softly. 'Hüseyin had complete control over those girls' lives. They had no family in this country, no one to whom he had to account for their whereabouts. If they displeased him, he could simply make them disappear. Why kill them in his own house, pitch them off his own roof on to his own doorstep, for all the world to see?'

'You know,' said Shaw in a thoughtful tone as they descended the stair to the third-floor gallery, 'I asked myself that very question a dozen times, when I come acrost a planter that's beat his wife to death with a curtain weight, or a woman that's cut her husband's throat while he's asleep in bed an' left the body there layin' in its blood. An' generally I don't get a very good answer.'

They emerged on to the gallery, the courtyard a gray well beneath them in the drenching rain. The roofs of the service buildings that surrounded it on three sides were typical New Orleans structures, slanting inward from a high outside wall, like the roofs of sheds, rather than ridged down the center as the roofs of houses were. January had heard outsiders opine that this style had been adopted to keep slaves from climbing over into the next courtyard to safety, but in fact – because the service wings of the buildings next door would be constructed in exactly the same way – there was nothing to keep a determined slave from scrambling up one side and then down the other into the next property.

In this case the effort would be complicated by the fact that the building which housed the kitchen – and, he guessed, the laundry – backed on to the yard of a livery stable, with no structure behind it and a two and a half story drop from its outer edge. Not an insurmountable problem, he reflected, going to the gallery rail to look out across the kitchen roof – the service buildings being only two storys in height, and the main house rising above them like an island set in the sky.

From here he could see down into the livery stable yard behind the kitchen and note that a two-story ladder lay along the ground there, easily long enough to serve.

'I ain't sayin',' Shaw went on, 'that some ill-intentioned rat-bastard couldn't'a sent a letter beggin' that the house be cleared for the evenin', to permit of nefarious fiscal dealins in the study, an' then lugged them girls over the roofs from Pavot's attic. Could happen.' His heavy Conestoga boots clattered on the next flight of steps down to the second-floor gallery beneath. 'But I'd still like to have a good hard sniff around the premises, 'fore we leave.' He turned his head and spat his tobacco chaw down into the courtyard below, lest chewing it in her presence offend a lady.

The Lady Jamilla awaited them in her husband's study on the second floor, Ra'eesa in attendance. Both women were veiled, and it distressed January to see the unmistakable signs of illness in the Lady's darkened and swollen eyelids, as well as the marks of tears.

'My lady Jamilla,' the tutor introduced with a bow. 'May I present Lieutenant Abishag Shaw, of the City Guards? And M'sieu Janvier . . .'

'M'sieu Janvier and I are old acquaintances.' She inclined her head in welcome as both men bowed. Her French had enormously improved. 'Please be seated. Thank you, Lorette,' she added as the disapproving housemaid appeared in the doorway, bearing a tray of tea and sugar cakes.

There were men in New Orleans who would have refused to sip tea and eat sugar cakes if a black man was doing so in the chair next to him, but Abishag Shaw wasn't one of them. In any case, January guessed that the Lady Jamilla was insufficiently acquainted with the intricate etiquette in play in New Orleans society which prevented such a situation from ever arising. It was almost, he reflected, like being in Paris again . . .

But he resolved to explain these niceties to this woman, lest she incur social damage later.

By the expression in the maid Lorette's sour eyes, he guessed that she might well beat him to this.

'How is my husband?'

'As well as can be expected, under the circumstances, my Lady. Lieutenant Shaw is here in his official capacity,' January went on, 'and I can assure you that he is a man of honor whom you can trust with your life, as I have more than once trusted him with mine. I am here only as a friend, to offer whatever help you may need in finding the true killer of those poor girls. Who, I am bound to say, despite my account of his character, the Lieutenant is perfectly ready to believe *was* your husband.'

Something that might have been a smile flickered in the corners of those dark eyes. 'Such is his duty.'

'I am glad to hear you say so, M'am.' Shaw's French was worse than execrable, but the Lady inclined her head to show that she understood. 'That makes it easier. Will you have any objection to my searchin' this house?'

A slight crease of puzzlement appeared between her brows, but she said, 'None, M'sieu.'

'You feel able to talk about them gals? An' I begs pardon,' he added, 'if'fn I don't know the customs of your country. I purely do not mean to offend.'

'It is not the custom in my country,' returned Jamilla, 'for a woman to pretend that her husband does not have concubines . . . as it is, I understand, in yours. Your question does not offend.' For a moment her brow twitched, and her fingers suddenly shook, where they fidgeted with the edge of her sleeve.

'When my husband's enemies gained power in the court of the Sultan, so that he knew that he must leave, he gave all the women of his household a choice: to remain with him, or to go to other homes. His other two wives, the ladies Marayam and Utba, both had family in Constantinople, and my husband gifted them with sufficient gold to ensure they would find other husbands – or at least find a welcome in the homes of their brothers. One concubine,

Raihana, chose to go with Utba, for over the years they had become dear friends. She is as a second mother to Utba's two daughters.'

She moved her hand as if she would sip her tea, but her fingers trembled so badly that she barely touched the handle of the cup before giving up the effort.

'I chose to remain with my husband. Noura and Karida had no family, and no other protector. I think Noura would have stayed in the East if she could, yet she is a . . . a troublesome girl.' Exasperation rather than anger tinted the soft voice. 'She has no malice in her – had none,' she corrected herself. 'Yet neither Marayam nor Utba would have her with them. Nor did my husband wish to abandon her, for she was very comely. And young, not yet twenty. Karida was a few years older, gentler in soul, yet easily led. She had been a Christian, and she renounced her faith, I think, only because it was expected of her.'

As she spoke January looked around him at the study, which was furnished – like the parlor next door – very much in the Western fashion, the tables French, of brass-mounted mahogany, and with only a single Wilton carpet on the floor instead of the piled rugs of Eastern custom. The rosewood desk he recognized as local, the work of M'sieu Seignouret on Rue Royale: Hüseyin would have sat there, he thought, while his bearded and bespec-tacled visitor Mr Smith sat in the chair now occupied by the lady. Very likely, he thought, Hüseyin had had the letter of introduction in his hands, asking about this detail or that . . .

And when Hüseyin rushed downstairs, how easy for Mr Smith to simply pocket it before he stepped out on to the back gallery, hurried down the stairs, across the courtyard while Hüseyin was dealing with the angry men already accusing him of the murder, and out the carriage gate.

'I have heard many ridiculous things that are believed in this country,' *Sitt* Jamilla went on. 'My husband did not keep us locked up, though of course we did not walk about the streets. Every week, sometimes oftener, he would have Nehemiah harness the carriage and take us out to walk beside the lake, or along the . . . the little river . . .' Her hand flickered in a ghost of her old swift-ness of gesture.

'The Bayou St John?'

'Even so. Thank you. The Bayou St John. Always with Ghulaam

and Suleiman in attendance, of course. Noura asked, many times, to be permitted to go out shopping, as from the windows of her room she saw other ladies do along Rue Bourbon, and she pouted when this was forbidden to her. But my husband is a man of the old ways and would not hear of it. He would buy us – any of us – whatever we asked for, but he would not hear of us dressing in the fashion of this country, or leaving off the veil.'

'An' did Miss Noura,' asked Shaw, 'come to know anybody – any man – here in town?'

'No one. As I know no one save M'sieu Janvier. It is my husband's belief that for a woman her family should suffice.'

'Well,' said Shaw grimly, 'he ain't alone in that. It's right Christian of him, as a matter of fact. An' was you surprised, M'am, when Miss Noura an' her friend disappeared a few nights back?'

A small sigh escaped her, and her brow contracted in another flash of pain. 'Not really. My husband was invited to a dinner on Friday evening, at the home of a Christian, a planter here. Thus my son ate his dinner after the custom of our country, which my husband does not wish him to forget. The two *sarârî* – the young ladies – and I served him in my husband's apartment upstairs. Later we three all ate in the same chamber, which adjoins the room where Noura and Karida slept. I will show you the place, if you will.'

She rose and led the way out on to the rear gallery, Ra'eesa padding silently behind them. Suleiman followed, face dark with disapproving puzzlement. At the foot of the stairs another man barred their way, very tall and chubby in his baggy crimson trousers and long, embroidered coat. He barked a question in a soft alto voice, and Jamilla replied in the same mixture of Arabic, Greek, and Turkish that was spoken in Constantinople. January thought he heard her call him Ghulaam.

Ghulaam shook his head, ready to die in defense of the stair. Suleiman gave him a sharp order, and with a sullen glare, the eunuch stepped aside. He was, January observed, armed, not only with a short cutlass worn openly at his belt, but also with a pair of pistols – *who is he expecting to storm the harîm?* He fell into step behind them as Jamilla led the way up the stairs, leaving Suleiman at the bottom.

Even so, January recalled, on Bellefleur Plantation in his

childhood, no field hand was permitted to set foot in the Big House, on pain of being beaten bloody – a stricture which included every child in the quarters, even if their parents were employed inside. To each country its own custom.

Four rooms made up the private quarters of Hüseyin Pasha and his women, a floor above the level of the rooms around the court-yard, and from these four rooms, as had been the case on the upper floors of the house in Paris, most Western furniture had been removed. Low divans ringed the walls, widened only slightly to provide sleeping space. Armoires – the only local objects that remained – held the bedding that would be laid out at night. Through the French windows beside the stair, as they came up on to the third-floor gallery, January recognized the pillows he'd hidden under, ten years ago in the house on the Rue St-Honoré, gold and bronze and cinnamon silk, and the sight of them was like a hand placed around his heart. At the downstream corner of the house, the Lady led them into a chamber which had been painted in brilliant persimmon orange and furnished with a divan and cushions of black and white. Costly lamps hung over a low table of inlaid ebony; a low stand held cups and bowls, and equip-ment for the making of coffee.

Layers of piled-up carpet sighed beneath their feet. With Ghulaam growling like a suspicious dog at their heels, she led them through this chamber and into the room that had belonged to the two concubines.

Muslin curtains divided it in two, after the fashion January had seen in servants' dormitories in Mexico. A single armoire set between the two cubicles held the bedding for both, and each small section was furnished with a couple of inlaid chests, to hold the girls' possessions. Though the whole of this upper floor smelled faintly of frankincense, January thought that he would certainly detect it, had two dead bodies been concealed anywhere up here, or in the attic above, even for a day.

'Did they take any of their clothing with them?' asked January as Ra'eesa opened the chests to let him look inside.

'Only what they wore that night at supper,' replied Jamilla at once. 'Those were the clothes they had on when their bodies were found, saving only their veils. Those were not found. A woman, you understand, Lieutenant Shaw, does not go veiled within her own household, or before men who are related to her: her father, her brothers, her son.' As she spoke, she lifted clothing from the chests and spread it out on the divan: fragile chemises of nearly transparent lawn, silk trousers, embroidered coats of crimson and indigo. Many shawls: some cashmere, as fine as silk, and some heavier wool, or thick cotton, oiled against rain.

'What is this?' From the side of the chest Jamilla brought out the largest and heaviest of the shawls, and exclaimed as she spread it out: 'What have those girls been doing?'

And Ra'eesa said something that January remembered Ayasha would say, when one of the cats would try to woo her with gifts of deceased mice.

The shawl – originally a pinkish buff color patterned with blue – was filthy, grubbed all over with reddish-brown dirt, as if it had been spread on bare ground. January carried it to the window, brushed his hand over it, dislodging a shower of particles. 'Brick dust,' he said. 'And common dirt . . .' His fingers found bits of broken shell as well.

At the same time Ra'eesa cried, '*Qabîh*!' and brought from the other chest a dark-red shawl, similarly soiled.

'Wherever they had them wraps, M'am,' murmured Shaw, 'I think it's safe to say they been outside the walls of this house.'

FOURTEEN

J amilla gathered the dirty fabric in slender fingers. Between veil edge and veil edge, her dark eyes clouded with doubt. 'To the best of my knowledge neither Noura nor Karida passed the gates of this house unattended since our arrival. It is clear now to me—' She broke off and put her hand to her head with a wince of pain.

'My lady?'

'It is nothing.' She shook her head quickly. 'A headache. They have grown worse, since coming to this country. For all that your countrymen boast of it, it is not a healthy land.'

Ra'eesa glided from the room, hastened the length of the gallery to the French doors of Jamilla's chamber at the far end.

The Lady forced her eyes to smile, but her fingers twisted at the edge of her sleeve. 'It is clear now to me,' she went on, 'that we were deceived. Saturday morning Ra'eesa woke me, to say that Noura and Karida had run away during the night. All the shutters on the outer doors and windows of the house were still locked and bolted from within. My husband and Suleiman and I have keys. Likewise the carriage gate on Rue des Ursulines, and the gate of the passageway on to Rue Bourbon, were locked. Yet I suppose that if one truly wished to escape, a way could be found.'

She motioned them to follow her on to the gallery again. 'I did not think of it at the time, but they could have gone over the roof to the attic of our neighbor Pavot without much trouble. It would be a simple matter to bribe his servant to leave the window open.'

'I take it Ghulaam slept Friday night in his chamber?'

'He did. But if one escaped through one of the windows of the central attic, one could climb past Ghulaam's dormers, if one were careful – or desperate. Which I promise you,' she added earnestly, 'the girls were not! Noura was selfish and greedy, as a child is, but she was not defiant. She always got her way with smiles or tears. Karida—'

Jamilla's eyes softened and flooded with unshed tears. 'Karida only wanted to be good, and to be liked.'

Shaw asked, 'Was the windows of the main attic unlatched?'

'No.' She frowned. 'So they couldn't have—' They reached the stair at the end of the gallery, where January had already noticed that one had only to climb over the gallery rail and drop down a few inches, to reach the kitchen roof. It left, of course, the question of what they'd used for a rope to get down – a rope which could easily have been fixed to the kitchen chimney . . .

'Thank you, Ra'eesa.'

The serving maid had reappeared from the Lady's room, bearing a tray on which a tiny cup was set. *Sitt* Jamilla took it and drank – a few soup-spoons-full of dark liquid – with a frantic eagerness that told its own story and pierced January to the heart with pity and regret, even before he smelled the bitter, swoony odor of the medicine.

Opium.

His glance crossed Shaw's. No wonder the escaping girls had had no trouble stealing their mistress's jewels. By the intensity of the smell, they could have taken the sheets off the bed without Jamilla waking up.

But a moment later, the Lady asked, her own gaze on the kitchen chimney, 'Could they have gone down into the yard next door? The place where the horses are . . .'

'The livery,' said January. 'And yes, I'd thought of that already.'

'They had my jewels,' she said, with a trace of bitterness in her voice. 'So it would have been simple also to bribe the slaves there to help them, and to let them out the gate. And since those shawls tell us that they had, indeed, found some way out of the house before Friday night, I think they must have had a protector, someone they could go to.'

'Or thought they could go to,' murmured January. Beyond the gallery, the rain still fell, gray and cold in the dreary tail-end of the afternoon. In the Place des Armes the clock struck three. And Fitzhugh Trulove's ball opened at eight, in the English planter's very elegant house out on the Bayou Road . . .

'First thing we'll need of you, m'am,' said Shaw, 'is a list of the jewels that was taken, theirs as well as yours. Times bein' what they are, won't be long 'fore some of 'em shows up on the open market.'

'I shall have such a list for you tomorrow.' *Sitt* Jamilla led the way down the stairs to the gallery below. Lamps had been kindled already in the parlor. Through the French doors, January could see Suleiman sitting in one of the hearth-side chairs and across from him – bent gravely over a book on his lap – a boy who had to be Hüseyin Pasha's son.

Shamira's son.

Jamilla called through the door to the tutor, who stood at once and came to the gallery. 'These gentlemen are to be admitted to whatever part of the house they ask to see. Please tell the servants that they are to be obeyed, as if they were the master or myself—'

January could just imagine the expression on the maid Lorette's face at that information.

'—and are to be admitted to the house, and given complete freedom, at any hour of the day or night. Ghulaam—' She turned to the eunuch, and – presumably, by the look on his face – repeated the order in whatever language it was that the man spoke.

'Please let me know, Lieutenant,' she went on, 'if there is anything whatsoever that you require, of me or of any other member of the household, that will assist in bringing justice for my poor husband. For he would no more have harmed those girls than he would have raised his hand against his own children. It is not in him to do so.'

Then she turned, rather suddenly, and reascended the stairs to the private floor of the house. Ra'eesa and Ghulaam followed her, close and cautious, as if she had fallen before when taking this particular medicine. And January cursed that he didn't know enough of the servants' language to ask them what had originally ailed Jamilla and how long it had been since she had slipped into the clutches of a medicine that was worse than many diseases.

For the short remainder of the afternoon, January and Shaw worked their way methodically through the house, trailed by Ra'eesa and Suleiman and frowned upon by the elegant Lorette. January spoke to the servants – the maids Bette and Desirée, the quadroon cook Louis and the Turkish cook Iskander, André the kitchen boy, and the stable staff, Nehemiah and Perkin the groom, and learned little that he had not already either heard or deduced.

'And you can bet,' said January, when he rejoined Shaw in the stables after the last of these interviews, 'that if Nehemiah suspected Lorette of even *thinking* about concealing some kind of secret, or if Lorette had been kept out of that ballroom over the stables or the loft above it and thought she could get Nehemiah into some kind of trouble over it, they'd have crippled themselves trying to get to me to tell me all about it, to the ruin of the other.'

'That bad?' Shaw prodded with his boot at the loose heaps of straw along the stable's inner wall, near where a narrow service door opened on to Rue des Ursulines. January had heard all about the service door from Lorette: about how Nehemiah the coachman would thieve feed and harness-leather and medicines for the horses, and how he'd sneak them out through there after dark to sell to that scoundrel Sillery who worked at the livery. Nehemiah, for his part, had been eloquent on the subject of Lorette's own depredations on household stores such as sugar and coffee – Louis the cook being her lover – to the extent that on the fateful Sunday night, she and the other maids had 'boosted' nearly a half-pound of cinnamon, and almost twice that much coffee, and they had then gone with them to take tea with Lorette's cousin who was a housemaid to the Marignys. None of the three maids would dream (they said, and Nehemiah rolled his eyes at the assertion) of spending their evening out at so rude an entertainment as *The Red Rover* at the American Theater.

January sighed. 'Don't they understand that they're all slaves together?' he said. 'That it doesn't matter how fair you are or how many white grandparents you have?'

'Well, it sure don't matter to your mother.' Shaw held up the little stable-lantern he carried – it was densely gloomy along the back wall by the hay – and stroked the nose of one of Hüseyin Pasha's beautiful chestnut carriage-horses who put its head over the edge of the stall, to see what was going on. 'I got more white grandparents than she does, an' I ain't got a civil word out of her yet.'

'You're an American.' January felt the jambs of that locked service-door in the almost-dark, fingered the battered bolts, turned over the padlock in its hasp. Through the door, he could hear the scrape and swish of iron wagon-tires on the pavement of Rue des Ursulines, the clatter of hooves as they slowed to turn through the gate into the livery stable yard, only a few feet away.

A man cursed, then said, 'I ordered them bags delivered last week, boy—'

Still, January was well aware that his mother tried to pretend that she'd never had children by a fellow slave on Bellefleur. And even the short time that he'd sat on the Board of Directors of the Faubourg Tremé Free Colored Militia and Burial Society had given January a wealth of infuriating experience as to who considered themselves superior to whom at the 'back of town'.

He came back over to Shaw, where light fell from the stable entrance from the courtyard, and examined what he'd picked up on his fingers at that dark service-door in the corner.

As he'd thought. Sawdust.

'Well, you may be right, Maestro,' admitted Shaw as they left the house and made their way back toward the Cabildo again in the thinning rain. 'An' I sure couldn't find a place in the whole of that house where them girls could have been kept without somebody seein' flies or rats makin' a beeline for the place, even if they was curled up into a trunk.'

He thrust his hands deep into his pockets and spat into the brimming gutters as they passed across them on the makeshift bridges of plank that were, at last, being replaced all over town by regular pavements and drains.

'The whole story is ridiculous.' January tucked tighter beneath his jacket the little bundle Suleiman had handed him, warm and slightly greasy from the kitchen: bread, cheese, vegetables and goat meat for his master in the prison. At the best of times, January was well aware, the food in the Cabildo was inedible, and what meat there was in it would be almost certainly be pork.

'An' yet,' Shaw went on, 'Oliver Breche is damn clear on his story. He says he'd been doin' the shop's books late, in that front room over the shop, an' when the rain quit, he opened the windows to get some air. He saw light in the dormer, though the rest of the house was dark, he said, an' was apparently admirin' the general effect when the sash was throwed open. He saw Hüseyin Pasha framed in the window – he says – with the body of a girl in his arms. He says he recognized him by the lamplight in the attic behind him an' was transfixiated with horror as our friend the Turk chucked first one, then t'other of the girls out. He knew the Turk, havin' provided Mrs Hüseyin with medicines these past four weeks—'

'So he's the one.'

'Pharmacy's right there.' Shaw nodded across the street at the darkened bricks of the building, the round glass globes of the great display retorts in the windows. 'He said there was no mistakin' what he saw.'

They reached the corner of Rue Royale, where the iron street-lamp creaked in the wind on its crossed chains above the intersection.

'Which leaves us with the question,' Shaw continued, when they'd gained the banquette – and the sheltering abat-vents of the houses – on the other side, 'of where Hüseyin did hide them girls' bodies.'

'Or the question,' countered January, 'of why young Mr Breche would lie.'

'There is that. Not to mention the question of how you can see a man's face on an overcast night by light in the room *behind* him.'

Oliver Breche's motives were elucidated a few moments later, when Shaw and January – after another plunge through the thin sheets of rain that sluiced down on the Place des Armes – reached the arched colonnade of the Cabildo and stepped once more into the chilly shelter of the watch room. Rain generally had a damp-ening effect on the combativeness of Gallatin Street and the levee, and on this gray tail-end of the afternoon the big stone-floored room was relatively quiet.

Quiet enough that, as January stepped through the door, the first thing he heard was a young man's voice raised in anger. 'That's ridiculous! The man murdered them! How can you argue that, having perpetrated so shocking a slaughter upon their innocent bodies, he now has the right to reclaim even their poor sweet flesh for his own foul purposes?'

'M'sieu,' sighed Sergeant Boechter, behind his tall desk, 'those two young women were, in effect, members of M'sieu Hüseyin's family. I believe that his wife wishes to bury them, not cut them up and serve them to Hüseyin for his dinner.'

'Listen to yourself!' The young man before the desk flung up his arms. 'You pronounce this obscenity, and you don't even understand what you are saying!'

Beside January, Shaw stopped, his sparse, pale eyebrows drawing down over his gargoyle nose. 'Well, fancy that,' he said.

'How can you give them back to their murderer?' cried the young man – smallish and plump, with fine light-brown hair already thinning back from his narrow forehead. 'When I am offering those poor lost souls the resting place in my own family's tomb?'

January's eyes met Shaw's, and his eyebrows raised. 'Is that who I think it is?'

Shaw nodded. 'That's Oliver Breche.'

FIFTEEN

'Well, now.' Shaw ambled up behind the young man. 'That is mighty neighborly of you, Mr Breche.'

Breche's mouth pursed like a rosebud trying to make a fist. 'It is only Christian—'

'But she warn't a Christian,' pointed out the Kentuckian. 'Did you know her?'

'Well, I – I saw her, of course.' He was one of the worst liars January had ever seen. The weak blue eyes flinched away from Shaw's pale gaze, and those soft nail-bitten hands fumbled with each other and then took guilty refuge in his pockets. 'I prescribed for the Lady Jamilla, and naturally when I came into the house I would see her – I would see them both. Like indigo ghosts on the shadowed loggia—'

His features contracted at the memory of that first glimpse of forbidden beauty. 'Her eyes met mine above their veils, filled with despair and loneliness; speaking eyes that said a thousand things. Later I would see her at her window, gazing hungrily into the world of the living from which pagan enslavement shut her out. How could any man who *is* a man not pity her? How could any man deny her the single scrap of freedom, that she might at least lie in the tomb of a free woman, rather than be given back to those who had bought her body and her beauty . . .'

'That gallery's near forty feet long,' remarked Shaw, and he scratched under his hat. 'Kind of a far piece, to see despair an' loneliness in somethin' as little as an eye.'

Breche's lip curled. 'I dare say *you* couldn't recognize them at the distance of a yard. A rich man's sins always find forgiveness—'

'If you mean, money has ways of purchasing transgression, sir,' put in January, with careful diffidence, 'you are quite right. And curiously enough, I have every reason to believe that the coachman Nehemiah was paid at regular intervals to unscrew the hasp from the service door of the stables—'

Shaw snapped his fingers, like a stage bumpkin suddenly enlight-
ened. 'You know, January, now you speak of it, I *did* wonder who
was bribin' the man. I thought that jacket he had on looked awful
new an' swell.'

'Let's go back and ask him.' January had wondered if Shaw
had observed the newness – and the bespoke fit – of the coachman's dark-red coat.

Sergeant Boechter had lighted the gas jets behind his desk just
in time to illuminate the flush that crept over Breche's face. 'And
what if I did join her?' Breche demanded sulkily. 'What if I did
contrive it, that hearts destined for one another could meet? Though
we were born on different continents, of different faiths and
speaking different languages—'

'Your father know of it?' inquired Shaw.

Breche's round little chin came up. 'We would have told him.'

'I'm sure he woulda been thrilled.'

Since one of the few opinions January had heard old Philippe
Breche deliver – he avoided the shop, having reason to suspect
that the old man adulterated his camphor with turpentine – had
been that 'goddamned Protestant Jews' should be turned over to
the Inquisition, he suspected that the apothecary would not have
welcomed a Muslim daughter-in-law, be the circumstances of her
rescue never so romantic.

Breche snarled, 'Much you know about it, American!' and January,
as the lover drew in breath for further observations, asked gently:

'Did she plan to run away to you?'

'She did.' Breche shot a resentful glare at Shaw. 'Friday night.
I waited for her, nearly all night in the shop.'

'She could get out of Hüseyin Pasha's house, then?'

The apothecary emitted an angry titter, like a boastful child.
'Of course! Cupid is a mighty deity, when true hearts love! I'd
pay off Nehemiah to let her out that side door that goes into the
stable. And Sillery – Mr Valentine's nigger, from the livery –would
unlock the gate to the yard for us, so that we could go in and . . .
and have a private place to speak.' He glared at the other men,
defying them to read anything but honorable friendship in such
trysts.

Given the minimal French of which Noura was capable, January
guessed their meetings had little to do with speech, or honorable

behavior either. But he knew better than to interrupt this flow of information by saying so.

'Because of the lamp above the intersection, we didn't dare even cross the street to the shop, for fear of being seen from the house. It's just a step, from that service door into Valentine's yard. She told me there was another way she'd go out on Friday, because she would be carrying her things.'

January's glance crossed Shaw's.

'You got no idea what way?' asked the Kentuckian, and Breche shook his head.

'And I take it,' said January, and he found it an effort to keep the anger out of his voice as he asked, 'that you'd made sure that the Lady Jamilla's medicine would keep her from discovering that the girl was slipping out at night?'

The apothecary giggled again. 'Child's play! All I had to do was slip a little opium into her medicine, then gradually raise the dose. I know it couldn't have been she who discovered the escape. No –' the smugness at drugging an unsuspecting woman vanished in an agony of anxiety again – 'it must have been *he*, who surprised my beautiful Noura as she fled. All day Saturday I watched their windows, but they were shuttered fast. Imagine my agony! Not knowing, fearing, picturing every horror that I know the Infidels do to women who escape from their harems!'

January longed to ask him where he had the information about what the Infidels did, though he suspected the source was novels of romance. His sister Dominique had a dozen.

'All Saturday night I watched, my bleeding soul crucified with fear. Then Sunday night, when the rain ceased, as I stood at the window, bending the whole of my heart and my gaze upon that dark house, the glow of a lantern sprang up! The attic window was thrown open, and framed in it I saw the Turk, with Noura's body in his arms! His face was twisted into an expression of jealous rage, more like a beast's than a man's! I cried out in horror as he flung her down, and the next instant he reappeared with the other girl, like a dead butterfly in her veils! As I watched in terror he shrieked a curse upon her and hurled her down as well!'

'An' you saw all that,' marveled Shaw, 'at a hundred an' seventy-seven feet, an' two storeys up from the balcony where you was standin'. An' heard his curse at that distance in open air.'

'I did!' Breche stamped his foot. 'He learned of her flight and killed her – killed them both! – in jealous rage—'

'I ain't sayin' he didn't,' replied Shaw soothingly. 'An' if'fn he *did* catch them girls absquatulatin' in the middle of the night – *with* his wife's jewelry – he'd have the best of good reasons to be sore-assed about it. All I'm sayin' is, that rich as he is, he's gonna bring in a fancy lawyer who's gonna tear your story apart, so you need to be good an' clear. *Did you see his face?*'

'I did.' Breche's soft fists clenched. 'As clearly as I see yours. I know it was he. Who else would wish to kill her – she who was so innocent and beautiful? And why? Only vile jealousy that she would have found love beyond his loathsome clutch!'

'An' she never spoke to you of any reason, any other thing that was goin' on?'

The apothecary shook his head, as if he did not even understand the question. As if there could be nothing else, but what concerned him. 'It is a cruel world,' he said after a moment. 'We were twin souls, Lieutenant Shaw, hearts born for one another, brought together by a miracle. You must grant me what I seek: permission at least to lay my beautiful Noura in the tomb where I myself will one day lie! Where my bleeding heart already lies, waiting for her!'

'You pusillanimous sons a' Belial!' bellowed a voice as three City Guards dragged through the Cabildo doors a powerfully-built Kentuckian whose breath and clothing January could smell across the room. 'How dare you lay your pussified French hands on a true-born Salt River Roarer! *Wee-hah*! You come on an' take me if'fn you can! I killed more men than the smallpox—'

'By breathin' on 'em,' muttered Shaw, and he strode toward the melee that ensued just within the doors.

Breche's grief disappeared in an expression of disgust, and he moved toward the doors as well, keeping his distance from the affray.

January followed. 'One more question, sir, if you will? When you would meet with the Lady Noura, did her friend ever come with her? The Lady Karida?'

Breche made an impatient gesture at what he clearly regarded as a side issue to his bleeding heart. 'I think so. Sometimes.'

'Do you have any idea what she did, while you and the Lady Noura spoke together –' he congratulated himself on sounding like he actually believed these encounters had been platonic – 'in the stable yard?'

'She kept watch.' Breche's self-evident tone led January to suspect that this was another piece of fable gleaned from romances. 'Kept guard on the door, lest we be discovered.'

Which would make more sense, January reflected, in a country where girls weren't perfectly free to come and go once they stepped outside . . . And in circumstances where they didn't have the coachman Nehemiah on hand to act as lookout.

They both stepped quickly back as the True-Born Salt River Roarer hurled one of his captors sprawling past them, yanking – as the man went flying – the cutlass from the constable's belt. The other Guards leaped clear of the now-armed prisoner, and Shaw – timing his swing precisely – stepped in around the slash of the blade and caught the keelboatman a punch on the jaw that lifted the man's feet from the floor. January guessed the prisoner was unconscious before he hit the flagstones. He certainly put up no kind of fight as Shaw relieved him of his weapon.

When January turned back to speak to Breche, he saw the man had moved away toward the Cabildo doors, where he had been intercepted by the fat, protective form of Burton Blodgett.

Shaw saw this also, swore as only a Kaintuck could, and made a move to intercept them. But one of the Guards yelled, 'Get him in the cells before he comes around!' and Shaw glanced back. And in that moment, Blodgett put a plump arm over Breche's shoulders.

'My dear Mr Breche, you must forgive my eavesdropping, but the tale you told wrings my heart! Depend upon it, the *True American* will not rest until this terrible wrong has been righted . . .'

Together, the two men stepped out into the rainy dusk.

Since the portions of the Cabildo which had been piped for gas lighting over the past few years did not include the makeshift morgue beneath the stairs, January arranged with Shaw – when the Kentuckian returned from bestowing the True-Born Salt River Roarer in the cell allotted to white men – to come back early in the morning and examine the bodies of the dead girls.

Six o'clock was striking from the Cathedral as he crossed the Place des Armes. The rain had ceased, but masses of clouds stirred above the bare branches of the pride of India trees on the levee, and the wind smelled of more rain to come. When January reached his house, it was to find Rose in the workroom over the kitchen – which in more prosperous times had served as a classroom – engaged in a long and complicated experiment involving sulfur, soda, and arsenic, and his niece Zizi-Marie in the kitchen itself, looking after Baby John. Gabriel, January's fourteen-year-old nephew, was making dinner, something he could do with considerably better results than either Rose or Zizi-Marie.

Hard times being what they were, January had contracted with his sister Olympe – whose upholsterer husband hadn't worked since March – to take her two older children into his household, relieving Rose of a good deal of household drudgery and Olympe of the necessity of feeding two extra mouths.

Hard times being what they were, January's acquisition of five hundred dollars in hard silver – wages for risking his life over the summer – meant that, with most banks in the city either closed or issuing nothing but paper, it was better to have a few more people in the house at all times, other than Rose and the baby. In that fall of 1837, New Orleans had suddenly become filled with men who were very interested in who had money in their houses, and January was well aware how swiftly word got around. The owners of every grocery knew who paid their bills and who was living on rice, beans, and credit; every man who sold hay, or coal, or candles had a slave or two who had nothing better to do than keep his or her ear to the ground. Gangs that had previously only worked the docks – stealing cargoes or trunks or a hog or two – now found themselves obliged to extend their field of toil to houses as well. *Hell, they got SOME silver in their house, an' I got none . . .*

In addition to Gabriel and Zizi-Marie – on cold evenings like this the kitchen was by far the most comfortable place in the house – January found a young man named Willie, who was currently acting as a sort of sous-chef for Gabriel, cleaning bones, feet, and feelers from the pint or so of mixed fish and shellfish that lay on a couple of sheets of newspaper on the table. 'Dinner be ready in ten minutes, Mr J,' said Willie, in English, which was all he spoke. 'I set the table, just like a fancy butler, an' I go fetch Miss Rose the minute you say.'

'You'll do nothing of the kind,' retorted January, and he leaned – carefully – into the glowing hearth, to fill a basin of water from the copper at one side of the flickering coals. 'You'll get your supper and go back under the house where you belong. You got to be less helpful when you're on the run,' he added, with a grin to take away any sense of banishment from the words, and Willie grinned back. 'Let other people help you for a change.'

Willie was the property of a planter named Gosse in Plaquemines Parish, and he was hiding out in one of the two tiny rooms that January had walled off the sides of the storerooms under the old Spanish house. Advertisements containing his description, under the heading RAN AWAY, were in every newspaper in the city. In a night or two, those who made up the greater chain of slave runners in Louisiana would smuggle him on to a boat going north. 'Riding the underground railway', it was beginning to be called. Heading north to freedom.

Sometimes January wondered if he and Rose were both insane, to be mixed up in the organization.

'Nonsense,' said Rose, when January voiced his concern after dinner. 'There's a far greater likelihood that I'll kill everyone in the house with one of my experiments, than that some slave taker is going to report us for sheltering runaways.' In the bedroom's warm candlelight she cradled Baby John to her breast, while January changed clothes for Mr Trulove's ball and a series of clinks and giggles from the dining room punctuated the cleaning-up process. Without her spectacles – for which their month-old son had developed an almost instant fascination – Rose's green-hazel eyes lost their daytime look of brisk efficiency and became, in the shadows, like a mermaid's eyes, sea-colored and dreamy.

'Yes,' agreed January. 'But that isn't the point. You take good care with your experiments. I'd trust you with a mountain of gunpowder. But we don't know who might hear a rumor, or spread a rumor, of the rooms beneath the house. It was my choice to get involved in slave running . . .'

'Disregarding my screams and pleas to the contrary?' Rose stroked Baby John's back as the child slipped into sleep.

January lifted the baby, to allow her to stand and adjust her clothing: the infant (*MY son! My SON—!*) so tiny in his enormous hands. Rose put a hand on his arm, kissed him lightly with a touch that he felt through the whole of his skin, like electricity, and adjusted the white linen stock around his neck.

'As you said yourself,' she reminded him with her quicksilver smile, 'now is the time that we need to remain on the good side of God.' She put her spectacles back on – and with them, the calm face she showed to the world.

Still carrying the sleeping Baby John, January followed her back out to the dining room. Willie had once more emerged from beneath the house and was drying the dishes that Zizi washed in a basin on the long table. 'Miss Zizi tellin' me, you're helpin' out this heathen that killed two of his wives?' inquired the runaway.

'A Muslim is not a heathen,' corrected January patiently. '*Rose* is a heathen.' Rose hit him with the dish towel. 'And those girls weren't his wives. They were his slaves . . . and as his slaves, they had no rights. So why kill them?'

Willie thought about that for a moment, brow furrowed. He'd been a cane hand, and New Orleans was the first time he'd seen more than a hundred and fifty people in one place in his life. 'You mean he coulda sold 'em if he didn't want 'em around?'

'That's right. There's something funny about all this, even if I didn't know the man – and didn't know he would not have killed those girls, any more than I'd lay a hand on Zizi or Gabriel if I'd learned they'd stolen from me. I'd put them out of the house—'

'We'd never steal from you, Uncle Ben!' protested Gabriel. 'Mama'd kill us!'

'*I'd* kill you.' Rose gathered a stack of dried plates to take back to the pantry. 'I have been waiting for *weeks* for an excuse to grind up your bones for chemical filtrates, which are *extremely* expensive.'

'Save their hair,' January reminded her.

Rose raised her brows enquiringly.

'Their mama told me, if you had to kill them, save their hair to make gris-gris with.'

'Thank you,' said Rose serenely. 'I'd forgotten.'

But January's certainty of Hüseyin Pasha's innocence – not on grounds of character but by simple logic – did not appear to be shared by the very people who'd invited the man to their suppers and had exclaimed at his wit and erudition only a week before. If he heard his mother's observation about the insane jealousy of

Turks repeated once that evening, he heard it a score of times – and that, only within earshot of the little orchestra, behind its rampart of hothouse palms at one end of the enormous Trulove ballroom. Heaven only knew how many times it was made in the rest of the room.

'The man always terrified me!' The Widow Redfern's diamonds flashed as she shuddered, exactly as if she hadn't flirted with *that heathen brute* – in her ponderous fashion – at a half-dozen balls and receptions at which January had played. 'The look in his eyes! Cold, without pity—'

January wondered if she read the same novels that his sister Dominique and Oliver Breche did.

'It is the Mark of the Beast.' The Reverend Micajah Dunk, whose Salvation Church – largely paid for by its most prominent parishioner, the Widow Redfern – was one of the few establishments in New Orleans that year that seemed to be doing well, took her hands in his black-gloved grip, with the license presumably extended to Men of God, and gazed down into her eyes. 'One can read Evil in the face of the Infidel, no matter how gorgeous the gold and crimson that covers the serpent's back.'

The widow gazed up at him in holy awe.

As usual, Fitzhugh Trulove's reception attracted both the old French and Spanish Creole planters – whose wealth dominated the city and the lower parishes of the state – and the newer American businessmen who had come with the American purchase of the land. Trulove was an Englishman who had bought his plantations – he owned four of them – in the days of Spanish rule some thirty-five years previously, and as such was acceptable to both groups. And as usual, the crowd in the red-columned ballroom had divided itself with the symmetrical precision of a lady's coiffure: Marignys, Verrets, Roffignacs, Prieurs on one side of it, their backs turned with resolute insouciance upon the Bullards and Butlers, Ripleys and Browns on the other.

White-haired, pink-faced, and hearty in his long-tailed coat of blue superfine wool, Trulove moved between the groups at the side of his slender chilly wife, and now and then gave the polite nod of a stranger to the gorgeous German opera-singer who was his latest mistress, clinging to the arm of an embarrassed clerk.

Around the Reverend Dunk, the wives and sisters and grown-up daughters of the American planters, the American brokers and factors and cotton buyers and steamboat owners, all nodded and whispered their agreement, as they did at any pronouncement he made. Any Protestant congregation in New Orleans tended to be predominantly female in make-up, but the Reverend Dunk's sermons in particular held a fascination that January could only attribute to the man's feral physical power and melodramatic sense of theater.

'My heart bleeds,' Dunk went on in his somber, beautiful bass, 'when I think of those poor girls, held prisoner in that terrible house, clinging together, trembling, at the sound of his footfall . . .'

And on the other side of the room, Dr Emil Barnard, the most fashionable up-and-coming physician of the French Creole community, took a scientific rather than a melodramatic view of the sensation. 'It has been empirically proven that Turks are of a more primitive emotional make-up than European men. One has only to examine a Turk's hands, with their blunt fingers and coarse shape, or the characteristically animal shape of their ears, to see—'

'You know, I noticed that, the first moment that I saw him!' cried the young planter Hercule Lafrènniére.

'Myself,' added the sugar broker Charles Picard, 'I wondered from the first how the Turk came by that fortune of his – if indeed he ever had as much as he was rumored. They say that when the pirate nests of Algiers were taken, tens of millions of dollars in gold disappeared – gold that was taken from ships of all nations, when their crews were sold into slavery.'

'I understand that when a girl escapes from a harem,' whispered Madame Lafrènniére, 'and is retaken—'

She sank her voice as Cécile Philipon, Granmere Roffignac, and two of the Viellard sisters drew near to hear the horrific details.

'I hope it shall be remembered in Hüseyin Pasha's favor when he applies for entry to Paradise,' murmured Hannibal Sefton as his long, thin fingers adjusted the pegs of his violin, 'that mutual slander of his name brought a truce between the Royalistes and Orleannistes of this community. Lafrènniére hasn't spoken to Barnard since the Bourbon Kings lost their throne for the *second* time, and I understand Barnard's wife has visited voodoos to cross the house of Philipon over there. Now look at her whispering with Philipon's wife. In another hour one of them will actually go over to trade rumors with the Americans.'

'I got five cents says they don't go that far.' Jacques Bichet wiped the mouthpiece of his flute and hunted through his music for the next dance.

'Done.' Sefton dug in his pocket. '*Back-wounding calumny the whitest virtue strikes* . . .' He produced a couple of Mexican reales. '*What king so strong can tie the gall up in the slanderous tongue?*'

'You got all kinds of money, since you give up drinkin',' remarked the flautist admiringly.

'Good Lord, man, you don't think I ever *paid* for any of those drinks?'

'How'd you stay so drunk all the time, then?'

'I haven't the faintest recollection. *Amicus meus* –' the fiddler turned to January – 'might we impose upon you to hold our wagers?'

'Don't let anyone hear about you saying a Frenchman is going to speak to an American, then,' said January, holding out his hand for the money. 'Or you'll be called out by every French Creole in town. *Allons*,' he added, and he struck up the opening bars of *L'Alexandrine* on the splendid Trulove piano. 'Let's see if we can get them thinking about something besides slandering an innocent man.'

SIXTEEN

The dancing went on until almost dawn, though most of the Americans left at two. Jacques Bichet won Hannibal's five cents off him, the satisfactions of back-wounding calumny taking precedence over mere lifelong political feuds.

In addition to this, there were the usual wagers among the orchestra as to the number of challenges to duels which would be issued during the evening: two, with some discussion as to whether to count the confrontation between the Reverend Micajah Dunk and the newly-arrived Baptist preacher the Reverend Doctor Emmanuel Promise over the attention of the Widow Redfern.

'Dunk did say that Satan would sweep Promise into the ovens of Hell with a Great Broom,' pointed out Hannibal, who had bet on three challenges. (The other two were perfectly routine quarrels: a Royaliste planter whose sister had been asked to dance by a Napoleoniste, and two American lawyers whose mutual accusations of graft, bastardy, Whiggery and unnatural appetites had begun in the courtroom last month and had been continued in the 'Letters to the Editor' columns of the *True American* ever since.)

From the doorway of the kitchen, to which the musicians had been suffered to retreat for ten minutes between sets, January could see the lights and carriages at the front of the house and hear voices raised in furious altercation: 'Damn it, Swathmore, you got the goddamned sand to come to me to issue a challenge for Butler? After you closed down the Trade an' Enterprise Bank an' ruined a thousand good men in this city—?'

'Don't tell me their seconds are going to challenge each other to a duel also,' January murmured, and Hannibal said instantly:

'In that case *that* makes three challenges—'

'That makes *four*,' pointed out Cochon Gardinier, the second violinist, perched corpulent and sweating on a corner of the kitchen table – he'd wagered on four – 'if Preacher Promise calling on God to blast *that glittering Lucifer* Dunk with His Holy Light counts.'

'If we're counting name-calling,' objected Jacques, 'we're up to about fifty!'

And the Trulove servants – trotting back and forth from the house with trays laden with Anne Trulove's two hundred and ten settings of blue-and-yellow Bow china and enough silver spoons to armor a regiment – all clamored in agreement or dissent, like a cut-rate Greek chorus. They'd all had money on the possibility of duels as well.

'A specific call for God to blast a *creeping minion of Evil,*' Hannibal said, quoting Promise, whose gentle manners and ascetic beauty – like a martyr in a Bible illustration – had clearly entranced Mrs Redfern, 'counts as a weapon, if it comes from the lips of a Man of God. *Ye shall be able to quench all the fiery darts of the wicked,* God has promised his saints . . . And the Reverend Dunk responded in kind, you recall, with a very clear demand that God burst Promise's guts asunder and devour him with worms, as God so obligingly did with Herod Agrippa in Acts. *Possunt quia posse videntur . . .*'

He got to his feet and coughed, one hand pressed to his side in a way that January didn't like. In the red glow of the hearth where the wash-up water heated, the fiddler's eyebrows stood out very dark in a face chalky with strain, and despite the heat of the kitchen he shivered. If opium had made Hannibal a slave for half his life, January reflected grimly, at least it had kept the pain of his illness at bay.

'If them curses was weapons,' inquired old Uncle Bichet, and he sipped the beer Mr Trulove's butler had provided for the musicians' refreshment, 'how come both those *execrable shapes* – like they called each other – wasn't blasted out of their shoes then an' there in the ballroom?'

'They both missed,' replied Hannibal at once. 'Their aim was terrible.'

Upon their return to the ballroom, January was entertained to observe that while most of the Americans had taken their departure, the Widow Redfern remained, and so perforce had the little court of gentlemen which always surrounded her. This included M'sieu Maillet – coincidentally the youngest and most handsome of the Board of Directors of the Planters Bank of New Orleans and also the only one in that organization who was unmarried – and the elderly planter Alfonse Verriquet, whose French Creole family, according to January's mother, had threatened to disown him if he continued to court the extremely wealthy American. The Reverend Dunk was still there as well, glowering possessively on one side of the group, and the Reverend Promise on the other. Both pastors, in between admiring the worthiness of Emily Redfern's soul, glared daggers at one another, smothering yawns of exhaustion as the small hours of the morning advanced. But neither was willing to leave until the Widow called for her carriage at three.

At which point Cochon suggested the musicians all repair with their wages to the Buttonhole Café – which like all establishments operated by *librés* was supposed to close at sunset – for breakfast.

So it was that as soon as the fog had burned off and the sun had risen high enough over the low pastel town to provide light into the morgue, January returned home, bathed, shaved, kissed Rose, picked up his satchel of surgical tools, and made his way to the Cabildo through streets that smelled of sewage and spilled liquor. A rumpled and sleepy-looking Shaw slouched at his desk, reading a smudgy newspaper which he passed silently to January.

WHAT COST A YOUNG GIRL'S LIFE?

A shocking crime of singular callousness was perpetrated late Sunday night in the very heart of the French Town. A Turkish gentleman, H—P—, recently come to this city, being displeased with two of his lesser wives, was seen to strangle them with a bowstring and cast them down from the window of his house into the street, behavior certainly not uncommon in the murky alleys of Constantinople but horrifying in the extreme in these freer climes.

His punishment a foregone conclusion, you will say? No such thing!

For when the witness to this bloody deed attended the Cabildo to offer provision for burial for these unfortunate daughters of the East – and to give testimony against the potentate whose gold has made him the cynosure of society since his arrival last month – he was met with mockery and derision, and hustled from the halls where the French still

hold sway with the strongly-worded implication to keep
himself out of the affairs of his betters . . .

'There's a letter from him, too,' remarked Shaw, and he spat in
the general direction of the sandbox beside his desk. 'An' from
Breche hisself.'

He removed his boots from the desk's surface, stood, and bent
his long body back and forth to crack his backbone. The watch
room, still blue with the remaining shadows of the night, stank of
burnt gas and vomit; a couple of prisoners were mopping the place
out under the sour eye of a City street-cleaner.

'And no mention, I suppose –' January followed him to the
courtyard doorway and stepped aside to let pass the line of prisoners armed with buckets and shovels, bound for the gutters at
the back of town – 'that the city has this potentate in custody?'

'You think that'd make a difference?' Shaw lit a couple of
candle lanterns from the nearest gas jet. The cupboard-sized morgue
beneath the courtyard stairs – which had previously done duty as
an auxiliary cell, a spare infirmary, and storage for the shovels
and buckets of the gutter cleaners – was windowless.

Even allowing for the morning's cold, January braced himself
as they neared its door.

The sweetish reek of decaying flesh met them even as Shaw
turned the key in the lock. *Thank God it's winter.* Nothing, of
course, could be done about roaches. Not in New Orleans. When
the gray light fell into the little chamber, a dozen of the huge insects
took rattling flight from the cracks of the two coffins on the trestle
table within and blundered clumsily around the walls. Despite most
of a lifetime in New Orleans, January loathed the things.

'I had a look at them girls yesterday mornin', soon as it was
light enough to see.' Shaw used the side of his hand to sweep
away the rat droppings that surrounded both coffins, and he untied
the ropes that held the lids in place. 'They was stone cold, an'
stiff. This rigor's passing off now, but it was clear their joints had
been forced – the rigor in 'em broke – elbows, shoulders, hips,
knees. Their wrists an' ankles an' necks was still locked up hard.
You can see by the way the blood's pooled in their flesh that they
was laid on their sides at some point, likely curled up.'

'Likely,' assented January softly.

He lifted the first girl from her protective box.

She must have been beautiful in life. January had seen enough death – in the yellow fever plague-wards, during his years at the Hôtel Dieu, in the years of the cholera – to be able to look past the bloating and discoloration of mortality and see beauty still in the delicate bones of the face. Her long hair, deep coffee-brown and rinsed with henna to give it red glimmers that bordered on the color of burgundy, trailed down over his arm; traces of kohl crusted the shut eyelids.

'Her clothes is in that box over in the corner,' said Shaw. 'That's Miss Noura; she was wearin' the pink. Karida was the one in green. Far as I can tell, neither one was raped, but have a look at Miss Noura's hands. She put up a fight.'

January turned the soft fingers over. The nails were just beginning to loosen in their beds, but under them he could discern bits of blood and hair. From the battered leather surgical satchel, he took a pair of fine-nosed tweezers and a small square of white paper, such as apothecaries – and his sister Olympe – twisted up drugs in. With greatest care, he extracted the tiny wads. 'Ever look through a microscope?' he asked as he worked. 'Rose has one . . .'

'Them things the doctors at Charity use, to look at tiny worms an' such in drops of water?'

'Exactly. Ever looked through one at a human hair?' He folded the paper delicately together. 'A black man's hair is different from a white man's. I'm wondering if the hairs from a man's arm are that different.' He pushed up his sleeve, held his forearm next to the Lieutenant's.

'Don't do no good lookin' at me, I got hair like a little girl.'

'I'm also wondering how different a white man's hair would be from a Turk's. The other girl fight?'

'Nah. By what M'am Jamilla said, doesn't sound like she would.'

'You'd be surprised.' Breathing as shallowly as he could, January examined Noura's body all over with Rose's magnifying lens: palms, feet, throat. 'This wasn't done with any bowstring. Looks like the bowstring was done after they were dead. Was a bowstring found in the room, by the way?'

'It was. There was two or three others in Hüseyin's study – both horse hair an' deer sinew – an' Hüseyin's bow hung up, unstrung, on the wall of his room. But I did wonder if a bowstring would bruise up flesh like that.'

The narrow ligature had sunk into the skin of the throat like a wire into cheese, but there was no bleeding. The flesh was bruised under the clayey discoloration, and it would be impossible now to determine whether the bruises around it had been made by a man's hands.

Impossible to prove it in court, anyway.

'Which means – I'm *guessing* – that she didn't struggle against it. That she was already dead. Somebody seems to have gone to a great deal of trouble,' January added as he laid the girl back into her borrowed coffin, 'to put the crime on Hüseyin.'

Shaw folded his long arms. 'I'm thinkin' so.'

'Look at this.' January lifted Karida's body from its box, laid it on the table where the light fell through most strongly from the door.

Outside in the courtyard, one of the sergeants grunted to someone – presumably the first slave of the day led to the whipping post – 'Strip off, honey,' and January set his jaw and willed himself not to hear.

Shaw moved a step closer as January turned the girl's hand over.

'Nails were all broken.'

Shaw frowned. 'I didn't see—'

'They were broken days before she died.' Gas and fluids were beginning to collect under the skin, rendering that graceful hand cold and slightly squishy. 'Look how much shorter than Noura's they are, and how uneven. She's had time to file them neat.'

'Don't sound like they was made to do the floors.'

'No. No calluses on either one, so whatever Karida was doing with her hands, it wasn't done regularly, or for long. Let's see their clothes – and especially their shoes.'

The girls' garments had been fouled by the wet pavement on to which they'd fallen, but, held to the light of the doorway and examined meticulously with Rose's magnifying glass, they showed no sign of tearing or stress. From the baggy folds of Karida's *salvars*, January picked a splinter of wood, and two more from Noura's. 'Down near the ankles,' he said. 'Look, here's another splinter in Karida's shoulder.' He carefully turned the heavier wool of the *entari*. 'It's hard to tell whether there was much abrasion on the palms, but if there was, it wasn't enough to break the skin. What does that tell us?'

The Kentuckian's eyes narrowed for a moment, as if he were reading animal tracks. 'They climbed down from the kitchen roof with that long ladder that's layin' in Valentine's livery yard, not a rope.'

'And here's a moss stain on Noura's shoe, and horse dung. More dung on Karida's. What do you know about Tim Valentine?'

'That he's a scoundrel.' Shaw helped January lift Karida back into her box, settled the lids on both girls and roped them fast. January remembered the rat droppings. 'I got a note this mornin' from Mr Harik—'

January raised his eyebrows a little at the proper use of the tutor Harik Suleiman's name and, as usual, wondered where Shaw had found out how it should be.

'—sayin' M'am Jamilla's asked him to make arrangements for the burial of the girls.'

'That's one in the eye for Breche.'

'An' won't we hear about it, next issue of the *True American*.' Shaw paused outside the morgue door to let January follow him out, locked it behind him. 'There bein' no Mohammedan cemetery here, she said she figured the best for 'em would be with the Jews on Rampart Street. I guess they allows Gentiles that's married Jews to be put in that little boneyard of theirs, so there's no danger of God rainin' fire an' brimstone on the place, the way he would if'fn they was put away among the Christians acrost the street.'

Shaw's voice was dry. So far as January knew, the Kentuckian was a Protestant – most Americans were – but he had never, he realized, heard his friend refer to his own faith or belief in God, if he had any, at all. Perhaps, like Rose, he was an intellectual Deist. But he could have been a Druid, for all he'd ever voiced an opinion of anyone else's religion, as most Catholics and Protestants of January's acquaintance were all too ready to do.

'As for Tim Valentine,' Shaw went on, 'we had him in a dozen times over the past three years, for bustin' up saloons or gettin' in fights over cards. Mr Pavot, what leases him the back part of his lot to extend the livery yard, has swore out complaints against him for not payin' his rent, an' once for nearly killin' a slave. That didn't come to nuthin', since Valentine swore he was just givin' the woman a couple of licks for thievin'.' He opened the lantern's slide, blew out the candle.

Though the morning was cold, and the water in the trough in the Cabildo yard icy, January was grateful for the chance to wash in it. He suspected he'd have to boil his shirt, to get rid of the smell of decay.

'Treats his horses good, though,' Shaw went on. 'His wagons an' buggies is always in first-rate shape, an' clean as your Ma's dishes. That slave of his, Sillery, has been brung in a dozen times, for theft an' bein' out after curfew. Far as I know Tim beats him hisself. He's got three of 'em: Sillery, Delilah, an' Jones. No wife, five kids, the youngest three an' the oldest sixteen; the boy seems to do most of the work at the livery these days. Since the banks crashed I hear Tim's been borrowin' money all over this town. Care to walk on over there with me?'

'I would,' said January, though he felt in his bones the gritty ache of staying up too late. 'I think I'd like to hear what Mr Valentine has to say about the events of Sunday night.'

'As would I.' Shaw set down the lantern on his desk in the watch room and collected his hat. 'Problem is, last time anybody seen the man was Friday – the day them gals disappeared.'

Burton Blodgett was sitting on a bench just outside the Cabildo's great double doors, reading that day's English-language edition of the *New Orleans Bee*. As January and Shaw emerged he rose to his feet, stretched like a man who has all the day before him, yawned, and fell into step about five yards behind them. Shaw's eyes narrowed for a moment, and his glance crossed January's. Then as they reached the corner of Rue St Philippe, he dug in his pocket and produced a couple of reales.

'Ben, I thank you for your information,' he said, not loudly, but loudly enough that their eavesdropper could certainly make out the words. 'I reckon I'll be seein' you around town?'

'That you will, sir.' January touched the brim of his hat. He supposed that if he knuckled his forehead and bobbed in a bow, Blodgett would think it only right and appropriate. 'I thank you, sir.'

'You keep out of trouble now, Ben.'

January manufactured the big, bright grin that as a child he'd reserved for his master's friends. 'Yes, sir.'

Shaw continued along Rue Chartres with his hands in his pockets; January loafed on up Rue St Philippe in the direction of the swamps at the back of town. He crossed Royale, Bourbon, turned downstream along Rue Dauphine, and estimated that he reached Rue des Ursulines and turned back toward the river at about the same time that Shaw – with Blodgett still in tow – got to the front door of M'sieu Pavot's house on Rue Bourbon, a locale which Blodgett already knew about.

The gates of Valentine's Livery stood open on to Rue des Ursulines. January stepped quickly through them into the yard, looking around him with an air of slightly bewildered innocence.

As he'd suspected, where the lot formed an L – the extension of the yard rented to Valentine by Pavot – there was a small door in the fence that separated Pavot's truncated lot from the rented-out extension. If there hadn't been a door there Shaw would simply have to scramble over the fence . . .

'Can I help you, sir?' A thin red-haired youth emerged from the stable.

'I'm looking for Mr Valentine.'

'I'm Mr Valentine.' The youth shaded his eyes and looked up at him, with a slight air of defiance, as if expecting laughter at the assertion. Shaw had said sixteen, but this 'Mr Valentine' didn't look a day over fourteen, if that. 'Magus Valentine, at your service with the best conveyances and the finest horseflesh you'll find in the city.'

'And Mr Tim Valentine is . . .?'

'In Baton Rouge this week. He should be back Thursday.'

The door from Pavot's side of the fence opened. Shaw slouched through and handed money to someone behind him, presumably Pavot's obliging servant Jerry. January glanced around him and observed that the livery yard occupied much of the center of the block bounded by Ursulines, Bourbon, Dauphine and St Philippe. A ragged line of the back walls of kitchens, stables, and outbuildings hemmed it in, two and sometimes three stories tall, and with the addition of the back half of what had originally been the Pavot lot, the whole must have occupied some ten thousand square feet, half again the area of the average city lot. Most of that space was occupied by a long stable, a number of fodder sheds, and – across the carriageway that led out to Rue des Ursulines – a large coach house, whose upper floor, to judge by the lines of washing hung from its windows, served the Valentine family as their dwelling place.

Shaw ambled over to January and Magus Valentine, taking in all these details with that deceptively mild gray glance. 'Your pa got a key to that door, son?'

'Yes, sir.' Under the brim of the boy's cap, the hazel eyes grew wary.

'Keep it on his key ring?'

'Yes, sir. It's always locked.'

'*Always* is a big word.' Shaw spat into the dirt. 'When did he leave?'

'Saturday morning. He took deck passage for Baton Rouge on the *Daffodil*. I was tellin' this gentleman he should be home Thursday or Friday.'

'What time you lock up the yard last Friday night?'

A small straight line appeared between the boy's reddish brows. In the cast-off hand-me-downs of a much larger man, Magus Valentine reminded January for some reason of the beggar-boy Poucet, of whom he had not thought in years. *That combination of cockiness and wariness, the air of being always ready to run for it?* Or was it only because of the four smaller children clustered at the foot of the stairs that led up to the gallery above the coach house, watching him as Poucet's little gang had done?

'I'd have to get the book, sir, but I think the last team came in at nine, the moon being just short of full. I locked up the yard, and it took us about a half-hour to get them rubbed and bedded down and the harness stowed.'

'*Us* bein' you an' your Pa?'

'Yes, sir. And Sillery, sir.' He nodded across the yard, where a barrel-chested little man with Ibo features was raking together soiled straw he'd pitched out of the line of stalls.

'An' nobody can get into the yard nor out of it, 'ceptin' through that gate –' Shaw gestured in the direction of the carriageway, which ran between the back of Hüseyin's coach house and the long side of Valentine's – 'or through the door to Pavot's yard?'

'No, sir.'

'Anybody else have the keys? Barrin' your pa?'

'Mr Pavot has keys to his gate, being that the land's actually his from that chimney –' he pointed to the roof of Hüseyin's kitchen – 'on back. Who should I tell Pa,' added the boy doggedly, 'was askin' after him?'

'Name's Shaw. Lieutenant of the City Guards.' For a moment he studied Magus Valentine's face, and the boy's eyes shifted. 'You mind if my friend an' I take a look around?'

'No, sir.' The boy's glance went to January again. This time the fear was unmistakable.

Why scared?

And why of ME? Why not the white man who has the power?

'You keep them lanterns lit all night?' Shaw nodded toward the iron brackets that projected from the front of both stable and carriage house.

'No, sir. We snuff 'em, last thing we lock up. Sillery sleeps in the stable; Jones and Delilah – she's Sillery's sister – sleep in the coach house next to the tack room.'

'An' you – or your pa – you didn't see nuthin' goin' on in the yard here, late Friday night?'

'No, sir.' The boy's voice had a wary patience to it, as if he would not be tricked or pushed. 'From my window – it's the one up there –' he pointed – 'I can see the whole of the yard. I wake up two, three times in the night, just to have a look, make sure the horses are all right.'

'An' you heard nuthin' Sunday neither?'

The boy's eyes shifted again. 'Nor Sunday neither, sir. Anything I can show you gentlemen, whilst you're here?'

Shaw and January went over the stables, the coach house, and the yard, and even up into the coach-house loft, which had been roughly partitioned into two chambers, one for the owner of the premises – it had a bed – and the one in front for everyone else. In addition to a pile of straw ticks and blankets in a corner it contained a table, at which, as they entered, the next-oldest child – a bright-eyed red-haired twelve-year-old girl – was carving up half a loaf of bread.

'Maggie, we got any money at all for beans?' the girl said. 'We—'

'I told you not to call me Maggie.' The boy fished in his pockets,

glanced worriedly at Shaw, then went to the packing boxes that
made up the room's shelves and dish cupboard and took out a
ledger book. 'I'll go round to Mr Braeden with his bill again,' he
said. 'We'll get somethin'.'

In the coach house below, January counted two buggies, a wagon,
and a stylish fiacre. As Shaw had said, they were all clean as his
mother's dishes, and moreover, the floor between them was swept
as well, a good deal cleaner than some parlors January had been
in. A tack room was partitioned off the coach house, and beside
it, a second cubicle served as the dwelling for the second groom,
Jones, and his wife Delilah. As he walked around the great open
space of the coach house, January felt them watching him from
the doors.

Last of all he and Shaw took the ladder from where it lay along
the stable wall and propped it on the wall just below the chimney
of Hüseyin Pasha's kitchen. It took the two of them to move it,
and when Shaw climbed up to have a look at the wall and the
chimney January again could feel the eyes of the three livery-yard
slaves on his back.

'Nothing?' he asked quietly, when Shaw descended.

'Rain washed away whatever there was.' He started to lower
the ladder down and was forestalled by Sillery and Jones, who
came to assist. Stepping back, Shaw went on softly, 'If them gals
helped theirselves to all the jewels they could lay hands on, that
kind of money buys a lot of silence.'

'Maybe,' agreed January. 'But even allowing that Tim Valentine
is a scoundrel, I don't think there's enough food in the house for
anyone there to have been bribed.'

Shaw returned to Rue Bourbon through the little door in the fence
and thus through to the Pavot house – outside of which, presumably,
Burton Blodgett still waited like a faithful dog. January took a last
look around the livery yard and wondered what he was missing.

From the coach-house door, the three slaves watched him still.
The children stood in a line on the gallery, watching also: when
one of them would have spoken, the red-haired girl shushed him.

Magus Valentine emerged from the stable and crossed to the
coach house, but was intercepted by Sillery.

January would have given a great deal, to know what words
were said.

SEVENTEEN

'So, do you think it was Sabid?' asked Ayasha.

They sat in a dark corner of Carnot's garret. The painter had finally talked Ayasha into sitting as a model, and the few candles that, as usual, Carnot's guests had been requested to furnish to the Shrovetide pancake-feast glimmered in front of the half-finished canvas: Susanna and the Elders, with Ayasha looking anything but innocent as she clutched a gauzy drapery to her breasts. It was sufficiently late in the evening that the noise from the Rue Jardinet below had finally grown quiet. Only the soft click of dominoes penetrated the gloom of the big chamber, and the murmur of voices in talk. Somewhere the bells of St Bernardins chimed two.

'What would Sabid be doing in New Orleans?' asked January. 'That was ten years ago.'

'Ten years isn't forever, *Mâlik*.' Ayasha folded up Noura's dirtied pink veil, tucked it into her sewing basket. 'Passion doesn't change, neither love nor hatred. In the East, it's shameful for a man to forgive an enemy, or forget a wrong that was done him. Where is Sabid now?'

January opened his eyes. By the gray light that came through the jalousies of the window it was after noon. For a moment – as often happened, when he slept in the daytime and woke suddenly – he did not recall where he was, though the smell of burnt sugar and mold told him *this is New Orleans*.

A soft clucking – a tiny fretful whimper – drew his eyes to the willow basket crib at the foot of the bed, and he saw his son asleep. Tiny and soft, achingly beautiful, and January felt the years in New Orleans, the years with Rose, come back on him like a descending weight. And in that first moment, though he hated himself to the core of his being for it, he could not stop what he felt.

He wanted Ayasha back.

And all the dividing years undone.

*   *   *

It took him several minutes of lying there, staring at the creamy plaster of the ceiling and the pink folds of the looped-back mosquito-bar, before he felt able to get up and go out into the parlor. He heard Rose in the dining room (to which the room behind the parlor had been reconverted, from its former use as a classroom) – the muted creak of one of the cane-bottom chairs, the clink of a cup on a saucer. Reading. He could almost see the way she propped her cheek on her fist, the pale gleam of the daylight in the oval lenses of her spectacles. Outside the French doors, beyond the high gallery, a dray rattled by, driven full speed up Rue Esplanade as if it were a Roman chariot. The wailing cry of the milk lady rose, alien and weightless, words transformed into a long African holler such as the men would call from row to row of the sugar fields when he was a child.

Across the wide street – one of the widest in the city – their neighbor Bernadette Metoyer called out to the milk woman; Bernadette was his mother's friend, a handsome demi-mondaine whose banker lover had absconded that summer, leaving her and her sisters to pick up the pieces. Yet Bernadette's rich alto voice drew him back to the world of present friends, present loves. Reminded him that his mother had commanded his presence, and Rose's, for coffee that afternoon – the Metoyer sisters would be there also – and if he wanted to have a look at the hair he'd taken from beneath Noura's fingernails, he'd better do it now.

He drew a deep breath.

The pain passed, and he folded the dream away.

'Have you compared hair before?' Rose unlocked the door of her laboratory above the kitchen, the small room warm from the hearth beneath despite the chill of the day. 'We really should get a sample from Shaw or Hannibal, to compare. My hair is close to a white woman's, but to be honest, I wouldn't want to bring anything into a court of law until I was sure.'

She took the key to her microscope box from the drawer of her workbench, lifted the box to the table by the windows where the light was best. The workbench had begun life as an apothecary's cupboard, its myriad of minuscule drawers stocked with probes, tweezers, packets of sulfur, or bottles of quicksilver or acid. The microscope was the first thing she'd purchased, back when they'd had money: Swiss, brass, and formidable. 'Remember too that we're probably looking at arm hair rather than head hair. The texture will be different.'

'I've looked at hair,' said January. 'But I've never had call to compare with a man's life at stake. It may tell us nothing.'

From another drawer she took slips of glass, and tiny tweezers, concentrating as she prepared the slide.

'Have you specifically compared a white man's hair with a black man's?' Rose, January knew, had volumes of notes on her microscopic observations, dating back years. There were times that he suspected that if Rose were confronted by the Destroying Angel and offered a choice of her husband or the microscope, he – January – had better pack an extra shirt to wear in Hell because that's where he'd end up.

'Oh, heavens, yes. The girls are always comparing each others' hair. It's my surest way of teaching them how to prepare slides.' She clipped a strand from her own walnut-brown curls, sandwiched it between slips of glass, and removed her spectacles to put her eye to the top of the tube. 'See how round that is?' January looked – making radical readjustments in the focus, since Rose was near-sighted as a mole. 'Now look at yours.'

January withdrew his eye from the eyepiece, blinking, as Rose changed slides.

'Yours is flatter, oval, see? The nappier the hair, the more oval it is in cross section. Now here's our friend's . . .'

January drew back again with an exclamation of disgust. He realized he should have expected that the fragments of flesh and blood around the retrieved hair would be alive with tiny larvae that suddenly looked as big as earthworms under the glass.

'Don't be a sissy.' Rose removed her spectacles again to have a look. 'It looks round.'

'I thought so, too.'

'Which doesn't mean the man isn't *sang melée* – just that he has *good hair*, as my mother calls it. He could be a brown-haired white man as well.'

'And the skin – if that *is* skin – is so discolored by blood under the broken nails that we can't tell what color it is,' finished January glumly, when after half an hour of changing slides and comparing samples he returned the microscope to its box. 'Which means that it could be anyone from John Davis –' he named the owner of the French Opera House and one of his most consistent employers – 'to Hannibal. And that could include Hüseyin Pasha, his valet, his son's tutor, the kitchen boy, and probably the American cook.'

Rose locked the box and replaced the key in its drawer. 'But at least now we know it couldn't include Shaw,' she pointed out as she washed slides in water, dipped from the jar in the corner, then in alcohol. 'Or Oliver Breche, more's the pity.' She set the glass slips neatly in the rack Gabriel had made for her from old forks, to dry. 'Or even Burton Blodgett, though I wouldn't put it past him to have done it just to make a good story.' She wiped her hands and followed January from the laboratory to the gallery above the kitchen.

'Don't suggest it to him.'

'But speaking of Hannibal – and of hair . . .' A frown clouded her forehead as she paused at the top of the steps. 'Is there any condition that you know of – or any drug – that shows itself in a man's hair? I know arsenic gets into the hair and makes it shiny; is there anything that will change the texture and make it limp and dead-looking?' She looked up into his eyes for a moment, seeing in them, January knew, his own arrested look. 'It isn't my imagination, is it?'

'I thought it was mine.' January was silent, trying to call back to mind that slight change in their friend's appearance, and whether the fiddler had seemed quite himself.

Which in fact, January reflected, he *had* . . .

'I've never heard of a malady that would do something like that to a man's hair,' he answered at length. 'Not so suddenly, and all at once.'

'A drug, then? I know he hasn't been well, but I've seen no sign of his going back to opium . . .'

January shook his head and wished for the thousandth time that there were something that would still Hannibal's coughing fits but would not bring with it the deadly temptations of euphoria.

'Where is he living?' She pulled her shawl close around her as they descended to the crooked little yard. 'Could it be something in the atmosphere of a place, the way the phosphorous in match factories is supposed to ruin the mouths of the girls who work in them? I understand that Kentucky Williams has a new fancy man who probably objected to Hannibal's sleeping over her saloon—'

'A properly brought-up lady,' replied January severely, 'has no business knowing about fancy men.'

'This from a man who spent last winter playing at the Countess Mazzini's *ganeum* . . . Well,' she added as they ascended the back-gallery steps, and her cool primness melted into a smile. 'I see someone's awake.'

'We were coming up to get you.' Zizi-Marie held out Baby John to her. The infant – a solemn little professor of philosophy whom no one would *dream* of calling Johnny – had not been crying, only gazing out at the yard with those wide brown worried eyes.

Rose gathered up her son in her arms and carried him toward the bedroom to feed him, before their departure for the Widow Levesque's. January moved to follow – he loved to keep Rose company at such times – but Gabriel, reading the same issue of the *New Orleans Bee* at the dining table that had occupied Burton Blodgett earlier, looked up as January came through the dining room and said, 'Have you seen this, Uncle Ben?' He held it out.

January cursed.

The paper Shaw had shown him a few hours ago had been the *True American* – notable for its attacks on the French Creole aristocracy, whose wealth still ruled New Orleans despite American efforts to gain more say in the city government.

The *Bee*, however, was the French paper. In addition to decrying the unwillingness of the City Guards to search for *the mysterious 'witness' CLAIMED by the Haut Ton to be in a position to completely exonerate the Infidel Turk* . . . the letter to the editor written by 'The Friend of the People' insisted that the entire affair was fueled by the desire of the rich to buy out the city lots of the starving poor with Turkish gold. *Why else the eagerness of both Mayor Prieur and Captain Tremoille of the Guards to believe the suave assertions of this foreign Midas who has so frequently been a guest in their homes?*

There were, January knew, quite as many men of French and Spanish descent in New Orleans who had been impoverished by the bank crashes as there were Americans – men frightened enough, and angry enough, to blame those whom they had once regarded

as their leaders. It was they – the 'Friend of the People' trumpeted
– who had been victimized by *the wealthy planters, the rentiers
and landlords and the bankers whose establishments have yet to
repay a single penny of the savings which they cynically stripped
from the hard-working folk of this city . . .*

*   The cry goes up: if a man of wealth is seen to be punished, will
this not drive investment from the city? Better these two lost lambs
perish unavenged, than that the City* (videlicit, *the planters and
landlords and bankers) should sustain any loss . . .*

And, of course, at his mother's nothing else was talked about.

'Those letters are the most poisonous concoction of insinuation
and lies I've ever read!' January replied, to Virginie Metoyer's
earnest declaration that she had known all the time that Hüseyin
Pasha was up to no good. 'Why is it that everyone assumes that
because a man is a Mohammedan that he is ready to casually
murder two human beings the way you or I would step on a roach?'

'It is their way.' Babette – the third-born and prettiest of the
Metoyer sisters, resplendent in a new silk tignon that was topped
with an astonishing cloud of pink ostrich-feathers – regarded
January with wide brown eyes. 'The Turks are brought up to
despise women—'

'Who told you that, exactly?'

She stammered, discomfited, and Rose came to her rescue by
handing January a plate with a slice of cake. 'Now, Benjamin, you
know perfectly well that you have read *far* more poisonous concoc-
tions of insinuation and lies during the election last year.'

January drew in breath to retort, then let it out and inclined his
head to Babette. 'I'm sorry,' he said. 'That was execrable of me
to get angry at you, for what that "Friend of the People" wrote in
his imbecile letter.'

'You must admit,' added Agnes Pellicot – the Widow Levesque's
former rival among the free colored demi-monde and, since the
bank crash, her most assiduous friend – 'this story of a mysterious
witness who *just happened* to vanish at an inopportune moment
is a little ridiculous. Why hasn't he come forward, if the whole
transaction was innocent?'

'And it's quite true,' added Virginie, feeding a finger-full of
butter to one of Livia Levesque's two exceedingly fat yellow cats,

'that every man of wealth and position in this city defends the Turk because of his gold.'

When January opened his mouth to protest that *every man of wealth and position in this city* had been slandering the Turk like a parcel of schoolgirls the previous evening, Bernadette – the eldest of the sisters and, at nearly fifty, still the closest thing January had ever seen to Original Sin – cut him off with, 'Precisely the reason they're going to let that dreadful man walk away free. We all know perfectly well that first, Mr Smith never existed, and secondly, that they're going to let the Pasha go because they're hoping he'll invest in their businesses. If he dies, God knows who's going to get that money. The nearest Mohammedan Orphanage, I dare say.'

During the inevitable speculation about where the *Mohammedan plutocrat* had acquired his gold, and where he had it hidden ('I've heard he has great jars of it buried beneath the floor of his cellar!' 'Don't be silly, Babette, there isn't a house in New Orleans that *has* a cellar . . .') January forced himself to sit back and regather his perspective, noting that one of the Metoyer sisters had acquired a new lover . . . and a wealthy one, to judge by Babette's new tignon and Virginie's very beautiful new French shawl. Bernadette was, as usual, quietly dressed in plain aubergine silk, but under the edge of her close-wrapped dark tignon glinted new earrings, solitaire diamonds of well over six carats apiece. Moreover, there was something in her manner, sleek and pleased with herself.

'It's driving Agnes Pellicot out of her *wits*,' reported his sister Dominique, when he and Rose walked her to her own little cottage on Rue Dumaine after everyone had imbibed as much tea and gossip as they could stand. 'She thought she'd just concluded the bargain with some American for Marie-Niège, and yesterday his cotton press and warehouse closed down and he's had to leave town . . . and, Agnes says, she'd already bought Marie-Niège a new set of dishes for the house – Crown Derby, and the most *beautiful* Chantilly pattern! – and silk for three dresses, and M'sieu Cailleteau at the sign of the Golden Rabbit won't take the dishes back. Which is *monstrously* unfair of him—'

'It goes to prove, I suppose,' remarked Rose, 'that your sister Olympe's curses actually do work. I understand Marie-Niège went to her and begged for a spell to stop the match, which she didn't feel she was able to tell her mama she didn't actually want. I shall have to keep that in mind.'

'Well, these days one can't afford to be choosy.' Dominique paused before the door of her cottage, bought for her – in the usual arrangement – by a stout and still-wealthy sugar-planter. 'I don't think anyone I know has been placed in *months*, and in fact poor Iphigènie Picard was told by Hercule Lafrènniére that they would actually have to *part* – because of money, you know – and her mother is just *furious* . . . So it drives Agnes *wild* that Bernadette is still able to find a protector on her own, at her age . . . though she may very well be sharing him with Virginie and Babette,' she finished matter-of-factly. 'The way they did with Mr Granville.'

January said, 'Hmn.'

And where lay the difference, he reflected as he and Rose continued on their way toward their own house, between such businesslike negotiations by the well-dressed mamas of Rampart street, and Shamira's mother, who had obliged her daughter agree to concubinage, that there might be money to educate her brother and keep her mother in a modicum of food?

Where else could a girl go, in Cairo or New Orleans or in the swampy wilds of St John Parish? What could a girl do, except thank God that she was beautiful enough to be given the choice between selling her body for a decent return, or spending her life cleaning out someone else's chamber pots?

He glanced at Rose, seeing – despite her ironic amusement at the follies of the world – sadness in her eyes. The school she had taught – the school she hoped to teach once more if anyone in this world ever had any money again – was a quixotic absurdity in this world, offering to instruct young girls of color in such stupidly useless subjects as history and chemistry, literature and logic, mathematics and microscopes: subjects for which Rose's own tough mind had hungered as a hunting dog hungers for meat.

No wonder we went broke, January reflected with a sigh. *Why can't we let them be bored and ignorant and have done with it? What good will it do them, or us, to know that nappy African hair has a different shape than a white girl's silky curls?*

'This came for you, Uncle Ben,' Zizi-Marie greeted him as they came up the steps to the front gallery, and she held out a folded sheet of paper. 'At least I think it's for you. It was stuck under the window in the parlor.'

American, January mentally identified it even as he unfolded the sheet. Americans never understood the Creole rules that only animals came into the house through the French doors of the parlor, instead of through the bedroom of their hostess or host. Personally, he had never understood why, but this had been so firmly beaten into him as a child that it still made him slightly edgy when he saw American men do so, in the houses where he had – up until the bank crash – taught piano to little American children . . . Not that he, as a black man, had ever been allowed to go in through the front opening of any house, French or American, not even his mother's. *It wouldn't be right*, was all his mother ever said about it when he'd asked.

The handwriting was unfamiliar.

> *Mr January,*
>
> > *The pears you ordered from Boston have arrived. I will give myself the pleasure of holding them for you at my office on Peters Street at the corner of Poydras, this evening at 6.*
> >
> > > *P.B.*

Rose said, 'I'll tell Willie to get his things together.'

Pears from Boston meant the slave runners.

EIGHTEEN

January half-expected that the meeting-point with P.B. – whoever that was – would be at one of the warehouses that lined the river below Peters Street. The code was a simple one, but the neighborhood, upstream of Canal Street in the American sector, was one to which he didn't go any more than he had to.

He could think of few buildings in that neighborhood that weren't warehouses – except for an occasional saleroom where slaves were put on display. Upriver from the market, each cotton factor and sugar exporter had his own warehouses, sometimes his own wharves. In flush times bales or barrels would be brought in on steamboats, the cotton stacked so high on the decks as to completely cover the barn-like superstructure. Even in hard times like these, cotton was big business . . .

And that business demanded slaves.

And when a white cotton-farmer paid eleven hundred dollars for a slave, he wasn't going to listen to that slave's protests that he was really a free musician from New Orleans who'd been captured and drugged while walking around the streets of the American quarter like an idiot one night. *Yeah, sure you are, Sambo.* And since that white man's friends and in-laws and – more importantly – his creditors would constitute any judge, jury, and law enforcement in the district, it was unlikely that protests would garner the hapless victim anything but a beating.

Even by day, January hated to go above Canal Street and into the American town. By night it terrified him.

In the French Town, there were free blacks who could attest to his freedom, and French Creole judges who would believe a free black a lot sooner than they'd believe an American.

Above Canal Street he was in enemy territory, eleven hundred dollars in the pocket of any man who had a gun.

The code used by the slave runners in New Orleans was a simple offset. Six o'clock meant eight. Poydras Street actually meant Lafayette.

The penalty for helping slaves escape from their rightful owner
was five hundred dollars – enough to sweep away everything
January owned. House, hope, his son's chances of a decent life in
the world . . . Given the wrong judge and the certainty of an all-
white jury, he wasn't at all confident that the court wouldn't find
some more serious penalty for a black man . . .

And if the matter wasn't brought to court, but only settled by
angry slave-owners themselves in some alley at night, the consequences could be worse yet.

'You sure this ain't a trap?' whispered Willie.

January wasn't, but he breathed: 'We'll be fine.'

'Who's this Mr Bredon, that signed my pass?' The field hand
fished in his jacket pocket for the paper, to be presented to anyone
who asked them, that said he was on business for his owner.

'Never met him,' said January, which was a lie. Judas Bredon
was one of the men who coordinated slave escapes from New
Orleans; the man who had asked January to join those who helped
the fugitives. January carried his legitimate free-papers tucked into
one boot . . . and a completely illegal knife in the other. At eight
o'clock on a December night the river fog reduced visibility among
the warehouses to a few yards, and the stench of sewage, garbage,
and cattle pens masked the burnt sugar and smoke of the refineries;
the air was so thick that it was almost palpable in the swaying
glimmer of his lantern.

The glare of cressets around the wharves dimmed away behind
them. The clop of hooves faded; January heard the sloosh of the
river around wharf pilings.

Music drifted through the fog.

At first he thought it was a work chant, men wailing African
words they'd learned as children as they worked late to unload
cotton. But there were too many voices, women's as well as men's.
Words took shape in the darkness.

Go down, Moses,
Way down in Egypt land.
Tell old Pharoah:
Let my people go . . .

The building on the corner of Peters Street and Lafayette had
probably been a cotton warehouse until the bank crash. It was
brick and unprepossessing, the windows of its upper floor shuttered

tight. Those on the lower glowed with the dull orange gleam of
lanterns. Fog drifted through the topaz gleam of the open doors.
Against that grimy light, January saw men and women, either
slaves or the roughest sort of artisans and dock workers.

He thought: *It's a Protestant church.*

Yet the music pulled at something in his chest, like the sound
of the waves had the first time he'd seen the ocean.

At his mother's that afternoon, between bouts of slandering
Hüseyin Pasha, he'd heard all about Letty – the Metoyers' maid
– who was American-born and Protestant, to the great contempt
of not only the three Metoyer sisters, but also their Louisiana-
born Catholic cook. *I tell Elise to show a little Christian charity to
the girl, but honestly, she does bring it on herself, you know . . .
Oh, I don't know what kind of Protestant – there are about a
hundred of them, aren't there? Methodists and Lutherans and
Baptists, and heaven only knows how they can tell each other
apart . . .*

And the chuckle in Virginie Metoyer's voice had been like the
flick of a whip.

*It seems like it's harder and harder to find a good Catholic
maid these days . . .*

He and Willie moved into the doorway.

When Israel was in Egypt land,

(*Let my people go . . .*)

Oppressed so hard they couldn't stand,

(*Let my people go . . .*)

Voices called and answered, the familiar patterns of a thousand
old songs that January remembered from the village ring-shouts
as a child. His mother's voice came back to his memory, sweet
as a bronze chime, though these days she denied she'd ever gone
to such diversions . . . . Like the field hollers of the men in the
roulaison, when truly, he thought, they were *oppressed so hard
they couldn't stand . . .*

And like the hollers, like the ring shouts, like the field songs
whose words served to warn runaways in the woods when the
riding boss came by ('*Wade in the water . . . Run to the rocks
. . .*' Which actually meant: *The Man's comin' with the dogs . . .*),
he recognized at once that this hymn was in code.

Only, this time, the code wasn't escape.

The code was hope, and the hope smote him like a blow with a club.

God knows our names.

He won't let us be slaves forever.

He saved the Children of Israel, and he'll save us.

January had attended Protestant meetings before and hadn't been impressed. The sight of the sinners on the 'anxious bench', down before the preacher, writhing and sobbing at the thought of their sins, had filled him with distaste and with contempt for the Americans who felt they had to turn the state of one's soul into a show. He had felt as separate from the ranting of the preacher on that occasion – several years ago, now – as he had felt when he'd watched that ecstatic young girl in pink silk and jewels, at the Convent of St Theresa in Batignolles . . . As he'd felt when, as a young man, he'd been drawn by the music to the slave dances at the brickyard on Rue Dumaine and had seen men and women reeling and shouting under the influence of the African loa and West Indian rum.

There was an 'anxious bench' in this makeshift church, but the preacher wasn't trying to convert anyone on it. And in an odd echo of the voodoo dances – to which Protestant blacks were not welcome – January looked around him and saw nothing but faces as dark as his own. Not even the polite *crème café* of the *librés*, nor the dusky *sang-melée* hues that everyone in New Orleans, white and black alike, preferred.

These were the American-born slaves: more African of blood than the *gens de couleur libré*, so shut out of their society; not Catholic; not French; and utterly without power.

God knows our names . . .

The man at the pulpit was young. Somehow, January knew it was the P.B. he was here to see, the man who was risking his life to get men like Willie away to a country where they could be free. His voice was strong, and though he spoke in the ranting, over-familiar style favored by the white Protestant preachers, he was an excellent speaker. Men and women called out, 'Amen!' and 'You tell us, brother!' as they did during storytelling times, either at parties at the back of town or when January had been a child in the Bellefleur slave-village: not for them the respectful silence of the Mass.

'The Children of Israel had forgotten God's law, and so God sent them harsh masters, cruel masters.' The preacher's hand made a long slashing gesture, calling all eyes. Lanterns flanked his makeshift podium. Against their glow January could barely see his face. 'But God relented and sent them a Law, for all men to obey. Even as he sends his Law to us all now . . .'

Code, thought January. His eyes traveled over the room, and even in the dimness he picked out the white countenance of the man sitting on a chair near the pulpit: the white preacher whose congregation sponsored this midweek meeting for the slaves. Most denominations in the south forbade black preachers to have their own congregations, so that young man who spoke so beautifully was – and always would be – merely a 'guest' of the white pastor.

'If we follow that Law, we can all hope for our reward in Heaven. We can all hope to become the Children of God, welcomed into his bosom, taken up like Elijah in a chariot of flame, never to have toil or grief or pain any more . . .'

And maybe – January could hear it as clearly as if the preacher's thoughts radiated from mind to mind throughout the room – *we won't have to wait for Heaven, but can escape at least a little of that toil while we're still here on Earth . . .*

'We must be faithful. We must have hope. God knows our names, brothers and sisters – for you are all my brothers and sisters. You are all EACH OTHERS' brothers and sisters. God knows where every single one of his children lives, what they do each day, who they love, and what dreams they dream at night. There isn't a word you whisper in prayer that God doesn't hear . . .'

Could that white preacher, sitting there smiling, really be that stupid? *Probably*, reflected January. Whites didn't grow up with that sense of the world being one way and everyone saying it was different. Didn't grow up with the sense of a double universe, visible and unseen equal and alike, laid over one another like two colors of light. With a sense of coded meanings that sounded innocent and really meant *wherever you are hiding, brother runaway, duck down NOW 'cause the Man's coming . . .*

He knew full well that no state government would permit an all-black church, for precisely that reason. Hope was too strong a thing to let it go blazing up on its own. You had to make sure the whites kept an eye on a black man preaching hope . . .

And he smiled as the congregation burst into song again, right under that smug nose:

Swing low, sweet chariot,
Coming for to carry me home . . .

He glanced sidelong at Willie's face and saw – almost with a sense of shock – the wide eyes, the tears flowing down silently. Willie, too, knew that home wasn't Heaven.

Home was where he could be free.

Willie and January lingered as the congregation drifted into the night. Curfew was at ten. January guessed that more than a few of the men and women here had slipped away without their masters' knowledge and had to hasten back before the master returned. From the shadows by the door, he recognized Bernadette Metoyer's little housemaid, Letty, and Sillery, Jones, and Delilah from the livery. He nodded a greeting to a tall young man named Four-Eyes he'd met while playing piano last winter uptown, and others that he'd seen when he went to the uptown grocery where, after hours, the American-born black musicians would go to play American tunes with African rhythm, syncopated and wry. Up by the pulpit, the young preacher was besieged with handshakes and those who clustered close to speak. As he and Willie slipped through the knots of men and women, January saw the pastor's face slick with sweat, like a man who has been working the *roulaison* furnace. The sweat also made his hair look black, curly like Rose's rather than nappy (*What does it look like under a microscope?* he couldn't stop himself from wondering) and soaked to dripping points.

January smiled. No congregation of Africans was going to listen to a man who stood still while he preached.

And his face had a glow to it, an inner joy that January understood. He had felt like that, those nights playing for his own people at the back of town, when the music would take hold of everyone in the room like magic, and they'd dance the moon down out of the sky.

Rather to January's surprise, he recognized the white preacher as the saintly-looking Reverend Doctor Emmanuel Promise, who had come so close to pulling the Reverend Dunk's hair last night over the attentions of the Widow Redfern. He, too, beamed, with patronizing pride at his . . . *Pupil? Dependant?*

'You're doing quite marvelous work here, Paul, quite marvelous.'

Promise stepped in as one parishioner moved away, in front of the next woman in the line.

Having better manners, she didn't object. Or maybe she'd just been severely schooled that you didn't object to whatever a white man did.

'You know, it's quite piquant to hear so moving a message delivered in – shall we say – the language of the country?' He chuckled at his own little jest.

The young Reverend Paul smiled too, but he looked a little embarrassed – *as well he might*, thought January.

'Thank you, sir.' His speaking voice was soft, with the accent of New England. 'I hope and trust you understood that no disrespect was meant—'

'No, no!' The Reverend laughed again: a tall, slender man with the refined features of an emaciated saint. 'When St Paul taught in Athens he spoke Greek, and when he preached in Jerusalem he spoke Hebrew. You must call the straying sheep in the language they'll understand. This is quite an impressive congregation you have for these Tuesday meetings, and when the new church arises, you can be sure they will have a place there.'

'Thank you, sir.' The young man wiped his face with a spotless handkerchief – any other African in Louisiana would have had a bandanna. The light, long bone-structure of a Fulani was overlaid with at least two crossings with whites. The expression of eager naivety made him look very young, and even without it, January guessed, he wouldn't put the pastor's age above twenty-five.

When the Reverend Promise moved off, and the last four or five of the congregation had shaken hands and thanked the young preacher, January at last moved forward. 'Excuse me, Reverend – are you the Reverend P.B.? I'm here about the pears.'

The Reverend turned, with a different sort of brightness in those speaking brown eyes. 'Then you must be Mr January.' He held out his hand: soft, though the grip was strong. A scholar's hand.

He'd never cut cane in his life.

'Welcome. Thank you – and welcome. Paul Bannon. And you'll be Willie?' He turned to January's companion.

'Sir.' Willie shook hands, with a confidence January had not seen in him before, his uncertainty wiped away by strength and quiet pride. 'Thank you, sir. What you said up there – I never heard the gospel preached, sir. Marse Den back home didn't hold with it, an' new Marse – Marse Gosse – lived too far from any town.'

'I'm glad I spoke words that helped you. And I'm sorry,' added Bannon, with a quick smile, 'that you won't be staying on to come again. You're going to be traveling with a family named Thomas. I'll take you to the wharf as soon as I lock up here. Mr January, I hope we'll meet again.'

'We will.'

'Ben—' Willie shook January's hand. 'Thank you. I won't forget this. Not ever.'

'We hold these meetings here every Tuesday night Mr January,' continued Bannon, 'if you'd care to join us. I won't ask if you've found the Lord,' he added a little shyly, 'because just you coming here, as you have, tells me that you have.'

'He found me,' said January.

'That's the thing about God,' said Bannon. 'He has all the time there is, so He's willing to look for as long as it takes. Anybody here going back to the French town?' he asked, turning to the last of the worshipers as they filed out the door. 'Excellent . . . Jerry, Matt, Mariah. You won't mind walking with Mr January? You all mind how you go.'

NINETEEN

It wasn't until January and the man Jerry had bid the other two goodnight, and crossed through the Place des Armes with the Cathedral clock striking curfew, that January realized that his companion was, in fact, the slave of M'sieu Pavot. Jerry had mentioned his mother being sold earlier in the year, but it was only when he said, 'I got a little extra time, if I don't get seen by the Watch. My master's in Baton Rouge—' that January said, with a start:

'You're Pavot's Jerry, then!'

Jerry grinned sidelong. 'You musta heard all the row-de-dow Sunday.'

'I'm sorry,' said January at once. 'That was stupid of me—'

'No, no.' The young man shook his head. 'If the house had caught fire, you'da heard my name the same way.'

'You think he actually did it?' January inflected his voice like a stranger agog for sensation, not that of a man seeking information.

'Mr Breche from the apothecary saw him.' The account was clearly good enough for him.

'Was you in the front of the house when they fell?'

'I was in the kitchen in the back. I'd checked the whole front of the house just before sunset, like always when Mr Pavot's away. But he's been gone most of the week, an' it's cold in that house! In the kitchen at least it's warm.'

And somehow less lonely, thought January, recalling how Willie would risk his freedom – and the well-being of every one of his benefactors, though that thought had clearly never occurred to him – to emerge from beneath the safety of the house and sit in the kitchen, only for the pleasure of hearing other peoples' voices, of knowing he wasn't alone.

They crossed Rue St-Philippe, January following the young servant along Rue Bourbon with the air of a man fascinated by the inside story of great events.

'Wasn't 'til someone came ringin' on the doorbell, shoutin' about the murders, that I knew anything had happened. I came out, an' there was everybody on the street crowdin' around already, an' Mr Breche kneelin' beside the bodies, weepin' an'—'

Jerry froze in his tracks as a man's voice ahead of them shouted, 'Heathen whore-bitch!' and there was a dull thunk, of something thrown against shutters.

January thought: *Shit*.

A single oil-lantern hung on its crossed chains above the intersection ahead. In the isolated pool of its yellowish glow, five or six men and two women were visible, clustered in the street in front of Hüseyin Pasha's house. Dim needles of gold marked the shut jalousies of a second-floor window, and the reflected gleam slithered on the bottle one of the women held in her hand. A man threw another bottle at the passageway door. It splintered.

'You hear me, you goddam devil-worshipping murderer?' yelled one of the men. He staggered, cupped his hands around his bearded mouth. 'You suckin' the mayor's arse, to keep out of jail where you goddam belong?'

'Damn it,' whispered January through his teeth, 'Hüseyin is *in* jail.'

'Really?' Jerry sounded genuinely surprised. 'Didn't say nothing about it in the paper.'

'That's because the paper is written by a conceited clown who loves to get people stirred up.'

Jerry looked startled. 'They wouldn't print it if it wasn't true, would they?'

One of the women pulled up her skirts, half-squatted, and pissed on the threshold of the door, to howls of laughter from her companions: 'That's showin' him, Ginny!'

The man who'd thrown the bottle took something from his belt, and both January and Jerry retreated into the inky shelter of the doorway of Philippe Breche's shuttered-up pharmacy. A shot cracked out in the misty night, accompanied by the splintering crash of the window glass behind the shutters. January thought of Jamilla, lying in her bedroom upstairs. Of the three maids and the eunuch Ghulaam, and of the other servants whom white men could probably shoot without anyone inquiring who'd done it . . .

Wondered if Oliver Breche, in his room above the shop, could hear these first fruits of his craving for revenge.

And of course, reflected January bitterly, the City Guard was nowhere to be found.

He was just about to duck out of the sheltering doorway and head for the Cabildo when a woman appeared from around the corner of Rue des Ursulines. She walked calmly and alone, a basket in one hand, as if all the night were hers to do with as she pleased. By that alone, January reflected, he or anyone in the French town would recognize her, even before she came near enough the feeble street-lamp for its glow to outline the seven points of her tignon: a thorned halo around her head, a crown of flame.

Jerry whispered in shock, 'Holy shit, that ain't . . .?!'

January nodded. All the voodoo queens wore their headscarves tied into five points. Only one wore seven.

The woman ignored the drunken whore as if she weren't there, stopped before the passageway door. Something in her demeanor silenced the men – one of them approached her and began to speak, but she only looked at him, and he stepped back.

She took a piece of chalk from her basket and began to draw on the door.

Fear as well as belligerence tinged the drunk woman's voice. 'What you drawin'?'

'I'm drawin' death.' The deep alto was utterly matter-of-fact.

The drunk woman and the men looked at one another and did not reply.

Jerry whispered, 'Is that Marie LeVeau?'

'Oh, yeah.'

The other whore was *sang melée*, Indian features as well as African mixed with white; she said nothing, but backed away. The others were white, and Americans, but knew hoodoo when they saw it. Whether or not they believed in its power, January could see that none of them was willing to go up and touch those signs.

One of the men finally asked, 'You puttin' a curse on the house?'

LeVeau turned. In the shifting shadows of that single lantern over the street, her dark eyes seemed fathomless, inhuman as a snake's. 'What do you think?' Then she turned back.

She marked the door, then the shutters of each window in turn:

crosses and hearts, circles and stars, the curving track of the Damballah Serpent. Black chalk and salt, gunpowder and rum – the smell of them drifted faint on the heavy air. The strong, sudden sharpness of blood as she drew something small that squirmed from her basket and cut its throat.

The Americans drew further back.

January recognized the signs of Maitre Carrefour – an aspect of the master of the crossroad, Papa Legba; of Ogun and the Baron Samedei; and of the dreadful Marinette of the Dry Arms. LeVeau sang soft and guttural in her throat as she worked. So silent had the rowdies fallen that January could hear clearly, African words blending with French.

The Americans left, pretending that they did so of their own accord. Their feet tapped wetly on the brick banquette. They didn't start speaking, all the way back down Rue des Ursulines. Foggy silence closed in.

'You want to come inside?' whispered Jerry when they'd gone, and he nodded across the street toward the Pavot house. Marie LeVeau had gone around the corner on to Rue des Ursulines, to mark the carriage gate, the stable door.

'I'll head home. Last folks I want to meet now is the Watch.'

'You take care, then.' And, as if he feared to be seen by LeVeau as he crossed the street, Jerry darted over the way at a run. January watched him as he unlocked the little passway that led to Pavot's rear courtyard; heard clearly the clank of the key turned again, the snick of the bolts.

Only then did he come out of the black niche of Breche's doorway and cross the street. He knew Mamzelle Marie – his sister Olympe was her pupil and friend. And he was a good Christian and knew that God's strength was greater than those crosses and triangles in black chalk and graveyard dust . . .

He might even have been brought to touch them, if someone had offered him money to do so. His family needed the money.

But it would have to be a great deal of money, he reflected. And good Christian or not, he'd go visit Olympe afterwards, to have the cross taken off him, just in case.

Mamzelle Marie came around the corner again with her little basket as he neared the door.

With her, a little like the skeletal Baron Cemetery himself in his too-large frock-coat and much-battered chimney-pot hat, was Hannibal Sefton.

'I earnestly hope you have money to pay this lady, *amicus meus*.' The fiddler coughed, one hand pressed to his side. 'I promised her two dollars, and an extra fifty cents for the inconvenience of coming out at this hour on short notice – *amicus certus in re incerta cernitur*. And in truth, I haven't a dime.'

'*You're* paying her? To do *this*?'

'It got rid of them,' said Hannibal reasonably, 'didn't it?'

Wordlessly, January dug in his pocket. He had a dollar fifty. 'Can I give you the rest tomorrow?'

Mamzelle Marie smiled like the Serpent in the Garden. 'I trust you, Ben. It's not that I don't know where you live.' From her basket she took another flask and emptied some of its contents into her hand. In the street light January could see it was reddish: brick dust. The color of life. She knelt and began to mark crosses, small and almost invisible, at the bottom corners of the vèvès she had drawn.

Cynics throughout New Orleans were wont to say that Mamzelle Marie made half her money taking curses off the houses that she'd been paid to put curses on. They didn't often say this to her face – and they generally didn't say this after it got dark.

'When I came by your house,' said Hannibal, 'with that Aeschylus translation Rose is working on for M'sieu Landreaux at the bookstore, Rose was kind enough to offer me supper. She asked me: would I walk past this house on my way home, to make sure all was quiet?'

Hannibal generally scrounged quarters in the attics or store sheds of the bordellos and saloons in the Swamp – the violent and filthy district out beyond the edge of town that had grown up around the turning basin of the Carondelet Canal – and earned food money by playing for such of the customers as were sober enough to appreciate it. He had lately augmented this income by forging free-papers for runaways, and by doing a little gambling, but steadfastly refused January's offers of attic room in his own house: *Who's going to send their daughters to Rose's school, if word gets around I sleep under your roof?* Between them, Rose, January, and January's sister Dominique at least made sure he didn't starve.

He went on, 'I came around the corner and found Pig-Nose

Dick and Waddy Page and their friends assembled, and rather than
attempt reasoning with them, I thought perhaps if they thought
the house sufficiently ill-wished without further effort of theirs,
they might go away. It *is* a cold night. It would perhaps have been
cheaper if I'd asked them to accompany me back to a saloon, but
I suspect Soapy Jansen had turned them out—'

'I didn't think any saloon keeper in this city would turn anyone
out.'

'You've never seen Pig-Nose in his cups. I'd have gone to your
sister, but she's clear on the other side of the French Town—'

Lantern light shone suddenly around Hüseyin Pasha's door,
which opened a crack. The tutor Suleiman's face appeared.

'It's all right,' called out January quickly. 'They're gone, and
this –' he gestured to the marks that covered the shutters – 'might
actually serve to keep others away for a time.'

'Please,' said the tutor. 'Come upstairs, if you will, sir. And
you, Lady—' He bowed to the voodoo queen.

Marie LeVeau made a final mark on the inside of the door and
shook her head. 'This naughty man –' she flicked Hannibal's
shoulder with the back of her reddened fingernails – 'called me
from my bed, with tales of injustice done to the innocent. And
indeed,' she added, 'the Grand Zombi whispers to me that your
master is innocent of that which they say he has done. Else I
would not have come.'

Her dark eyes moved, seemed to pierce the deepening fog.
'What I have marked, not all will draw away from. But for a time
at least, I think they will cross over to the other side of the street
and leave you be.' From her basket she took a bandanna and wiped
the brick dust from her fingers. 'Still I say to you, and to your
Lady, sir, that it is best that you leave this house. Evil has been
done here. Only Evil will come if you remain.'

'I think she's right,' said January, when the voodooienne had
melted into blackness and he and Hannibal had followed Suleiman
back along the passageway to the loggia. 'I'm amazed men like
your friend Pig-Nose would even be able to read newspapers . . .'

'Don't underrate them because they smell like privies. Even in
an outhouse you'll find a newspaper. And it only takes one literate
drunkard with a grievance against the rich to stir up a whole tavern
– or the whole of a street.'

Suleiman opened the door to the upstairs parlor, where a branch of candles burned on the marble-topped table. Movement further down the gallery caught January's eye, and in the shadows he saw a boy standing, a blanket wrapped over a pale nightshirt . . .

Suleiman saw him, too. January didn't understand the words he called out, but his voice was reassuring: *Everything's all right. Go back to bed. It will be better in the morning . . .*

The child vanished.

Hüseyin's child. Shamira's child.

'Thank you.' Jamilla rose from her chair as they entered the parlor, where the smell of fresh coffee lay thick on the lamplit air. 'You are kind.'

Hannibal bowed deeply. 'We were lucky, my Lady,' he said. *'Ignavus fortuna adiuvat.* Lucky that those Gallatin Street slush-buckets believed in Madame LeVeau's magic – at least in the dark and the fog they do – and luckier still that Madame believed my assertion of your innocence. Nevertheless—'

'Nevertheless,' continued January, 'those men are dangerous, and they'll be back. Not because they're angry about the murder of innocent girls, or even over the injustices of the rich, but because if there are enough of them, they know there'll be a chance to loot this house and get away with it. My advice to you, my Lady, is to close up the house and go to one of the big hotels, where they have a staff capable of turning ruffians like that out before they can make trouble.'

'What you say is true.' Above the edge of her veil, her eyes were heavy with sleeplessness, and by the movement of her head he guessed she'd taken opium preparatory to going to bed. Hannibal was watching her, too, and when she caught the arm of her chair for balance, his glance crossed January's, with a curious matter-of-fact compassion.

'Yet we shall need to sell this house, I think,' she went on, 'and if we leave it empty, will they not come the more quickly? Damaged, what will it bring? The former owner seized upon my husband's offer like a starving child on food; I think it had stood empty a year. For so many of us to live elsewhere—' She shook her head, as if she were trying to make her way underwater. 'I know not even how much it will cost, to find a lawyer to help my husband. Suleiman has been asking and has found none, yet, to take the case.'

January cursed under his breath.

'*Video meliora proboque, deteriora sequor*,' murmured Hannibal. 'Even if a lawyer believed in your innocence, why would he take the risk? If he loses, you'll be in no position to pay him. If he wins, Hüseyin Pasha will undoubtedly have to leave New Orleans anyway, and his attorney will stay on and never be hired again by anyone who believes your husband was guilty. *Our doubts are traitors, and make us lose the good we oft might win . . .*'

'And if we leave Nehemiah and Perkin here,' Jamilla continued, her voice groping over the words, 'will they not run away themselves? And if they prove loyal, will *they* not be in danger of being killed, or stolen like loot, by a mob?'

January was silent, knowing the truth of what she said. 'Nevertheless,' he said after a time, 'the City Watch has few men. At this season of the year there is trouble all over the waterfronts every night. Fear and superstition will keep chance drunkards away for a time, but the waterfront gangs know of your husband's wealth. If you remain here, it is worth their while to stir up a mob to attack the place some night. Better you should accept the loss of this place, take your husband's gold . . .'

'My husband's gold.' Jamilla sank down into the chair behind her, and her whole body quivered, first gently, then more and more violently, until she was shaking with uncontrollable shudders. 'My husband's gold. All of this then comes to that: my husband's gold.'

She put her head down into her hands and began to laugh.

Suleiman whispered, 'Madame—!' and January made a move toward her, then drew back as Ghulaam stepped fiercely out of the shadows, his hand on the hilt of his cutlass.

Ra'eesa sprang up from the floor in the corner where she had been sitting, ran to her mistress's side. '*Khânom*—'

Jamilla shook her head, her laughter dying away into sobs of exhaustion. 'Forgive,' she whispered. 'Forgive. Only that we are all in danger, because of my husband's gold. All blame us and hate us, because of my husband's gold. Come.' She raised her hand against Ghulaam's protest, and Suleiman's. Like a graceful phantom in her embroidered coat and silent slippers, she led the way out on to the gallery and up the stair, weaving a little in the light of Ra'eesa's candle, like a spirit barely able to find its way back to its haunt.

Shadows reeled as they entered her room, caught the filigree
of the lamp, the pattern on the quilts that had been tossed aside
from the divan when she'd been woken by the noise in the street.
A chamber had been partitioned from one side of the bedroom,
probably – guessed January – a nursery in some early phase of
occupancy of the house; Ra'eesa's pallet lay on the floor. On the
opposite side of the bedroom from this, a sort of alcove had been
built out of the side of the chimney and was furnished with latticed
doors for the storage of bedclothes in the Turkish fashion.

These doors Jamilla opened, and she knelt, to fumble at what
looked – in the wavering candlelight – like a knothole in the wood
of the floor.

Ra'eesa said something in Osmanli and helped Jamilla to stand
and step back. Then she herself knelt and opened a trap door in
the bottom of the alcove. Ghulaam brought the lamp close, his
own face a study in consternation and suspense.

There was a chest in the compartment under the trap door.

It was solid iron – January couldn't imagine how Hüseyin Pasha
ever gotten it upstairs – and about eighteen inches square. Ra'eesa,
though she steadfastly refused help, could barely lift its lid.

The chest was filled with dirt.

Dirt, and old bricks, and clamshells, such as every path and
road in Louisiana was paved with, in that gravel-poor country . . .

Everything, in fact, of which he'd found traces on those big
shawls that had belonged to Noura and Karida.

At the back of the dirt, a thin reef of gold pieces was heaped
up, perhaps a hundred of them, pushed to the back, as if they'd
been thrust away by frightened disbelieving hands.

The hands of someone who had believed, up until a moment
before, that the entire chest was filled with gold instead of rubbish.

Jamilla sank down on to the divan and laughed until she cried.

TWENTY

'Well –' Hannibal knelt beside the chest as Ra'eesa sprang to clasp her mistress in her arms – 'this explains why our two young ladies needed to make their exit other than through the stable.' He picked up a handful of the coins, let them drop with a sweet musical clinking. 'How many trips would it take, to carry that much gold down three flights of stairs and across the court? But, if they had help, two girls could lug it across the roof and down a ladder.'

'And we know they had help.' January leaned one shoulder against the corner of the mantelpiece and tried to purge from his heart his first, involuntary, and overwhelming spurt of impatience with Jamilla's frantic tears:

You still have two thousand dollars, Madame. Try finding out sometime that you have NOTHING but two dollars and fifty cents . . .

He crossed himself. *Holy Mary, Mother of God, lift this poison from my heart . . .*

What had Shakespeare said of it? *This yellow slave will knit and break religions, bless the accurs'd . . .*

And sour a man's heart with envy against the stricken.

Dearest God, forgive me.

He at least, at the start of the bank crash, had been surrounded by his friends and his family. He had not had his beautiful Rose in peril of being taken from him, had not been stranded in a foreign land . . .

He still had to swallow down the unhelpful urge to tell Jamilla that things could be a lot worse.

Instead he said, 'I think a return visit to young Mr Valentine is called for. His father is a well-known scoundrel who apparently owes money to everyone in town, and who coincidentally vanished the same night the girls made their escape. The only question is whether he was their murderer or a fellow victim.'

'Neither.' Hannibal stood up, took January by the elbow, and steered him to the door out on to the dark gallery.

'You know him?' January asked softly.

'Never saw him in my life.'

'Then how do you know what he was doing on Friday night? According to Shaw, the last person outside his own family to see him was the moneylender Roller Gyves. If the man gave him an ultimatum for the money he owed—'

Hannibal shook his head. 'He did give an ultimatum.' He glanced back into the bedchamber, where Ghulaam, Ra'eesa, and Suleiman gathered around Jamilla, barely more than shapes against the light of the single candle and the wavering lamp. 'But Valentine had nothing to do with those girls disappearing.'

January stood silent for a time, looking down at his friend, considering the implications of Hannibal's words. Suspicions that had percolated in his mind about the younger Mr Valentine resurfaced and fit together like pieces of a puzzle. From the black pit of courtyard below, Nehemiah's voice drifted up, reassuring the frightened maids, and January shivered at the knowledge that the first course of action open to Jamilla would be the sale of the American servants. Maybe they'd be lucky and someone in town would have the money to pick up a good coachman, a good house-maid, cheap.

But the likelihood was greater that only those who needed farm labor would be buying. *A coachman won't get you money. A cotton hand will.*

'And did "young *Mr* Valentine" tell you this?' He marked off the name with the inflection in his voice, and by the way that Hannibal glanced up at him, January knew that his suspicion was correct.

He wondered if Shaw had guessed also.

No wonder, he reflected, *I thought of Poucet . . .*

The fiddler shook his head. 'I know because it wasn't Tim Valentine that Gyves saw. It was me.'

It was slightly more than three-eighths of a mile from the house of Hüseyin Pasha to January's doorstep on Rue Esplanade. Had he not known every step of the French Town he doubted he could have found his way there, for by the time he left the big house on Rue Bourbon the fog had thickened, and most of the inhabitants of the quarter had locked up their shutters and gone to bed.

Still, he walked with his heart in his throat, one hand extended to touch the walls as he passed before them – *stucco, that'll be the Rastignac cottage; brick, with six sets of shutters new-painted, the Philipon town-house. That gap's the passway into Pélisser's yard* . . . His ears strained for every sound in the muffled air.

When first he'd come to New Orleans as a child, his mother had cautioned him not to go across Canal Street into the then-tiny American faubourg of St Mary: 'They're American animals there; you stay away from them.' That same year the American President had bought Louisiana from the dictator of the French. Only a few hundred Americans had lived in New Orleans then, connected with the trade down the river. Even when he'd left – fourteen years later, in 1817 – they had been more a nuisance than anything else. He had mistrusted them, but didn't fear them.

When he'd come back from France, it was a different matter.

January walked swiftly, silently, with pounding heart, and climbed the steps to his own gallery with a sense of having escaped from some terrible peril, to be clasped in Rose's arms.

'Evidently Tim Valentine has been dead for about three months,' he said, after he'd explained what had delayed him – it was almost ten thirty by this time – and Gabriel had brought the cold remains of supper from the kitchen. 'At least, when his children started hiring Hannibal to impersonate him in dealings with moneylenders – when Hannibal and I got back to town in October – they said he'd died the month before. They buried him under the stable.'

He glanced toward the dining-room door. After initial reassurances he'd sent his niece and nephew from the room, but he could hear, from time to time, the soft creak of feet in the back parlor.

'Well, I'm sure he was no loss to the community.' Rose poured a tisane from the tea pot, sugar and mint sweet in the soft candle-light. 'I trust Hannibal conducted these interviews sufficiently disguised to avoid later embarrassment if they encountered him in a bar room?'

'False whiskers and bleached hair,' said January. 'And I presume an American accent – which he does astonishingly well . . .'

'Hence that queer look his hair has had, that worried me so much.'

'He could get the wherewithal from any woman on Perdidio Street,' agreed January. 'I've never seen tresses the color of Russian

Hetty's, for instance, growing out of any human head. He re-dyed it afterward, to cover the henna. The children are all redheads—'

'And all under age, of course.' Rose propped her chin on her fist. 'And thus would find themselves in an orphanage, while everything their father had owned disappeared into the pockets of his creditors. When the oldest is finally of age to look after her brothers and sisters—'

'Oh, you guessed that secret?'

Rose cocked a glance at him over the rims of her spectacles. 'I've only been past there once or twice,' she said, 'not having any call to rent a horse and carriage . . . But I've seen enough Shakespeare to take a guess about the so-called "young Mr Valentine's" true nature. *I am all the daughters of my father's house, and all the brothers too . . .* She's hardly the first female of our acquaintance to have masqueraded as male.'

'You've done it yourself,' pointed out January with a smile.

'Well, only to travel. But if I were faced with the prospect of arguing before a court of law that I should be granted ownership of a heavily mortgaged property and custody of four younger brothers and sisters, I would much rather do so in the character of a boy than a girl. How old does "young Mr Valentine" claim to be?'

'Sixteen, I think Shaw said. She looks about thirteen.' January finished the dish of his nephew's excellent jambalaya and wiped up the juices with bread. 'But the slaves, of course, back up her story. They know they'll be the first the state would sell to pay off Valentine's creditors.'

'Which means –' Rose went to fetch from its place beneath the sideboard the china basin to wash the dishes – 'that you're not going to be able to believe a word that anyone says to you there.'

January sighed. 'Not one word,' he agreed.

As January suspected she would, Maggie Valentine denied any knowledge of anything that had happened in the livery yard on Friday night, or Sunday. 'We lock up when the last wagon comes back, and that's the truth,' she insisted, when January and Hannibal went to the livery yard on the following morning. 'That was just after nine on Friday.' Without the hat – which she removed when they retreated into the gloom of the coach house – her thin, boyish face still had an androgynous look to it, in its frame of short-cropped red hair.

'I locked up the yard, rubbed down the team, then we all had supper and went to bed.' She put her arm around Emily – the twelve-year-old girl who'd been carving up the only half-loaf of bread on the premises at January's previous visit – and looked in desperation from January to Hannibal and then back. 'Sunday we had more custom, even with the rain, but the last teams came in not long after dark. That's really all I can tell you. It's all I know.'

It wasn't. He saw it in her eyes, and in the faces of the other children, grouped close around her. They were terrified. And would have been so, guessed January, even if there had been no murder between Friday night and Sunday. He'd seen beggar children on the New Orleans wharves, sleeping behind cotton bales and fighting with older beggars for promising scraps.

He remembered the winter Chatoine had frozen to death, down on the Quai St-Bernard.

Maggie faced him like an ill-armed, too-young knight squaring off against a dragon she knew she couldn't defeat. But she was ready to die trying. 'Yes, I was wrong not to report Pa's death, and I guess it's wrong of me to pass myself off as a boy, though I honestly don't see it's anybody's business but my own. I really will be seventeen next year—'

'If you want, we can dig Pa up and show you he wasn't murdered,' put in Emily helpfully.

The two boys – Roger and Sam – and three-year-old Selina all nodded.

'He just drank himself to death,' Maggie went on. 'Lots of people do that. Hell, he had so much liquor in him I'll bet he ain't rotted yet. But I will say,' she added, and raised that tough little chin, 'if those poor girls had come to me, asking would I set up a ladder so's they could get out of where they were, I'd have done it. And anyway they *couldn't* have got out on Friday, 'cause he killed 'em an' pitched 'em out the window right there in the house Sunday night.'

'We think,' said Hannibal, 'that they might have been taken away and brought back.'

'Who'd do a blame silly thing like that?' demanded Maggie, and her fear momentarily dissolved in genuine perplexity. 'Dangerous, too. If they took 'em away, why not just dump 'em in the bayou?'

January shook his head. 'That's one of the things we're trying to find out. Does anyone else have a key to the gate?'

'No, sir.'

'Not Sillery?' He had watched how the wiry little head-groom spoke to Maggie, when first he and Hannibal had entered the yard asking for her. He'd heard the man call out to her, to get that roan rubbed down first before anything; had heard him snap: *You got to get that fodder bill paid this week, or we're gonna have to sell one of the nags . . .*

He'd seen her expression. She was scared of the slave. He could bring her world down in ruins with a word.

But now her jaw tightened hard, and she said, 'No, sir. We have just the one. I keep it in my pocket.'

And January was perfectly well aware that keys could be stolen and copied, particularly if before they'd been kept in Maggie Valentine's pocket, they'd been kept in the pocket of a drunkard who might be found passed out on a hay bale any afternoon.

Yet if Sillery – or either of the other two slaves – had done more than take a bribe to open the gate and raise the ladder in the dead hours before dawn, would they not have taken the stolen gold and disappeared themselves? New Orleans was a port. Ships left for Mexico, New York, Europe every day. Admittedly, it would be more complicated for three black fugitives than for three whites, but with sufficient gold a great deal could be done.

'Were you aware that Sillery was taking money to let one of Hüseyin Pasha's concubines meet with her lover in the carriage house in the afternoons?'

A flare of pink stained those high cheekbones. 'I – sometimes I wondered,' said the girl. 'I'd find things – once an earring, the kind I've never seen around the town before. Another time a man's handkerchief, in the tack room. I know Sillery always has money. Probably more than me,' she added wryly. 'I thought it might have been one of the servants in the Pasha's house, or maybe one of his wives. But I didn't see any harm in it. And I wouldn't have told on those girls,' she added, 'even if I'd knowed.'

Sillery was even less forthcoming. The yard had been shut and locked by nine o'clock both nights. *Ask Jones here, and 'Lilah, if you don't believe me . . . Ask Miss Maggie. She'll tell you.* The dark eyes that regarded January were wary but calm.

And slaves, January knew, were always wary in the face of questions. When the truth of a black man's guilt or innocence mattered to so few whites – when the consequences of how a white man would take *any* piece of information could be so arbitrary and so devastating – how could they not be?

'She knows something,' said January as he and Hannibal emerged on to Rue des Ursulines again. 'Or suspects. The girls didn't flee until the small hours of Saturday morning. Sillery and Jones could have raised the ladder for them, carried the gold down without knowing what it was, harnessed a team and for all we know driven them to their destination—'

'Given the efficiency of the City Guards,' put in Hannibal, 'it's unlikely they'd have crossed their path.'

'Personally,' January added, 'I wouldn't like to go into court with a story about the girls running away and then mysteriously being brought back. Maggie's right. It was dangerous – and stupid – for the murderer to put himself into Sillery's hands that way. Why *not* just dump them in the bayou?'

Hannibal shook his head. 'I'll tell you this, though. Hüseyin Pasha's odalisques weren't the only ones using that carriage house as a *maison d'assignation*.' He dug in his pocket, produced a necklace of cheap beads, such as slave women wore. One of them, rudely-painted black and white, looked like it had come from Africa. 'This was in a corner near the back.'

The charcoal man, leading his little white donkey along Rue des Ursulines, crossed over the street to the river-ward side as he approached them. On this gray and chilly morning, January was interested to note how many people were doing that, dodging drays and wagons if necessary, to avoid walking near the vèvès written on the walls of Hüseyin Pasha's house. Even in daylight they looked ominous, scrawled crookedly across shutters and doors. The shopfront that occupied the corner rooms of the ground floor was also shuttered fast, the renter – January recalled the place sold fans and gloves – having no doubt realized that between scandal and voodoo, he had better find another place of business.

As they passed the courtyard gate, the coachman Nehemiah emerged with a bucket of whitewash. 'I've contracted with your sister Olympe to come back after dark and renew the signs,' said Hannibal. '*Sitt* Jamilla agrees that it's best that the household doesn't appear to realize that the signs may have the effect of keeping potential troublemakers away . . . the point being how many of them are likely to read this.' He took a newspaper from his pocket and held it out: it was the *Bulletin*, not the *True American*, but the long letter on the editorial page about the rich men of the city defending an Infidel Murderer was initialed B.B.

January cursed, but in fact only one person lingered on the corner of Rue Bourbon to gawk at the house, and that person, January saw, was Abishag Shaw.

'Suleiman said as how you was here last night.' The Kentuckian stepped back to let a couple of slave women pass, crossing themselves even as they stared at the house. 'One of our boys came by just after dark an' cleared off a couple of two-legged alligators an' their girlfriends then. But there ain't but twenty of us on the night watch, an' eight of them I couldn't set to keepin' schoolboys out of a candy shop. You seen what it's like down on the levee these days, Sefton.'

'Indeed I have,' agreed Hannibal. '*Chaos, rudis indigestaque moles* . . . One reason I agreed last night to take up my residence temporarily under the Lady Jamilla's roof.' He nodded across the street. 'That, and the fact that Russian Hetty turns out to have a boyfriend she didn't tell me about – not that I would dream of laying so much as a disrespectful finger upon the hem of the lovely Hetty's garment.'

'M'am Hüseyin holdin' up?'

'As well as can be expected,' said Hannibal grimly. 'She asked me about breaking free of the opium habit – and I fear I could give her little encouragement that it would be easy. She has the shakes this morning, but hasn't taken any yet. It isn't a condition in which I'd care to try running for my life across the roof ahead of a drunken mob myself, but then a state of stupefaction wouldn't be much help either.'

'Damn Breche,' January whispered. 'He should try being a slave to the opium bottle, if he thinks it's so clever of him to start feeding it to her . . .'

'Oh, he is.' Hannibal regarded him in mild surprise. 'I thought you knew. Walk past the shop's rubbish bins sometime. Somebody in that house is going through four bottles of Gregory's Soothing Syrup a week, and something tells me it isn't old master Philippe. Nasty stuff, all sugar and treacle, and not nearly the punch that a good spoonful of Kendal's Black Drop will give you.' He shook his head in disapproval at the young apothecary's juvenile taste in drugs.

'You got a gun?' inquired Shaw.

'Hüseyin Pasha has a number of truly formidable fowling-pieces.'

'I'll send you over somethin' with a little more meat to it. That wouldn't be your sister's work –' Shaw nodded across the street at the vèvès – 'would it, Ben?'

January shook his head, neglecting to say that by tomorrow morning it would be. The whitewash Nehemiah was applying did little to cover the marks, for the stucco was originally a clear, pale blue and the shutters red. While speaking to Shaw, January had observed the passers-by, and he had to agree that though many stopped and stared, even Kaintucks who knew nothing about what the signs meant kept their distance. A second layer of marks over the whitewash would only increase the eerie appearance of the house – the announcement that the place was sufficiently accursed.

Sufficiently, at least, for those whose only intention was to vent upon the helpless their own anger at the rich.

'How long before Hüseyin goes to trial?' he asked. 'And has any progress been made in finding out about this Mr Smith?'

'None,' said Shaw. 'Nor is there like to be. I sent off letters to the newspapers in Mobile an' Baton Rouge, but if our bird came in disguise – an' damn few businessmen walk around wearin' beards like a keelboat captain's – stands to reason he had some call to do it. Just as it would stand to reason for anyone wantin' to start up a bank to go to Hüseyin, him havin' just about the only specie in New Orleans.'

'Not any more, he doesn't.' January recounted what they had found – or rather, what they had not found – in the alcove in the Lady Jamilla's room. 'It looks like the girls sneaked dirt and bricks out of the livery yard a little at a time in their shawls, when Nehemiah let them slip out so that Noura could meet her beloved. They'd carry up the rubbish late at night and substitute it for the gold while Jamilla was asleep.'

'Well, them clever little minxes.'

'I'm guessing they hid the gold in the divans in their room,' put in Hannibal. 'It's what I'd have done. Even one piece would be enough to win Sillery's assistance, for such things as putting up ladders and lugging heavy bags across kitchen roofs in the middle of the night. Far easier to lower the gold by a rope wrapped around the kitchen chimney than lug it down through the house in the middle of the night. I can't imagine why they didn't wait until Sunday night, when they knew the servants would be out of the house, but they didn't.'

'The only problem,' concluded January, 'is that we have not discovered one single shred of proof of any of this.'

'All we *have* discovered,' added Hannibal, 'is a splendid reason – far better than mere jealousy – for Hüseyin Pasha to strangle our larcenous damsels and toss them out the window . . . as the imaginative Mr Breche is going to point out if we take this to court. So it perhaps behoves us—'

'It behoves us nuthin'.' Shaw shoved his hands into his pockets and spat. 'Monday afternoon Mayor Prieur sent off a letter to the Sultan's consul in Havana, askin' him to send somebody to fetch Hüseyin Pasha an' deal with him elsewhere – Constantinople, for preference. Captain Tremouille's like an old maid with an engagement ring: it gets us outta the whole shootin' match, an' the word is now that we just hang on to the man, 'til the Sultan's Guards come an' take him away.'

'And leave his family as targets for the rest of New Orleans to shoot at.'

'That,' said Shaw, and he spat again, 'we have been told, ain't none of our business no more.'

TWENTY-ONE

'I know the Consul.' Hüseyin Pasha leaned against the rusted filth of the cell bars, tired resignation in his voice. 'Like everyone whom the Sultan appoints these days, he sees me as . . . old-fashioned. Obstructionist.' He sighed and rubbed at the fresh cut beside his left eye. 'Nevertheless, he knows me. I can only hope that he will not assume – as will any men here who would make up my jury – that I would simply murder two members of my family out of jealousy . . . and certainly not that I would be so stupid as to pitch them from the front window of my own house.'

There was a sharp rattle of wings and a three-inch roach buzzed across the room; the Turk struck it out of the air with an exclamation of disgust, crushed it underfoot. 'I suppose I should be glad of this,' he continued wearily. 'At least the man Breche will not come to Constantinople and babble his fantasies before the judge.'

The stink of the cell nauseated January, even where he stood in the icy corridor outside. The cold did a little to damp the fetor, but through the bars he could see that, despite it, the straw underfoot crept with insect life. Some of the wards of the Hôtel Dieu in Paris had smelled just as bad during the cholera, but at least the roaches had been smaller.

'Will it be safe for your family to follow you there?'

'The Sultan is not a man to kill the family of one whom he condemns.' Hüseyin unwrapped the package that January had brought him as he spoke: in addition to paying a call on the Valentine children, January had set forth that morning with a package from Rose, wrapped in clean newspapers: bread, cheese, apples and bottles of ginger beer. 'I suppose I should be grateful, that this is not the modern way, the Western way. But there is the chance that my goods will be confiscated and my beautiful Jamilla, and my son, left destitute. Moreover,' he added, 'it is clear to me that I was . . . How do you say it in this country? That I was "set up", maneuvered into this position, though by whom I do not know . . .'

'Is there any chance,' asked January quietly, 'that your enemy

Sabid is behind this?' For a moment he had what felt like a memory, of Ayasha's voice – *So, do you think it was Sabid?* – and the ache of something lost . . . 'Where is Sabid?'

'Until two weeks ago, I had thought him in Germany.' On the other side of the cell, two of the other prisoners shouted at one another over whether or not someone named Violet was a whore; a third prisoner yelled for them to shut up. Down the corridor, in the white men's cell, a thin, frantic voice screamed: *Get 'em off me! Get 'em off me!* January wondered if Dante had ever spent time in a prison before writing about the sounds and smells of Hell.

'I have friends, naturally, who have kept me apprised of Sabid's movements. He has never regained his position at the Sultan's court, and he holds me responsible for this.' Hüseyin finished the cheese, drank the ginger beer thirstily and wiped the droplets from his mustache. 'Thus at least I do not need to fear him if it comes to trial. At the end of last month I received word that Sabid had left Munich; my correspondent knew not his destination. Believe me –' the Turk's mouth quirked sidelong – 'this is a thought that has crossed my mind as well. Yet it sounds as if my poor Noura had begun to plan her sins well before Sabid could have reached this country, if it was indeed he. And how would he have known of their intentions?'

January shook his head. 'And it seems very – very *elaborate* – for something which could be done as easily with a rifle some afternoon when you rode in the country.'

'This is so. As for the man Smith – yes, he could have been paid to arrange with me that the house would be cleared. Looking back on it, I should have been more on my guard. But he was not the first, you understand, to ask for a quiet audience with me. Nor the first to ask that no one be in the house to see him come and go.'

'Was the letter he sent you in English, or in French?'

'French. But that is something which anyone in the city could have told him of me,' he added, as if even in the intense gloom of the corridor he could see the thoughtful look that narrowed January's eyes. 'He was doubtless friends with any of a thousand businessmen here. What he said to me – that, within a year or two, cotton prices would recover and all men would clamor for loans to buy new land – is what everyone has said, at every party and *ziyafet* since I have come here.'

January was silent, turning this over in his mind. A man who disguised himself, to call on someone who had never seen him before . . . A letter written in French . . .

'What is your advice, my friend?' The prisoner wrapped the last of the cheese and bread in the newspaper, set them aside. To purchase the goodwill of his cell mates, January guessed. 'Think you that my son and Jamilla will be in danger, once I am gone and this *nuti* of a journalist can gain no more readers for his newspaper by slandering me?'

'I think they will be safe,' January replied slowly. 'They can take a smaller place in the Marigny quarter and live quietly. It is a district of foreigners: Germans and Russians and Italians. I will put myself at your lady's disposal, to help with arrangements. When public feeling has died down I'll introduce her to friends in the French Creole society, who can help her.'

'Good.' Hüseyin ran a hand over the graying stubble of his hair. 'Since I am to be taken away, I think it a better use of your time, my friend, if you would be so good, to look after *Sitt* Jamilla for me, and my son, and our servants who have been so faithful to us. After all, if this Mr Smith would cover his face with a beard and lie about his name to see me, he will hardly go to Constantinople to speak for me.'

'But he will send his affidavit,' said January firmly. 'As will the Lieutenant, regarding the distance from M'sieu Breche's balcony to the window. As will I, and my friend the fiddler Sefton, asking whether, if you had killed those unfortunate girls because of their theft, you would not have put the gold back in your chest. All these can you show your judge—'

'And my judge will say,' said Hüseyin with a bitter smile: '*Here is a man who wishes to keep the old ways of Islam strong in our Empire, rather than turn its rulership over to politicians who see only law, and not into the hearts of men.* Just as they say here: *Here is a man who does not worship the Christian God – he must have done this evil thing.* Or: *Here is a black man.* Or: *Here is a woman.* And of course there is a very good chance that my judge will not be able to read French. If Allah wishes me to survive, he will guard me and keep me, my friend, and all that the Sultan can do will fall

away. If Allah does not wish me to survive, all that *you* can do will
not preserve my life. Care for my family.'

When January descended the stair and crossed the Cabildo courtyard to the watch room, Shaw solemnly handed him a wrapped-up
bundle of umbrellas. 'Your friend at Hüseyin's house said he'd
need these.'

January took them with a nod. It was illegal for a man of African
descent to carry a weapon of any kind, even a walking stick. He
guessed, by the length and weight of the bundle, that it contained
a rifle, which he duly delivered to Hannibal at the house on the
Rue Bourbon. As the woman Lorette conducted January up the stair
to the second-floor parlor, he heard the sweet fantasias of Hannibal's
fiddle, drifting down from the floor above, and guessing what was
going on, he asked Lorette, 'Is the Lady Jamilla ill?'

'Yes, sir.' A great deal of her haughtiness of Monday was gone.
She looked tired and strained – and who would not, January
reflected, with rumors going around among the slaves, and the
near-certain knowledge that she, and they, would all be sold, to
God knew where, in a wretched market? 'Sweating, and sick, and
wanting him beside her, poor lady, just to talk – an' that nasty
beast Ghulaam sitting right there with his sword, like he didn't
trust either one of them . . . What the hell's the matter with those
people?'

January paused in the door of the parlor, and shook his head.
'What the hell's the matter with *any* people, m'am?'

The woman sighed, her wide mouth setting for a moment in
wry agreement. 'You got a point there, sir. I'll fetch him down.'

January returned to his own home to find Rose beneath the house
with two new 'visitors', a young man named Del and his wife
Peggy. Surprisingly, Peggy had a child with her, a girl just under
two. It wasn't usual for slaves to escape with children that small:
'—but our master gone off to New Iberia for three days, an' we
had the chance . . .'

'It's all right.' January prayed silently that it would in fact be
all right. 'I'll see what we can do.' With Baby John in the house
at least no one would question it, if a child's cries were heard . . .

'But the last thing we need,' he sighed as he undressed that night, 'is for people to be coming around here looking to collect the bounty on escaped slaves.'

'I shall speak to your sister in the morning,' promised Rose, taking off her spectacles, 'and have her put curses all over this house.' And, when January rolled his eyes: 'Some people are never satisfied.'

I'll have to write to Rose.

The thought came to January suddenly as he sat in the window watching the last of the thin spring sunlight on the rooftops of Paris. Birds skimmed above those mossy tiles. The sweet, clear question of the bells of St Séverin, answered by the reassuring bronze voice of Notre Dame.

Happiness at being home again, which made him want to weep.

Ayasha, sewing in the last of the daylight; she sat in the other side of the window's aperture, black hair bundled up carelessly into a crest on the crown of her head, stockinged feet tucked against his. Her gold thimble flickered against the silver needle, the delirious waterfall of blue-and-white silk that streamed from her lap to the floor. It was his turn to cook supper, and he'd been turning over in his mind what was in the cupboard and if he'd have to go down all seventy-two steps to Renan's to get bread—

—and then the thought came to him: *I'll have to write to Rose.*

Guilt and horror and a terrible confusion flooded over him as he realized he didn't even remember how long he'd been back in Paris, or whether he'd told Rose he was coming back here . . .

John! What about John?

The thought that he'd left his son – even for Ayasha – turned him sick. *How could any woman walk away from her child?* Ayasha had asked him as they returned home from the L'Ecolier house on that Sunday afternoon in 1827, and January knew she spoke true. So how could he have left Baby John? How could he have left Rose . . .?

I'll have to go back to them . . .

Yet the beauty of this place, this city – this world where white men didn't call him *tu* like a dog, and where he could walk any street in the city, and risk murder, perhaps, but not enslavement. The thought of leaving it twisted at his heart . . .

Someone knocked at the door. 'Uncle Ben?'

Waking was like dropping a yard down into darkness.

'Uncle Ben?'

Gabriel's voice. The panicked confusion of his dream left him disoriented. He felt Rose move beside him, heard the clack – saw the blinding spark – of flint striking—

From the parlor Zizi-Marie screamed, *'Uncle Ben!'* and there was the crunching rip of nails pulled from wood, the thunk of a window thrown open.

January came out of bed fast and silent, shot through the door into the parlor past his nephew, caught up a chair – thank God for Rose's ability to light a candle, to give him that fragment of golden light . . .

The rear gallery and the high walls of the yard kept any light from silhouetting the men in the French doors of the rear parlor, but one of them had a bullseye lantern. January charged them, flung the wooden chair full-force to disrupt their aim if they had a gun, caught up another chair and shouted.

The men turned and fled, back through the French door, out on to the gallery.

Hollers, cries, and a woman's voice yelling: 'Damn you snot-suckin' thieves!' Peggy and Del, from under the house.

January sprang through the French door – where the light of Rose's candle didn't penetrate, and the thieves had dropped their lantern – grabbed a handful of somebody's jacket. A fist scraped his jaw in the dark. He struck back, his blow connecting meatily with the side of someone's head. He tried to sling the man against the door jamb, but somebody kicked him hard in the knee and he stumbled, cursing. Peggy had not once stopped swearing nor repeated herself. Under the house, her little girl Alice screamed in terror.

Someone fell down the gallery steps to the yard, and Del yelled, 'God damn it!'

Footfalls rattled on the stair.

Then light as Peggy set up the fallen lantern and yanked off the slide. At the same moment Rose appeared in the French door with two more candles, backed up by Gabriel with the fire poker. *Thank God he didn't come out earlier and start swinging that thing.*

'I heard them on the gallery.' Zizi-Marie came out behind her brother, the quilt from her bed wrapped around her over her nightgown.

When Rose's school had had nearly a dozen students, they'd slept in a dormitory in the big old house's attic, but because of the cold, January had moved two of the beds downstairs, so that Gabriel could sleep in one of the former classrooms downstairs, and his sister in the other.

'Me, too,' agreed the boy.

'We heard 'em go up the steps,' corroborated Del as Peggy darted down the gallery steps – which, being old, creaked and clumped like a cord of wood dropped out of a cart – to fetch up tiny Alice. Inside the dark house behind them, January heard Baby John wailing. Rose shoved one of the candlesticks into his hand and hurried back inside.

'We thought for a second it was the patterollers,' Del went on – the term American slaves used for the bands of whites hired by the white planters to ride the roads by night in search of runaways, 'but then they didn't say nuthin', just started crunchin' at your shutters with a crowbar. Look, they dropped it here.'

He knelt, Peggy moving close behind with the dark-lantern, and picked up a short iron pry-bar that January was damn glad had been dropped in the confusion. It was *not* something he'd have wanted to catch between the eyes.

'And look here, they got your candlesticks!' Peggy straightened up, a pair of silver candlesticks in her hand. 'Damn friggin' thieves – and they'd got your money!' She strode a step further along the dark gallery, bent to pick up a wash-leather bag that jingled heavily with silver. 'Better check if they got anythin' else—'

'But they didn't get into the house,' protested Zizi-Marie.

'And those aren't your candlesticks, are they, Uncle Ben?' Gabriel took them: graceful work of the previous century, each embellished with a garland of tiny shells and roses. He held them close to the candle in January's hand. 'I've never seen anything like these in your house.'

In the rear parlor Rose had kindled all the after-supper reading-candles on the sideboard. January checked the hasp on the French door's shutter – it had indeed been forced with the crowbar – then re-entered, for the night was freezing. Zizi-Marie had already gone to build up the fire.

'But how'd they get your money?' Gabriel dumped the leather bag on to the table and brought the candles over. It was English coin, all of it silver crowns and half crowns, unusual in New Orleans where a great deal of business was still done in Mexican reales.

January said, with a curious prickling sensation on his scalp, 'That isn't my money.'

'I've heard of thieves breaking in to steal.' Rose came to look over his shoulder, Baby John in her arms. Once his mother's arms were around him the infant seemed perfectly content to have everyone in the household milling about at – January glanced at the clock – three in the morning. 'But never to give money away.'

'Haven't you?' said January softly. 'I have. And I think I need to find Shaw and hand this over to him – without getting anywhere *near* the Cabildo – without a moment's delay.'

TWENTY-TWO

January took Peggy, Del, and little Alice to spend the remainder of the night in the back room of a disreputable 'grocery' out beyond the 'back of town', on land which up until recently had been the Labarre Plantation. The term 'grocery', in much of Louisiana, also included gambling and the sale of alcohol on the premises, but of course *every* establishment in New Orleans included gambling and the sale of alcohol on the premises – and in Django's case it also included a back room where the black musicians who played the uptown American whorehouses could get together in the small hours, play music, drink beer, and talk about lazy nothing until they'd unwound enough to go home and sleep.

It was an unnerving trek in the misty blackness, but at this pre-dawn hour even the keelboat hoo-rahs from the Swamp had drunk themselves into oblivion, and in December one was reasonably safe from alligators. The City Guards, as Shaw had pointed out, numbered only twenty for this municipality and never came this far back from the river.

'I wouldn't ask this of you,' he told Django – who, as he'd suspected, they found still awake, sweeping the front gallery in the clammy, drifting fog. 'But I have reason to fear the house'll be searched.'

'We'll be movin' on in a day,' promised Del.

'Stay long as you please.' Django shrugged: tall and thin, gray-haired and covered with tribal scars. He had a voice that seemed to come from a Titan imprisoned at the bottom of a well. 'Make no difference to me.'

January spent the remainder of the night sleeping on one of the tables, with the silver candlesticks and the little sack of English coin under the rolled-up jacket he used for a pillow. Though the back room reeked of beer, and of the dried marijuana some of the country blacks smoked to relax, the old Yoruba kept a clean place, and his half-dozen cats were at least a guarantee against the rats that were to be found everywhere in this district. Not long after first light January woke from troubled dreams and tiptoed on to the back gallery, to wash in the freezing water from the barrel there.

This part of the Labarre lands had supposedly been divided into lots for development, but the bank crash had put paid to that scheme for the time being. The marshy ground was sheeted with ice, and the thinning fog mingled with the stinks of woodsmoke fires from the squatters' shacks built here and there among the woods that still mostly covered the area. A few hundred yards upriver lay the part of town that everyone called the Swamp – brothels, barrel houses, flop joints and gaming hells where the ruffians from the keelboats spent their money and their time. From Django's back gallery he could smell the untended privies. This area lay slightly deeper in the woods, on the edge of the genuine swamps – the *coprière* – and functioned as a hideout for runaways and a sanctuary for those who could afford nothing better.

Despite the cold, he stayed out on the gallery until Gabriel appeared, with the morning fully bright and the fog burned off but the silence of sleep still thick as a fairy's spell.

'They say at the Cabildo, Mr Shaw's gone down to Chalmette,' reported the boy, and he uncovered the food he'd brought with him: a crock of last night's rice and beans done up in a towel, with a couple of sausages and a double-handful of freshly-boiled shrimp thrown in on top. 'There's a revival meeting there. Protestants.' He shrugged dismissively. 'But one of those preachers says – I guess it's in the newspapers, too – that another one of 'em has been stealing money.'

January rolled his eyes. 'Would this be the Reverend Dunk? Never mind,' he added as his nephew shook his head in ignorance. 'Doesn't matter. Would you tell your Aunt Rose I'm all right so far, and that I'm going down to Chalmette – and that I promise I'll come back and get her crock back from Django as soon as all this is straightened out?'

'Doesn't matter.' Gabriel grinned brightly. 'She gave me a cracked old one, in case it doesn't come back. There's banana leaves in the bottom, to keep it from leaking.'

'Your Aunt Rose,' said January, 'is a wise woman.'

I have to write to Rose . . .

The words echoed briefly in his mind, and because of them he tore a page from his notebook, and with a stub of pencil wrote: *A virtuous woman is a crown to her husband – her price is far above rubies.*

He folded it up and wondered: *And what is the price of a virtuous husband? I have brought her nothing but trouble . . .*

'Tell her to be careful,' he said. 'And that I love her. I'll be at your Aunt Dominique's tonight—'

'Does Aunt Minou know this?'

'Not yet,' said January, 'but you're going to tell her on your way home. And you tell your Aunt Rose that I hope to be home tonight.'

'You know what's going on?' asked the boy as he turned to go. 'Or who those men were?'

'I don't know who they were,' said January. 'But I think that – like that preacher down in Chalmette that Mr Shaw's gone to see – somebody's trying to get me thrown in jail.'

He left the crock of food for Del and Peggy – less a percentage for his own breakfast – and made his way cautiously riverward through the bright chill sun of the new morning. Though it filled him with uneasiness to do so, he kept upriver of Canal Street. Thanks to the enmity between the Americans and the old French Creole aristocracy, these days this portion of New Orleans had a completely separate police force and city council from the French town, and they would almost certainly have heard nothing of any charge against him. He was stopped twice by City Guards with demands to show his Free Papers, but evidently nobody was looking for him for stealing silver candlesticks and a sack of English money just yet. The loot, distributed in a money belt under his clothing and bound rather painfully to the calves of his legs, felt like it was burning a hole in his flesh, and he knew that if he were caught with it on him, it was going to be impossible to explain. But he couldn't think of anywhere safe to leave it.

Damn them, he thought, not knowing who *they* were . . . *Damn them, damn them.* He felt as if every man he passed – and as he neared the river front he passed hundreds – could hear his heart pounding, could smell the guilty sweat that drenched his face despite the day's brisk chill.

He remembered the way Breche had giggled, when he recounted

how he'd casually driven the habit of opium like a barbed fish-hook into an innocent woman's flesh, just so that he could meet his mistress undetected.

Was there more to it, he wondered as he walked, *than a concoction of stupid romantic dreams?*

He recalled old Philippe Breche, shouting into the back of the shop at his son: *See if you can get it right this time . . .*

How far would almost a hundredweight of gold pieces go, in buying the young man his freedom?

A romantic ass, or a malicious schemer? Breche was certainly, with Burton Blodgett's help, making damned certain that Hüseyin Pasha wasn't going to start hunting for his stolen money in the apothecary shop down the street.

January was almost certain there had been two men who'd broken into the house. One chance in two, then, that Breche would bear the mark of the struggle on his face.

Old Philippe Breche was short, January recalled. Stocky, but shorter enough than Hüseyin Pasha that the Turk would almost certainly have commented on it. Otherwise, he would be a good candidate for Mr Smith: it would make sense that he'd disguise himself behind false whiskers and spectacles, to conceal a face that his victim might see on Rue Bourbon any day.

Had it been coincidence, that Smith had requested a meeting on the Sunday night after the two girls had disappeared? A meeting that virtually guaranteed that his host would have no witnesses to speak for his actions and whereabouts, alone in that great house on that rainy night?

Yet he was almost willing to bet that Breche knew nothing more about the events of Friday than he'd said: that he hadn't been the one who'd bribed Sillery . . . Possibly, that he had known nothing of the gold. If Noura was clever – 'troublesome' – she might well not have told her lover of it, particularly if she planned to break with him as soon as she could find a better protector.

And where did the pliant Karida fit in?

Buzzards circled overhead as he skirted the cattle pens that lined the river; cold wind blew across the water. The girls' faces returned to him, waxy and stiff and beginning to discolor.

Fabled for their beauty by men who'd never seen them, who'd offered Hüseyin money for them sight unseen . . .

Why bring Karida in on it? Or had she found out Noura's plans and simply included herself? Had she, like Shamira, only wanted a life where she could choose?

And who among us has that?

He turned the facts that he knew, the surmises and possibilities, this way and that, like a puzzle box in his mind.

Sillery knows Jerry – he'd seen them at the same church. *He'll have a copy of the key to the door into the Pavot property.*

Was it Sillery's plan from the start? The slave was certainly in a position to take the girls anywhere in the dead small hours of Friday night, though it left the problem of how he'd gotten them back into the livery yard sufficiently early on Sunday night for them to be thrown out of the window at ten. Yet the man was clever and had his two fellow slaves – Jones and Delilah – to act for him.

But to implicate Sillery, thought January, *I need unshakeable proof. Or I will be destroying the lives of those children for nothing.*

Poucet's face flickered through his mind, and Chatoine's – brave as little soldiers. Poucet had died in the cholera epidemic, fourteen years old, a few weeks before Ayasha's death. And Carnot the painter had been killed on a barricade, in the revolt that had finally thrust the Bourbon kings again from their mismanaged throne. The happiness he had felt in his dream twisted at him, like the thorned tentacles of some monstrous sea-creature, wrapped around his heart.

He reached the Tchoupitoulas Road, made his way downstream along the batture. The river was high, the pebbled gray stretch of beach that lay below the levee narrowed to a walkway of a few yards. Above Canal Street it was all cotton: in ordinary years he would barely have been able to thread his way through the unloading bales. Now most of the wharves had only one boat, or stood empty. At five cents a pound, sale on the wharves wouldn't cover the cost of shipping it from Missouri. Already – though it wasn't yet ten in the morning – many of the stevedores had given up and crossed the road to the taverns.

January found the man he was looking for on the levee below the Place des Armes, where the fishermen put in from the Gulf. As he came at last below Canal Street he moved more carefully, watchful though he guessed that if the Guards were on the wharves at all, they wouldn't be looking for an accused burglar, but for the gangs that stole cargoes.

Natchez Jim was at Auntie Zozo's coffee stand, under the brick arcades of the market, a sturdy handsome man with the features that January identified as Wolof ancestry – as his own father had been – and graying hair braided into dozens of plaits: *couettes*, they were called in the country. 'Hell, I had no downriver cargoes three days now,' said Jim, when January spoke to him. 'Barely pays me, to bring in wood into town. So sure, I can take you down Chalmette.' He shrugged. 'If those boys of mine –' he nodded at the two youths who helped work the oars – 'had anything better to do with their time, I couldn't pay 'em.'

The boys finished their coffee, grinning, and followed them down to where Jim's wood boat was tied. As they rowed into the current that swept past the dark-hulled ocean ships docked down-river, January relaxed at last. The brown opaque water widened between the *Black Goose* and the shore. Under the bright-blue sky with its drifting masses of clouds, the town seemed small and very low, for all the growth that the newspapers bragged. Houses of pastel stucco, green and gold and pink, a little faded against the dark-green monotony of trees. Brick warehouses, cotton presses, mills – a scattered line of newer wooden dwellings, where one planter or another had sold off his cane fields to the immigrants who crowded to this fever-ridden city, in the hopes they'd make a fortune or at least a living.

In the hopes they'd forget the world they'd left behind?

January's mind caught painfully at the wink of an image – gold thimble, silver needle, silk of blue and white – that surfaced for an instant and then vanished, as all around them torn-off branches, whole tree-trunks, chunks of earth held together by grass, bobbed and surfaced and vanished in the thick brown floodwater forever.

When they got close to the low white wooden buildings that marked the landing at Chalmette, some fifteen miles downriver, January pulled up the legs of his trousers and untied the silver candlesticks from his shins, then dragged up the money belt from beneath his shirt. 'Well, my, my, my, what have we here?' inquired Jim, and January shook his head.

'It ain't how it looks.'

'Not going to contribute to the salvation of souls?' Jim's eyebrows quirked up 'til they almost vanished under his blue cotton bandanna. 'Not going to assist the Reverend Promise in the great work of guiding toward the Light them that's lost in the dark swamps of Popery? Ben, I'm surprised at you.'

'Where's Promise got his tent pitched?'

''Bout a dozen rods back of the levee, on the other side of the trees.' Jim leaned on the steering oar, the heavy current fighting them every foot to the little wharf. 'You go up the path, you'll hear them singing, if you can call it singing . . .'

Further than a dozen rods back of the levee, reflected January, there wasn't anything *but* swamp. As he climbed the path his eye sought the place on the rise above him where he and the other members of the free colored militia had crouched behind redoubts made of piled cotton-bales, waiting for the British soldiers to come out of the fog.

If Ayasha's death seemed to him like something that had happened yesterday, that night march, that cold clammy waiting in the darkness, felt as if it had happened to someone else. To some other boy of twenty who'd clutched his musket in numb fingers and had wondered: *Do I have what it takes, to play a man's part . . .?*

Who WAS that? A boy who went to Paris, vowing never to return to the land where he'd been born a slave.

He came to the top of the rise and heard the singing.

My faith looks up to Thee,
Thou Lamb of Calvary,
Savior divine;
Now hear me when I pray,
Take all my sin away,
O let me from this day
Be wholly Thine!

Men and women milled around the big white tent pitched at the edge of the trees. Monday's rain had left the ground a clayey soup; everything was smirched and spotted with red-gold muck. Others moved back and forth from the smaller marquee set nearby, where trestle tables had been put up. Nearly as many tables again stood in the open air. For slaves, presumably . . . There were at least as many blacks as whites in evidence. Was the seating going to be separated in Heaven as well?

As he came closer, a man's voice boomed from within the tent, passionate and theatrical:

'If it isn't enough for your hearts to know that you have kindled the fire of salvation in nameless souls who but for you – but for your loving help! – would have been damned to the outer darkness, let me ask you this, then: of what use is that silver that you cling to with such desperation? Of what use is the gold that binds you like a chain and drags you down? Jesus said: *My son asked you for bread, and you gave him a stone* – no, not a stone, but a brick of solid gold! What father among you, what mother who sits there listening to me, if your child begged you for bread, would give him a brick?'

The voices rose behind him, not singing now but humming, a formless sweetness like wind flowing over empty country.

January stepped through the door of the tent – careful to choose the one around which the slaves clustered. At a guess, if he tried to enter by the other opening he'd be pushed out by a white salvation-seeker. After the clammy chill outside, the tent was warm, and every bench that formed a semicircle around the makeshift pulpit was packed, mostly with women. Whites and blacks sat crowded elbow-to-elbow, swaying and moaning as they listened. Behind the pulpit, more worshippers – white as well as black – were on their feet, eyes closed or half-closed, bodies rippling in a sort of snake-like, private dance.

'Look at the people who hang on to their silver and their gold!' Promise swept one powerful arm, as if to conjure such sinners before his listeners. When January had heard him speak on Tuesday evening, his voice had been soft and refined. Now it was pitched to carry, with the clear tenor power of a trumpet. 'Look at the aristocrats, at the bankers, at the wealthy of the world, so blinded by the dazzle of gems that they cannot see the path that leads to the gate of Salvation!'

'Dear God, save me!' wailed a voice from the 'anxious bench', down in front, the bench where a dozen women sat quivering and writhing as if in pain.

And most notably, January observed, the plump black-clothed figure of the Widow Redfern.

'God, save me!' She jerked to her feet as if dragged, flung out her arms. 'I have sinned—!'

'Do you truly want to be saved?' Promise sprang down from the pulpit, graceful as a dark-robed angel, and seized her by the hands, drew her to his breast like a lover. His long, dark curls hung into his eyes, dripping with sweat. One dancer behind him burst into tears; two others began to spin, their arms held out and their huge, bell-shaped skirts swirling like enormous flowers.

'Your lips say one thing, but what is in your heart? Oh, my dearest sister, what does your aching heart say? Will you be saved? Or are you like the Rich Young Man of the Bible, who came to Jesus wanting to be saved, but then could not let go of his wealth?'

'I want to be saved—!'

For some reason January remembered the girl in the Convent of St Theresa, radiant with self-sacrifice and the exultation of being the absolute center of attention.

'The rich care not if a man is a Papist or an Infidel, even,' shouted Promise to the congregation, 'so long as he's rich and they think they can get some of his money! They're perfectly happy to welcome into their houses bankers who've cheated every man in this city out of the wherewithal to feed his family! Murderers who start each morning by spitting on the blessed name of Christ—'

January whispered, 'Damn it,' and made his way across to Abishag Shaw, who stood, arms folded, at the back of the tent. The Kentuckian was always ridiculously easy to find in a crowd because, other than January himself, he was the tallest man in the room.

Shaw raised his eyebrows at the sight of him. Before he could speak a word January took the Lieutenant's hand, slapped the bag of English coins into it, then shoved a silver candlestick into each of the Kentuckian's coat pockets.

'You looking for those?'

'Well,' remarked Shaw, and he spat into the trampled grass along the edge of the tent, 'somebody sure is. An' they did say as how you'd be the man who had 'em.'

'I thought so. Someone tried to break into my house at three o'clock this morning. My nephew and I managed to repel them before they got inside, but we found these on the back gallery, dropped in the scuffle. I think I blacked the eye of one of our visitors . . .'

'Oh, that you did.' Shaw emptied a few coins into his palm, turned them with his dirty thumb, and nodded. Presumably, thought

January, the reason that English coins had been selected for the booty: fairly uncommon, but easily identifiable. 'He come into the Cabildo this mornin' with the story of how you'd broke into his house, robbed him an' struck him, an' him a white man . . .'

'Was it Breche?'

'The apothecary?' Shaw raised his brows. 'Not hardly. Feller name of Tremmel. Owns a cotton press an' a couple boats.'

'*Who*?' January stared, taken aback. 'I've never heard of the man in my life.'

'Well, he's heard of you. He didn't just say a great big tall black feller broke into his house, neither. He said he knowed you, from seein' you at the house of a friend a year ago, teachin' that friend's daughter piano.'

'Who was the friend?'

'Franklin Culver.'

January was silent. He had indeed taught Charis Culver piano for three years.

'So less'n you can produce two white men who'll swear they was with you at three o'clock this mornin',' Shaw went on gently, 'it is my duty to place you under arrest.'

TWENTY-THREE

January said – a little uncertainly – 'That's ridiculous.' But his heart beat faster and he felt disoriented, as if, standing on some high place, he had felt the floor beneath him crack. From childhood he had known, and feared, the power of white men before the law.

It was assumed by the courts – as it was assumed by nearly every white man January had ever met – that a black man would lie.

'I know it is.' Shaw spat again. 'But that ain't my business. An' that ain't my decision. They's white men all over this town who'll testify to your character—'

A man entering the tent behind January thrust him aside with a violence that almost rocketed him into Shaw's arms, and a voice like thundering Jove boomed, '*Whoremaster*!'

Down at the front of the tent, the Reverend Promise – with one arm locked like an iron band around the Widow Redfern's ample waist and one hand gripping her wrist as he wrestled with (presumably) the Devil inside her – looked up in shock.

His face changed as he recognized, in the tent doorway, the Reverend Micajah Dunk.

'Antichrist!' he shouted, and he shoved the widow behind him for protection.

Dunk stormed down the aisle flanked by a flying squad of his own beefy parishioners, his dark brow contracted into a storm of righteous wrath. 'Beelzebub!'

'Spawn of Mammon!'

'Micajah!' sobbed Mrs Redfern, and she held out her arms. Her black-veiled bonnet had fallen from her head in her struggles with her inner sinfulness, her blondish-gray hair tumbled in thin ribbons over her shoulders, like that of an elderly princess welcoming St George. The Revered Promise seized her as she tried to step forward and again interposed his body between her and her former mentor.

'I charge you in the name of the Father, and the Son, and the Holy Spirit, to release the hold thou hast upon this woman—!'

'Behold how Satan will quote the Scripture unto his own ends!'

Promise turned to the congregation, swept his arm like Moses commanding the sea to part. 'Wilt thou stand by and suffer the Servant of the Lord to be mocked?'

A dozen men leaped to their feet and charged like warriors at the Reverend Dunk and his disciples, tripping over the feet of others on the benches on their way.

Shaw said, 'Well, I will be dipped,' and plunged down the aisle into the fray.

Though he knew that Rose would never forgive him for leaving before he learned the outcome of the battle, January turned promptly and left the tent.

Natchez Jim and his cousins looked up from their domino game as January strode quickly down the path from the levee. 'You find your man?'

'I did indeed.' January got into the boat. 'And returned to him the goods to be taken back to their rightful owner. Now I'd appreciate it if you and your boys would forget you ever saw me.'

'We ever saw who?' Jim grinned and put a long, stout pole into January's hands. 'We'll just say it was a little bird, helped us get this bull-bitch boat back up to town.'

It was, as January had feared, many hours of poling and bushwhacking – literally pulling the boat along by means of overhanging branches and half-submerged tree-trunks – before the *Black Goose* returned to New Orleans. Sometimes there was enough wind to put up the wood boat's sail, but even so, only by steering in close along the banks could they make headway against the ferocious currents of the river's winter rise. He was exhausted and famished by the time they reached the levee by the French Market again, and chilled by the sweat drying into his clothes. Jim and his crew joked with him and laughed that they'd make a river man of him yet ('My wife will kill you if you do . . .'), but January noticed they walked with him along the levee as far as the bottom of Rue Dumaine through the gathering dusk, looking in all directions about them for the City Guards.

And among the dark hulls of the ships drawn up to the deep-water wharves there, a red flash of flag caught January's eye as the river breeze lifted it . . .

The star and crescent banner of the Sultan.

January whispered, 'Shit.'

He said the word again when he came within a hundred feet of the house of Hüseyin Pasha. In spite of the renewed vèvès that Olympe written over the doors and shutters last night, men and women loitered on the corner across the street. The men were of the stevedore type, mostly white but with one or two blacks among them, whose clothes and bearing, as much as their more pronouncedly African features, made him think they might well be American-born. The women weren't the dockside drabs he'd seen Tuesday night, but working women in shabby calico, the kind of women who took in washing or sewing in order to feed their families while their men worked on the docks.

He felt their eyes on him as he crossed the street to the house door, pounded on it with his fist.

After a long time – someone must have looked down from one of the upstairs windows – an eye he recognized as Hannibal's appeared in the judas, and he heard the clank of the lock, the scrape of bolts drawn back.

He stepped inside quickly, conscious of two men and a woman crossing the street after him as Hannibal slammed the door behind him and shot the bolts. Someone pounded on the door as January followed the fiddler down the passageway to the courtyard. 'The Watch have been by twice,' reported Hannibal as they ascended the stairs to the gallery above. Looking down into the shadowy courtyard January saw Nehemiah briefly appear in the kitchen doorway, carrying what looked like the handle of an ax or shovel. Perkin the groom came out of the stable to see who was in the court, then disappeared again. January wondered if the hasp on the side door of the stable, so many times unscrewed and reattached, would hold against a determined attack.

'Breche was on the corner earlier,' Hannibal went on, 'talking like he was running for office. I think the Watch told him he was in danger of arrest, because he hasn't returned, but everyone's been back and forth to the shop.'

January cursed in Arabic. Ghulaam, standing guard outside the door of the parlor, said, '*Âmîn, hâbib*,' as they passed through into the parlor.

Jamilla, properly dressed and veiled, sat on the Western-style sofa, but the visible hand-breadth of her face was pallid and beaded with sweat. The boy Nasir stood beside her, a look of agony on his round, snub-nosed face. As Hannibal and January entered, the boy asked in French, 'When it gets dark they'll come, won't they, sirs?' He cast a quick glance at the swift twilight already gathered in the windows. 'When the Watch are all down at the taverns?'

'I think so, yes. *Night's black agents to their preys do rouse* . . . and I'm sure they won't make a move until the house is actually broken into. Can't arrest people for standing on the street corner, can you? Not whites, anyway. You haven't seen Shaw by any chance, Benjamin?'

'He's still down in Chalmette,' said January grimly, 'as far as I know. At least, no steamboat passed us from that direction. But I suspect he'll have his hands full. My Lady, with your permission—' He took Jamilla's hand, felt the pulse of her wrist. 'How have you fared?'

'Mr Sefton warned me that it would be difficult.' He could see the attempt at a smile in her eyes. 'All these years I have taken care to keep away from *afyûn* – my mother, and my father's concubine, were much given to it, you understand – and now to be caught that way by a Christian. I'm sorry,' she said at once. 'I am weary. I should not have spoken ill of your faith.'

'Having come from a Christian gathering this afternoon,' sighed January as he brought the candle close to look at her eyes, 'I have no words with which to refute you, Lady.' And he recounted, briefly, the events of the day, which had started in the small hours, and was glad that the account of the riot in the revival tent drew a whispered laugh from her.

'Who is this Tremmel?' asked the Lady, when January had finished. 'And why does he accuse you? Might he be this Smith, that came to see my husband—?'

'I thought of that,' said January. 'Because it's clear to me that Mr Smith – as *Smith* – doesn't really exist. Like some other people I could mention –' he glanced trenchantly at Hannibal's bleached and recolored hairline – 'he was invented . . .'

He stopped as a thought struck him.

He looked back at Jamilla, and at the boy beside her.

'He was invented to get something from my father?' asked Nasir. 'Like a spirit, called into being from smoke to accomplish a task?'

January was silent. He felt as if he should be shocked, but he felt no shock. Only a kind of irritation at himself, such as he felt sometimes when he'd been searching all over the house for his hat or his gloves or a piece of music, only to find it in the obvious place.

'No,' he said at length, aware that Jamilla and the boy were both looking at him, troubled by his silence. 'No, I don't think Tremmel is Smith. In fact, I've just realized who Smith might be. It doesn't help us tonight, and I'm not sure how much it will help your husband—'

'It will not help him,' demanded Suleiman, from a chair beside the fire, 'if a man can be made to testify that he was with my master at the moment that Noura and Karida were thrown – were *seen* to be thrown – from the window?'

'Thrown by whom?' January, still kneeling by the sofa, half-turned to face the tutor. 'We've already established that Breche couldn't have seen the face of the man who did it. It could as easily have been you or Ghulaam.'

'We were at the theater! And may Allah curse the night that we went.'

'Allah has already cursed that night,' said January softly. 'The court will say that if it was not your master, it was one of you acting upon his orders. The unfortunate girls had been dead a day already. This is a big house, and everyone in town knows it's a big house. They will say: *Big enough to keep the girls locked somewhere without anyone seeing or knowing that they were dead.* If I can find—'

In the deeps of the house, pounding started, fists hammering on the door downstairs. Ra'eesa, who had sat silently at her mistress' side, ran to the front window to look down, and Hannibal dragged her back as a brick crashed through the glass of the window she opened. The sound of glass breaking in another room told them other bricks had been thrown. January said, 'Damn it,' and Jamilla spoke quickly to Suleiman, who strode to the parlor's French doors and yanked the shutters closed against a sudden hail of bricks.

Suleiman shouted something, and January – already at the next window, leaning out to pull the shutters to – heard Ghulaam's light tread on the gallery. A moment later, as January leaned out to shut the next set of shutters, he saw the eunuch doing the same from the study next door.

'Better bar them,' said January as he and the tutor strode through the dining room to the garçonnière wing. 'One man can boost another up on to the balcony.'

'I have commanded it, yes.' By the time they and Ghulaam had shuttered up every window of the schoolroom and young Nasir's bedroom, and returned to the parlor, Ra'eesa had lit candles against the thick gloom and was trying to talk Jamilla – by the sound of it – into going up to her bedroom.

The Lady shook her head, pale as ash.

Outside, feet clattered on the gallery stair. Lorette, her voice frantic, called in, 'Mr Suleiman, they're beatin' on the side door of the stable!'

'*Ahku sharmoota!*' Suleiman strode to the corner of the room, where two six-foot, silver-mounted blunderbusses stood: they must have been eighty years old. 'Lorette, get Bette and Desirée in here.'

'Get the gold,' commanded January. 'Put it in a sack, or a couple of pillowcases. Hannibal, do you think you can talk Maggie Valentine into raising up that ladder from her yard? Bribe her if necessary – you can certainly bribe Sillery. Have you rope, Suleiman?'

'In the stable.' The tutor plunged through the door, and January heard his feet on the stair.

Desirée, the youngest of the maids, whispered, 'They wouldn't hurt M'am, surely . . .'

'Don't you think it,' returned January. 'Three years ago when a mob broke into the Lalaurie house over on Rue Royale, the coachman tried to go back into the house and was beaten to death. Hannibal, with me—'

He caught up the rifle Shaw had provided, and they descended the stairs at a run.

'Have you ever climbed down a rope before?' January asked. 'Wrap it around your arms, put a turn around your body, brace your feet on the wall—'

'I have descended from enough windows on knotted bed-sheets,' replied the fiddler with dignity, 'to understand the principles.'

'Well, you'll have to work fast, or the mob may turn on Valentine as well.'

'Not if they have a well-stocked house to loot, they won't. *Pecuniae obediunt omnia* . . . . When I compounded with the despicable Mr Gyves to get another three months' grace on the late lamented Valentine's loan, Mags swore she owed me whatever I cared to ask of her, so I think hiding space in the lofts isn't too unreasonable a boon. And you, sir,' Hannibal added, turning abruptly in his tracks to face Nasir, who had followed them down the stair and across the court, 'belong upstairs with your mother—'

From inside the stable came the crashing of what sounded like hammers or crowbars on the door, and the terrified neighing of horses. A single lantern burned above the stalls and showed January Perkin the groom and Iskander the Turkish cook as they struggled to hammer wood wrenched free from the sides of the stalls against the small outer door. Nehemiah said, 'What about the horses, sir?' turning to Hannibal as the only white man present.

'They'll be stolen,' said January simply. 'And we'll give the police a description to get them back. They're not more important than anyone's life.'

'If they break in,' added Nasir firmly, 'get the lantern out of here, so it doesn't fall and set the place on fire.'

'Rope,' said Hannibal, and at the same moment January saw a coil of it on the wall. He caught it down, tossed it to the fiddler, who seized Nasir firmly by the hand and dashed across the court-yard again.

'Hold them as long as you can,' said January to the two stablemen. 'If they do break in –' there was another crash, and even in the near-darkness he could see the door jerk on its hinges – 'don't fight. Hide in the dark and slip out as quick as you can. We're getting Madame and the Turkish servants out over the roof. They're the only ones who'll be in danger.'

'Yes, sir.' Perkin looked uncertain about taking orders from a black man instead of a white one, but bowed to the voice of authority.

January stepped out into the courtyard, now deep in darkness.

A little light filtered down from the house gallery above, but it was only because he was watching the roofline of the kitchen that he saw Hannibal, a few minutes later, make his scrambling way from the third-floor gallery across the steep slates to the kitchen chimney. He put his head into the stable again, said to Iskander, 'You'd better get up there and help them collect anything of value they want to save.'

The cook – an immensely dignified gentleman with a long mustache – said, '*Ibn-kalb*,' handed January the hammer he'd used to pound the re-enforcing planks into place, and went.

'Where the hell are the City Guards?' Nehemiah emerged from the stable, panic in his voice.

'Probably on their way. But I'm guessing they think Hüseyin Pasha is as guilty as everybody else in this town does, between that idiot Breche and those damn journalists.'

'I swear he didn't harm them girls – damn!' he added as there was another rending crash in the dark of the stables. 'I'm just hopin' those fools don't fire the place, nor hurt the horses.'

'When they break in, you slip out past them and head for the Cabildo. You, too,' he added, to the kitchen boy who'd come running up, butcher-knife in hand. 'You'll probably meet the Watch on the way. Damn it,' January added, at the sound of another crash, and he glanced back up at the kitchen roof. Still no sign of Hannibal. Mobs had always frightened him – perhaps the reason he'd never been a wholehearted participant in the impassioned rhetoric that had been so freely slung around in the cellar of the *Chatte Blanche* and a dozen other illegal political gathering-places in Paris in the late twenties. Old Lucien Imbot had remembered very well the crowds of Parisian poor storming in triumph down the Rue St-Antoine with human heads impaled before them on pikes, and the ballet mistress Marguerite Scie, as a little girl, had been in La Force prison when a mob had decided that the Revolutionary Tribunal was too slow about bringing enemies of the Revolution to trial.

Even less did he trust mobs of whites in Louisiana.

Now he darted across the courtyard, climbed the gallery stair. The worst thing he could do, he knew, was use the rifle he carried: white men would kill him for that. But he guessed that the Lady Jamilla, at least, stood in danger of being beaten to death, and probably the boy Nasir also, as well as any of the Muslim servants who would try to protect them.

He heard another, louder crash from the stables, and a man emerged into the darkness, dashed across the court toward the stair. At the last second January recognized Nehemiah as the coachman clattered up the steps to his side, a piece of lumber held like a club in his hand.

The next moment men poured from the stable door and across the court toward the stair.

Behind him he heard Nasir's voice in the parlor cry out something – some sharp order – in Romanli; was aware of the women retreating up the gallery stairs to the third floor. *They'll be cut off*, thought January as Nehemiah reached him, turned at bay with his makeshift weapon. Suleiman joined them, a silver-mounted musket in hand, and Louis the American cook.

Damn it, if anybody fires they'll kill us before we can reload . . .

A shot cracked out, and the first man to reach the bottom of the stairs crumpled, clutching his arm and screaming. The next four men tripped over him.

From the kitchen roof, Abishag Shaw's voice called out, 'Next man gets it 'tween the eyes.'

The last of the twilight in the sky silhouetted him, tall and thin beside the kitchen chimney. Two smaller shapes flanked him, just emerging up the ladder from the livery. Lanterns flickered in the blue darkness of the courtyard below as City Guards came in through the stables and the carriageway. Enough light, thought January, to enable Shaw to make good his threat. He'd seen the man hit his target at a hundred yards in starlight.

From behind him, Suleiman touched his shoulder. 'From my master's bedroom at the end of the gallery, a stair goes down to the shop below,' he murmured. 'Here is the key—' It was pressed into January's hand. 'Return it to my Lady when you can.'

January handed him the rifle and the hammer that he still carried, and touched his hat brim. 'Give her my thanks,' he said. 'Tell Hannibal, if the Lady needs a place for herself, her son, and her maid tonight, to take them to my house, which is not far from here.'

'*Shukran.*' The tutor bowed. '*Assalamu alaikum, wa rahmatullahi.*'

'*Walaikum assalam.*'

January strode soundlessly along the gallery to the French doors at the end and was out of the building and walking innocently up Rue St-Philippe before Shaw and his minions finished arresting the rioters in the courtyard.

TWENTY-FOUR

From Dominique's beautiful little cottage on Rue Dumaine, January sent a message to Rose. He didn't think Shaw would actually be watching his house, but he wouldn't put anything past the Kentuckian when the man was on the scent of a wrongdoer – even one whom he himself, personally, didn't think had done any wrong.

So when Rose came to Dominique's the following morning, she was duly dressed in a shirt and pants belonging to Gabriel, with a wide-brimmed hat pulled on over her hair. For her part, Dominique was fully prepared to receive her and lend her one of her own dresses, since Shaw would immediately suspect any tall youth emerging from the January residence with a bundle of petticoats and corset, and follow accordingly.

'Honestly, p'tit, you're worse than your nephew.' Dominique shook her head disapprovingly as she considered the five candidate costumes which her maid had brought down from the attic, arranged tastefully on the bed. 'You're going to get yourself into real trouble one day – and Rose is just as bad . . . What do you think of the pink delaine? Rose always looks so attractive in pink, but the sleeves are *terribly* out of date – what can have possessed me to make up anything so *hideous* as those great silly pumpkins? And that gauze is simply absurd . . .'

Having heard his younger sister's ecstasies three years ago on the subject of the gauze-covered sleeves whose globular tops measured nearly two yards in circumference, January wisely held his peace.

Instead he said, 'I *am* in real trouble, Minou. Or I will be unless I get to the bottom of who it is who's trying to make the world think that Hüseyin Pasha killed his two poor concubines.'

'Maman says that a Turk would think nothing of killing wives who had offended him.'

'And Maman has spoken to exactly how many Turks in her lifetime?'

'Do you like the straw-yellow? Oh, no, the lace is loose – if

I've told Thèrése once I've told her a thousand times . . . How about the gray?' She lifted several acres of translucent skirt in slender fingers: like an adorable bronze Aphrodite, but kinder than that capricious goddess ever was. 'I can't *think* why I bought it, gray doesn't suit me in the *least*, but then it doesn't suit Rose either . . . Oh, but if you put a pink tignon with it . . . Thèrése, run back up to the attic and bring down my other gray, and the brown sprigged challis . . . Darling, *everyone* knows how jealous the Turks are. But it did seem to me that it was an *extremely* stupid thing to do. Yet who else would have? Who *knew* them, who could have gotten into the house? I mean, people generally don't go around killing total strangers, do they?'

'That,' said January, 'is exactly what I'm trying to—'

'You sent fo' me, suh?' Rose appeared in the doorway that communicated, through baby Charmian's room, with the rear yard – since no tall, skinny *sang melée* boy would have been permitted to enter the house through the French door that opened from Dominique's bedroom on to the street. She made a somewhat more Shakespearean boy than Maggie Valentine did, being taller enough than Gabriel that his borrowed trousers showed off slender ankles. But, like Maggie, she was thin, and she took care to slouch and scratch her bottom and use the slurry *mo kiri mo vini* French of the cotton patch and cane field.

'*Who saw Cesario, ho!*' quoted January solemnly.

'I hear tell you wants to burn down a house, suh?'

'Only burgle it.'

'P'tit!' said Dominique, shocked. 'If that's why you asked me to invite Bernadette Metoyer for tea this afternoon . . .'

Rose put on her spectacles and removed the hat. 'Well, that's no fun. As far as I know I wasn't followed, Ben . . . Oh, Minou!' she exclaimed, her eye lighting on the dresses as Thèrése brought in another wicker hamper and began laying out more over every piece of furniture in sight. 'How beautiful! We shall arouse suspicion instantly.'

'Silly.' Dominique smiled with pleasure at the compliment. Had she been a pigeon, reflected January, amused, she would have fluffed her feathers. 'I've had those for just *ages*.'

'Well, we *shall* arouse suspicion,' amplified Rose thoughtfully, 'since I'm four inches taller than you.'

'Oh, it won't take but a *moment* to let the hem down . . .'

January didn't comment on the length of time it would take to re-sew some twenty feet of seam, but merely asked, 'Did you bring the rocket?'

Rose produced it from her trouser pocket. 'The casing is tinned iron,' she explained as January took it gingerly. 'What the British Navy puts up beef in for long voyages. There should be no danger whatever of actually setting Bernadette's house afire—'

'*Rose!*' protested Dominique.

'—but smoke should come out in clouds.'

'No one is ever going to *speak* to me in this town again!'

'If I'm correct about what happened – at least in the study – at Hüseyin Pasha's house last Sunday night,' said January, 'I think we can count on no word getting back to Bernadette about the smoke in her parlor curtains.'

Bernadette Metoyer and her sisters arrived an hour or so after that. It was not a long walk – the three women shared a yellow stucco cottage across Rue Esplanade from January's house. January and Rose retired in silence to the nursery as Dominique rustled into her bedroom to open its French door to her guests – Rose now respectably attired in Dominique's second-best pink delaine frock and looking as if she'd never evaded possible police surveillance in the guise of a boy in her life. Bernadette, January was interested to observe through the smallest crack in the nursery door, had on another dress that he'd never seen before – amber silk shot with darker notes. Ten years of living with a dressmaker had forever heightened his awareness of what people wore and what it meant. Ayasha could pinpoint a man's income by the lace of his wife's collar.

Babette and Virginie also wore new shawls.

Speculation was rife in the New Orleans demi-monde as to whether the fourth sister – Eulalie – had, despite her marriage to a bank clerk, also been involved with Bernadette's former patron, the banker Hubert Granville, but none of the Metoyer sisters were forthcoming on the subject. Virginie had gotten a house out of the affair, which was now bringing in a handsome rent while its owner lived with Bernadette.

'Darling, what's this I hear about Benjamin being sought by

the police?' demanded Virginie. 'Surely he didn't have anything to do with those poor concubines being murdered?'

'I hear he's a good friend of the Turk – oh, the little darling!' Babette added, for Dominique had taken the precaution of having Charmian's nurse bring the little girl into the parlor, to forestall the inevitable demands to enter the nursery.

'Is it true that the mob that broke into their house last night killed the family and all the servants?' Bernadette tried to school her voice to sound concerned when in fact all she wanted was to be the first with the best information.

'How is my Lady?' whispered January as he closed the door.

'Not well.' Rose's face clouded as they stepped through the nursery's French doors into the rear yard, then followed the passway around the 'swamp' side of the house and so out to the street. Gabriel's clothing she had left under Dominique's bed: it had served its purpose. 'I could kill that lout Breche. And your news that the Turkish ship has already put into port has added a great deal to the . . . the desolation of spirit that she suffers. Hannibal is with her, and her son – only, he isn't her son, is he?' she asked. 'He would be Shamira's son.'

'He would be,' said January thoughtfully. 'But I don't actually think he is.'

Rose regarded him in surprise.

'I think Shamira's son,' said January, 'never existed . . . Rather like Mr Smith.'

They made their way cautiously up to Rue des Ramparts, and thence circuitously back to Rue Esplanade. Gabriel met them on the corner: 'No chickens so far.' Meaning, *police*. He nodded down the street. 'Zizi's keeping watch down toward the river, and she just signaled me a couple minutes ago.' He looked as if he were enjoying himself hugely.

'I hope you're right,' said January. 'Considering what we're about to do is illegal, the last thing I need is the Watch right at hand.'

Two streets away he saw Hannibal come down the gallery steps from the big Spanish house and stroll up toward them: he was also, January noticed, keeping a sharp eye about him. He had a basket in one hand, containing a pineapple and a half-dozen crawfish. 'Shouldn't be difficult,' he said, when he reached them. 'The

Metoyer cook's been out three times just since the ladies walked out, to chat with the scissors grinder, a girl selling berries, and Phlosine Seurat's maid who happened to be passing by. She also walked back to the kitchen when the charcoal man came by, to chat with him. If I ask her opinion about the crawfish when I deliver the pineapple, ten to one she'll take me back to the kitchen for a consultation.'

'Good.' January hefted Rose's tin cylinder in his hand. 'What's *in* that thing?'

'Mostly saltpeter and sugar,' replied Rose cheerfully. 'With a little gunpowder to make it stink.'

'I can throw it,' offered Gabriel.

'Absolutely not. The last thing I need is for your mother to put a cross on me for getting you in trouble.'

'I thought you said we wouldn't get into trouble,' challenged the boy with a grin.

'I've been wrong before. Hannibal, the minute you hear Rose shout, you run to the house and be there at the bottom of the stair. We need a white man for a witness.'

'I warn you I charge for court appearances.'

They crossed the street. As it turned out, that was actually the most dangerous item of the program: Rue Esplanade was one of the main arteries of trade from the lake to the River and twice the width of most streets in the town. Between the drays and carriages, the water sellers and strollers and goods wagons, there was no way Gabriel and Zizi-Marie could have spotted Abishag Shaw, had he really been on January's trail.

Looking like any respectable couple out for a promenade, January and Rose idled a few houses down while Hannibal strolled up to the yellow cottage with his basket and rapped at the French door that opened into the Metoyer parlor.

He would not, of course, have been admitted into the parlor from the street, had any of the Metoyers been home, nor would he have dreamed of asking to be so. But a gentleman did not rap at the window of a lady's bedroom.

The door opened and Elise emerged, small and wrinkled and cunning as a Roman empress in the arts of intrigue and gossip, and succumbed in five seconds flat to Hannibal's feckless charm. She emerged from the house and ushered him through the passway to the yard, for a consultation in the kitchen about whether the crawfish in the basket were wholesome or not.

'How long is the fuse?' murmured January as he and Rose approached the house.

She held up two fingers, and they stepped through the unlocked French window – he half expected his mother to appear and shriek at him for entering through the parlor . . .

Soundless as spies they passed into the dining room, hugging the walls where their footfalls wouldn't creak. The stairs from the attic descended through a 'cabinet' next to a French door, through which, in the yard, Hannibal could be seen chatting amicably with both women servants in the door of the kitchen.

A careful housewife, Rose turned over a silver tray on the highly polished cherrywood of the dining table to protect the finish. On this she set her smoke bomb, lit the fuse, and both she and January retreated through the door into Babette's bedroom.

Black smoke belched forth with the stink of gunpowder. It was followed at once by a rolling cloud of white smoke, pouring from every nail hole in the tin. Rose dashed into the dining room, feet clattering in panic, and shouted, 'Fire! Fire!'

From the yard behind, Hannibal took up the cry, 'Fire!'

At the door of the cabinet stair, Rose cried, 'Hubert, run! Fire!' and stepped back into the bedroom, at the exact moment that Hannibal yanked open the door from the yard.

A man raced down the stair, slammed through the cabinet door. A tall, stout gentleman, whose ruddy complexion and red-gold beard-stubble matched extremely ill the black dye still lingering in his hair. He wore shirtsleeves, trousers, and a handsome lounging-robe of green and gold brocade, and he skidded to a horrified stop at the sight of Hannibal in the doorway. It took January and Rose mere seconds to dash through Bernadette's room, out to the street, and back into the house through the parlor French door, and their victim hadn't moved.

'My goodness,' cried Rose as they plunged into the smoke-filled dining-room, 'is that Mr Granville?'

The still-smoking bomb was borne into the yard (*'I can't imagine who would have done such a thing!' 'It must have been those boys we saw running out of the house and down the street, Rose!'*)

When January said quietly, 'Mr Smith, I presume?' the banker Hubert Granville glowered, but consented to cross the street to the January house to continue the interview. Far too many neighbors were appearing – to be greeted with Hannibal's shocked tale of malicious boys – for the defaulting banker to wish to remain in the home of his former mistresses.

'I wouldn't have left the man to be hanged, you know.' Granville scowled, but accepted the cup of coffee Rose brought him – brewed by Gabriel, since Rose, though she could judge to the weight of an apple seed how much sulfate of copper to put into a blue fire-work, couldn't, as Shaw privately put it, *make coffee for sour owl-shit*. 'My partners and I would have hired some fellow to come forward and be Mr Smith, if it had come to trial. And since Hüseyin's the Sultan's friend, he's well out of it if all that happens is he goes back to Constantinople.'

'But he isn't the Sultan's friend,' said January quietly. 'I doubt he'll be hanged when he gets there, because I don't think even the Sultan would believe that fool apothecary's affidavit, but your not coming forward has placed his family in jeopardy, if nothing else.'

'You think they'd have freed him, if I'd come forward and said: *No, I was sitting with the fellow the whole time?*' The banker's small blue eyes glinted shrewdly. 'Or would they just say: *Here's a man who'll swear anything, in order to get his hands on the Turk's gold*, and clap me up as well?'

January was silent. He knew Granville was probably right.

'Was that what you were doing there that night?' asked Rose. The failure of the Bank of Louisiana nine months previously had wiped out virtually everything she and January owned, except the house, yet her voice was calm and reasonable, recriminations being useless at this point. January knew Hubert Granville was an honorable man by his own lights, and as honest as bankers were capable of being. If he had – as he was widely accused of doing – specu- lated in cotton, railway shares, and Indian land with the bank's money, it was no more than what every other member of the bank's board had done.

And he hadn't *had* to come back to New Orleans, to try to re-establish a bank. There were planters – and men of considerably lower social standing – who would almost certainly shoot him on sight.

More to the point, thought January, he had remained in New Orleans, hidden at the Metoyer cottage, following to see what would happen to Hüseyin, when he could have fled back to Mobile or Baton Rouge from the Turk's very doorstep, washing his hands every step of the way.

Granville took a praline from the plate Rose offered him and turned it, with surprising delicacy, in his chubby fingers. 'Six of us on the board of the bank have been trying to put assets together to reopen. We've been writing to investors about it for months. It will be a few years before we're able to repay former investors—' He lifted his hand as January drew in breath to say something that probably shouldn't have been said to a white man. 'You can believe that or not, and it doesn't matter so far as last Sunday night is concerned. I came into town –' he fluffed at his cheeks, where he'd previously sported a jawline Quaker beard – 'suitably decorated, to meet with the Turk.'

'After asking him to get rid of the servants for the night.'

Granville nodded. 'I arrived just after dark, and we talked for about two hours. I remember it rained while I sat there. I explained to him that my bank had been involved in the crash, and that it was imperative no one saw me. He'd had the letter out during our talk, and I snatched it up from the desk the moment he was out of the room. Too many people know my hand.'

'So you were with him,' said January, 'when the shouting started in the street?'

'Oh, God, yes. The shutters were closed, but we both heard the girls fall. When the first struck the ground Hüseyin started up and said something in Arabic – it must have been something like: "What was that?" – and he stood half out of his chair for a minute, listening. I knew his wife was in the house and he'd mentioned she was unwell – I think we both feared it might have been she who'd fallen. Then there was the second sort of thudding crunch – horrible sound! He was already starting toward the door when people began shouting in the street.'

'And that's when you fled?'

The dyed eyebrows bunched at the word. 'I thought there had been some accident. Not 'til the following day did I learn he was accused of any crime. But people were coming in. I could not be seen.'

'You let yourself out the carriage gate?' Rose poured him another cup of Gabriel's very excellent coffee.

Granville nodded again. The request for factual information rather than recrimination for his flight seemed to reassure him. 'I waited on the stair, and as soon as Hüseyin went into the passageway to the front door I crossed the courtyard and let myself out the carriage gate. It's around the corner from where the bodies fell.'

'And no one saw you go?'

'I dare say some did,' grunted the banker. 'But they were too busy running to the four winds themselves. I was nearly knocked down by a wagon coming out the gate of the livery yard—'

'Wagon?' said January, startled. 'What? *Who* was running to the four winds?'

'Slaves, I think.' The big man shrugged. 'Saw 'em sneaking into the livery yard as I came down the street when I arrived. Half a dozen wagons, there must have been – one of the livery hands opened the gate to let 'em in – and God only knows how many on foot. Not my business.'

Not your business unless you're trying to work out how the real killer got two dead girls up to the Pavot attic and thence across the roof . . .

'More my wife's line,' the banker went on. 'It's not our business how our servants worship, and as far as I'm concerned it shouldn't be anyone's. Damn shame that they have to sneak out and meet in a stable, if they want to sing a few hymns and hear a sermon that isn't all larded up with Popish nonsense, if you'll forgive me saying so. There's no harm in it. The man was ordained by a proper church, and they'd never have done that if he were a troublemaker.'

Dazzled and a little shocked – seeing in his mind, for some reason, the cold exultant face of Mother Marie-Doloreuse, as well as the darkness of that stable yard into which one wagon could have been driven among many, bearing the corpses of the girls – January asked, 'What man? You're telling me there was a meeting in the livery yard that night?'

'In the carriage barn there, I guess.' Granville shrugged. 'I understand they have a dozen meeting places, all over town. Myself, I think it's to the niggers' credit, that they'd take that much trouble to get themselves to proper worship instead of those heathen dances in Congo Square.'

'What man?' asked January again.

'What's-his-name, that black preacher. Paul Bannon.'

TWENTY-FIVE

'*Credo quia absurdum*,' said January grimly. 'I believe because it is absurd.'

'Tertullian said that,' remarked Hannibal.

'The man obviously never taught a girls' school.' Rose glanced from the paper in her hand to the gateposts of the handsome houses along the Bayou Road, seeking the residence of the Reverend Emmanuel Promise.

Pavot's servant Jerry had had only the vaguest sense that Paul Bannon lived 'someplace in the Marigny', and January had been unwilling to pursue enquiries with the servants at the livery, lest word get back to Bannon that January was still at large. It would have been easy, January reflected, for a minister to ask slaves in the household of Mr Tremmel to set up some kind of false scenario that had implicated January in theft.

He remembered Daniel ben-Gideon, like a great, soft Persian cat in his gray evening-dress at the Tambonneau ball: *I've always had great admiration for the organization of the Holy Church. It's astonishing what they can get people to do . . . One would think they all had guilty consciences or something.*

'God gives some men the gift of golden voices,' he said thoughtfully. Their feet crunched on the shells that paved the Bayou Road, and to their left, the bayou shimmered in the morning sunlight like a sheet of greenish steel. 'Sometimes they go into politics, and sometimes into religion, but it doesn't seem to make much difference. They can get people to do things.'

'*I say unto one Go, and he goeth; and to another, Come, and he cometh . . .*'

' . . . *and unto my servant*,' January continued, elaborating upon Hannibal's quote, '*take this bottle of opium and this Western dress to a girl named Shamira on the Rue St-Honoré whom you've never seen before and never will again, and behold, it is done . . .*'

'Considering what some men do with that gift, I find it hard to imagine that it's God who hands it out.' Rose drew her borrowed pink skirts aside from the wet weeds at the edge of the roadside ditch. 'Perhaps my notion of God is limited.'

'Perhaps it's only evil fairies,' surmised Hannibal. 'As Pope Urban the Second found out when he preached the First Crusade, *deus vult* seems to cover a multitude of sins. This appears to be the place.' He stopped at the head of a carriage drive that stretched back through a copse of trees.

To the right of the drive land had been cleared for a lawn, though the project seemed to have been abandoned before the cypress stumps had been pulled. The house was in the American style, two stories, long and box-shaped, with a porch across the short end equipped with pillars in the hopes that these – and the inexpensive coat of white paint – would induce people to exclaim how great a resemblance it bore to the Parthenon of Athens. It rose from straggling thickets of palmetto and elephant ear suggestive of not having enough yard help, though when January, Rose, and Hannibal followed the carriageway to the back of the house, January took note of the fresh droppings in the stable yard, so the Reverend Promise was making enough at least to keep horses and presumably a groom.

But the whole of the property bore an air of neglect. Only two servants – the groom and a woman who might have been the cook – sat at the table outside the kitchen in the mild winter sunlight. The instant the visitors emerged around the side of the house the groom sprang to his feet and walked with purposeful stride back to the stable ('*I'm getting on about my work, sir, I wouldn't THINK of sitting and taking a rest . . .*'), and the woman also started to rise, a sort of tired two-stage motion that shouted to January *mid-back pain: probably chronic . . .*

'Please don't get up.' January crossed the yard to her.

She cast a quick glance toward the house, then another – warily – at Hannibal, who immediately retreated and looked at his watch. *I have no interest in how other peoples' servants spend their time and wouldn't DREAM of splitting on them . . .*

'My name is Belloc – my wife . . .' January made no mention whatsoever of Hannibal, who idled in the background. 'We're seeking the Reverend Mr Bannon, and we hoped that someone here might know where he could be found.'

'He lives on Caza Calvo Street, just past the big cotton-press, a brown house in the middle of the block.' The woman glanced at the house windows again, and January saw the flicker of fear in her eyes. 'River side of the street. I'm sorry it's a long walk for you . . .'

'It's a beautiful morning,' said January, which was true. The wind that blew in from the Gulf brought an almost springlike balminess, a relief from the gripping cold. By the woman's speech she was American-bred. When she shook his hand in parting he saw the fresh galls of a strap on her wrist bones, the kind of wound a slave takes when she struggles against bindings as she's beaten.

The wound was echoed in her eyes. He wondered if there were a way of letting Emily Redfern know about this, and if the widow would care.

If you don't keep discipline there's absolutely no dealing with servants . . .

Or maybe that was a truism she only applied to her own household staff.

'I'll bet he doesn't let his own servants out to attend the Reverend Bannon's services,' he said, with quiet wrath, when they had once again gained the Bayou Road.

'By the look of it,' replied Rose calmly, 'they couldn't contribute to the building of his new Tabernacle anyway, so why bother? I'm sure there is more holiness to be gleaned by sweeping the Great Man's floors.'

January reminded himself that to assume that a man was a murderer just because he was a hypocrite was exactly the same as assuming he was one just because he was a Turk . . .

And a black man could as easily be a hypocrite as a white.

It wasn't until they reached Caza Calvo Street, a few blocks back from the river in a shabby district of small cottages permeated with the odor of backyard chicken-runs, that he understood fully what had happened to Hüseyin Pasha's concubines.

Standing on the opposite side of the street from the brown house in the middle of the block, he said quietly, 'It was Promise who killed them.'

'Yes,' Rose agreed. 'This house is too small.'

Nearly every dwelling in New Orleans – with the exception of the old Spanish houses like January's, and the town houses of the rich – was built exactly alike: four rooms, two cabinets, and a half-story loft. You walked straight into your host or hostess's bedroom from the street and were ushered into the parlor; if man and wife owned the cottage, the man's bedroom would be closer to the river, the woman's farther, even if only by feet. These rules were as immutable as the ones about who walked through which doors.

But there were also houses in New Orleans that were essentially half-cottages. One room on the street, one room in the back, and the loft. Your kitchen, at the other end of the backyard, would be barely a shed, and there was no building to house servants because if you were living in a half-cottage you couldn't afford servants.

You probably couldn't afford to feed the two small children playing with toy bricks on the doorstep, either, much less the older girl – she must have been seven – scrubbing the step with brick dust, or the older girl yet – twelve? thirteen? – who emerged from the single dormer above the front door, lustily singing a hymn, to shake out bedding and lay it over the window sill to air.

'It doesn't mean Bannon wasn't in on it,' pointed out Hannibal quietly. 'And it doesn't mean that he won't inform the police of your involvement with the slave runners, if he thinks it will protect him or his master.'

January opened his mouth to say, 'I'll take that chance,' and closed it again.

The chance was not his to take.

'If it was Bannon who – um – proverbially stuffed the silver cup into Benjamin's luggage,' said Rose, 'as Joseph in the Bible did to pay back his obnoxious brothers, he would have known that he had a far better accusation to make, and one that would actually stick.'

'But one that would backfire on to him,' said January. 'I think you're right. The accusation came from Promise, and Promise probably hasn't the slightest idea of what Bannon is up to with helping fugitives. Myself, I think it's worth trying . . .'

'So do I.' Rose put her arm through Hannibal's. 'If things go wrong I will claim to be Hannibal's mistress and say that I've never seen you before in my life.'

'Why do I feel like this is an opera and I'm your valet, Benjamin?' inquired the fiddler as they crossed to the door.

The little girl sprang up from scrubbing the step as they approached. Contrary to tales January had heard, there was no 'secret

sign' written on the house – as there was none on his own – to alert
slaves that this was a way station. Yet he wondered, looking up
at the bedding in the dormer window, whether in the twilight a quilt
might be hung out, on nights when 'company' was expected, even
as Rose would put a quilt out over the rail of the gallery to mark
the house.

In so tiny a house, the children had to know.

'Is your Papa home?'

The little girl nodded. The tiny boy abandoned his bricks and
toddled through the single French window that was door and window
and all things else, for the front of the house couldn't have measured
nine feet, and called out, 'Papa!'

A woman emerged an instant later – Rose's age, neat as wax,
smiling welcome – and beckoned them into the tiny parlor. Before
she could even finish the sentence, 'Please come in . . .' or January
could introduce himself and his companions, Paul Bannon emerged
from the bedroom, tugging down the dress of the baby he held.

Concern sprang into his face at the sight of January, and he
handed the infant to his wife – 'You, sir, are a hero,' she said, and
kissed him.

'Mr January. Dearest—' He turned to Mrs Bannon, who gathered
up the toddler and disappeared at once into the bedroom and so,
presumably, through to the yard. 'Is all well?' he asked at once,
and his glance went from Rose to Hannibal.

January said, very quietly, 'I don't know. It depends on what
you can tell us about the concubines of Hüseyin Pasha, and
what you were doing on the night they escaped.'

Paul Bannon closed his eyes for a moment; his breath went out
of him in a sigh. He asked quietly, 'How did you learn?'

'Never mind that now,' said January. 'Did you arrange it?'

Bannon nodded, a slight movement. Pain creased his face. 'And
I wish I'd had both hands cut off,' he said, 'before I'd done it. I
don't think he would have harmed them if they'd stayed in his
house.'

'You think Hüseyin Pasha killed them?' January tried to keep
the disbelief out of his voice, but by the way Bannon looked at
him he could tell he hadn't succeeded.

'Who else would have?' He sounded genuinely surprised.

Rose said, 'Tell us what happened.'

Bannon brought her a chair. It was chilly in the house, but no fire burned in the little fireplace. Fuel was clearly something to be conserved for nightfall. There was a settee in the parlor, and a crippled-looking footstool. Hannibal solved the seating conundrum by perching one flank on the corner of the sturdy table that took up a good deal of the center of the room. January settled himself at one end of the settee; the preacher at the other.

Bannon folded his slender hands. 'I know you're acquainted with Jerry Gosling,' he said after a moment. 'Mr Pavot's man. Do you also know Sillery Hodge, who works at the livery behind Pavot's? He's hard,' he went on, when January nodded, 'but his heart is good. It's been difficult for me to learn, the depths to which this curse of slavery rots the souls of even the best-hearted of men. Before I left Boston I hadn't the slightest concept what it does – what men do, and become, as a result of knowing that at any moment everything could be taken away from them. I dare say—' He looked up and met January's eyes with shyness in his own. 'I dare say you could give me lessons in the subject.'

'I dare say I could.'

'Well.' He sighed again. 'Sillery. He's been a member of my flock since I've been here in New Orleans. When the owner of the livery is away – as he often is – he'll open the gates after the curfew hour, so that we can use the carriage house for meetings. It's useful, because he also has the key to the Pavot yard, so our congregation can slip through from two directions and draw less attention to ourselves. But in the daytime, he was renting out the carriage house for other purposes . . .'

'To Miss Noura,' said January quietly. 'So that she could meet her lover.'

'Exactly. I was conferring with Sillery one day when she came in, to wait for Mr Breche. Her French was very halting, but I had studied a little Arabic in seminary. Please don't think too harshly of her, Mr January. She was only a young girl and had been raised to know no better. She said that her fellow concubine, Karida, had been a Christian and now felt herself in danger of God's displeasure for renouncing her faith. The next time Noura slipped out, she brought Karida with her. Karida and I talked in the stables, while Noura trysted with her beloved in the carriage house. That afternoon Karida returned to the arms of Jesus Christ.'

'And was that when she decided to escape?'

Bannon nodded. 'I made arrangements with the Reverend Promise,' he said. 'His house is large enough, and he only has the one servant woman and the groom, so Karida could hide there in safety while she learned English. Dr Promise said that he would seek out a respectable family to take her in. He knows many extremely prominent families here in town, and there are many who will do whatever he asks of them, in the Lord's name.'

Including accuse me of theft and assault on a white man, reflected January, *and plant evidence in my house to make the story stick . . .*

'Did you know they planned to rob their master?'

A flush crept along the minister's cheekbones. Even if both his parents had been deemed 'Africans' in Boston, he probably had two white grandfathers and probably all his great-grandfathers were white. What had they thought of their son, January wondered, those quadroon parents whose parents before them had somehow managed to get to Boston, to make enough money to give their children a decent living? What had they said to him, when he'd told them: *God has called me to go to the South, to preach His word to the souls there whose names God has forgotten?*

'Dr Promise said that there was no shame in "despoiling the Egyptians", as the Israelites did when God led them to freedom.' Bannon's voice halted over the words. 'I didn't agree. But he pointed out that it would be far easier for him to find a family willing to take in Karida if she wasn't penniless, particularly in these times. And even if she hadn't taken some of the Turk's gold, I suspect Noura would have done so.' He sounded like even speaking that truth about the dead girl troubled him.

'I can't imagine old Philippe Breche would otherwise have countenanced a match between his son and a Muslim girl who barely spoke French.' Hannibal folded his hands on one bony knee. *'Thou ever young, fresh, lov'd and delicate wooer, whose blush doth thaw the consecrated snow that lies in Dian's lap! Thou visible god . . .* It certainly explains why Breche was sitting up in agony for Noura on Sunday night.'

'Yes,' said January. 'Sunday night. You helped the girls escape on Friday—?'

'Sillery went up the ladder to the kitchen roof and helped them down with their luggage. It was the dead of night, and Valentine was away—'

'Did you already know you were going to be holding services in the carriage house on the Sunday?'

The minister shook his head. 'We were going to meet in a barn on the old Allard plantation, but Dr Promise warned me at the last minute that that barn had been put back into use. Now, at harvest time, it's hard to find places to meet. The sugar houses and cotton warehouses are all in use, even in these times. To tell you the truth, I wasn't sorry to be meeting at Valentine's. I hoped – and I know it was foolish of me – that somehow the girls would change their minds, would decide again to take the chance and flee . . .'

'Change their minds?'

'This was after they'd gone back,' said Bannon. 'I'm sorry. I'm not telling this very well—'

'*Gone back*?' January repeated. 'Gone back to Hüseyin Pasha?'

'Yes.' Guilt and distress again darkened his eyes. 'Dr Promise said only that they'd changed their minds – that they were foolish girls and longed to return to the luxury of sin. But I know Karida was never happy with the thought of stealing from her master. The Friday night, the night of their escape, when Sillery loaded their bags into the wagon to take them to Dr Promise's house, she said to me: *It is wrong*. And though I understood why it had to be, I could not disagree with her.'

He pressed his fist to his lips. Outside the door, his children laughed at something and a puppy barked: the sounds of play, of joy.

'I should have spoken then. In the daylight – sitting here now – I can tell you a score of places in the Bible where God clearly states that it is perfectly acceptable, even righteous, for His children to plunder the goods of unbelievers, if by doing so they will save themselves. But since that moment when I came around the corner on to Bourbon Street and saw those poor girls dead on the pavement, every night it comes back to me that I should have spoken. They returned to their master of their own free will. Would it have made a difference to his wrath, if they had not compounded their escape with robbery? Even though they returned his gold as well . . .'

'How do you know this?' asked January. 'You say the girls went back – and returned the gold. How do you know?'

'He told me,' said Bannon simply. 'The Reverend Promise.'

They walked back along the levee, the swiftest route to the Cabildo. 'It should be simple enough to confirm,' remarked Hannibal as they wove their way among packing crates and drays, pipes of French wine and boxes of English tools, scissors, hats. Downstream of town the cane fields were being burned after harvest; the smoke dyed the air yellow, gritted in the eyes. 'His Holiness can't have disposed of the gold because it would implicate him immediately. There aren't lashings of Turkish lira in circulation.'

'Which would be why he had to put Hüseyin out of the way,' added January grimly. 'So long as Hüseyin Pasha is in New Orleans – or probably anywhere in Louisiana – the Reverend Promise can't spend the gold. He can't say: *The Turk gave it to me*, so long as the Turk is there to tell his side of the story. And I don't suppose he would trust any man with the secret, if he hired someone to help him melt it down.'

He glanced sidelong at the young preacher walking beside him. Bannon's face kept a wooden expression, but the tautness of his mouth, the bleak bitter gaze that seemed to stare through the stacked cotton-bales, the small gangs of Russian and British and Spanish sailors, were almost painful to look upon. Apart from whatever trust Paul Bannon had placed in Emmanuel Promise as a man and a man of God, January felt himself reminded that if Promise were arrested, Bannon would lose the white church that sponsored his ministry.

He would become just one more black man trained for a position that the custom of the country would not let him fill: rather like January himself.

But it was Bannon who said, in a small voice, 'Did he ever mean to use that money to build a church at all?'

It was the first thing January had thought of. Hannibal and Rose as well, he would have bet money. But neither of them reacted with the exclamations of good-natured sarcasm that either would have employed had they been alone.

This was a new discovery for Bannon.

January said gently, 'I suspect not.'

Bannon took a deep breath, then let it out, as if with it he expelled his dreams.

Kindly, Rose said, 'We won't know until his place is searched.'

'How he could—' Bannon began, but broke off as January froze in his tracks. 'What is it?'

What is it? January turned the question over in his mind, wondering what to reply.

He hadn't seen the man's face in ten years. And it was only a glimpse, on the deck of the handsome little brig that stood at the wharf. The man was turning away, hidden in a moment by the crimson flags of the Sultanate of Constantinople. A stevedore jostled January, and he stepped aside as if in a dream. Was it unreasonable that a man who had been in the employ of one of the Sultan's former favorites would later in life go on to work for the consul in Havana? Particularly if he had experience of the West?

Two more men crowded past him. The brig was loading: barrels of water, of ship's biscuit, of salt beef. Men shouted from the deck to *stir a stump you lazy bastards* . . .

The man January had glimpsed returned to the rail, and this time he was sure of it.

It was the scar-faced groom with the gold earring, whom he had last seen ten years ago in the wine cellar of the house of Sabid.

TWENTY-SIX

'**B**en?' said Rose.

He drew a deep breath, with a sense of enormous and terrible clarity.

The one thought in his mind was: *And what are you going to do?*

He had met Hüseyin Pasha on only a handful of occasions in his life. The woman whose life the Turk had saved was dead. The fact that the brig – he saw the name *Najm* painted on her bow, and beside it what was probably the same in Arabic – was taking on water meant they were sailing within the hour.

He had only to turn his head away and say: *Sorry. I thought I saw someone I knew, but I was wrong . . .*

Ayasha had risked her life for a young girl who was alone and a slave, for the sake of her own memories of slavery and helplessness.

And the man who had let his mortal enemy go free into the world had been given back into the hand of that enemy, by those who said: *He must be guilty because he is a Turk. Because his skin is dusky and he does not worship as we do.*

January took another breath. *I have a wife and a son*, he said in his heart, to the man who had handed him that letter in that cellar in Paris . . .

Or to that man's wife, and that man's son.

God damn it . . .

'I don't think the man who claims to be the Sultan's representative from Havana is telling the truth,' he said.

The other three only looked at him, not yet aware of what this meant.

'Hannibal—' He was surprised at how calm his own voice sounded. 'Find Shaw at the Cabildo. Tell him to have the credentials of the Sultan's representative checked. I have good reason to think they're forged. The man who claims to have been sent by the consul in Havana is a man named Sabid al-Muzaffar, a personal enemy of Hüseyin Pasha's, who means to cut Hüseyin's throat and drop him overboard as soon as they're clear of New Orleans. Tell Shaw what the Reverend Bannon said: that he should search Promise's house as soon as he can, but that first he has to prevent Hüseyin Pasha from being taken on to that ship. All right? Rose—'

He stripped off his jacket as he spoke, followed by the cravat that he usually wore as a way of marking himself as different from the rough-dressed workers on the docks. 'Find Natchez Jim. You know where he usually puts in, just below the market? Tell him I'm going aboard the *Najm*, in case Shaw isn't at the Cabildo. Tell him to follow the *Najm* when she puts out, follow close enough that they don't dare drop a body overboard. I'm going to try to free Hüseyin and go overboard with him. We'll need Jim to pick us up.'

'I'll go with Rose,' said Bannon. 'Jim – he's the owner of the *Black Goose*, isn't he? – may need a couple more men, and I can probably find some on the dock who'll go if I ask them—'

'Another Centurion,' mused Hannibal. '*I say to one Go, and he goeth . . .*'

'And I say to you *go*—'

'And I goeth.' The fiddler fished in the pocket of his old-fashioned cutaway coat and brought out a thin roll of tattered silk, which he placed in January's hand. 'I won these off Slippery Jovellanos at faro last week. You remember how to use them?'

Through the silk, like a little bundle of bones, January could feel the skeletal shapes of a set of picklocks. 'I guess we'll find out.'

'I trust you've made your will,' said Rose as Hannibal vanished among the sailors, drays, and cotton bales.

'First thing when I get back.'

'Fat lot of good that'll do me when your mother claims the house.' She added his waistcoat to the bundle.

'Tell her I've left town and will be back in six months—' January pulled off his boots: most of the men on the levee worked barefoot despite the cold, and he knew he couldn't afford to replace them if he left them behind on the ship when he went over the side. 'Then hire somebody to be me.' He kissed her, swift and passionate – Bannon looked shocked – trying to keep his mind from the fact that he might very well get himself killed on the *Najm*.

That he might leave her a widow, Baby John an orphan. *And for what?*

Do unto others as you'd hope to God somebody would have the decency to do unto you in this benighted country . . .

From his boot he pulled his knife, which it was illegal for him to carry but which he was never without, and thrust it into his waistband, under his shirt. Then he glanced around, made sure no one was looking, and picked up the nearest sack from a pile left on the wharf. He joined himself on to a group of stevedores carrying similar sacks up the gangplank on to the black-hulled brig and didn't look back.

The *Najm* was about a hundred feet long, of which less than eighty was deck. She was the kind of low-built, sleek vessel made for pirating among the islands; two years ago January and Rose had traveled to Mexico on a ship much like her. The crew – Cubans, in whom Spanish and Indian blood was mingled with greater or lesser degrees of African – clustered around the hatch amidships where the water kegs were being lowered. The forward hatch that would lead down to the forecastle was shut.

An awkward arrangement for the men who slept there . . .

The fo'c's'le was the place January would have stowed a prisoner, particularly one he didn't plan on taking farther than the river's mouth at Balize.

He descended the aft companionway into deep gloom barred with dim daylight. Beyond a door, light from the open hatch showed him two crewmen settling the water barrels. There was little cargo, only stores; in this weather it could take a week to reach Havana. Two tiny cabins, barely closets, flanked the captain's quarters behind him. One of them upon investigation belonged to the ship's carpenter, whose chest contained a pry bar. The other – allotted to the mate – held a sea chest, the hasp of which January simply wrenched free with the bar. He had no idea how long it would take him to pick a padlock: Hannibal could do it in seconds, but his own time ranged from five minutes to infinity.

There was a pistol in the chest, and a horn of powder. He bent the hasp back, turned it to the wall. Worthless if he was going to remain on board for more than a few minutes . . .

And I have it on Bannon's authority that the Bible says it's perfectly appropriate to despoil the Egyptians . . .

Men scrambled up the companionway to the deck. An officer

shouted. Someone else bellowed in sloppy cane-patch French that
this is it, you lazy bozals, time to ficher *this tub . . .*

One thing about brigs: it took a lot of men to set their sails,
particularly against a headwind such as the one now blowing up
from the Gulf. The currents around Algiers Point were treacherous,
and the crew would be picking their way among steamboats,
packets, ocean-going craft and wood boats like the *Black Goose*,
all angling for space at the docks . . .

January stepped through into the now-empty cargo-hold, then
through into the smaller hold just aft of the fo'c's'le, where, as
he had suspected, hammocks and sea chests taken from the fo'c's'le
had been heaped higgledy-piggledy, to clear the room for the
prisoner. The hatch overhead was closed, increasing the gloom.
He wriggled himself down between sacks of corn, barrels of water,
pulled a couple of spare sails over himself. Something indignant
wriggled away from his foot, and squeaked. *If worst comes to
worst I can always claim I'm a slave on the run . . .*

If Sabid's men didn't remember his face as clearly as he recalled
theirs.

Virgin Mary, Mother of God, he prayed, *PLEASE let Rose have
found Natchez Jim.*

*PLEASE let Hannibal get to the Cabildo in time to speak to
Shaw . . .*

Voices on the deck. The thick planking muffled them, but he
heard feet descend the aft companionway a few moments later.
Mingled with the creak of belt- and boot-leather, the clink of chains.

Hüseyin Pasha said something quietly in Osmanli, and, sharp
and steely, the voice of Sabid al-Muzaffar replied.

They passed through the aft hold, and from his hiding place
beneath the canvas, January caught a fragmentary glimpse of
Hüseyin's brown hand and torn and grimy green pantaloons. Sabid
added something else as they passed him. Listening carefully – the
purposeful uproar of launch had begun on the deck above – January
heard the clack of a key in a lock, the woody creak of a door.

The jingle of chain. Another metallic clack.

Men passed him again and ascended the companionway to the
deck. The decking underfoot dipped as the river took the *Najm*
and they luffed away from the wharf.

Hannibal quite obviously hadn't located Shaw. Perhaps – judging by the time it would take the fiddler to walk from the blue-water wharves to the Cabildo – he had met Sabid, his guards, and his prisoner on the way.

And here's where Dauntless Dick charges into seventeen enemies armed with nothing but his sailor's knife and his virtuous American courage . . .

Through the wood of the bulkhead, he could hear Hüseyin praying. '*In the name of Allah, the most Compassionate, the most Merciful. All praise belongs to Allah, the Lord who is the Creator, Sustainer, and Guide of all the worlds . . . Thee alone do we worship, from Thee alone we seek help . . .*'

Ayasha had taught January the words in Arabic, practically the only part of the Qur'an she knew by heart.

He slipped from beneath the sails, crossed to the shut door in two strides. Voices drifted down through the grilled hatch-cover: orders shouted in Spanish and Arabic, running feet, the creak of rigging. In his mind January pictured, like a desperate conjuration, the low dark shape of the *Black Goose* disengaging itself from the tangle of wood boats and keel boats and steamships and sloops, hanging off the *Najm's* stern . . .

In his mind he made Sabid say to his officer: *We can't kill him until we're clear of the town . . .*

Hugging the wall – though there was little chance of anyone looking down through the hatch cover – he scrambled over boxes, sacks, kegs to the door.

'*Sahib* Hüseyin!' he hissed.

There was a judas in the padlocked fo'c's'le door, but the blackness beyond it was impenetrable. The voice stopped, and metal clinked.

'Hüseyin, it's Janvier!'

A whisper from the darkness, '*Ya-allah.*'

January wedged the pry bar under the hasp, leaned on it with all his strength. 'Are you hurt?'

'Bruises only, my friend. But the chain is locked to a staple in the wall. How many are with you?'

'Just me.'

'*Ya-allah,*' said the Turk again. 'They will come to fetch me soon, do not risk—'

'Not 'til they're clear of the shipping.' January panted as he

worked the pry bar deeper, braced shoulder and thigh against the
door and pushed again. The wood gave with a splintery crack that
he could have sworn was audible on the deck. 'It's the middle of
the afternoon. Sabid will hardly dump a man's body in full view
of every steam packet and cotton importer from here to the Balize.
He isn't really working for the Sultan's consul, is he?'

'Would any official have set sail so promptly? I doubt the consul's
secretary has even yet put the Police Chief's letter into the consul's
hand. No, Sabid has friends at the consulate in Havana, so heard
of my misfortunes while he was in Vera Cruz. He pays well for
information. He claims my arrest was none of his doing, but—'

'He's telling the truth.' January pushed the door open, slipped
into the tiny chamber as he fumbled from his trouser pocket the
candle end he always carried, the tin of matches, and Hannibal's
picklocks. The cell was smaller than a whore's crib and reeked of
bilge water. The iron staple bolted into the wall would have needed
an ax to chop loose. 'Hold this.'

He pressed the pistol into Hüseyin's hand, lit the candle. 'And
this. Good, it's a slave shackle . . .'

'And this is a good thing, my friend?'

January bent over the iron tube, probed with the flattened T-bar
picklock. 'It's a simple thing,' he said grimly. 'It has to be, because
there are so many of them required for the trade. I have a collec-
tion of all the different sorts of screw keys – at present reposing
in the storeroom under my house – but a friend showed me how
to pick these . . . Got it.' With delicate care, he turned the screw
mechanism within the tube. Hannibal could pick this type of lock
with one of Rose's hairpins while carrying on a conversation about
who had actually written the *Iliad*; January fought to keep those
tiny, invisible pins in contact with the equally tiny probe.

'One would think,' murmured Hüseyin gently, 'that you are
versed in robbing other men of their property in this fashion.'

January glanced up at him, saw amused enlightenment in his
eyes. 'I've been known to violate a law or two, M'sieu.'

'The ways of kismet are mysterious. If—' His head turned
sharply, and January heard it, too: feet on the companionway,
voices in Spanish—

January blew out the candle, turned the picklock gently . . .
Wrapped his hand around the loop of the shackle to muffle the

grate of its teeth sliding from the iron tube. He heard his companion's breath go out in a whisper of thanks, gave him his knife and thrust him against the bulkhead to the left of the half-open door, then stood to the right with the pistol held as a club.

For a split second he feared that the crewmen would simply turn around at the fo'c's'le door and go back up to the deck: *My lord, the Turk has escaped . . .*

But they came running instead to make sure. January would have liked to let all of them come into the cell before attacking, but when the second man came through the door he had the wits to turn around and saw Hüseyin, cried out an instant before the Turk stabbed him. Thus January had to plunge out through the door – not knowing how many were outside – to keep them from simply slamming the door again. There was only one other in the forward hold and he'd already turned, racing for the companionway.

He was a small man, and fast, and used to moving with the pitching of the deck. But January knew that his own life was at stake, and the knowledge gave him wings. He leaped over barrels, boxes, kegs, caught the man a foot short of the bulkhead and slammed him against the timbers with all his force. Whether the blow killed him or not January didn't know. He heard someone on deck above the open aft hatch shout something. Hüseyin burst from the cell at a dead run, bloodied knife in hand, and January raced full tilt through the aft hold, up the companionway – *if they close the hatch we're dead men . . .*

A man was silhouetted against the daylight, slamming the hatch above him. January fired the pistol at a range of about five feet, and the man jerked back, those around him leaping clear. January burst up out of the hatch, dodged sideways from the inevitable shot and stooped to tear the dying sailor's knife from his belt. *And a lot of good that's going to do . . .*

Hüseyin Pasha sprang up the companionway and fired – *one of the men at the cell must have had pistols* – at almost point-blank range into the sailors and guards clustered near the aft hatch. A musket ball tore a chunk from the hatch molding inches from January's chest, and past the milling confusion he glimpsed Sabid, standing on a coil of rope near the mast, reaching for another musket from a man behind him.

'This way!' January flung himself at a guard where the crowd was thinnest. He slashed with his knife, heard another pistol close beside him, then Hüseyin was at his side, swinging the empty pistol like a club. Someone grabbed January's arm, and January turned, punched his assailant with the whole of his force, plunged for the rail. '*Jump!*'

He was in the air and headed for the water before he realized that he had no idea whether Rose had been able to locate Natchez Jim or not.

Another shot, and he struck the Mississippi like an arrow.

And thank God the current here's too strong for gators . . .

He came up, gasping. Musket and pistol balls hit the water around him; men lined the *Najm's* rail. Sabid's green coat was not among them.

Hüseyin was swimming strongly toward him, brown stubbled head like a bobbing coconut on the dun-colored waters, fighting the current that swept them both toward the sea.

More shots behind them. January turned and saw the low black hull of the *Black Goose* skimming toward them like a somber Valkyrie, with Rose's spectacles flashing among the men clustered at the bow.

Crimson banners flickering against the smoke of the burning cane-fields, the *Najm* swung over out of the wind. The massive current of the river carried her downstream, past the landing at Chalmette and away toward the sea.

TWENTY-SEVEN

E ven with all sails set to the smart wind that blew from the Gulf, it took the *Black Goose* the rest of the short winter day to fight the current back to New Orleans. Wrapped in rather grubby blankets in a corner of the deck, Hüseyin Pasha listened in silence to Bannon's account of Karida's reconversion to the religion of her childhood, and of what the Reverend Promise had considered the appropriate destination for money belonging to unbelievers.

'I should like to think that he meant that gold to go toward the building of his church,' said the young preacher quietly. 'That he was merely misguided – culpably, criminally so – rather than simply . . . greedy.' He turned his face away as he said it, looked out across the sugar fields, where the trash of harvest smouldered – leaves, cane tops, weeds – that the ash might nourish next year's crop. When the *roulaison* was done, the bagasse – the crushed waste of the cane scraped from the grinding wheels – would be raked into huge mounds and fired as well, so that from the levee the whole of the land had the appearance of the sixth circle of Dante's Hell: Dis, the city of the damned.

'It didn't take much for the Reverend Promise to convince Karida to extract the gold from your chest, little by little, over a period of weeks,' January said, to cover the younger man's bitter silence. 'She'd gather whatever she could from Valentine's yard, while Noura met with Oliver Breche. Maybe Noura had already started this, before she met Breche . . .'

'I would not put it past her.' Hüseyin sighed. 'I knew it of her, of course – that she was a minx and a schemer. But, she had a vision greater than I realized.'

'One she could not have accomplished,' pointed out Rose, 'in Constantinople.'

'And perhaps not in America,' added January. 'I suspect that if Promise hadn't killed her for the gold, Breche's father might well have taken it from her. She planned well: hiding the bricks and shells and clay in a corner of the stable, under the hay, then moving

them up a little at a time at night, when your Lady slept under
the spell of Breche's opium.'

'For that,' said the Turk softly, 'I owe him a reckoning. Will
she be well? So many ladies of my country fall under that spell.
You are a physician, my friend—'

'Would that I could speak words of reassurance to you, my
friend,' said January. 'It takes . . .' He shook his head. 'I do not
know what it takes. My friend Hannibal the fiddler has not touched
it for over a year now, but what his fate will be if his illness
reawakens, I don't know.'

'Nor can any man.' The Turk folded those heavy, brutal hands.
'So we must assume that our ignorance also is the will of Allah.
And having robbed me – they put the gold in their own room, did
they not, until the night of their escape? – these clever girls had
only to fix the night of their leave-taking with this Christian *imam*,
whose followers –' he glanced at the silent Bannon – 'it seems
were as deceived as they.'

'We won't know until his house is searched.' January had
resumed his boots, waistcoat, and jacket, but still shivered, for the
wind that streamed up from the Gulf was sharp as a knife blade.
'But yes, I think so. And after he had killed them, and hid their
bodies in his house, it was likewise easy for him to arrange that
the Sunday meeting of the Protestant slaves should take place in
the livery carriage-house, so that he could drive a wagon with the
girls' bodies in it into the yard unnoticed in confusion and darkness. And, of course, Jerry would be at the service. Promise could
get Pavot's key from Sillery and pass through the house with ease.
We may never know if the girls told him that their master was
meeting with someone Sunday night. But Promise must have learned
that you would be wanting your gold and would find that it was
gone before he could make arrangements to get it out of Louisiana.'

'My poor Noura.' Hüseyin sat silent for a time, staring across
the yellow-brown water at the smouldering lines of fire in the
darkening afternoon. The steam-packet *Montezuma*, gaining behind
them for the past hour, sloshed past in great clouds of smoke and
churning of paddles, small figures on the deck pointing at the
brightly-painted Creole houses beyond the levee, the keelboats
working their way up the banks.

Even as he himself had looked, January remembered, leaning

on the rail of the *Duchess Ivrogne*, when he had returned at the end of that cholera summer of 1833. Gazing at the land he had remembered for the sixteen years he'd been in France.

Curious, he thought. For four years now he had recalled as if it were yesterday the day of Ayasha's death. But only recently had those other memories of Paris stirred to life.

He wondered if Hüseyin Pasha – ten years older than himself – dreamed with similar clarity of the house on the Rue St-Honoré, and of Shamira's face.

'And depending on how much Noura told him,' said Rose softly, 'or Karida – who sounds like she had a confiding nature – he might even have guessed that Oliver Breche would still be watching the house on Sunday night, desperate for news of Noura, so would be a witness to the supposed murder of the girls.'

'All the world who knows exactly how an Infidel Turk will behave toward his concubines.' There was no anger in Hüseyin Pasha's voice, nor even, January thought, bitterness. Just a deep sadness, that men should be as they are.

It was dark when the *Black Goose* put in at the wharf below the Place des Armes. Hannibal was waiting for them at the Cabildo, and he remained with January and Hüseyin Pasha at Shaw's desk under the glowering eye of the desk sergeant, while Rose walked over to Auntie Zozo's coffee stand in the market for a jug of coffee and a dozen slightly stale callas done up in a newspaper, the only thing any of them had had since breakfast. When Rose returned, Shaw was with her, consuming one of the fried rice-balls with sugar all over his fingers.

'The gold was there, all right,' he said, and he wiped his hands on the skirts of his jacket, lest it be said that he ate at the same desk as blacks. 'Close on to a hundred pounds of it, done up in a couple of carpet bags with these.' From a drawer of his desk he withdrew three necklaces, gold vermeil set with rubies, and two pair of elaborate earrings. 'There was a couple silk veils there as well,' he added more quietly. 'Mrs Hüseyin's already identified 'em as the girls'.'

'And will the courts believe this tale,' asked Hüseyin quietly, 'with only black men as witnesses?' His dark glance passed from January to Bannon, and then to Shaw.

'Oh, they ain't gonna be allowed even to testify.' The policeman dug in his pockets for a twisted quid of tobacco, bit off a chunk of it with strong, brown-stained teeth. 'But the judge for sure will listen to me. An' we have an affidavit from Mr John Smith – of the newly-formin' Merchants an' Citizens Bank of Louisiana – as to how he was with you in your study the night in question, before havin' to suddenly an' unavoidably leave town for Philadelphia. The affidavit was swore to by six or seven prominent citizens, many of whom was stockholders in the old Bank of Louisiana, attestin' that yes indeedy Mr Smith was their representative . . . It's amazin' what recoverin' that gold did for peoples' memories. An' the Right Reverend Micajah Dunk,' he added, 'has hinted to me that he knows dark an' terrible things about the Right Reverend Doctor Emmanuel Promise – whose real name in Boston was Lemuel Smart – that he might be moved to come forward an' testify to in open court.'

'I think there's a commandment about that,' warned Hannibal.

'T'ain't my business who's bearin' false witness against his neighbor,' returned Shaw. 'An' speakin' of bearin' false witness, Maestro, Mr Tremmel, upon hearin' that the Reverend Promise has been locked up in the chokey, recollected that he didn't see his attacker so very clearly after all t'other night an' has dropped all charges.'

'My mother will be crushed,' said January. He offered the last callas to Bannon, who shook his head, as if he barely saw what was passing in the watch room around him. 'She has a bet going with her dressmaker that I'll come to a bad end.' He handed the confection to Rose, who – knowing how dearly he loved the deep-fried balls of rice and flour – meticulously divided it with him.

Together they crossed the watch room and emerged into the wild, windy dark of the Place des Armes. The chimes on the cathedral clock spoke eight, and through the great doors golden candlelight shone as men and women moved about the confessionals. Mass tomorrow . . . January remembered the sailor he'd struck down in the hold of the *Najm*, not knowing if he'd killed him or not. He would have to confess, and be absolved, before partaking of the Host.

Bannon gazed into the church – into the light – with pain and bitter loss in his eyes.

'What will you do?' asked January. 'Are there others in New Orleans willing to sponsor your ministry to the slaves?'

'Promise was the only one,' the younger man replied. 'When I think of the money we raised for him . . . money most of them couldn't spare. The white gentlemen on the Church boards would rather keep slaves where they can see them: in the gallery, or the benches at the back. The white ladies who give money would rather think their *people*, as they call them, are listening to a white man's teaching, about a white man's God. *Servants, be subject to your masters with all fear; not only to the good and gentle, but also to the froward . . . For what glory is it if, when ye be buffeted for your faults, ye shall take it patiently? But if, when ye do well, and suffer for it, ye take it patiently, this is acceptable with God . . .'*

'Your Bible actually *says* that?' Hüseyin looked appalled.

'First Peter,' assented January.

'The founder of the Catholic Church,' said Bannon, without irony. 'I think I shall go into the countryside,' he went on, 'and preach God's word without a church. Preach it on the plantations, and in the woods. Some of the men I met on the boat this afternoon spoke of preachers who do that. Men of color. Men who don't really think that the greatest gift God can give a *darky* is to make him white when he gets to Heaven.'

'You ask Natchez Jim to send someone with you.' January put a hand on the preacher's slim shoulder. 'Until you know your way around, you don't go alone.'

'I won't.'

'And take these.' Hannibal dug in his pocket and handed him the little bundle of picklocks. 'You'll need them.'

When Bannon had gone on his way, and the four friends turned their steps toward the Rue Esplanade and supper, January asked, 'Will Sabid return?' He glanced at Hüseyin Pasha in the dull yellow of a street lamp's swaying glow. 'Or will the knowledge that forgery of diplomatic credentials can be proved upon him keep him away?'

'I fired at him in the thick of the fray on the ship,' said Hüseyin, 'and saw him fall. Whether he is dead or living I know not, and I fear I shall not learn until the least convenient time. Yet I think it shall behove me to take this moment of his weakness and see if anywhere in the wide world can hide me from him. My son I shall take with me, for only so can I protect him. If my Lady wife choose not to accompany me, Janvier, may I leave it in your hands to arrange for her return to Constantinople? Or to Paris, or whithersoever she chooses to go?'

'I will see her safe dispatched,' promised January. 'Yet I think, my friend, that she will go with you.'

'So I hope.' The Turk sighed and hunched his powerful shoulders against the cold wind. 'It has been too many years that I have taken her presence for granted, as one takes the air in one's lungs. Yet I think,' he went on as the lighted gallery of January's house took shape in the blackness before them, 'that I shall have done with concubines. I have not been so fortunate in them, as I have been in my wife.'

'How did you guess that it was Granville?' asked Rose, much later, when Hannibal had disappeared into the night and Hüseyin Pasha – bathed and fed and with his bruises cleaned – had retired to the bedroom that had been made up for him and his wife. Nasir and his tutor, and the faithful Ghulaam and Ra'eesa, had been given beds in the attic dormitory. As Rose laid Baby John in his wicker cradle, January heard the occasional soft tread of footfalls overhead. In the room behind theirs, Gabriel said something to Zizi-Marie. Tomorrow, January recalled, there would be another 'visitor' underneath the house as well.

He moved over to let Rose slip under the comforters at his side. The wind screamed around the eaves, yet the house itself seemed filled with silence, a dark ship in a lightless ocean.

All safe together, thought January, *for this time, in this night . . .*

Fathers and sons, wives and friends, secrets and time.

'Partly, it was when Hannibal spoke of being hired to play the part of Tim Valentine, for the convenience of Valentine's daughter,' he said. 'And seeing how he'd dyed his hair. But it didn't come to me how a person could be entirely invented for convenience – like Mr Smith – until I saw Nasir ibn-Hüseyin for the first time. Then I realized that Mr Smith was a fabrication, played by someone who couldn't let his face be seen in New Orleans . . . therefore, someone who was known. And I remembered Bernadette Metoyer's new earrings, and her sisters' new feathers and furbelows. It had to be Granville – and he had to be hiding in Bernadette's house.'

'And she's never going to speak to you or me or Dominique again, if Granville ever tells her how we flushed him out,' said Rose as she laid her spectacles aside. 'But what has Nasir got to do with it? He's a very handsome and well-spoken little boy and *nothing* like an absconding banker with four mistresses.'

'And nothing like his father either,' said January thoughtfully. 'Or his purported mother. Who he is like – strikingly so – is a young man I saw only once in Paris. He was the younger brother, I think, of a widowed female cousin in the household of the banker Jacob L'Ecolier: the household to which Hüseyin's concubine Shamira fled after she escaped. A widowed female cousin who had five children already,' he went on as Rose's brow pulled down over those lovely green-hazel eyes. 'And few prospects to bring up or educate the sixth.'

'You mean Shamira talked this woman into switching her child for Shamira's, when they both gave birth? I can see why,' she added quickly. 'Hüseyin Pasha is still a wealthy man – as *Sitt* Jamilla assured me in *very* solid terms after dinner, I meant to tell you . . .'

'Shamira had no child,' said January. 'The amount of quinine Hüseyin's lesser wife poisoned her with would have caused her to abort, and there was no sign of that. Shamira had planned to escape from the moment she heard that there was the slightest chance of leaving Constantinople and going to France. And she knew her master would take her with him – and give her all the comforts and favoritism she could ask for – if he thought she was carrying his son. But it meant that she would draw down on herself the jealousy of the other women in the household . . . And it meant that, once in France, she *had* to escape, before it became obvious that her pregnancy was a lie. It was her passage to freedom.'

'Do you think Hüseyin knows?'

January was silent, thinking of what he knew of that coarse-featured, ugly man who slept beneath his roof. The man who had wept for the concubines who had betrayed him. Who had given freedom to that fleeing girl in Paris – and had handed over the letter that would have destroyed his enemy, in order to save Ayasha's life.

'I don't know. He certainly saw the widow's brother when we were in L'Ecolier's house, though of course he may not remember. He might guess,' he said. 'But whether it would matter to him – whether he would only see the infant that was handed to him in Paris as the son God chose to give him, for reasons of God's own – that I cannot say.'

He leaned across Rose and blew out the candle.

Falling rain woke him, and the far-off chiming of the cathedral clock. Though he did not recall his dream, he knew it had been about Paris. The rain had quenched the smell of sugar from the air, and for the first moment, on wakening, it seemed to him that if he lit the candle, he would see the steep pitch of the mansard roof, the shallow dormer of the Rue de l'Aube, the armoire that had stood against the wall near the bed's foot, and beyond that, Ayasha's work table, the tiny tiled cook-range, the glow of the banked fire shining in the cat Hadji's eyes.

The memory of the place came back to him with such wrenching force that it took his breath away. It seemed to him that if he were to put his hand to his face, he would smell on it the sandalwood and frankincense that had always seemed to perfume Ayasha's hair.

He wrapped the quilt from the bed's foot around him, and his feet found their way in the darkness out into the parlor. He opened one shutter of one window, and though the moon broke through the clouds enough to show him the wet trees of Rue Esplanade beyond the dark frame of the gallery, mostly there was only darkness beyond.

A darkness that wasn't Paris.

As if he'd strayed from the proper road somehow through an error of his own and could not find his way back to the world he was supposed to occupy, he felt bereft, stranded and sick with grief. *There was nothing I could have done*, he thought. *I couldn't stay, when she was gone . . .*

He pressed his forehead to the window's framing, the pain inside him like a ball of broken glass.

Rose. How can I tell Rose?

Tell her what? That he loved a woman who was dead? Loved her still and forever?

This was something he'd never even told his confessor.

And if Olympe offered me a hoodoo, to uproot the shadow-flower of that love out of my heart, I would turn away.

The floorboard creaked. He didn't look around.

Rose asked, 'Can I do anything?'

He shook his head.

'Get you anything?'

'A heart that will do you justice?'

Her arm slipped through his. 'Hearts have nothing to do with justice,' she said. 'Or with waking life. Did you think I'd be jealous, when I hear you whisper her name in your sleep?'

His whole body heated with shame. 'I thought it was done.'

'How can it be done,' asked Rose reasonably, 'when it's part of what you were, of what you are? Does dreaming of her make you happy?'

He wanted to say: *No*, for her sake, but there is a truth that lives in darkness and he whispered, 'Yes.'

The gallery cut off the watery moonlight, so he could not see her face, but he heard the smile of genuine joy in her voice. 'I'm glad,' she said. 'We aren't responsible for where our dreams take us at night, or for our first thoughts when we wake in darkness. If we could change them I dare say we would.'

She went on, 'It isn't often, now, that I dream of the man who raped me. But I have woken, and lain in the darkness, shaking as if he had just left me lying in the woods behind my father's barn. Having been mauled by a wolf, even though I know to the core of my bones that the one who lies next to me is the kindest, the gentlest and most loving soul on this earth – the friend who loves me dearest and whom I most dearly love – all that my heart knows in that moment is that his flesh smells like a wolf's flesh, and if I reached out to touch him my hand would feel a wolf's pelt. And so I don't.'

He stared at her – or at the dim silhouette of her in the darkness – aghast that these were the dreams of which she never spoke; that this wound remained in her, that he had hoped would heal. *Had* healed . . . He could only put his arms around her, light and thin and gawky as a heron.

'Beloved . . .'

Helplessness filled him, worse than any fear of death.

'It's all right,' she said. 'It almost never happens now, and when it does, the . . . the dreadfulness passes more quickly. I'm glad I can tell you,' she added softly. 'I've felt so bad about it, as if there were something I could do about what I feel.'

Her head rested against his arm – high on his shoulder, higher than Ayasha's had been – and her hair smelled of chamomile and gunpowder, from some experiment . . . 'I'm glad when you dream, it's of someone you love. Would you like some cocoa, before we go back to bed?'